ADVANCE PRAISE:

"Anyone who thinks dystopian fiction is a lemon with no juice left in it needs to read *The Only Ones* to get that tingle back in the taste buds… How can a writer this good have waited so long for her due? Carola Dibbell's marvelous narrative has pace, emotional range, plenty of humor—some bitter, some sweet— and one of the most harshly enthralling narrators in fiction since Huckleberry Finn."

—Adam Mars-Jones

"One of the most beautifully handled aspects of Carola Dibbell's novel is the slowly unfolding way in which her narrator's deadpan gradually begins to reveal deeper emotion even as her maternally dystopic world is depicted. A fine book."

—Jack Womack

THE ONLY

ONLY

CAROLA DIBBELL

ONES

Two Dollar Radio
Books too loud to Ignore

TWO DOLLAR RADIO is a family-run outfit founded in 2005 with the mission to reaffirm the cultural and artistic spirit of the publishing industry.

We aim to do this by presenting bold works of literary merit, each book, individually and collectively, providing a sonic progression that we believe to be too loud to ignore.

TwoDollarRadio.com
twodollar@twodollarradio.com
Two Dollar Radio
Books too loud to Ignore

For my daughter, Nina

THE ONLY ONES

BEFORE I START, LET ME SAY REALLY FAST, DON'T worry. You're not in trouble. I will not track you down or hurt you—nothing like that. I just got a few things to tell you that you really need to hear, and you need to hear them from me, not someone else. Ok. That's it for now. Here we go.

1 THE LIFE

THE HYBROBUS STOPPED RIGHT BESIDE THE RIVER
checkpoint, like Rauden said it will. The driver wore a mask.

They generally check your Pass real good when you go out of
state, but this guy didn't even look—just took my bus coupon
and off we go. I guess whatever bad thing someone from where
I'm from could have, they already got it in New Jersey. I recognized the smell. Hygiene spray and smoke. It even stinks inside
the bus. Outside, the regular stuff—barricades, caution tape. I
think I saw some person look out a window at us, but that's it.
No one is on the street. Me, the driver, a couple passengers all
the way in back, it's like we are the only ones even alive out here.
At least I'm out of Queens.

Man! I am glad to be out of Queens.

We pass a bunch of houses burnt right to the ground. We got
that in Queens too.

I am glad to be on a trip. I never even been to this side of
the river. I been to Pennsylvania. Once. Well, I think I been in
Connecticut. But the van they took me in did not have windows.
Pennsylvania was in a Dome. I did not see a single Dome here.
Maybe they keep them in some other part of New Jersey. Here is
just burnt houses and smoke. Then the smoke is gone. The houses
are just empty. Then no houses. It is just a road, in Jersey, or I don't
know where. The road is in good shape. Snow is melting, and
everything is wet.

I woke up in a Terminal in a checkpoint called End Of Line, and outside a fat guy with a beard is standing in snow, saying to his Mobile, "She's here," and when he reached out to take the Pak I brought him from Queens, I recognized the hands. I saw them when he hired me. It's Rauden. The rest of him was in one of those stupid bubble suits clients wear when they come to do business where I work. We call it the Mound. If they come by boat, they could just wear a mask.

"The dropoff work as planned?" Rauden asked. "Nobody touched the Pak?"

"Just the guy who brought it and he got off the Mound real fast."

I am glad to be off the Mound myself. Cold out there. The girls all wear two coats because we got to stand right on the edge of Powell's Cove, in case somebody wants to hire us from their stupid boat. They come in boats so they don't have to go too far in Queens. Nobody wants to go too far in Queens.

There was a food stand at the Terminal shelter and after the guy put the Pak in his truck, he bought something which is called Chickn N Dumpling. I enjoy that.

I enjoy the truck! I never been in a truck. We head off on a big road through, like, snow, snow, snow. I been out in the sticks before—Pennsylvania was the sticks—but like I say, in a Dome. You don't see much from a Dome. Here it's mainly snow. They got a few burnt houses too.

We turn on a smaller road, with trees, then up a hill, and where a sign says, "DVM," we turn to a really small road of dirt, and the guy gets out at a gate where there is a, like, blinking light? Stands a minute in the road, like he is listening to something, then he shrugs and works some gizmo in the gate, which opens and shuts behind us when we drive on, up dirt and snow through bushes and trees, to a clearing. "And that's the Farm," he says.

I heard of it. When he sent me trip coupons, he signed off like this—

RAUDEN SACHS: The Farm.

It looks like a really big dirty tin can cut in half.

"Old school Quonset," he says.

Whatever.

It is very windy. There is a smell I never smelled.

A large woman with short orange hair and a large pink sweater is at a counter inside, watching TV and eating donuts, which are also pink. Rauden said her name was Janet Delize. Behind her was that kind of wall they call paneling, and in front was one orange sofa, plus chairs. The whole place seems to be narrow but long, and Janet Delize and Rauden and me seem to be the only people in it.

"If you'll bear with me while I do a quick product check? And I will need your Pass and ID." Rauden took them and the Pak and went through some door, and Janet Delize said, "Like to take a bath?" and took me through a different door past one dark room and a hall of freezers to a very small side room with a large sink right near a blinking green light. "Just climb right in." She said she will leave a clean outfit for when I'm done and take my old dress.

She's not taking my coat, I can tell you that. I foraged hard for that coat. Where I live it is low on people and food but forage is up the wazoo. Great big empty houses—just climb in a window, help yourself. What's going to happen even if somebody sees? We don't even got a working jail in Queens. Not in Bronx or Brooklyn either. It is a Hygiene thing. They burn them down.

I could hear Rauden coughing in back when I came up front to dry off in my outfit. Cough, cough, cough. He coughed like that on the Mound. I just look out the window. It is the kind that does not open. Then a phone rang and he yelled at someone.

I been looking out the window maybe ten minutes when Rauden showed up breathing so hard he got to lean his fat self on the door. "If you'll come with me to my office?" he goes. "I'm going to run a few tests—nothing invasive. Janet!" he yells. "Hold my calls. I'll be in the Box Room with the Subject."

Subject? So that is news to me. I didn't know I was the Subject. I thought I was the Courier. Courier, you take a trip. Subject, you don't know what is going to happen.

And that's ok with me.

ii

"I'm having some trouble calling up your files, Ms.—" Rauden pulls my ID from a pocket and reads off, "Fardo."

So this is Rauden's office. I had not been in an office like this. It is like a warehouse, but small. I had been in a warehouse. I had been in a tent. I been in labs and also boats, of course. This office is mainly boxes, cables, old gizmos, plus dirt, with pictures on the wall, one of someone who seems to be Rauden next to someone else who also seems to be Rauden. They are both holding baby pigs.

"I. Kissena Fardo." He's sitting at a desk and I am on a box, and he is reading off my ID. "What's the I for?"

"Inez."

"And they call you?"

"I."

He looks up from the ID and says, "I see." But like he didn't.

Well, get over it. That's what they call me. I'm lucky they call me anything.

He swipes the ID in a slot in the gizmo on his desk. "I'd like to do a little intake," and makes a big deal of saying, "I," then coughs, like he had trouble saying it. "It might help me access some medical information I can probably figure out on my own but this could save some time. Just basic background," he went on, typing in his gizmo and squinting at a screen. "Where you were born, grew up?"

Intake. Ok. I was not wild about intake. They ask a lot of

questions they expect you to answer for free. But it's part of the job. Just get it over fast. I told the guy I grew up in Corona, Queens, in a basement. I didn't know where I was born. Cissy Fardo brought me up till she died in the fire when I was ten. When I finished saying all that I just looked at the pictures on the wall.

"Well!" the guy said. He leaned back and got comfortable. "I think we're missing a few details," and he got so comfortable he starts scratching himself in different places under what he wore, which by the way I had not seen a Tech wear this before. They generally wear a white coat or bubble suit. This guy wore overalls. I never saw overalls so big. In forage, you generally just find small ones. You find those a lot. Nobody needs the small ones. "For instance," he goes, starting soft, then turns his chair around to look right at me and gets even softer, "your entire life between ten and now." Then he banged his fist on the desk. Boom.

Ok.

The phone rang.

He pushed a button under his desk and it stopped. "How old are you, by the way?"

I said I didn't know.

"You don't know how old you are?"

I shook my head.

He leaned back in the chair again and rubs his forehead, like I already wore him out. Well, that's his problem. He's the one who wanted to do intake in the first place. If it was up to me, I just as soon go straight to the so-called tests. Whatever they are, I'm pretty sure I will rather do it than intake. Let alone, sex.

He starts tapping his nails on the desk.

That is what they generally want where I work. A lot of people got the stupid idea if they have sex with a Powell's Cove hardy, they won't die—well, it is a pretty ignorant clientele. But that's not my problem. I did not like sex and tried to pitch other things, like blood or urine. I got no idea what they did with it. They even bought teeth sometimes. I think they wore them on a string, for luck. They even bought fingernails.

I'm pretty sure no one will ever spring for this guy's fingernails. They are cracked and funny. Tap, tap, tap.

"Thing is," he goes. "Typically, a simple ID will access some databases that I would very much like to explore and might be some Compensation for the fact the product in the Pak turned out to be," tap, tap, "completely useless—not what I'd thought I was getting, and quite a bit of what I did get was compromised, in fact," now he smacks the desk, "dead! Not your fault, but I'd like to see if I can get some return for my expenses—access to interesting files, possibly by running a few tests, but I need to know what I'm testing for. Some very basic history might help—labwork, illness—nothing is coming up from your ID or Pass. Can you tell me something about your vaccine history?"

I shook my head.

He put his head in his hands a minute and said, "This isn't going to work."

Right then, Janet Delize came in with coffee and the donuts on a tray. "Delmore called," she said, then leaned and whispered something, and he said back to her, "Can you just deal with it?" and she went off.

He did too. He went down the hall. I heard water running.

I had a donut.

It is pretty dark in here. No windows. Three doors though. One to the orange sofa room, one door shut, and one opens to the back where he had went.

He came back with his beard and hair dripping like he put them under a faucet, and is very bright and cheerful like, put your head in water, that really does the trick. "Yes! Let's give it another shot. I might be able to get at your files through some local grid." He's back at the screen. "Did you reside in any other areas than Corona?"

East Elmhurst.

He looked it up and thought a little. "How did you end up there?"

"The Vargas brothers took me when they bought me from foster care."

We could hear the phone ringing again.

"Bought you from?" he said. He sat still, like he had some trouble following.

See, this is what comes from running intake. They like to ask the questions. Then they cannot take the answer.

The phone stopped.

He said, "And," he still seems to be having trouble, "and after that?"

"They die when we move to Powell's Cove. Edgar Vargas have the TB. Well, they said it is the TB. It could of been that thing with fleas. Manny Vargas, they said they didn't know."

"Who said?"

"The Vertov brothers."

"Junior!" That's Janet Delize calling. "Junior!"

"Janet!" he yells. "Will you please fucking deal with it?"

She yelled back, "Delmore says now he heard horses."

Rauden punched his phone on so hard if I am that phone, I will punch him back. So this guy got a temper. I seen worse. Edgar Vargas was worse.

Rauden went into the other room to take the call, which I don't know why he bothered, because I can hear everything he says. "Calm down, Del. Just take a few deep breaths. You know they don't come out till dark." When he came back in he just sat in his chair and thought. Or I think he thought. When he finished thinking, he goes, "Yes! We're getting nowhere. There could be a jam on your regular ID. I'm going to run some pure code if you don't mind."

So I'm like, why would I mind? A Subject like myself? I run pure code all the time.

Like I got any idea what it is.

He wipes a stick in my mouth, smears that on a plate. Ok, I had done this before but we call it something else in Queens. You do it to get a Pass, so they are sure you're who you say you are and not someone else, who should be in jail. If they had a jail. He is sticking the plate in a slot in his gizmo when Janet Delize came through in a coat, and Rauden threw up his hands. "Janet, Janet, what is this? I need you here. I'm sorry if I was rude. But I do fucking need someone to take fucking Del's fucking calls."

She said she thinks Delmore's right. She was going home right now to check her home alarms, in case there really is a raid. "And you should check yours too," she said. "And watch your language." She went off. The front door slammed.

Rauden put his head in his hands.

We could hear a motor starting up outside. Also a noise I didn't hear before, like wind, but different than the wind I heard when we got here.

"Henry!" He's on the phone again. "Delmore thinks there's going to be a raid. Yeah, he's going ballistic. Janet thinks I should rig up some alarms. That green light hoo-ha in back? I thought it just ran the generator. Oh, right, that kicks off the old system. And I hook it up to the main system in front? Yup, I'm working with the Powell's Cove hardy. Like pulling teeth. I think she is a little challenged. Gotta go."

He looked through boxes in the Box Room until he found a long cable, plugged one end under his desk and took the rest down the hall. I eat another donut. When he came back, he said to his screen, "Oh, what's this now?"

I already saw it went black. That is how challenged I am.

He got under his desk, did something, sat up, and stared at the screen. "*Subject: I. Kissena Fardo. Location: Zone North.* So this is new. *Origins: unknown.*"

It is not new to me.

Outside, the motor sound got louder.

He just sat there tapping his nails. "Kissena." Tap, tap, tap. "What sort of name is that?"

The motor got softer, outside.

I told him it is where the bus stopped.

"So." Tap, tap, tap. "You were named for a bus Stop."

Oh, what is it with this guy? He got a problem with everything I say, like, who is even named for a bus Stop? Who do they even call I?

Well, tap this, fat guy. I'm not going to tell you why the bus stopped there or who was on it or why it's in my name. It is not your business. I just told the guy I didn't know.

He pulled a metal bottle from a drawer and unscrewed the top.

The motor sound outside got softer, then softer. Then it's gone. So I'm alone in this place I never been with some guy with a temper who got a bottle. It's not like I never did this before. It's how it works. It's not like I am scared.

He had a long drink. "Let's try something else. Have you been in close contact with, let's see, someone infected by, hmm, one of the Luzon viruses, say—even a lesser one like, well, Avian—I think I could test for that. TB is not relevant, hmm, and you don't know your vaccine history, or so you fucking say." He had another drink. "Help me out here."

Well, he looked so sad, I began to think, watch out. He could give up and send me home. Better think of something to tell the guy. "I could of had one vaccine," I said.

So he goes, "Bingo."

So I said but I don't know if he could find the file.

He had another drink. "Why not?"

I said Lonnie Vertov could of gave me a fake ID.

He had another drink. "And why would Lonnie Vertov do that?"

"If you are a minor."

He just held his hand out, like, this would matter because?

"It was a vaccine trial."

He was about to have another drink but stopped before he got it in his mouth. "What vaccine?"

I said I didn't know. And by the way, that's true. I did know they ran the test on a boat called *Flora May*, and the boat was in Flushing Bay.

He typed all that in his gizmo, then said, "Bingo," again. He stood and clapped his hands. "Sounds like some early version of Universal vaccine. I can use those antibodies as a Control and work from there."

Whatever.

At least the intake's over.

He leads me up front then around to where he had went to check my ID and Pass in a shiny little room called Lab 3, where he sits me on a table, sets up a syringe and I'm like, with this guy's nerves, what are the chances he finds the vein, but he does it fast and good. "These are express kits and we should see some results in minutes. Why not relax in front?"

He's putting on a mask and Hygiene gloves while I go back to the orange sofa and look out the window that doesn't open. It's starting to turn dark and by now I am sleepy. I started so early for this trip, all the way from Powell's Cove, and even once I got to Jersey, there is the whole hybrobus trip up.

The phone rang. This time Rauden picked it up. "Harold, hey! Daisy? But that's way early. What's the timing on her contractions? Harold, I'm a little busy. Can you try Walter or Sook? Get back to me if nothing works."

I could hear that wind real good through the window. It's still just light enough to see trees moving around in it. I also heard a bell. Then Rauden, breathing—you hear him breathe before you see him. He leaned on the door and looks like he is going to cry. "I'm not finding any Universal history in your blood. That seems incredible, if you've taken the vaccine. Are you sure you did?"

So I said they could of lied.

The wind is getting really loud.

He sat down in a chair like he is tired too. "What do you mean?"

"They could of gave a different vaccine than they say."

He is so tired. "Why would they do that?"

"It was a shady operation."

"How do you mean?"

"A Tech died."

"Died?" He sat right up. "How did he die?"

"Well, his eyes bled. His skin too."

"But—why would this happen from that vaccine? It almost sounds like symptoms of—" then he stopped and is, like, thinking, thinking, "but who would mess with that?"

Now I heard the whole building make a noise. Creak.

"Well the Tech was the only who died," I said. "The others just went to Emergency. I was ok."

"Wait—everyone got sick but you. And you were how old?"

The phone rang again. He let it ring.

I go, "Thirteen." Right away I wished I didn't say thirteen because he looks like he did about the foster care. So I said, "It could be fourteen." To tell the truth, it could be twelve. The look he gave me now, I wish I said sixteen. I wish I never told him anything.

The phone rang again. "Harold! Talk to me. And you tried Walter? No, I'll come! What? *Where?* Keep your eyes open and I'll see you in twenty," then, "Janet! Are you there?" He's just running around. "Will you fucking pick up? Daisy's having a breech birth—Harold's Daisy. And Delmore's not the only one who saw horses. Please come get the Subject. I have to leave her here." He went to Lab 3 and came out in a white coat like Techs usually wear, carrying a black bag. He wrote down a number for me and told me to call it from the Box Room phone and Janet will come get me. He said don't let anyone but her or him in, no matter what they say, and he went out the front door.

Then he came back and locked the door an extra way. I heard his truck drive off. I was alone on this empty, creaky Farm way out in the sticks. I been in worse situations, believe me. At least this one got heat.

I tried to call the number Rauden had left, but no one picked up. The Box Room screen was black again when I went in there to call.

I just went back in front and sat on the orange sofa and listen to the wind blow and the building creak.

Then I tried to call again.

The lights went off.

After a while, a phone was ringing. Not the regular phone. A different phone, near the freezers. Then it stopped. Then it rang again. This time it didn't stop. Finally I went down the hall in the dark and picked up this different phone. A machine said, "Backup system will be activated in one minute. Please pull the lever at the green light to confirm."

I put the phone down and felt my way past the freezers till I got to a green light which has a lever underneath I could see by the green light. I pulled it. The lights went on.

Something was hitting the window like rain, snow, when Rauden came in the front door, wet and excited, saying to the phone, "Two little heifers. Daisy's doing great." He seemed surprised to see me lying on the sofa. "Let me take a quick look around. Oh! Shit! What's this now?" That was from the Box Room. "Can I get back to you?" I could hear him moving all the way down the hall. Then all the way up to me. "Did you touch something? *And do not goddamn say you do not know.*"

I told him.

He sat down on the chair. "Henry! The old system was in place, storm knocked a cable out, that kicked on the old backup system and when the failsafe message went off, the Subject did what it told her to, and now the whole system's totally fucked. Password? What password?"

He heaved himself up and went back down the hall toward the green light hoo-ha. The lights went off. Then on.

"Yup," I could hear him say. "Her pure code was in the drive. And there was uncompleted bloodwork running. Let me check how that's doing." In a minute he was saying, "Please tell me how you knew that, Henry." Then, "You're kidding me. You're fucking kidding me." So he came all the way in front breathing noisy like he does and when he got to me, stared really hard, then said, "Dear fucking God," and sat down on that chair. "You're sure, Henry?"

So I'm in trouble now. I should not of pulled the lever. I should not of even picked up the different phone. He's going to send me right back to the Mound.

But he just kept talking to Henry. "You're saying I should pull her codes out, as a test?" He went in back. The lights went off, then on. "Then put her codes back in?" The lights went off, then on. I heard him say, "Dear God," then he came up front and stared at me again. "You're right! That's how it used to work. What a crazy piece of luck. I'll call Bernie right away." He walked around in a little circle, saying, "Yes!" a few times, then, "Bernie? Rauden Sachs here. Long time! Look, can you fit a Subject in for a checkup? Let's not go into detail on the phone but this could be something very special. Think you could squeeze her in between virgins? You still use the RV? We should make it by morning."

He went to Lab 3 again and came back with a regular coat, the Pak from Queens, and the Mobile.

"I!" So he could say it without coughing now. "Let's go!" I take my coat too and we head off into the night.

iii

The rain or snow was still coming down, and it is hard sloshing through the slush to get to the truck in the dark, but Rauden started talking before we finished sloshing, like I could even hear him, in the rain or snow.

"Guy who was the original owner of the Farm? And in case you wondered," he goes, like I even did, "it's not a working farm. Never was. Everyone just called it that." He stamped his boots on the side of the truck, then climbed in. "Dewey Sylvain." I climbed in too. "A very smart man. A little paranoid at the end," he starts the motor, "but who could blame him? Set up all kinds of security, alarms, failsafes, firewalls, worms, you name it." We go down the road, with the rain or snow hitting the windows and roof.

"Plus customized search programs, flag Alerts, buzzing hoo-has—the guy loved a gizmo! Some of this software goes back twenty, thirty years. Still works—well, what's left of it. My brother Henry used to call it SOTA, when we were kids. State Of The Art. Ha, ha. We weren't allowed to touch most of it, so now that we bought the goddamn place, we can't make heads or tails of it. What's the word, Larraine?"

We had stopped for the gate and he is on the phone. "Oh shit, oh shit. Well! I'm a-turnin' off my lights." He turned the truck lights off, said to me, "We do not want to attract attention on the roads tonight," and drove into a bush. He steered us out. Hit another bush and so on till we got to the road at the end that we had took from the Terminal? Then he stopped the truck, rolled down the window, leaned his head out and listened, and when he finished listening, drove us on this road but the other way from the Terminal, up a hill, or seemed to be a hill, in the dark.

There was a moon in the sky but so many clouds it was hard to see anything, and he drove very slow. He would roll the window down to listen. Once, after he had gone off the regular road to a smaller one, he said, "Better not," and backed us to the regular road again. "Larraine," he's on his Mobile, "I'm on old Route 9. Thought it was safer than the back roads."

So this is a front road.

By now some clouds have cleared. You could see the moon better and it showed some things alongside this front road, mainly snow and big snow puddles but also a few trees and fences, plus something burnt that I didn't know what it was.

"Larraine is way up in the hills," Rauden told me, "but she keeps tabs. Has a very SOTA tracking system. Ha, ha."

I just look out the window at the snow. He doesn't notice. He is on the phone.

"Those fucking cretins," he says, then, "I'll go the old way, past Hyman's place." He drove off this road onto some small road, very dark, where I think he hits a fence and also the wheel with his hand a few times, saying, "Fucking cretins!" till we end up on some other regular road but very soon are on a different road that seems to be wide, though bumpy, with trees very close, and right away he started coughing so hard he had to stop the truck and roll down the window. Then he started sniffing the air. "Oh! Shit!" he said.

Well, it was smoke—I smelled it too. He turned right around and backed us straight off the road into a mess of branches, turned the motor off, and jumped out in the dark. I heard him throwing something on the truck, maybe branches—I'm just sitting there alone till he is back beside me, whispering, "Not a word. Not one fucking word." And we both sat there in the dark with him putting one puffy finger on his lips, till I heard a sound I never heard before, and it got louder. Then louder. Like rocks that fall, one at a time, but fast, and I could see what looks like lights, but not exactly lights, getting closer. This is through trees in the dark and the lights seem blurry, like little fires? And the fires are bobbing up and down behind the trees with that sound getting louder, till it's not one at a time but all together, like all the rocks fell down right near me, BOOM, BOOM, BOOM, through the trees, and then it's gone.

But Rauden kept his fingers on his lips. He stayed a long time like that, then got out of the truck and walked a few steps in the dark, listening, both ways. Listen, listen. Now back in his seat. Slammed the wheel a few times with his hand, then said, "You have just had a first-hand sighting of the Knights of fucking Life." He took a few deep breaths like he had told Delmore to do. It seems to calm him down. "Just a bunch of very foolish local vigilantes who come out of the hills from time to time to burn our farms down."

Then he yelled again, "FUCKING CRETINS!" And he looked at me.

So I look back, like, cretins. Right. I know exactly what that is. Cretins.

He starts the motor up and is on the phone again. "The Ks passed right by the goddamn truck. Yup, torches and horses."

Man! That was horses?

"Seemed to be coming from—oh, shit, that's Harold's. On my way."

We race down that same dark, bumpy road till we turn down some other regular road that is so open we could see all the way to where a pretty big fire was showing a ways off down a long hill, and we went down that hill to there and could see other fat guys in overalls throwing snow and other things at the fire, and Rauden put the truck under some trees, got a blanket, told me stay underneath and do not move, and he went running to the fire, yelling, "Fucking cretins!"

It was a long time till I saw him again. I just stayed under the blanket and listen to shouts and smelled smoke, till I saw him right by the truck, and he put his head on it and cried. I guarantee I never saw a Tech do that. Then he kicked the truck. He already had one of those metal bottles out when he got in his seat and took quite a few drinks before we headed off to the regular road, or one of them. This time he turned the lights on—I guess whatever he was scared would happen already did. You could see this was a pretty big road, with hills on both sides.

"I mean, shit!" He kept smacking the steering wheel, and the truck would bounce around. "We're talking cows here. Cows! And, I mean—" he got the bottle from his pocket and waved it around, "—these wussies think they are so fucking hot? They should have seen the nuts who chased us out of Minnesota—one of those godawful End of Days groups from back then—we had to drive halfway cross the country to lose those fucking maniacs—we were in trucks—Henry and me, Dad, old Phil Delize and that whole group—landed at Dewey Sylvain's door in the middle of the night, Henry and I are little kids in our friggin jammies, Dewey took one look at us all, burst out laughing and said, what a bunch of rubes. That's how we got our name. You might have heard of us."

I didn't. But I don't say it. I just look out my window. We are passing a fence.

"Bernie!" On the phone again. "I'll be a little late. Yup, the Ks hit Harold's. Everyone's all right. They torched the barn but Harold and Weezie had already moved Daisy and the little Daisies into the big house. I'm going to check in with Walter and Larraine. Bernie came a little later"—What? Oh he is talking to me now—"on the run from Ohio. He was the only one of us who was a bona fide MD—Dad's group were DVMs—veterinarians, for God's sake—and Dewey Sylvain with so many goddamn degrees he couldn't remember them himself. That was the original rubes."

So let me stop a little minute and say something, because maybe from what I said back at the Farm you think, well this girl have done everything. Well, I did things that night I never did before, and one of them is, I never heard anybody talk as much as this rube talked. I never heard anything like it. Sometimes on the Mobile, sometimes to himself—it's like he cannot shut himself up.

"Ever see a baby?"

Oh! So he is talking to me this time. I shook my head.

We went under some trees.

I heard a baby crying in a building once. But I don't feel like telling him that.

He had another drink. "I saw Dewey Sylvain deliver one once. Back when there was still much need for that kind of work." He shut up a minute. "Real Renaissance man. He went out on a job with Dad once and delivered a pair of goddamn lambs! The guy was a research fucking scientist! Literally! Got his hands into everything. Used to say, it's all about the hands. To be fair, I don't think he was any better than Dad when it came to enucleating cells under a goddamn microscope! That's tricky."

Now out of trees.

Here is another thing this rube will do. He will say something, then look over at me like, you agree, right?

So I'm like, I agree. Sounds tricky to me.

Yup.

We pass, I think it is a house, but dark. No lights.

When he smacked the wheel this time, the truck slid sideways, and when he tries to steer the other way we slid almost to a tree on the other side, till he finally got us going straight, but we did go off the road, even with the lights, so many times that maybe you are starting to wonder do I have second thoughts about this job? And not because of the Knights of fucking Life, who were pretty interesting, to tell the truth, with those lights and that noise, and, I mean, they rode horses—horses! But how this guy drove? You could say I'm lucky to be alive.

Phone in one hand, bottle in the other, we go sliding back and forth across the road—the guy's steering with his elbows—bounce over a bump, and, splash! Slush at the bottom. Mess on the windows. He jumped out and cleaned them all around, front and back, and he left the door open, so I just smelled whatever is out there which, whatever it is, I never smelled it before. We head off again and he hit another bump and the whole thing happens again.

I never had so much fun in my life.

Bump! Splash! Slide!

Go through trees again. Hit something in the dark. Come out on a great big open space and now he shut up. He will do that sometimes. Talk, talk, talk. Then shut up.

He turned on a side road with one of those blinking lights like at the Farm. Some fat guy in overalls opens up and leads us down his road to a little house. Rauden set up a cable from the truck to the side of the house for a charge, and I went in where a woman in a long check dress let me use the toilet, and here's something else I never did, saw a toilet like that, so shiny. Jars with pink things in them. Pictures on the wall of little girls in hats.

Rauden had come in the house for a hot Beverage and bread while the truck charged, and the woman gave me some too while Rauden told them how Daisy is doing, and the guy told Rauden he heard an Inspector is coming around tomorrow, and Rauden says thanks for the heads up, Walter. So this was Walter. I didn't hear the woman's name. She didn't hear mine either. Rauden just said he's bringing me to Bernie. When he told them that, they just look the other way. Walter and the woman walked us to our truck and patted Rauden on the back. We're off.

You could see real good now with the truck lights, and the

moon helped too. There was a kind of metal tower far off. We seem to head toward it. Then we come around a bend so you can't see the tower any more but are turned so we got a view of smoke coming up even now from Harold's, behind a hill, and Rauden whispered, "Fucking cretins."

Then he shut up.

Ok, let me say something else about how this guy talked. You could not understand a word he said. Like DVM. So that is veter whatever. That is a big help, right? Well they are both doctor for animals. DVM and vet. They got a doctor for animals! Who ever heard of that? But sometimes you hear vet and it means GI, so watch out. Words could mean two things or more. MD is regular doctor, and you are going to hear about OBGYN which is another kind of regular doctor, though shady. IV, IVF, PBJ, SCNT, ASAP, ova, solos, sperms, somatic this, embry on that, plus you already heard enuke whatever. Rubes need to talk a funny way so no one will know what they mean or they will end up in jail or worse, but sometimes I think Rauden just liked to mix people up. And I will tell you this. It worked.

"Genes were Dewey's main interest. Got carried away some-times—well! Dad always said that first Subject in the modification Project would have died anyway, how things turned out in fucking Baltimore. Never figured out why that flu hit them so bad, when DC got out of it with just a few thousand deaths."

Ok, that worked. I am mixed up.

"See that?" Now he's pointing to something downhill on his side of the truck. "One of Dewey's later Projects—started in '42. That's two fucking years after the Big One. Most people who were still alive were just ready to roll over and die. Dewey said, let's make the best of our situation. We all felt that way. All the rubes."

I looked where he pointed, downhill. It seems to be poles coming out of the snow with fans on the end? Then big plexi boxes with something in them, maybe vegetables. You could see this real good under the moon. Then more poles, with wheels on them, going around and around. Then nothing.

"The college let Dewey teach here after Hopkins threw him out, and I guess he was lucky to get a job, but they were lucky too. Dewey would do fucking anything. Plants—soil—software. Very gifted hacker. And of course the medical work—not even in his area of specialization—brilliant guy. What he did for those poor little kids who ended up at the clinic here—well, you wouldn't know what he did even if I told you, but it doesn't always work. He got it to work. The problems those poor kids had—the thing with the eyes, dear God. Henry and I were barely in our teens but Dewey said bring them into the Project. They'll learn something about human beings. We fucking did."

Then he shut up and drove.

"Larraine? Wake you up? Could we stop by?"

We're heading uphill now, and on both sides are that kind of tree you would see in a picture of Christmas? He has been quiet for a little while but I guess can't stand it for very long.

"Do you see a lot of kids in Queens?"

So now I got to talk too. Ok. "Sure. The mothers like to hide them, but a lot of times you could see them hiding in the toilet in some park."

"In the toilet? What do they hide from? Vigilantes?"

"Inspectors."

"Inspectors. Do you get a lot of those?"

"Well, the ones from Staten Island Dome," I go, "not so much. That's Ethics. They got a uniform."

He shuts up, because we are going through a bridge that is like a little house, with walls, and makes a lot of noise to drive through. When we're on the other side, he says, "And what do Ethics do?"

"Take a bribe."

He laughed and laughed. "Ours too. But what is it about? Life sales?"

Ok, I'm not going to answer that. You're asking for trouble even talking about Life, let alone sales. You cannot sell Life. Unless you got a license. I just told the guy I didn't know.

"And Health Inspectors?" He has to steer hard around a big rock.

"No, you see them a lot. They are like, did you take your shot? Did your kid take her shot?"

"Nobody wants to take a shot?"

"Some do."

He needs to turn pretty hard now, how the road went. "I mean, you can't blame people," he goes, "what ends up in some of those damn vaccines. What happened to those poor kids Sylvain tried to help—well, that was more by way of their Parent's exposure—GIs, a lot of them, shot up to the gills with every kind of goddamn untested thing some mega could make a profit off—breaks your heart, but it was never as common as people thought. Vaccine Syndrome can be mild. Beats polio, for sure. Even measles are no walk in the park. Those stupid vaccine boycotts. Everybody wants to go back to the goddamn Stone Age! You have no idea what I'm talking about," he said.

I heard of it though. I heard of polio.

"That's why Sylvain went in the direction he went in, those last years." Now he is turning us another way, and I think there is a drop on my side, but he is looking at me, not the road, like—you agree, right?

I agree!

He looked back at the road and steered back from the drop. "He'd patch people up, they'd go back home and die of something else. And that was even before the Big Ones started coming through. Then they stopped coming up at all."

He steers the turn a different way, and now we're going uphill, and you could see the moon on my side. "The first Big One killed the market. It killed the fucking patients!" He shut up for a while. "Well, people did still come for Bernie. Nothing stopped anyone coming for what Bernie sold."

Then all at once something went flying across the moon. Whoosh!

It's birds.

I had seen birds before. But generally, you know, falling in Powell's Cove or right on the street. You would see their bodies on the street. You do not want to eat those birds. Some people did though. Whoosh!

"Lookin' good, Larraine," he says to the phone and we turn off onto a little road with one of those blinking light gizmos and an old woman in overalls comes to let us in. She got a big red face and long white hair.

"Got some goodies for me?" she asks Rauden.

"Just soma," he said and handed that Pak to her. "Sook's contact screwed me. Pigeon and gull."

She said, "I can work with that."

"If anyone can, it's you, Larraine."

They laughed and laughed.

"Want a look?" she said. "Oh, let her look too. If she's a candidate for Bernie, she's not even going to know what it is."

And she brings us around her house, which is like a tower that goes way up, with wires and lights?

And I want to tell you something. You are going to hear what people say about the girls like me, how we are exploited, got no self-esteem or worth or none of that, the life we live. They never say it's interesting.

Behind this tower is a very little house that is very warm where she had a glass cage of little fluffy things that is going, Peep! Peep! Peep! Peep!

Is that interesting or what?

Larraine lets us use her toilet. She gives us food for the road. Then we are on our way.

Do you want to know what's interesting?
Meatloaf.
We ate it when the road straightened out.
You know what else?
Pie.

I woke up and the door is open, and it's still trees outside.
Rauden came back fixing his overalls. I guess he pissed on the
road. We head off, downhill now. Still trees and rocks with snow
on them, and the moon sometimes, but in a different place. And
this guy is still talking, like he never stopped. Maybe he been
talking to himself the whole time I been sleeping.

"There'd been rumors for some time, even before Sylvain
started tracking them down. From the worst hit areas—LAX,
Rio, Manila. Queens, of course. Very mysterious—the profile
didn't read as conventional immunity. Odd fluctuations in cyto-
kine levels. Antibody anomalies. The whole thing could have
been a myth, but the rubes talked about it—Dad and Old Phil
knew quite a bit about livestock hardies, after all."

I saw a lantern on a pole.

"Sylvain was the only one to do the research. Set up a search
program that hacked into clinics and labs, and how it worked,
a test for certain modalities went out—Henry explained this to
me once—bloods, location, history, like that—and if three got
positive checks, an Alert flag would pop up in his system."

Behind the lantern, the road turned downhill sharp. Rauden
steered hard and kept on talking.

"Dewey liked to call them X-treme hardies, but for most of
us, they were Sylvain hardies. Thought it was just an old man's
fantasy. Even Bernie had his doubts, though Dad said the pair of
them had big plans. Sylvain had started buying up conventional
hardy product, male product. Dad had the idea there was some
dicey stuff too—viruses, maybe for testing purposes, kept them

in his goddamn shed. Dewey knew some dealer in Scotchtown, guy's still working, for all I know. We'd moved to Bovina by then, but we all kept in touch. Dad was worried—thought Dewey was losing it, guy kept muttering about footprints in his hardy search. With hindsight though, Dewey was probably right."

Now the downhill turn turns the other way. Rauden steers that.

"Maybe a month after Dewey made real contact with one of these so-called X-treme hardies—she was from Michigan—an Inspector showed up at Dewey's front gate."

I saw a little house in the trees. The little house got a light.

"Claimed Sylvain was in violation of some health or Ethics code—well, he probably was—we all fucking were—but to arrest the guy?"

That is the first lit-up house we have seen since Larraine's.

"And of course Dewey tried to bribe the Inspector, then got charged with that as well. A bunch of the old rubes went to try to get Dewey out of jail—old Phil Delize, Larraine's husband Rebert—what a sweet guy he was—and a few of the younger ones, maybe eight total. They threw them in the clinker too."

Rauden steered around the house with the light.

"Henry always said someone big was behind it. Maybe some mega who wanted to get Sylvain's hardies before him, and God knows what they'd do to them. The timing of the raid does work. And when Dad came down to sort things out afterward, it was clear someone had broken into the Farm."

You could see something red ahead through the trees.

"Henry thinks the flu that went through the jail was planted, but that seems excessive, even for those greedy motherfuckers. The Inspector died too. And the sheriff. Everyone in the place. Henry says that's what did Dad in too."

The red thing is a lantern.

Rauden stopped the truck there. Oh, man. He's crying again. "Just knowing about it," he said. He sat there at the wheel, crying.

I just looked out the window. It is not so dark out as before.

After a while Rauden wiped his eyes and made a turn on a different kind of road. This road is flat, got some houses on both sides, and some of them got lights outside, on trees, though you don't need them so much now. It's getting brighter.

"You may be wondering why I'm going into all this."

Wonder. Ok, where do I start?

"Well, with Dewey gone, old Phil's son Phil Junior took over the Farm—you met Phil Junior's widow, Janet—but the place was a mess—ransacked, partly burned. Most of Dewey's files had been destroyed, and what was left was so fucking booby-trapped with Dewey's own antihacking shit—viruses, worms— it wasn't worth saving, except for one little backup program that can be handy in emergencies—reads breaches very well and kicks off the backup generator when needed. Turns out to store backup for some of Dewey's missing files, which you definitely want to steer clear of since most of them come with individual anti-hacking devices that are certainly SOTA today—and one of these goddamn files was that old hardy search I've been mentioning, with that pop-up flag and a real doozy of a worm. How it works, the worm is in the actual flag, so it's only activated when the flag is triggered by the goddamn three modality thing—and what are the chances any goddamn code in your goddamn system is going to trigger that?"

And he gives me that look, like I agree, right? I agree.

We go across another bridge now, just small, across a little river, and on the other side is, like, rows of stores that show up real good because it's getting so light.

"I saw that worm today. Now what could have triggered that?"

I said I didn't know.

"Your pure spit code and fucking bloods," and he smacked the wheel again, like, three times. "Your code kicked off the hardy flag. Some fucking Courier!"

I didn't say a word. I thought I was the Subject.

It's already morning when we pull into an icy yard near a long building called Motel 16, and a big white truck is parked on the side, and a girl is running out crying and an old guy is standing at the door, shaking his fist at her. When he saw Rauden, he started to laugh, spread his arms for a big hug, and brought us into the RV that looks more like a regular lab inside than Rauden's place. It got cots and tables and counters and all that, and Bernie made a hot Beverage though he said none for me, in case he needs to put me out for a test, but he was nice. He wore a white jacket with short sleeves, though it is cold, but he had a kind of sleeve anyhow, of white hair, and he smelled good. Bernie says to Rauden, where they are sitting on stools with their Beverage, "So what is so special you must interrupt my tight schedule and drive all this way on such a dangerous night?"

Rauden leaned over and said something quiet.

"What?" Bernie looked over at me, surprised. "That old hocus pocus? Do not read too much into this, Junior. You know the man was not in his mind at the end."

Rauden whispered some more.

Bernie looked at me harder.

Rauden started to talk so loud I could hear it from my stool. "The fucking flag went off! The worm went up. Her bloods fit the fucking modality. I'm telling you, Bernie. Come up here, I."

I went and stood in front of them.

"Bernie! You are looking at a Sylvain hardy!"

iv

There is a TV in the Motel 16 room Bernie puts me in when he got done. The TV is broke. The window is broke too. The test was invasive.

I had worse.

He gave me pads where I, you know, bled.

"Too bad," he said when he left.

The window in the room got a hole. I could hear a sound through it. I went to check. Ice falling from the roof. I lay down again. Now it's crunch, crunch. I went to look again. An older woman and a man are crunching across the parking lot, over the ice, and went in the RV. The next crunch, crunch is them leaving, with the woman crying.

The next crunch, crunch is Bernie crossing with Rauden, who came back from errands in Ithaca. I ducked back on the cot and act like I'm asleep when they come in, with Bernie patting Rauden's back, Rauden looking shaky, and Bernie saying, "Too bad."

And that is when I got it. Whatever these guys thought they could do with me, it isn't going to work.

Bernie took food out of a little Locker and put it in a cooking box. He said it is Frank in Bean and gave me mine to eat on the cot. Him and Rauden ate at a table. With all three of us, it is not too cold in here. Frank in Bean was pretty good but not as good as meatloaf. Rauden mostly just sat without eating, but Bernie ate the whole time he talked to Rauden.

"I'm very sorry, Junior, but," Bernie goes, "she would have been a hard sell even without this problem. My clients are such dickheads—they insist on virgin Hosts. They do not understand a girl like," Bernie looks at me and nods. "And patching her up would not be simple. Even selling her ova will not be simple. These dickhead clients all insist on pre-pandemic product! And, you know, that one Dewey had dealings with? The Dearborn hardy? She had many problems, even besides the antibody anomaly. Compatibility, response. Her ova had some very serious problems, and there was another he heard had the same problems. Eat your lunch, Junior."

"No offense, Bernie," Rauden said and did take a few bites, "but are you sure there are no problems with those pre-pandemic embryonic viables you're selling those dickheads? Isn't that stuff twenty years old?"

"I am very careful with my freezers. Double generator backup. So? Sometimes it doesn't work." He looked across the room at me. "She would be a hard sell, Junior." Rauden looked too. I just look at my empty plate, and Bernie starts clearing up. "She has no Proofs! No history! No one has heard of Sylvain hardies!"

So I wasn't the only one.

"The ordinary tests are useless, as you have already seen. There is one that could work, but it is very, very risky. It is even risky to try to patch her up. Too bad," he said again. "The life these poor girls live, they will sell anything. Some of them," he lowered his voice, like I won't hear him if he does, "they are so exploited, their pimps have put them on the street since they were little girls. They do not understand their own worth. They sell parts of their own bodies. Most of them would be glad to be a Host. Nine, ten months? They are happy to be off the street. Too bad."

He went in the toilet to clean up and came out drying a dish on a towel. "Let's start her on shots ASAP. Beef her up. See what happens! Call me to schedule the Harvest. When we see how the Harvest works out, we will know how to proceed."

Rauden and me got our coats on and Bernie patted Rauden's back again. "So!" he goes. "You are going cross species! You'll have to do the shots yourself. I will be on the road. But I am sure it will be easier than the work you do with Daisy. That is fussy work. I have written the instructions for the timing and tucked it in the kit. Watch out for yourself, Junior. They say there is a new thing starting up though it is still overseas." He puts his arms around Rauden. "I miss your father still."

Then he gave Rauden a kind of kit and we're off, with Rauden just driving, not talking.

It's getting dark. The snow is turning blue.

Rauden didn't say a word, just drove, and we really been on the road quite a while before he said, real casual, "What did you get for it?"

So I thought, do not say anything.

He pulled over by a house we had seen on the way to the RV and he put his head in his hands. "This is not going to work," he said and turned the truck around. He drove to a place where there was a kind of shelter with a roof on poles over a bench and two lanterns on the sides. "The bus to Yonkers should come by in a few hours. You should be able to find your way to Queens from there," and he handed me a bunch of coupons. Before I climbed out he said, "Whatever they paid you for it, it wasn't enough." Then he drove away.

I sat on the bench.

It was pretty cold.

So I am going back to the Mound. So, whatever.

No vehicle passes.

It got darker. Colder too. Snow under my boots. Snow, snow, snow.

Whatever.

After a while some lights came down the hill in the dark. I stood up so they could see me, if it's the bus.

Man! It's the truck. Rauden jumped out, starts running right at me over the snow and now this rube is yelling, "And it's not worth a goddamn thing without you attached! What moron thought it was?"

I got up and ran.

He fell down in the snow.

I waited.

He pulled himself up by the pole that holds the roof up over the bench. The lantern lit him so you could see where he is covered in snow from falling.

I just wait in the dark, what he will do next.

He walked back to the truck. I heard him hit it with his fist. "And the mess they made taking it out!" he yelled from there. Then he came back and sat on the bench. I stay standing, in case he's going to run at me again. He just put his head in his hands.

When I am pretty sure he is not going to run again, I told him, "They gave me too much shots."

He lifts his head up and put the hands down. In the lantern light I could see his eyes trying to follow this. Then they change. "You were megadosed on hormones to maximize an egg Harvest."

"It broke."

"Your ovary," he goes.

"Then they went in to fix it and, well, the surgeon should do it but he died, so the Tech had to but really messed things up."

He sat a long time on the bench then said, "Who did this to you?"

"New Life labs."

"*New Life?*" He's like somebody poked him with a stick. "You worked with New Life? In that SOTA Dome in Pennsylvania? But—they have incredibly high standards. They're major players in the Life Industry. That's gotta count as some kind of Proof." He pulled himself up. "Come on, I."

He went somewhere in the dark. He came back and put, I think it is wood, in front of the truck, tells me to push while he starts the motor. Then I climbed in beside him and off we went, driving, driving all night till we come to a house which had a lot of levels and is shiny, with green covers on everything, and they put me in the basement. I stay there for two days till it is time to beef me up from Bernie's kit.

I had been beefed up before. In Pennsylvania, like I told Rauden, but also on some different boat. Not *Flora May*. They give you shots and pills and you puff up. It is not invasive.

The house he took me to is Janet Delize's house, and in the basement they have a cot. They have a window you could see out of if you stood on a chair. Which I did. Well what is this? It is a cow. I had seen pictures of a cow. This cow just goes walking by, with a bell.

And here is what I mean, you never know what will happen. I had done this before. Shots, pills, puff up, all of it.

I never saw a cow though.

v

They did it in the RV in the woods somewhere, in the rain. I woke up very zonked on the orange sofa, with Rauden wheeling by in some kind of chair and saying in a voice I never heard, "Now you're the genius, bro. But tell me this. How's somebody going to spring for just two eggs of unknown origin, no antibodies, no Proofs except some very funky software drama, and there is a very reasonable chance her eggs are subpar?"

That's how I got the news the Harvest didn't work.

I hear that same voice a lot, the next hour or so, and Rauden's voice too, both of them saying things like, we could try the Esperanza network. Bro, they are looking for white. Dude, she's a goddamn Sylvain hardy. But no one knows what that is! I'm trying conventional IVF with her ova and some of Sylvain's frozen hardy sperm. And, more than once, I hear Rauden's regular voice, like this, "Forget it, Henry. I'm not running that test."

When I woke up next, the one in the wheelchair is serving a hot meal that is red and yellow. "Give some to her, Henry," the regular Rauden said.

"Ok, bro."

So this other Rauden is Henry. He is Rauden's bro. He was the other one in the picture in the Box Room, holding baby pigs. He brought me the red and yellow meal, which is not that great.

It's still raining.

Rauden put the News on. "Dear God."

It's the new thing Bernie talked about, starting up in Mumbai, India. It is confirmed in Karachi and possible in Bandar.

Henry did not wear overalls like his bro, but a check shirt and has to wipe the yellow and red stuff off it after he ate. He also got it in his beard. "What about Parvi's friend from Toronto? You've had some dealings with her, right?"

Rauden had took off his boots and wore, like, sandals over socks. "Rini Jaffur, right. What a piece of work. Tragic situation. She had something else in mind. Still, I guess it's worth a shot.

"Out of reach," he said, when he came back from the Box Room. "She's in fucking quarantine. In Sydney, Australia."

"It got that far?"

"Just prophylactic, I'd say. Panic." He went to Lab 3 to check the thing he's mixing with the hardy sperm from Sylvain's freezers. If it works, that will be easier to pitch than a solo egg.

By the time he comes back, the TV News is saying it's official, it is a Pandemic. Mumbai Pandy. They name it from where it starts. There are new cases in Pune and Sholapur.

The two of them just sit and stare at the TV.

Henry said, "Reminds me of the first Big One—remember? Watching the News with Dad, talking about the numbers."

Rauden goes, "Dad said, the Plague had better numbers than this motherfucker."

"He was crying while he watched."

On TV, they are saying it got to Trincomalee. Rangoon. It already is in Karachi.

"That's what it was like hearing the names of all those places in Queens," says Henry. "Jamaica. Hollis. St. Albans. JFK. Flushing Airport. Powell's Cove."

Then they both turned to look at me. Oh, man. Now these guys are crying. Both of them. A long time they looked at me, with tears, until I look away out the window, where it's still night and still raining.

Then Rauden says to Henry, "Well! She's never known anything else." Then he went off to Lab 3.

I heard of it though.

I heard of the Big One. Everybody did. Not just in Queens. Everybody in the whole world heard of it. It just started in Queens. Then it went everywhere else.

Rauden came back saying, "Didn't work."

The phone rang.

While Henry and me bring the food things to this little kitchen behind Lab 3, we heard Rauden yell at Rini Jaffur from the Box Room. "Rini! No one is saying you didn't love your daughters. You've had a terrible, terrible loss. But please! Give this some thought."

He came back shaking his head and talking in a funny voice. "This was not what we discussed! This was not what we discussed! And Henry," he says to his bro, and is, like, almost giggling, "wait till you hear what she thinks we discussed."

Henry wheels off to a corner with him and they whisper.

Henry goes, "No way."

"I will say this for the woman. She has an open mind. She was convinced I could bring it off. Well! I probably could."

Ok, here I want to say, if you don't understand this part, don't worry, you will. Later, you will.

They just got very still. They stared at me. They stared at each other. Rauden put his hand on his head and even sagged, like somebody socked him. "Whoa!" he said.

Henry said, "Dude!"

Rauden goes, "Solve the egg problem real good. Plus! How pure would those genes be!"

What I'm saying is, this is really important. I just don't know what it means. Half what these guys say, I don't know what it means. Half what I say, they don't know what I mean either.

Rauden is wheezing, even though he sat down in a chair.

When he can breathe he goes, "Okay. I'm on it! I'm pitching Rini right now." He came back saying, "Out of reach."

Now they both sit down in the front room and look at me. Then they both started to giggle again. I'm just like, keep my eyes on Mumbai News. I mean, they are falling over, giggling.

"Bro!" goes Henry. "We have to get some better Proofs."

Rauden says, "Don't start, Henry."

It is getting light. Still raining. Henry is in the Box Room, doing research. "This test is a seal-tight Proof. Sounds like what Bernie meant."

"I'm not doing it."

"It works."

Rauden had been in front with me, but now he goes to the Box Room door and yells, "You know why? They put the girl in a bubble and expose her directly to unbelievable shit. If she's still alive when they pull her out, it works. I messed with this girl enough."

"Bro! How much better will it be for her to go back to god-damn Queens?"

"I'm not risking her goddamn life!" And Rauden storms off.

They are getting on my nerves.

Morning. Still raining.

Henry is not giving up. "How about this one? Hmm. That's a very nutty name."

"I'm not doing it, Henry."

"Seal test, something like that. Bro! Don't turn it off!" I could hear them bumping around and knocking things around. "Bro, stop. You'll crash it."

The lights went off. Then on. These guys.

Finally, I had it. "Seal *Room* test," I call out from the sofa. I think they could hear from there.

I heard nothing for a minute but the rain. Then I saw them in that Box Room doorway, both of them a mess, because nobody but me had any sleep. They looked at me, then each other, like, bro, I thought I heard the sofa talk.

So I say back to them, "Seal Room test. S-E-A-L."

Then they're like, dude. It did. The sofa talked.

"Like the animal?" Henry asked.

"*Like the goddamn room.*"

They're like, bro! The sofa cursed!

So I just said, "It is for Hygiene. You got to seal the room real tight, so the Tech is safe. But it is more like a bubble. You got to seal the bubble too." Then I go, "That I heard."

Finally Rauden came up to me and by now he is so tired he is shuffling in those stupid sandals. "I? Look at me. I'm going to ask you something, and you are not going to tell me you don't know. Have you done this test?"

Whatever. I did this test.

vi

So this part is about the Seal Room test.

"Where would I even find the equipment?" That's Rauden, giving everybody a hard time.

"You know the little bubble they blow up for quarantine, if they don't got a regular quarantine to seal you in?" They both stare at me for a minute. They are still getting used to me talking.

Finally Henry just laughed, and Rauden says, "Where would I fucking find one of those?"

Henry goes, "Middletown General. My pal Morty Moon has access."

"I'm not working with fucking Morty Moon."

Henry rolled his eyes at me.

"And the pathogens?" goes Rauden. "Where am I going to find pathogens serious enough to be worth our while? If I even agree to run this test?"

I go, "The shed?"

Henry laughs again.

Henry and I check out the shed. It finally stopped raining. He could wheel his chair across these big flat stones in back, if I help. The shed is smelly and dark, but he found the old freezer unit and pulled out some cryoPaks. "Hmm, what's the expiration date on product like this?" He reads off a label. "Pneumonic plague."

I said, "I been exposed to it."

He whistles. "Whoa. You are lucky to be alive."

Whatever. "It is airborne though. That is hard to control." I thought a minute. "I think they got a kit for this that is Hygienic for the Tech. It comes with the mask and all the rigging."

Henry thought about it. "I'll see what Morty Moon thinks."

When we get back inside, Rauden is already drunk. "I'm not doing this!"

I tell Henry, "Get the kit with a lock file that says what went in and out of her. If they are doing it for medical, it is Proof."

"Why else would they goddamn do it?" Rauden said from the Box Room.

I'm like, oh! The Box Room talks.

Between you and me, I'm not telling the Box Room why they would. He already had too much trouble with it. They do it for sport sometimes. Expose her to serious pathogens like pneumonic. Get drunk and place bets on how long she will stay alive. Sometimes they will use a filovirus like Ebola—that's easy to find. The pay is very good.

Henry goes to Middletown in his special van and when he comes back with the stuff, he brings me to the shed and shows me the kit. It looks ok to me. I help him put the bubble in there. We pump it up and get the seal ready. Henry rigged up a monitor and I dragged the cable inside to the Box Room.

"You could fix it to work express," I told Henry. "Forty-eight hours. Five days is better though." Five days for the test, plus a few before and after—I could be staying here another week for sure, maybe more. "You got to leave meals and Beverage for the Subject. Sometimes they put a TV in." In my dreams. "Five days, open the door. You could run her blood and urine tests before you let her out, if you like to be totally safe. She could even do the cleanup, for a Bonus."

Rauden just got drunk and said, "I'm not doing this." When he looked over the pathogen listing, he kept saying, "Dear God," but he cleaned himself up, had coffee, and seems pretty sober when it's time to start. He told Henry, "Nobody's on the fucking grounds but the Subject and me when I do this. If you're within five miles of this fucking test, you won't have to worry about the risk. *Because I'll shoot you, myself!*"

Ok. I'm in the bubble in the shed. It is a little cold but there is a heater, though not inside the bubble. A heater could melt the bubble. Rauden and me check the rigging for the IV and the mask. He goes back inside to check did the monitor work. I gave him thumbs up. The monitor worked. I put on the mask.

"Do you feel anything?"

The catheter.

He came back to fix it, then sealed the bubble. There is a light inside the shed but it is still pretty dark. The heater is ok.

Rauden's saying something in the monitor. I pointed to my ear. No sound. When he fixed the mic, I told him, "I did this before."

So here we go.

He took one of those noisy breaths and pulled the lever for intravenous. I almost couldn't get him to pull the airborne one.

The bad part of this Seal Room test is he is so afraid I'm dying here, he keeps waking me up. "I! You ok? Do you feel anything?"

I feel like I woke up. Man! Ok, I'm up. I take out a Breakfast Pak.

"I! Hello?" He's waving at me in the monitor. "When the surgeon died at New Life, was it from a test like this?"

This guy. Now I'm in one place and cannot move, and would you believe he's running intake again. I said I didn't know. Man!

"I still don't see how New Life made the contact. Hello?"

When does this guy sleep? I said, "The broker makes the contact when she is too old to pass." The Breakfast Pak is hard to open. "Then you get her tested."

"Too old to pass for what?"

I mix it with water from a jug.

"Cures? Virgin Cures?"

Oh, man. Who's he been talking to? He been doing research. I drank my Breakfast Pak and said I didn't know.

Besides Paks, I have MREs, PBJs, IVs, no TV, but I have old cartoon tapes.

"I heard about virgin Cures. Some evil broker has a stable of little girls he rents to end-stage sickos who think if they have sex with a virgin they won't die."

"*Unprotected* sex," I tell him. I'm watching a cartoon. "And she is not a virgin. That I heard." I watch the cartoon to the end. "She just got to look so young she fools the client. And even if he figures it out, what is he, going to call a cop?"

Rauden goes, "Dear God." This is what I mean about intake. Get over it, dude.

I told him, "If she is old enough to start the Curse, you could even time it around that. You got to pull out the hairs though."

"You're telling me they time the sex around her periods, so the client thinks he broke her hymen? And she's what, twelve, thirteen years old?"

I said I didn't know.

It could be eleven.

He's out of the monitor. I don't know where he went.

When I woke up next time, he's saying, "And when the bus stopped in Kissena, but it wasn't a regular Stop, were you the only one? I mean, on the bus?"

So he figured it out. That's his problem. From now on I just said I didn't know. Between you and me, it wasn't even a regular bus.

I woke up and see him in the shed in the middle of the night! The cable got unhooked. The monitor's dead. I mean, he is really at risk that close to me, even outside the bubble! He's just wearing regular clothes. He should wear something, a bubble suit. At least a mask. What is he thinking? Then it's fixed.

He's on the monitor. Do I feel anything? Here we go again.

When the test is over, he runs his own urine and bloods too, in case he got something. I mean, lucky to be alive, I wasn't the only one. He looks worse than I do.

I pour spray inside the bubble before he opens the seal. Then I take the bubble to a hole I had already dug in the woods where Henry told me and bury it.

Rauden got the first read of my bloods. "Nothing in the blood. No pathogens, no antibodies. Nada."

"Read the urine."

"Jesus!"

"It's safe. They're all dead." I had done this before.

"So this is how it works! I have never seen anything like this in my life!" He is reading from the lock file, which is, like, Proof, what went in, what came out.

So. We finally got something that works.

He lets Henry come over and even Henry has a drink. Rauden already had a drink. I will say this, he didn't drink anything the whole time of the test. He is still really shaky. Henry is wheeling all over the place. They are both excited. Now all they have to do is reach Rini Jaffur, but this time the problem is, wherever she is, systems are down, so they got to put me in a trailer in the woods, because Janet won't let me in her house in case I got something from the Seal Room test, and they don't think I should stay on the Farm because Rauden has to go to the clinic in Bovina and they don't want me in there alone.

Rauden is furious at Janet. Now he knows how hardy I am, he is worried am I cold? Wet? Hungry? Like, I am so hardy, he has to make sure I don't get anything! Janet won't even help make the vidCast for Rini Jaffur. I hear Rauden scream at Janet from his Mobile but she just leaves a bag off at the Farm with makeup, a comb, her daughter's old clothes in it. Rauden brings them to the trailer. We have to pin the clothes to fit. I have to clean up with water Rauden brings in a jug, dress, sit in a chair, look at the camera, and say, "My name is Inez Kissena Fardo. I lived my whole life in Queens and never got anything."

I was alone for two days while he's at the clinic. I stayed pretty much in the trailer. The trailer was ok. It had a burner, MREs. Beverage. No TV though. I only saw the Mumbai News when they finally let me back on the Farm. Twenty cities, six million dead. They say it got to China.

The vidCast just bounced back from Rini. Nada. We don't even know where she is. He's back from Bovina and I could stay at the Farm in the daytime. Rauden's just sending message after message to Rini.

"Rini, do you realize the odds against someone like her turning up?"

Away message.

He gets drunk and calls her. "She may not be the only one like her in the world. But she's the only one I've ever found! You are not going to get hardy talent like this, honestly, in your life."

He reached her!

He yelled and then I heard him say, "Well, how fucking ethical would it have been with goddamn Madhur? Sorry! That was very callous of me but you fucking know what I mean." He got off and punches everything he saw. "Damn that woman! Damn that woman!"

She sent a message saying she has changed her mind.

I hear him call her back. "You won't regret this."

She sent a message saying she has changed her mind.

It was the old message looping up.

From now on, he keeps leaving messages but nada from Rini Jaffur. "Rini! This could work!"

Zip.

"I'll fucking sell to someone else!"

Now she left a different message. She's stuck in Vancouver,

in some quarantine checkpoint. This all takes so long, I'm ok for another Harvest, and Bernie's back from Erie. This time the Harvest didn't work, period. They don't get anything. Not a single solo. Bernie took what they call a wedge, from the ovary, because that could improve ovary function, and you can freeze the wedge and use it for other things. It is invasive. Rauden gets so drunk Bernie won't let him drive, and when Henry gets us back to the Farm in his special van, Rini Jaffur left a message saying it will not work.

And I start to think she's right. It isn't going to work. None of it.

Host already wasn't going to work. I would of liked to be a Host. It sounded like real steady work. Now Donor isn't even going to work. Even Courier didn't work. What I brought in the Pak was compromised. It's not going to work, period. Rauden could even deduct expenses from my fee. So I end up with nothing. Still, I had seen a cow.

When Rauden woke me up in the trailer, shouting, "All right! Rise and shine!" then looks me up and down like Bernie did, and goes, "What can we do with you?" I thought this is it. He's sending me home. We head straight for Janet's house, and he's screaming at her door, "Fucking get over it! She doesn't have anything!"

Janet lets us in. She has different clothes for me that her daughter used to wear, a track suit she will stitch to fit while I get in the bath. Janet even cut my hair. There is white trainers for my feet that are too big but what am I, going to train? My teeth, just try not to open up my mouth too wide.

"I mean, what does it matter?" Rauden mentions, shaking. "That's environmental." He just mentions it to himself though. Janet Delize is too busy putting my lipstick on.

Now bring me back to the Farm. Rini Jaffur bought her way out of the Vancouver checkpoint, is so rich she could afford three planes to Ottawa, a ride to Albany, and a glider-drop to hit Erdelyi's field at three. She fucking changed her mind.

vii

You're going to hear very soon what Rauden has in mind to do, and maybe you will hear somebody else say he just did it for the money. I'm not going to lie to you. Money was involved. But it was always about more than the money. And when you see who Rini Jaffur was—well, it was her money. But she was more to it than that. Even later, when maybe you will think she's out of it? She never was totally out of it. She was always part of it. She knew what it was.

She walked right in the front room with big steps and came right up to where I was standing with Rauden. She wore a coat over, like, veils. The color of her veils is, if pink was gray, that color. The veils are wrinkled and her hair is falling down, but she does not seem to care. She's darker than me, especially under her eyes. Under her eyes is almost black, and I could see that really good, because she sticks her face close to mine, then looks at it hard, then steps back and looks me up and down like everybody does, but even harder. And maybe you think I am used to it by now. I'm not.

When she was finished looking, she sat down on the orange sofa and patted beside her.

So I sat down.

She asked Rauden, "You don't know anything?"

Rauden shook his head. "She could be anything."

She shrugged her coat off and it fell behind her. Then, like you would put a coat on, or, I don't know, a light on, she put a smile on. She shone it on me. Even her eyes were shining. It was like when you light a candle, when the power's off? "Don't you have any family?" she asked, and her voice was like a candle, bright.

I agreed.

"No mother? No auntie?"

I nodded, but thought about it and added, "But if I don't come back, someone will know."

Rini stopped smiling fast. "Rauden! What did you tell this girl?" She took my hand. She even stroked it. "Come. Did you think we mean to harm you?" There is no snow or rain outside the window now. There are even a few small leaves on those trees that was blowing around my first day at the Farm. It was still a little cold, even inside. But here, from Rini, it's warm. She's stroking my hand and leaning very close. "Do you understand exactly what will happen? Did Rauden say?"

I looked at Rauden.

"Rauden doesn't know this answer. Look at me."

And, I don't know why, all at once I could not talk. I just sat there. It is a little hard to talk anyhow without the teeth showing.

I heard Rauden saying, very slow, "Look at Rini, I. Tell Rini what I said."

So I looked at Rini, opened my mouth as small as I could, and told her, "Rauden will use my Life to make a child which will be yours."

They both seemed stunned when I said that, like something hit them on the head.

Rini smiled so hard at me her whole head shook. She said very soft, "Did you think we meant to take your life away?"

I said, "I would be paid for it."

Rini stopped smiling.

Finally Rauden moved. "Oh! Oh, I see what she means. She

heard something someone said about the Life Industry. It's not going to be your own life, Inez."

Well, how it turned out, nobody knew whose life it is. But I didn't know that. But I didn't have to know. I just have to keep my mouth as closed as I could and let Rini say whatever she is going to say.

"You will not see or know this child," and she went on stroking my hand. She leaned very, very close. "She will be my child." And now she squeezed my hand very, very hard. "How do you feel about this?"

I got no idea how to answer that.

Now she raised her voice. "*How do you feel about this?*"

Who knows? Who cares? Man! This is the worst intake I ever had.

She suddenly rose to her feet and began to pace. She wore sandals. She even is barefoot in them, even though it's still a little chilly, even though not so cold as when I got here. Finally, she stopped pacing, spun around and now she took those big steps back to me and sat down and took my hand again. "Now, I am going to tell you something that you do not know. I once lived in Siliguri, India, with my loving husband and four daughters, until my husband died from second Wave Luzon and I took my four daughters to my cousin's home in Toronto, Canada, where next Wave Luzon had already hit, though we did not know it till we landed. My daughters all died in one month. Four daughters. Now, you must tell me," and tears just popped out of her eyes while she went on, "and you may judge me for this, but you must understand what it is like to lose my husband and then four daughters in one month." Tears just kept rolling down her face. "I cannot bear to lose another child. I cannot bear to go through this if you will change your mind."

So now what do I do? I don't want Rini to cry, or anyone to cry. I had it with how much crying I saw since I been up here. But I don't even know what she means. I looked at Rini Jaffur and said, "I would be paid on delivery. So if I change my mind, I don't get anything."

Rini got very quiet. I noticed at this point *she* was looking at Rauden. I don't know why.

"We must tell her," Rini said suddenly. "I know we said she did not need to know, but I have changed my mind. Come. I'm going to tell you something else, and you may judge me for this, but when I lost four daughters in a month, I was mad with grief. When my final daughter, Madhur, died, I reached out to my husband's old schoolfellow, Parvi, who lived in Ithaca and knew rubes, because I dreamed of doing something with what was left of my last daughter that people tell me is unethical. Parvi sent me to this fellow here," and she looks at Rauden, "a DVM who Parvi told me was so unethical he might do the work."

I looked at Rauden too. He was rolling his eyes like Henry.

She just ignored him. "Do you know what I asked this rube to do?"

I didn't know.

"To make a new child from what remained of my last one's skin, and this child would be gene for gene Madhur's living replica. Did Rauden tell you that?"

I heard him say that name. The gene for gene thing, maybe not.

"Did he say some would call it a crime against nature?"

"Rini, I don't think this is absolutely necessary."

"What if it is a crime against nature? What if nature committed a crime against me? Four daughters! One husband! I say, go bury two daughters who are so young they cannot even speak. Then tell me what is ethical!"

I shot a really fast look at Rauden. He shook his head.

"Do you know what this rube said? He said, to do what I had in mind, it *is* unethical. He said I am just asking a child to be born who will die like the rest from one Pandy or another."

I was so surprised he cares if it's ethical, I did look right at

Rauden. Nobody else seemed to notice. They were looking at each other. Suddenly, they were both smiling. Rauden was saying, "She drove a hard bargain though."

Rini explained, "I was mad with grief."

Now it was like a song, where everyone knows the parts before they sing. Rauden went, "I asked her to consider something radically different. I said, Rini, it's not what we discussed, but at least you will end up with a child who at least has a goddamn chance of staying alive."

"At first I refused. This time it was me who said it was unethical."

I remembered that.

"But then I changed my mind. And I will tell you why. You see, while we discussed all this by phone and message, I was in Sydney, Australia, and then in Vancouver, in quarantine, watching on TV, like everyone, the spread of Mumbai, which everyone says is a variant of that terrible Luzon virus that killed my family. I watched on the News the bodies of corpses, and some of them were tiny children, babies, and I will tell you, I tore my hair, I scratched my cheeks! Do you know why I did these things?"

I said as quiet as I could, "Mad with grief?"

I don't know if she even heard. "It was because I thought," now she pointed a finger straight up, "whatever I do, this terrible disease will kill whatever child I have! It is my Fate! My Fate to be the mother of a child who dies of it. As Luzon Third killed the original Madhur, so Mumbai would kill the new child I would make from Madhur's skin, which would be gene for gene her living replica. It is my Fate that no child I will ever have will stay alive.

"And then I thought," and she grabbed me, "what is Fate?"

She kept grabbing me, so I said I didn't know. It turns out I was right!

Because Rini said, "Nobody knows! Fate *is* unknown. It is

unknown until it happens. Then, when it happens, you say, that was Fate. Fate is what happened. So then I thought, if I change what happens, that will change my Fate. I will change my child's Fate to someone else's Fate, who would stay alive. If I was ready to be unethical with my own daughter's skin, why not with someone else's daughter's skin?"

I forgot not to look at Rauden. I looked at him and asked, "The child won't be her daughter?"

"No, no, no!" said Rauden. "She means you. *You're* someone else's daughter."

Rini just went on, "I do not want a genius or a beauty star! She could be tall or short. Dark or fair. Smart or dim. All I want is one child who will stay alive. Is it so much to ask? So you must tell me," she told me, "what do you think of that?"

I said, "Am I a Sylvain hardy?"

Rini went stiff. "Why bring this up now?"

I said, "Are their eggs subpar?"

Rauden started to laugh and laugh and Rini to weep and weep so hard I wished I never said anything. "You must tell her," she gasped. "This is not some cow or pig or bird or treefrog. This is not tissue in a jar. This is a human being."

"Yes. Well!" Rauden cleared his throat. "It's not so much your," cough, cough, "eggs we would be working with."

I looked back and forth between them.

Rini wiped her eyes and told Rauden, "You must explain."

Rauden ran his hands through his hair. He cleared his throat again. "Well! Normally—if anything can be called normal any more—when the reproductive product is mixed in a dish, male and female, the female product, well, the solo, the egg, contains," he coughed, "genetic information. Genes! DNA! Like letters— A, C, G, T, which spell words—which tell the baby what it is. Through protein! The male solo too, sperm. Each gives half the genetic information, half the letters, the words. But we have something else in mind. We don't use the male solo. We don't use the sperm." And he looked at me and waited, so I will have time to get what he said.

Which I didn't.

So he just stood up and walked around the room. "You may well ask—will this child be half a child?"

I'm not going to ask that.

But Rauden bends over where I'm sitting and says, quiet, "It will be a whole child."

They both got really quiet now.

Then he takes a deep and noisy breath. Then he starts talking really fast. "We empty out that egg until it has nothing in it. Well! Mitochondria—which arguably makes the whole thing happen. Well, cytoplasm."

Rini is going, "Rauden, that is beside the point."

So he leans back and goes on, "How will this child know who to be, then?"

Ok.

Rauden opens both puffy hands wide, like here is the answer. "It will simply take its cues from somewhere else, not eggs, not sperm, but a single cell of a complete human being from, say, the skin, or breast—what we call soma! From a single cell from one Donor—say, you—from the nucleus of that cell, actually— which is the center, or boss, or instructions—the code—well! DNA—of that somatic cell from the skin, or breast—"

"Rauden!"

"Yes! And all that information from the single nucleus of that somatic cell will go into that egg which has—for the purposes of this discussion—nothing in it. And it will tell the child who it will be. Do you get that, I?"

Now Rini says, to me, "You must tell us, Inez."

This is not regular intake. This is like a game, where they know the answer, and I must guess it. I take a few deep breaths like Rauden told Delmore to. Then I give it a shot. "You want me to provide the egg with nothing in it."

They both look at each other. Then Rini sat up tall, like she is proud. "I will provide the egg with nothing in it."

So try again. "Bernie will patch me up, though it is risky, Rini will change her mind again, and I'm the Host."

Rauden just looked at me this time, hard, like, where did that come from, before he answered, "She wants a virgin Host. God help us all."

I'm running out of answers here. "I don't provide anything, but will still be paid."

Rauden coughed, the way he does. "You provide the soma, actually," he said.

Nobody said anything.

The Alert buzzed. Nobody went to pick it up. So I go, "Like the pigeon for Larraine?"

Rauden seems stunned again, like something hit him on the head. Finally he goes, "Well, yes! You could say that." Then he adds, "Like Daisy too."

Wait.

Rini said, "People will say this child is you."

I start to think I heard of this.

"Rini, the child won't be her. That's a physical impossibility."

"The child will look exactly like her."

Maybe I saw it in a cartoon.

"Well, so do twins. Take Henry and me. We even shared the same environmental factors in our upbringing and you know he's not me."

"You must tell Inez what that means."

"Well! Yes!" He mops his sweat off with a sleeve. "The environmental factors are—well! What happens in someone's life. It's someone's life, but—not the kind the Knights are on about—it's not a *thing*. Well—neither is Life. But environmental factors can legally be bought and sold." He seemed to have trouble following himself here.

I go, "You want to make a clone from me."

So now it's like they are both stunned, like what fell on their heads is a heavy box. They are never going to talk again, they are so stunned.

"Well!" Rauden gets out. "You can call it that if you want. We prefer SCNT. Somatic Cell Nuclear Transfer."

I look at both of them, like, that's the answer?

"You could just say Transfer," he goes, "if it's simpler."

"Clone sounds so negative," goes Rini.

"And then—we could go to jail. Or worse."

But Rini shut him up. "It does not matter what you call it. What matters is how Inez feels about it."

Not this again.

She pulls me around by my shoulders so I have to look right in her face. "You must tell me how *you* feel. Because there will be foolish people who will tell you she is you."

"For God's sake, Rini! Nobody's going to know! They'd have to see them in the same room, side by side."

But Rini would not let me go. "How will you feel, if they say the child is you?"

Man! How do I know? But she is not going to let me go till I come up with something, so I try. "I would feel, will I still be paid?"

Rini let go of me so fast I almost fell. She sank back on the couch. She looked loose and floppy, like an old rag. "Does this girl think only about money? Has she no self-esteem? No character? Has she no feelings at all?"

I'm never saying anything again! Every time I say anything, it is a problem. Even Rauden's eyes are closed.

Finally Rini whispered, and it is like a hiss, "Why do you do this? Why do you treat your life like something that can be bought and sold? New Life labs—my God! Will you do *anything* for money?"

Well, Rini knew more than me about Fate, but how it looked, she was a little challenged when it came to girls like me. But remember when I said she was a part of it? And I don't mean mito-whatever or even money. She was like an environmental factor. And I will tell you this. I never met an environmental factor like her. I did need the money, but I never gave any thought before why I do these things? I gave it now.

"I like to see what happens," I told Rini.

And I could see her eyes change when I said that, like, would someone do these terrible things just to see what happens? Then they change again, like, ok. There are worse things. "In school," I told Rini, "one of the Sisters said I could of passed, if I did the work."

"She gets it, Rini. She gets more than she shows," Rauden said.

But Rini got something else. She burst into tears and pulled me to her, right where her breasts were large and warm and damp under her dress, gasping, "She wants me to know her good points, in case my child is her!"

Well, I'm not even sure that's why I said it. I don't know why I said it. But I'm glad I said it if it worked for her.

I just know when Rini pulled back, and I could breathe, she looked down and said, "You must think about it and say is there any part you do not understand."

And I did think about it. Hard. Then I go, "If we have the same gene for gene, you know, DNA. If somebody runs her pure code ID, will it come up, *Subject: I Kissena Fardo. Origins: unknown?*"

Now Rini and Rauden are looking at each other the way Rauden and Henry did. Do sofas think?

Finally Rauden said, "It can be a problem. Henry and I have to deal with that sometimes. You can usually talk your way out of it. The conventional ID swipe is less of a problem. Henry will fix that when he rigs up her ID. Why do you ask?"

"I got a way to bump stuff off I could show Rini."

Now they are both staring at me.

So I just say, "That I heard."

Finally Rauden says, very polite, "Inez." He calls me that in front of Rini, like he doesn't want her to hear him call me I. "Will you come in the next room for a moment?" We get to the Box Room and, remember how Rini hissed? He hisses, "Did you bump something off your files?"

I shook my head. "Lonnie Vertov did."

"Can you call it back?"

"It doesn't all come back."

"You sit down at the goddamn keyboard and show me how to call your files back. You fucking show me now."

I sat down at the keyboard, swiped in my ID, and punched in a reverse code I saw Lonnie Vertov use.

"But!" Rauden's gasping, when files start coming on the screen. "You're nineteen years old! You were born summer of '40, right in the middle of the goddamn Big One!" He leans over me and starts punching in keys. Next thing I knew, up popped a bunch of test sites from—"Dear God! You have a track record!"—'52, so what's it going to be but clinic tests the Vargas brothers ran after virgin Cures, but before he can print anything, the screen goes ballistic, then blacks out.

Rini is saying, from the other room, "She wants this to work! Even after she is paid." She is totally sobbing.

Rauden looks like his face is going to fall off. I mean, he hardly slept for two months, now the system crashed, and, well, if he accessed my test records to start, how much more could he charge? Fifteen percent? He probably already cut the deal.

But he pulled himself up straight and turned right around in his chair. He pulled his face right up. And where he sometimes was a mess, like slush, now he was hard, like, I don't know, plexiglass.

"It goddamn *will* work," he said.

2 THE WORK

THERE WAS THIS HORROR SHOW CALLED *THEM* that came up a few years later. I used to watch it even though it was really stupid. Well, guess who *Them* is supposed to be? Clones. No one but Rauden and us ever said SCNT or Transfer or any of that. In this stupid Horror show, how you make a clone, you drop product in a dish and bingo, it's a clone. Well, it doesn't work like that. It usually doesn't work period. Let alone, first try. So try again. Still doesn't work. You just got to keep trying and trying. Sometimes it never works.

And that's true even the regular way. The regular way got all kind of problems. That's why Bernie does such good business. He sells product that doesn't work good any more—male, female, pre-pandemic like the dickhead clients insist on. Plus for an extra fee, he will hook you up with a virgin Host. Though it is pretty hard to find one who wants the work.

What Rauden got to do here is harder than that. It's very fussy, like Bernie said, and that's just when cows are the Subjects. Imagine how hard it will be with Rini and me. And we are talking about after they got the parts. Even the regular way, you need the parts. You could mix them in a dish or person, but either way you need the parts.

Rini is egg Donor, and hers worked very good—nobody even knew why. Maybe vaccine Syndrome was not so bad where she came from. Some OBGYN beefed her up in Toronto, and Bernie timed his circuit around that, so he's in Buffalo when she's ready to cross the border, and he did the Harvest there. He pulled fourteen! He had a friend in Buffalo glider-drop them to the Farm for an extra fee.

I'm soma Donor, and Rauden have been getting that from me while this was going on. How you get the soma is, you scrape mostly from the breast, but also ear or butt. Freeze it till you need it.

When Rini's eggs arrive, he took five of them and some of my soma to a place in the basement where no one was allowed but him, and he came back saying it didn't work. Tried again. Tried again. Did not work.

So Rini had to start again.

Me too. He wants to keep on running Harvests from me. I don't know why he bothers, with Rini's eggs working as good as they did. But it's ok with me. I am in no rush to get back to Queens. The food is great, the weather warmed up. Everyone's in a good mood.

A lot of new things is hatching in nearby farms, like remember what Larraine had in the cage that went, Peep! Peep! Now it's, Chee, chee! Hoo, hoo! Once Rauden took me with him on an errand, and I could hear some of them through the truck window. Wee! Wee! Ba! Ba!

Rauden calls them Endangereds. He says all of them are, even the heifers. Flus killed half, and the stupid antiPatho spray messed so bad with male factor, SCNT is all that works. It worked very good on pigs. Henry brought one baby pig around, called Delmore. Delmore had a bro named Marcus who had died. They didn't even eat him. The ones that didn't work, they ate them sometimes, and they are pretty tasty. Marcus, no. Mad with grief.

It looks like Mumbai was not going to spread as fast as they thought. It pretty much wiped out Sydney, Australia, though.

Janet really wants me to go home. I'm in her basement again, and she's nervous I will attract attention and there will be a raid, but my next Harvest is a bust, and Rauden says I got to stay another month and try again. "Come on, Janet," he tells her. "Once this girl is out of here, we're never seeing her again. We have to pull what we can from her while she's here!" So I get to stay another month.

There is flowers in Janet's garden and corn starting up in Rauden's up the hill behind the Farm. Henry says he should make ethanol but Rauden will use it for booze. He will make it in a tub.

Because my Harvest been so subpar, Bernie talks Rauden into trying a megadose. Rauden beefed me up so hard he got drunk and punched a wall. It's a whole week till he could use the hand.

Rini got some problems too. After Sydney, everyone thinks Mumbai is winding down, and for sure nobody heard of cases in America, North or South, but there is still a lot of panic and the border guards are so tough, Rini is worried, if she crosses from Canada for her next Harvest, they will never let her back. She has her Toronto OBGYN do the Harvest and glider-drop them over the border from there? But the drop got stopped and boy, she was on the phone to every contact she had, "This is not your mitochondria! This is my mitochondria!" but by the time the cryoPaks get to the Farm, well, the SCNT might not of worked anyhow, how things been going. Who knows why it didn't work? But it didn't. So then they got to start again.

Bernie is missing. No one knows why.

In July, a different shady OBGYN ran my Harvest, in Cahoonzie. That megadose really worked! They get twenty. Twenty! Rauden's so excited, he wants to do another round, but Janet said not a chance.

So that's it.

"You have your Bonus?" We're in Lab 3, where Rauden is going to take one last bit of soma before I leave. "And don't forget that bag Janet fixed up for your ride home."

I said, "Dude! I know."

He is going to scrape the soma from my breast, the left.

"How good are the Zone North public Boards?" he asked, while he wipes my breast down, for Hygiene.

I said, "Ok, if they don't crash."

"Well, check your messages when you can." He gave the topical and we wait for it to take.

It is very early and always cool inside Lab 3 though it's going to be a hot day. It's very quiet because we're the only ones around. I don't know where Janet went. Rauden looks like he is having a hard time thinking of things to say, if you can believe it.

"What will you do when you get back to Queens?"

I said, apply to be an Opener. The pay is good and you are off the Mound but first must pass an Interview and purchase starter equipment. I could use the Bonus Rauden's giving me for that.

He's getting the scalpel ready. "You open suspicious packages from drops?"

I agreed. "In case some bioterrorist put a pathogen in. You could also do deCon cleanups, in houses where somebody died, or sometimes you clean up after antiPatho spray."

"What sort of pathogens?" he asks.

But his scalpel hand is shaking so hard that I tell him, "Come on. What am I, going to get Anthrax? *I already been exposed.*" And I gave him a little poke.

That got a smile. His hand is steady enough now to do the scraping. He did this so many times by now it's not even invasive. He put the scraping in a dish and I just waited on the lab stool with my breast out.

What happened now, Rauden did something that really surprised me. After he put a cover on the dish and started to wipe the blood off my breast with a cloth, he said, "Well, watch yourself. We're still not absolutely sure how this Sylvain hardy business works."

So I'm like, whoa. Why would he tell me that? He's never seeing me again. Why would he even care?

And I guess it is because I was surprised, or maybe just I will never see him again either, I start to think if I got something to ask, better ask it now. "What will you do with those eggs?"

"The Cahoonzie Harvest?" he goes, like he's surprised too. Like, Cahoonzie? That's the last thing in the world I would wonder about. "Well!" He finished wiping off my breast with an antiPatho wipe. "I suppose I'll try another stab at conventional IVF—you know what that is—test tube babies, even though we do it in a goddamn dish—I'll mix your eggs with frozen sperm from Dewey's old collection—just to see what happens. I have fresh male product too." He put a bandage on. "That should hold you." He put the scalpel and things where they went. I pulled on my shirt. He headed for the freezers with the soma dish in his hand.

But now I got started with the questions, I keep asking and asking, while I follow him to the freezers. "And if the, what you said, IVF doesn't work?"

He is opening drawers. I think he's looking for empty cryoPaks. "Well! I might try a bit of cloning. Enucleate a few of your eggs and transfer some nuclei from your soma."

Man! I really got used to how Rauden talks. "With nobody's product but mine?"

He finds a cryoPak, puts the covered dish with my breast soma inside, writes on the outside with a pen, and puts it in a freezer drawer. "Yes, it would be a," he coughed, "single Donor SCNT. It's done sometimes." He shuts the freezer drawer and heads to the Box Room.

Well, I just kept on with the questions. It's like a chasing game I used to play with Cissy Fardo, so long ago. I followed him to the Box Room where he sat at his gizmo and punched keys, and I sat on a box, like the first time I was ever in this room. "And if that works?"

He doesn't even look up from his screen. "If I get results using your eggs and soma, hmm. Well, I could use it therapeutically, of course. It can be very effective on damaged tissue, for instance I could use it to patch your," he coughed, "uterus, in case we ever need you for Host." Once he started coughing, he kept coughing so bad that he went for water in the room where I had the bath and he had put his head under the faucet, my first day at the Farm. This room was so small, I have to squeeze myself in behind him while he drank from the tap.

"If Rini wants a virgin Host," I go, "why would she pay to patch *my* uterus for Host? I'm never going to be a virgin Host. Did she tell you to patch me up for Host?"

"She doesn't know," he says, between gulps. "She doesn't need to know." Then he stood up from the tap. "I'd just be doing this on my own time—for science. Just to see what happens." He wiped his beard off, looked at his watch and seemed to be thinking. Then he gave me a smile I never saw him give anyone, even Henry. "Want to give it a try?"

I said sure.

So he went out to the freezers and got a few cryoPaks from the drawers, then grabbed lab suits, Hygiene gloves and masks from a closet, and we suited up. He headed down the hall behind the green light, with me following as fast as I could, to where three steps I never knew were there led down to another hall, very dark and cool. We came to a door to a little room. He told me go in this room. One wall had an inside window that I saw Rauden through in a minute, in another little room, where he lit one dim light. There were buckets, metal boxes, a table with a machine on it, and a monitor he turned on. I could see his fingers in it. I feel almost like the Seal Room test, the other way around.

He gets on a seat and fiddles with some things, sliding around, because the seat has wheels, like Henry's wheelchair. I sat on a stool in my room. Then he stopped sliding and just put his hands in his lap and sat.

I saw a different Rauden, all at once. Normally the guy is so nervous, you think he can't do anything, then, when he takes blood or spit or soma, he moves fast and clean? But it's not even like that. He didn't move at all. He sat very, very still, and I sat, period, both of us in dark rooms, not saying anything, with a window in the wall between, a long time.

Then he moved. He took the dishes out of the cryoPaks, put one in a kind of cooker, punched a button, pulled a mic, and whispered, "*Defrosting ova!*" I heard something beep.

He put the dish in the machine. It came up on the monitor, with four circles in it, clear except for a smaller circle in each that got dark stuff in it. "*Enucleating ova!*" he whispered. Well, what is that? A stick starts poking one of the clear circles. Poke, poke, poke. Then it got inside. It kept poking, till it poked the smaller dark circle. Skoosh! The dark stuff went up in the stick, the stick went away. Another one came back. The whole thing happened three more times. When he was finished, Rauden looked at me, over the mask. He seemed excited. I was too.

He whispered, "*Extracting nucleus from somatic cell!*" He did it with a dish of blobs. He got the dark stuff out of them with sticks.

Now it's the first dish, with the first four clear circles, empty. "*Ready to transfer somatic nuclei to prepared ova,*" he goes. Then he sits very still. Very, very still like before he started. Then he says, "Here we go." Back comes a stick with dark stuff in it, poking one circle. Poke, poke, poke, poke, so gentle, till it got in, then skoosh, the stuff went down the stick and when it skooshed out, it was that same dark little circle again, but inside this circle now. He did it with all of them. It took quite a long time. Then he looked over the mask, and even with just eyes you can see a great big grin. "Now for the shock!"

He squirted something on the circles. He lifted the whole

dish of circles and put them very careful in a large plexi box, shut the top, patted it, then tiptoed from the room. I went out of my room too, down the dark hall to where a different door was open to outdoors and Rauden sat in the sun on some green steps near a tree covered with leaves. We were inside so long I forgot how sunny the day is, but there are shadows too, and a small breeze.

He already took his mask and gloves and even glasses off and now he closed his eyes. I almost think he would of gone to sleep for once, but the phone rang inside. He still looked relaxed when he was through taking the call. His skin even looked better. He looked shy. Music was playing. "I always like Sonny Rollins, after I do nuclear Transfer," he told me. "That's with an O."

Ok.

And he lit up a cigarette. Where did he find that? He smoked it in the sun and when he finished, leaned back on the Quonset metal wall and told me a lot of things. He said if it works, the things he just made start splitting maybe in a day or so, the way it works the regular way, or is supposed to. If you were going for multiples, you separated at whatever cell number, up to eight, you had in mind. He did this routinely. "The first cloners used human hair for the separation."

I'm leaning on the Quonset metal too. "What do you use?"

He turned his head and gave me a really long look. If I had to guess what he was thinking, he was thinking, who'd believe her, even if she told? "Sound waves."

He can be sure I'm not going to tell anyone that.

I just closed my eyes and felt how warm the Quonset metal is, from the sun. "How long before you know if it worked?" I asked and don't even open my eyes.

"Forever," he said. "This is so totally experimental. It would take the child's entire life—maybe the child's child's life—to know if it really worked. Well! It's still an open question what it does to all the fucking livestock we made! Not that they die young, though some have, and there is that business with the telomeres—well! You don't need to know about that." And he was quiet for a long time.

There went the small breeze again moving the branches of the tree, and this shadow from them is moving over us where we leaned, like the shadow was tickling us. I honestly think I never been out in a nicer day than this.

"But if it doesn't work, period," he said at last, "we'll know that in a few days, if they die."

He went back inside to check the box.

So. He got everything he could from me. I have to go back to Queens.

We could still hear the music behind us when we headed down the road in the truck. "What do you think is going to happen?" I asked.

He said he didn't know, and we both laughed, like now Inez is asking the questions and he's the one who says he didn't know. "If we get working viables," he added, "there would be a Bonus, if you came back."

We're brushing up against the bushes he hit that first time, driving in the dark. This time it's in the sun.

"Why would I do that?"

"Well!" he coughed. "To patch you up for Host."

"You know that's never going to happen."

"Give me a break, I."

We're back on the regular county road.

"And if what you did today does make, you know, viables that work?" I went on. "And they are the only ones you ever get?"

He waited awhile to speak, going down the regular road. "Well, Rini drives a hard bargain. But she does have an open mind."

"It won't be her mitochondria," I said.

"I, will you give me a fucking break?"

I didn't say anything until we're on the big road that goes to the Terminal. Then I say what I was thinking, and I think he was thinking it too. "So you think if they work, what you made today, she will want them to be her kid? Even if it's not her mitochondria or what she discussed?"

He got to fix the shade in front of him, because we are driving right into the sun. "I think she will."

I guess I thought so too.

So that's it.

I went home a different way, across the river at Newburgh on a bridge they let you cross on, then down through the Bronx. Because of Mumbai cautions, they hose you with Hygiene spray at the Bronx city line, then again at Queens, where it is really hot and smells worse than ever. I walked carrying my winter things in the bag Janet fixed for me, all the way from Flushing Main Street past the burnt houses and caution tape that is always on Northern Boulevard to where I had been living, near Powell's Cove on a little side street half burnt to the ground where no one lived but me. The little side street seemed different. I don't know why it did. I was still the only one who lived on it. I was still the only one in my whole great big empty house. It seemed different.

The city seemed different too. Of course, there are new Mumbai cautions at Zone crossings and extra checkpoints and barricades, but I thought it's possible, what's different was me.

I checked for messages regular like Rauden said. I mainly used the 14th Avenue Board across Flushing Bay from the old airport, but got nothing for so long, I tried the Board on Flushing Main Street that sometimes works a little better, and bingo. It's one of those messages that come with a talking vid of guess who? Rini Jaffur, going ballistic.

"This is not what we discussed! This is not what we discussed!"

And that's how I found out it worked.

ii

It must be early September when I got this deCon job in Forest
Hills. By now, I been doing Openings and deCon ever since
I took the Interview at Iron Triangle Bazaar and passed with
flying colors. I used my Bonus on the bubble suit they make
you wear even though I don't need it because I am a Sylvain
goddamn hardy, but no one in Queens knows what that is. I
even had enough coupons left to buy a fancy bag to carry the
bubble suit around in. The pay is good. I already moved from
my old neighborhood and have been crashing in an empty unit
in Flushing near a few people and even stores, not those stupid
food and water Lockers you got to use in Powell's Cove. I'm off
the Mound. I really got a different life.

So, I'm just walking around Forest Hills with my fancy bag,
when it hits me, hey! Why not see if the Austin Street Board
works? The Zone North Boards been down all August, and I
have not got any message from the Farm since Rini Jaffur. I
tried every Board I knew—14th Avenue, Flushing Main Street,
even Little Neck. Nothing worked. It's Queens. But this Board
looks pretty good. I swiped my ID in a slot, the screen lit up, and
what is this? Four messages in a row.

1. Get back to me.

2. Something happened.

3. I! Will you fucking contact me? You need to get your ass up
to the Farm ASA goddamn P.

4. There will be a Bonus.

Well, I just jumped on the first hybro I could make and head up to the Farm.

It didn't leave till the next morning. I spent the night in a bin in Jersey, by the river checkpoint. Well, I spent worse nights.

By the way, in case you think I did it for the Bonus, I didn't need that Bonus. I got a good job now. I just wanted to see what's going to happen.

Janet Delize met me at the Terminal. She said Rauden's at some DVM emergency in Shinhopple, and she told me all the news on the way to the Farm. She had a new hairdo. Bernie is in jail in Johnson City. They got another shady OBGYN, in Port Jervis. They found a virgin Host for Rini that Bernie had checked out before he went to jail, but by the time they followed up, she wasn't a virgin any more and didn't want the work anyhow, so Rini said she will be the Host herself, that way she can be sure the Host won't run off with the kid.

By now we're back at the Farm, where I forgot how windy it is, and Rauden is already waiting in the truck. "Let's go, I," he yells, and off we roll to Port Jervis like I never even left, with him picking up where Janet stopped.

The new shady OBGYN implanted Rini with the four viables Rauden made my last day at the Farm. Rini went into shock. They pulled her through, but Rauden could only talk her out of trying again because he ran out of viables. While he mixed up a new batch, he researched some details about the Dearborn hardy Compatibility anomaly and found out that sort of hardy could be toxic to anyone who didn't have Compatibility to her. It looks like the new viables have that same anomaly. And he gives me that look he used to give when I can't understand a word—do you agree?

I agree!

He goes on, what if you're the only one who has Compatibility to them?

I agree.

Then I'm the only one who could be the Host. Nine months, all expenses. He researched how to patch my uterus that way Bernie said is risky. The new OBGYN will try it out.

The new shady OBGYN lived in a house off the main road and worked from an office over his garage. He laid me on a table and scraped tissue from my uterus. It was invasive. We drove back to the Farm in the dark and Rauden waited till we got there to call Rini with the new plan. She hit the roof—this is not what we discussed, Inez will run off with the child. But she got over it. Rauden said he knew she would.

He thawed out two of the new viables, mixed them with the tissue scrapings, and he will culture them. This is a little hard to follow but Rauden says I don't need to follow, I just need to go with him back to Port Jervis in ten days on an empty stomach, lay down on the table where they stuff what he mixed up into me, and stay on my back for three days, but when I stood up, everything fell out. I lost a lot of blood and passed out. When I came to, Rauden was on his Mobile yelling, "Fuck you, Rini! She could have bled out!"

Like that is really going to happen.

We drove back to the Farm.

Still, it didn't work.

I was pretty sure I will get sent back to Queens once I could walk but Rauden said stick around, now I already made the trip. We could run another Harvest.

Well, maybe you are starting to think Rini was right. I got no character. No self-esteem. I blew off a good job in Queens just because I want to see what's going to happen. First of all, I didn't mention this but Opening is boring, and deCon is worse. And by the way, Rini got so much self-esteem, she was ready to go into shock *twice* just so she could Host her own child, and wait till you hear what she got in mind to do now.

"Rini, are you out of your goddamn mind?" I was sleeping the Port Jervis thing off on the sofa when Rauden woke me up screaming at her on the phone. "I may be out of my depth here but while I've heard it's always a challenge to be a good mother I'd have to guess offhand IT IS FUCKING IMPOSSIBLE IF YOU'RE DEAD!"

She wants to draw my blood and put it in her by transfusion so she will get Compatibility from that.

She hung up.

Janet made Rauden call back and say he's sorry—you can't talk to a client like that or they will take their money and go. Well, Rini did get over it, but still. It's not like anybody knows what to do. Rauden is on the phone to Henry every day.

Janet heard of some guaranteed virgins available in Homer.

Rauden says, Janet, for God's sake don't you understand anything? That's not what it's about. So now he has to say he's sorry to Janet too. At least he doesn't have to say he's sorry to me, but even if he did, even if he says he's sorry to all of us, that doesn't help the main thing.

We cannot find a goddamn Host. I don't know why they're even bothering with my Harvest. He already has twelve viables left on ice from the Cahoonzie group that nobody knows what to do with. Rini didn't work as Host. The virgin didn't work as virgin. I work as Donor but if Host doesn't work, none of it works.

And to tell the truth, it looks like it won't. We went so far and after all that, it's not going to work.

Then Henry showed up one day with some guy in whiskers with a check shirt and diagrams, Rauden says, I, come along, and we all go to Four Corners and look at what he got. His name was Lucas. He lived in a Quonset at the bottom of a hill with mud, a few pigs and a cow and a shed. He took us in the shed and we checked the thing out.

Henry is looking at the hardware. Rauden is looking at some tubes. Lucas is pretty much just looking at me, but he explains to Rauden, "They pump the stuff in from some cow. You give her shots."

"What's the track record?" Rauden asked.

"Last time all four worked."

Rauden whistled.

"Whose product?" Henry asked.

"Violet 4."

They all nodded at that, like, oh! Violet 4.

"And how did they come out?" That's Rauden.

Lucas shrugged. "Alive. Three of them still are."

When Rauden came back to the Farm he told Janet to track Rini down and get her on the phone. He had a plan.

Well, when you hear what the plan is, maybe you will think this is so open minded, our head blew off.

Even Rini, on the speaker-phone from Toronto, shouted, "This is beyond unethical! Even for cows it is unethical."

"Let's not split hairs, Rini."

"Put Inez on. You would do this, Inez? Did Rauden say how long it's going to take?"

I said it's ok with me. The deCon work is freelance. I could pick it up again when this is done. Rauden is mouthing at me, "Pitch her, I," but all I could think of to say was, "Don't you want to see what will happen?"

Rini didn't even know if she did want that. Maybe she didn't.

You can be sure that Rauden did. At this point, I think he would of gone ahead even without her. It's true Rini already put some money down but nobody ever signed anything. It was my product. It was his time. It was even his storage. But come on. It's her child.

He kept on her case. "I don't say this Host always works, even with livestock," I heard him explain on the phone, "but the great thing is, it's technically not alive. So it can't die." Then, when he finished coughing, Rauden added, "And then, obviously—it's not going to run off with the child."

We all knew why he said it. It was her bottom line. We all really knew she would agree in the end. She was mad with grief. Maybe this plan is not the best one Rauden ever had, but face it. It's the only one left.

iii

It took about two weeks to get the parts for this new plan and the whole time, Rini is calling two, three times a day to say she changed her mind. "It would not be my genes! It would not be my womb!" She is on speaker so everybody hears. "IT WOULD NOT EVEN BE MY MITOCHONDRIA!"

"Rini!" Rauden yelled back. "It's an adoption. An *open* adoption—so goddamn open you can watch the whole nine months through a high-powered scope right up till the kid is goddamn born! But when it is, Rini! This child will be very, very special. Gotta go!" And he's off to buy a new backup generator.

What will be special, Henry says to me, is if after nine months in that cockamamie hoo-ha Lucas dreamed up, the kid is still alive.

Uh oh. Rini again. She got the same idea.

"What if my child dies before she's born?"

"We do multiples!" Rauden just got back with the generator. He is wiping sweat off his forehead. "Five. That's more than I've ever done with cows," he tells Henry and me, "but Rini doesn't need to know." Rini already has enough trouble getting behind this hoo-ha plan, without the cow details.

She stopped calling for a while. I think she had some meetings.

Leaves were falling when Rauden drove me to Port Jervis for my Harvest. An even dozen eggs! He just froze them for now.

He froze everything—he even had froze the uterus tissue that fell out of me in Port Jervis. He's going to thaw that for this new thing. It's going to need a lining. The regular way got a lining. They want to make it as regular as they could. They are even going to mike my heartbeat in.

Rini again. "This is not what we discussed. I do not need all five. Inez must take one." Remember she was afraid I'll run off with it?

"Will you give me a break, here?" Rauden is trying to hook up the new generator. "What's Inez going to do with a child?" But she hung tough and finally he just said fine. Inez will take one child. But he told me don't worry. It's never going to happen. Some of them will die for sure, and one of the ones that dies will be the one Rini said is mine.

When Lucas showed up with the last parts, him and Rauden put the thing together in the basement. Remember those little rooms three steps down where I watched him make viables? You go from there down more stairs to a big dark basement room behind a door no one will even know is a door if they don't already know it is. We been fixing this room for days. They had to rewire and put paint on the walls and floor. They let me help paint. Rauden and Lucas put up a wall inside so it will be two smaller rooms, one what they call a rec room next to the inside room where everything is going to happen, and they put a glassed window in this wall, so you can watch.

They brought in two sofas, six chairs, one card table that Janet did not need. There will also be a monitor like Rauden had when he made the viables. You need a monitor to scope to because what's going to happen will be very small, at least at first.

Ten viables are on ice to thaw as needed. They will use five, to start. Each will have its own section so he can take out any that die without touching the others, but there was a sort of layer they would share, a track made of plexi, the soft kind. The section walls are plexi too, and the whole thing looked a little like an orange, the sections of an orange, except there were just five sections. They're not calling it an orange though, or even Host. They call it the tank.

They had a frame for it to hang from, which was on wheels, so you could move it, and there were springs. Henry put a thermometer outside the tank so you could read how warm the tank is. It had to be warm. The lights mattered. It had to be dark in the room. But you had to see a little, so they put in special orange lights. The backup generator worked. The backup for the backup generator worked. It still required manual override in case of an outage, but this is not a problem. Someone would be there all the time.

The Port Jervis stuff is thawed and in place. They set me up on IV and did a few dry runs with my blood.

They gave me a shot.

There was a problem with some of the tubing. Rini had arrived but couldn't stand the suspense and while Lucas got a replacement, she went off to Goshen. She would come back to witness the implantation. Man! She had her own hybrocar!

Ok, the new tubing worked. They called Rini in Goshen.

The Port Jervis OBGYN and Lucas are already in the tank room with Rauden when she gets there, looking very pale. Henry was called to Albany sudden on a job, so it is just those three. She went up to the window with those great big steps she takes, and Rauden showed her the viables through the window, in dishes. He wore a bubble suit. So did Lucas. The OBGYN wore a green suit and mask. Rini nodded at all of them, then extra to Rauden, and he starts.

She already picked the names out. She made Rauden write them on the tank.

Ani, Berthe, Chi-Chi, Lily, and Madhur.

Rini sat on the sofa with me.

The first part will take a few hours. They will squeeze the viables down tubes, till they get to the tank. One viable to each section. They got no idea how long the next part will take. We'll only know when the wire lights up. If it does. Each section got a special wire that Henry dreamed up. It isn't regular, but who's going to say no to that? The regular way, you got to wait a long time to find out if the nesting worked.

Lily died right away. Rauden thawed a new viable and squeezed it down a new tube but she died too. So it is a problem with the section. They left it empty. I was really worried that Rini will be mad with grief but she was ok.

Ani, Berthe, Chi-Chi, Madhur.

She even was ok when they had to replace Chi-Chi. They called the replacement Chi-Chi. Rini took my hand.

Janet Delize put sandwiches on the card table. The OBGYN came out for a break and ate one. Rini ate nothing.

I had to eat my sandwich with the hand she didn't hold. I took a nap with her holding it.

Berthe lit up first.

Rauden said that's when he knew it's going to work. Janet says it is bad luck to say that, but what did she know? What did any of us know? We never did anything like this, none of us, even Rauden. Even Lucas, when it comes down to it. We don't even know when Ani and Madhur stuck, like, one minute nothing, the next, they stuck. They lit up.

Now everyone is getting excited. Will it work with Chi-Chi? We're not supposed to shout. When Chi-Chi lit up though, we did, even me.

Everyone really liked Chi-Chi!

Four lights showed in four sections of the tank. "They all goddamn worked!" said Rauden.

Except Lily.

Ani was mine. Rini was ok with just three. I could still have one, she says. Unless one of the others die. Then Ani will be hers.

We weren't supposed to go into the room for five days, then Rini was allowed to pay a visit. I wasn't supposed to go into the tank room at all because I might bond, but I went in with Rini because someone had to.

They made us wear masks, in case we give the viables something even though the tank was airtight and come on, these are Sylvain hardies even if you couldn't see them. It was hard to see anything. It was nice in the tank room though. It was so dark and warm.

Rini seemed happy when she came out, but she was nervous still. Rauden was nervous too. He kept working but his hands shook. Lucas and Janet Delize was all right. I was all right too. I was excited.

You know how I been saying, it's interesting? Horses, meatloaf, cows? Nothing since I ever got up here been as interesting as this.

Rauden was so interested he was dropping things. He was so interested, Henry had to come back from Albany to help. The Port Jervis OBGYN already left. Henry was around a lot.

We all sat in a row in the rec room, watching the monitor. We drank coffee and Beverages. Donuts, chips.

"Like watching the grass grow," Henry said.

He and Rauden began to giggle.

The suspense was too much for Rini. She went for a drive.

The feeding traffic was arranged like this: They stuck the IV in my arm, with two sites, which ran both ways, out, then in, attached to bags. One bag took my blood, which got things in it to nourish the viables. The other bag brought the used blood back from them.

Rauden said, "The child doesn't exactly eat the product that comes in. It doesn't use its mouth. Even when it has one. It takes the product in and turns it into, ahem, itself. Herself. The product is like letters of the alphabet. She turns them into words. The words say what her body is. Well! Who knows who says what?" Everyone tried to ignore Rauden when he talked like this. It was interesting though.

The used blood got hung in its bag from my IV and piped back into me. I couldn't keep giving blood without getting blood back. I had to stay alive too, or it wouldn't work.

Well, we been doing this for three weeks now, and I am.

Ani, Berthe, Chi-Chi, and Madhur too.

It's November. There is early snow. I am allowed to go upstairs and look. Henry made a loop of my heartbeat for while I'm gone. Janet thought anybody's heartbeat would work, but Rauden didn't want to take the chance.

When I got back downstairs, I conked out on the sofa. I was so tired.

Five weeks in.

"I! Come and see!" The viables got tails. Rini is at the monitor. She says they look cute. Henry said they looked like shrimp. I never saw a shrimp, but who cares? Just let me lie down.

"It's the hormones, bro. How bad she feels is a good sign."

Rauden worries I am going into shock.

"It's regular!"

Rauden would like to filter the blood coming back to me, but that would mess with the hormones. The hormones is a message the viables send to me, like, "I! Conk out. Breast! Hurt very bad." It worked.

"Don't worry, bro," Henry pats Rauden's hand. "She'll stay alive."

So far, so good.

Rini had a business emergency and went back to Toronto. Henry rigged up a special vidPhone in the rec room so she can call night or day.

It's December.

We got an emergency too—an unknown van sets off the old system alarm near the gate! It's an Inspector! Rauden says everyone be quiet as a goddamn mouse. Shuts the rec room door tight and went out to deal with things. Janet got scared. Henry got silly. He wheels right up to the window and is whispering to the tank, "Chi-Chi! I heard that. You are so grounded." Everyone got the giggles, even Janet, but after that she was spooked and did not want me to leave the basement at all, in case somebody sees me and asks questions. She wants me to stay downstairs the whole rest of the time, so no one will know. She even wants to lock the basement door.

"For God's sake!" Rauden says. "You can't lock a person in a basement for nine months."

Henry said, "Afraid she'll get sick, bro?"

That got a good laugh.

It snowed again.

Rauden sent Lucas off. He was getting on everybody's nerves, how much staring he been doing. Stares at me then at the viables' picture on the monitor. Then me. Then viables. Then into space.

When he's gone, Janet starts doing it!

"Oh, not you too, Janet!" Rauden goes. "Janet, they are as different from her as I am from Henry. If they're her, I'm Henry. Yes! We have things in common—there is a certain predisposition. But that's all it goddamn is."

She kept doing it though.

"What do you think, I?" Henry asked. "Are they you?"

Henry called me I. Lucas did too. Rini called me Inez. Janet did not call me anything, most of the time.

I just said whatever. I don't even know what the big deal is, who is who? They could be me if they want. Why would they want?

Rauden could sleep on the other sofa now Rini's not using it, but he does not seem to sleep. I would see Henry sometimes sleeping in his wheelchair. Rini woke us all up, anyhow, calling at all hours, are they still alive?

Yes, Rini. They're still alive.

Sometimes she just wants to change her mind about who will get what child. She was the only one who thought they will all be born.

And to tell the truth, just before Christmas, the one called Berthe died. Nobody even knew why.

She was ten weeks in.

Rini wanted to come down from Toronto but Rauden said what is the point? He put what is left of Berthe in the freezer.

So there were three left. And none of them were mine. Henry went to Quarryville. He had a job. It snowed.

I missed Berthe. Man! I cried. Rauden says it is the hormones. When Rini asked me how I feel, I cried. Why would I miss Berthe?

Twelve weeks in.

Maybe it was Ani I missed. She was still alive. But she wasn't mine any more, because she had to replace Berthe. To tell the truth, I never took it serious, will Ani be mine. I didn't even know what it meant.

On New Year's Eve, Delmore heard horses and we shut the rec room door and Henry stayed with me in the room quiet as a mouse while Rauden waited upstairs with a shotgun.

False alarm.

There is also a false alarm about Mumbai hitting Ottawa, where Rini had gone for a meeting, but it took weeks till they figured it out and all that time she's stuck in quarantine.

In Macau, it's real. Mumbai took half the city.

Rauden rigged up a TV Signal to the monitor so we could follow the News. Taipei too. Then a big jump and Mumbai took out what's left of Luzon.

Rini kept calling from Ottawa because what else is she going to do from quarantine? I told her Ani, Chi-Chi, and Madhur are still alive, but she wants to know how I am. I said I'm tired. She said put Rauden on.

He yelled at her. "Rini! She doesn't want the goddamn child!" And he is right.

What am I going to do with a kid, the life I live?

I watched Ani very careful though. She moved. Sixteen weeks in.

Sometimes I thought about how it worked with Rini. How first she wanted gene-for-gene Madhur. Then Rauden talked her into my soma and her mitochondria. But when Rauden got viables from just me, she wanted them. Even the regular way, how it used to work, maybe you end up with a kid you didn't plan. You changed your mind.

When Rini called, I told her Ani moved. She wants to hear about Madhur. I told her Madhur moved too. Chi-Chi too.

Between you and me though, Ani moved the best.

They are swinging on their, you know, the cord. They all got one and Rauden says how useful the cord is if you remember to save it, but nobody does. Ani did the swinging first. But now they're all swinging. I showed Rauden. Is it regular? He looked it up and said it is. "No need to tell Rini, though."

It snowed again.

It's not a false alarm in Seattle, Washington. Two hundred

cases confirmed. So it hit Mainland. But back in India, where it began, is worst. It hit all over again. It spread every direction.

Nineteen weeks in.

She was a little smaller than my hand. They all were.

Cases in Chicago.

It snowed and rained. Rained and snowed. I had a really deep sleep and when I woke up, Chi-Chi was dead in the tank.

Rini drove the hybrocar straight down from Toronto which took four days with border problems and the weather. When she got to the Farm she strode into the rec room like a big curtain, walked up to the window, and scratched her cheek till blood dripped on her clothes. It dripped on the floor. She tore her clothes. She began to walk up and down the rec room, holding up her bloody hands and making a noise. It was awful.

Rauden went upstairs. When he came down, he was drunk. "Get her out of here," he said.

They hooked up my heartbeat loop and I went with Rini for drives. It was almost five months since I even went outdoors. We looked at scenery. It was cold and wet. When we got back to the Farm she was raving and moaning again.

It was like, when she looked at the ones who were still alive, she just saw the ones who weren't. She seemed to get nervous looking at Ani and Madhur. Maybe she was thinking of Berthe and Lily. Maybe the original Madhur. Maybe the sisters.

They had heartbeats.

Rauden was drunk. He kept drinking even after Rini finally left. He was even popping pills. He was cold and sweating all the time. If you accidentally touched him, you would want to wash your hands, that's how slimy he was from cold and sweat. Even Janet Delize was concerned, because if Rauden went off the deep end, the whole thing wouldn't work. Sometimes he was totally out to lunch. I had to remind him to check the IV bags. I don't know who had the idea, set him to work cloning again. I think it was Henry, calling from Albany. Henry said, give him a Project. That will keep him sober.

There were still viables in the freezers, twelve eggs from my Port Jervis Harvest and a lot of frozen soma. He had trouble getting it to work at first. That worked almost better—he had to be totally sober to concentrate. He tried conventional IVF with male solos twice. That never worked. He had to try two times before the nuclear Transfer worked. Then he got eight working viables, split those to multiples of four, and when it's all done, thirty-two new viables went in cryoPaks upstairs.

Well, maybe you wonder, wait a minute. Thirty-two viables, just made to keep Rauden sober? How ethical is that? And by the way, what's going to happen to them? Maybe they are not me, or Ani, or Madhur, but face it, they will be at least a little similar, right? Don't I care if they are ever born? Well, I'm going to get back to you on that.

For now, those viables are in the freezers, and I'm in the rec room. Ani and Madhur are in the tank, twenty-two weeks in, and Ani is blinking. I wasn't feeling so great. Generally it is Rini who calls to say, "Did Inez have her milk Process? Did she have nourishment?" Now she's forgetting to call. Rauden is getting on my nerves. He can't give up this toxin business. Nobody ever did a full-term study of the Compatibility anomaly. What if there is a late-term toxin that is going to kill me now? I am like, oh shut up, Rauden. All the things I been exposed to in my life, and I am going to die from Ani and Madhur who are not even born?

But I'm getting ahead of myself. Because Ani died in the tank at twenty-six weeks. So Madhur was the only one.

When Rini got the news, she drove down to the Farm and stared at Madhur for a long time, and everyone is worried, here we go with the cheeks but she did not even have fresh blood, just scabs from Chi-Chi. She took my face in her hands. She did not scratch my cheeks. She just looked down at me. Then she unhooked me, took my hand, and we went upstairs to tell Rauden he could only freeze a small piece of what was left of Ani, and she would take it with her. It belonged to her. We burnt the rest, to ashes. We had a ceremony in the woods. Even Rauden went. He seemed really nervous. He wasn't drunk though. Lucas came back to keep an eye on Madhur and the tank.

Rini took me for a long drive when the ceremony was over, to a hilltop where there was an old farm, or used to be a farm, which was burnt. We got out and walked around and we threw Ani's ashes in the wind. It was starting to be spring now, but windy. Rini's skirts and veils were flapping hard. She was ash-white; her lips were practically purple. There were large black shadows and hollows around her eyes. Her hair was dirty.

She turned to me, in the wind. "You must promise me," she said, and she had to shout for me to hear, "if something happens to me, you will take the child."

"What could happen?" I shouted back. But, to tell the truth, I could think of things. She looked like death.

"You must promise!"

"Rauden—"

"Rauden would sell the child! Promise!"

Finally I said, "Rini, I don't think you get this." I didn't think I'd be a good mother. The only thing that was worth anything about me was that after all I'd been through, I was still alive, and I didn't even pass that on to the original Ani who would of been mine.

"No, you must promise!"

She hung so tough that in the end I promised if anything happened, I would take her child. I mean, what are the chances? Right? But everything the two of us said here is going to be a very important environmental factor for what happens, in the end. For now, she brought me back to the Farm, then went back to Toronto to make preparations. Madhur's birth was approaching. She had to start work on the shady papers.

Rauden was going nuts. "You can't leave now! It is the last trimester. The birth could be any time!"

"No, I must go."

So she drove off. When Rini had a plan, ok, maybe she changed her mind. But no one else could change it for her.

Rauden had preparations to make himself. The Port Jervis OBGYN totally disappeared. Rauden and Henry had a bad feeling about him anyhow but thought they should have someone for the birth. Lucas had overseen tank births, but just with livestock, and Rauden himself had only delivered livestock the regular way. Then Janet Delize had a plan.

It seemed her cousin used to be a midwife. That might be good enough. It's not like all the extra things OBGYNs knew would matter, with the tank delivery. And it's not like even Lucas knew how this is going to work. None of us did. All any of us knew was that it was the twenty-eighth week and Rini's child was still alive.

They tried to have Rini show up for the Interview with Janet's cousin. They couldn't even get her on the phone. She sent a message she will trust our judgment. It sounded funny. She never trusted our judgment before.

Janet Delize's cousin had a very wide face and middle, a gray sweater, and a long skirt. Her name was Mariah Delize. She was a little bossy, but we weren't about to call the shots. If she wanted to call the shots, she could. It's not like other shady midwives were knocking on our door, you know?

The first thing Mariah did was pray, and she tried to get all of us to pray with her, including Rauden. Rauden refused. Janet and I got on our knees. Rauden got drunk. I heard him shouting at Mariah Delize from the hall. "She's not the mother. Technically, she's not even the birth mother. She's the Original."

Mariah Delize just shouted back. "I don't care if she's the boy next door! I want her at the birth!"

Maybe it wasn't even a birth.

Mariah Delize went away, then, till the time. Rauden went on a bender. Rini could not be reached. We got messages. We didn't get a call. Did she get sick? Mumbai had just hit Chicago.

Madhur was drinking, I don't know, whatever was in there with her.

We had six weeks left, or eight weeks, who knew how to count? No one was exactly sure how we would know the timing, but Mariah thought we didn't have to know, Madhur would tell us.

Which she did.

One day in May, the tank began to move until the frame rocked on the springs. I don't know why it did.

Janet watched the rocking and checked her watch. "That's way early," she said. It was just like Daisy.

They tried to call Rini in Toronto. They tried her in Ottawa. No one was there. They tried to call Rini's Mobile. It didn't work.

When Mariah Delize showed up, the first thing she did was play a tape of women screaming who are doing this the regular way.

Rauden was furious. He didn't want to attract attention by the screaming. Mariah said shut the door, that's what it's there for.

Rauden didn't trust Lucas, but in the end he called him. He really wanted to get the squeezing right. They didn't squeeze the tank direct, just some tube which went around the tank and made the whole thing rock harder.

Meanwhile, Rini Jaffur was nowhere to be found.

Mariah and Rauden are looking at their watches, for the timing. Janet just waited on the side. The frames were rocking. The tapes were screaming. I was supposed to be in the other room, listening to the screaming through the wall. I was supposed to breathe deep. I don't know why the women on the tape were supposed to scream. I don't know why Lucas and Rauden were supposed to squeeze. I don't know why I was supposed to breathe deep. I wasn't the father. I wasn't the mother. I wasn't even the birth mother. I was the Original. I didn't know what that was. I just sat there frozen in my chair, breathing deep, until the phone rang.

It was Rini, on the phone. The vid was dark. You could not see her at all. "Who is screaming?"

"It is the tapes." I told her the baby was on her way.

Rauden was screaming too. "You make her get her ass here, fast!"

I tried to make her hurry. I told her she would miss the birth. She said something had happened to her. She was in Delhi. Then she hung up.

"In Delhi?" Rauden said. "What's she doing in Delhi! They're dying like flies in Delhi. Shit, shit, shit, shit, shit!"

"The squeezing is too weak." That was Lucas.

They didn't know what to do. Rauden took a chance, give me a shot, what Lucas calls estro. They gave it a little time, then they draw my blood, send it back to the tank. So, my own messages went back to the tank, where Madhur is the only one of all five left. It didn't work. The walls in her section didn't change.

Finally, they stopped giving it to me. They just put it right into the track in the tank. It didn't work. They put it in her section wall.

They drew blood from the tank and put it back in me in case there was a message, which there was, I felt something, in what's left of my uterus. They had me squeeze what Lucas had been squeezing, which was a ball that went to the tube around the tank. Squeeze each time I felt something. That is good for the baby's brain, supposedly, but also could help her pop out. The regular way, she is supposed to pop through a regular hole, what Rauden calls cer, cer, anyhow it didn't work. The regular hole is in the regular uterus, but this isn't regular anything. It's liner from what fell out of my uterus in Port Jervis inside a wall that Lucas made a hole in, but it didn't work. It didn't stretch enough. They didn't want to just cut through and pull her out, like what they do the regular way when it doesn't come out the regular way. They tried everything they could. Mariah just reached her hands right in the tank and squeezed the wall. She had gloves on. You could see the top of the head, with hair, but Mariah couldn't pull the head through. They didn't know if I should keep squeezing too, or it might confuse the baby. None of this hurt me. I was glad they didn't make me try to scream. The tape screaming was already too loud. Finally Rauden said, "Turn that goddamn thing off," and Janet did, so then I just heard Mariah Delize grunting, and Rauden muttering, "Dear God!" and, "Shit! Shit!" Then I heard Janet say, "That's not her heartbeat!" It was mine. They had the heartbeat miked, but it was the wrong heart, mine, and when they got it all sorted out, they could tell something was wrong with hers. Finally they just cut right through the track, put their hands in up to the bloody wrists, and pulled her out. She was still alive.

iv

There is some kind of noise.

Static, from the monitor. You can't hear anything else.

Man, I conked out.

When I woke up, I could see them through the rec room window bending over, from the back. The static is still on.

Now, I don't know how it worked for you, when you were born. I don't honestly know how it works for anyone, anywhere. All I'm saying is, what happened now, I never saw anything like this.

They had a little suit for her, white, with arms and legs. It has a picture of, I don't know, I think it is a duck.

I mean, they cleaned her up first. She was a mess. But, you know, alive.

That I saw.

I only saw what shows through the rec room glass. They don't think I should get in the tank room too, in case I bond. If I gave milk, they would take the risk. I didn't give milk. I don't know why I didn't give milk. I don't know why I would of if I did. All I know is, she needs milk from somewhere if she's going to stay alive. They are putting a really small bottle of, I don't know, milk Process, in the mouth.

When they were finished, she was still alive.

They put her in a box, what they call dry tank, or incubator, like I had seen those tiny Endangereds in at Larraine's, that first night. It has glass in front. I have glass in front too, the rec room glass. They put a gizmo over her face so she can breathe. It worked. She woke up two hours later, still alive.

Then they are cleaning her up again.

Mariah says I should hold her, once. Nobody else wants me to hold her. They are afraid I'll bond.

They would, like, sniff when they held her. Someone was singing.

I did hold her once. I didn't bond. I gave her back to Mariah right away. I was afraid she's going to slip right through her clothes, they are so big. Janet said the way she's eating, they would not be big for long. When she ate, everyone stood around watching her eat.

She was two days old, still alive.

I still slept on the sofa. Rauden still didn't sleep at all. He was a wreck. Janet too. A tank is one thing. A baby makes noise. Someone could hear her. Someone could figure out what we did. To tell the truth, she didn't make that much noise. Janet was even concerned, something is wrong with her, she does not cry enough. Mariah Delize said, "What does she have to cry about? What a nice home she has here."

She was just saying it to keep us from thinking what had happened.

She was three days old, alive, and Rini was gone.

This is not a viable, or embryo, or whatever she used to be. This is a child. A child needs to live somewhere. A child needs a home.

When Rini finally called, Rauden was so furious, he could hardly speak.

So it was me who did the talking. I was angry too. I told Rini, "You missed the birth."

I don't know where she is but the vid she came through is

really bad. You could hardly see her face. You just see something dark. It goes, "How was it?"

I told the dark thing that is Rini, "Hard." I didn't know, compared to what. But I wanted Rini to feel bad she wasn't there.

"And how is the child?"

"Alive." I didn't think she deserved more than that.

"Thank God! Thank God!"

She sounds so happy, I broke down and told her more. I told her the baby had twenty-four bottles. Janet and Mariah Delize did the feedings.

She had fingernails.

Rini says, oh! Bring her to the screen, but Mariah's sleeping, Janet is out on a break, and Rauden and I were nervous to carry a baby that far. The connection went.

We felt a little better she called at all, but we still didn't know anything. We all just waited for Rini to call again.

Mariah went home. Janet did all the work now. She didn't really like me to touch the baby too much, and she thought Rauden would drop it. Janet didn't seem to get much sleep. Rauden got no sleep, but then he never did. By the time Rini called back, we were all so tense, I didn't even want to hold the phone. But Rini said she would talk only to me. "You made me a promise," Rini said.

I was really angry now. "I didn't steal the child. I didn't even bond! Was I the only one who made a promise here?"

For a long time, Rini didn't say anything. Man! Where is she finding these vidPhones? You could hardly see any part of her, everything is so blurry and dark. "That was not the only promise you made."

Now I don't say anything.

Now neither of us did. Then her voice goes, really soft, "If something happened." Now even softer. "Something has happened."

Remember she used to say, how do I feel? I felt something then. It was not good. "What happened?"

"I found Madhur."

"Your daughter Madhur?"

"She is my daughter now." She had found two older girls in Delhi who had survived Mumbai and Luzon too. The oldest one's name was Madhur. She had adopted them at once and changed the other one's name to Madhur too. "I went halfway around the world to make Madhur," Rini said, "and she was waiting here at home."

Remember everybody was squeezing Madhur when she was born? That's how I felt. Something was squeezing me. "What about *this* Madhur?"

"I give her to you."

I just went and got Rauden.

"Rini. You really must stop changing your mind."

You could see some blurry thing shake in the screen. It's Rini's shoulders. She is weeping. "I have made up my mind. I have found my daughters."

"Oh damn you, Rini! Damn you!" Rauden got so mad he almost choked. "I knew something would happen if you went off in the last trimester."

"What happened is my Fate!"

"What about your other Fate?" I said.

"Fate is what happens!" What happened was, Rini changed her mind. "In my heart I have always known this was not my child."

"Rini!" I said. "If you take her, she will be."

I could hear her sobbing. "I feel so responsible. I brought this child into the world."

I told Rini, "Then keep her!"

Rauden told her, "This is a real child, Rini. Someone must goddamn take her."

"Inez is not real?"

I go, "Rini! This is a special child! Don't throw her away on me."

She goes, "This child is gene for gene your living replica. Now tell me this—if she is gene for gene your living replica, how is she more special than you?"

I didn't know how to answer that. I was pretty sure she was more special. I just couldn't explain why.

Janet was very upset. "You just can't let her take the child." Janet thought I might do something really stupid. I did too.

Rauden was sitting on a sofa with his head in his hands. He was already exhausted. Now this. He looked ready to pass out.

"Rini!" I go. "If you don't want this child, at least let someone else have her. Rauden could find someone."

"Rauden would sell this child," she goes. "This is not Rauden's child to sell. I bought this child already! This is my child to give! I do not give this child to just anyone. I give this child to you."

Rauden said, "Oh shit, oh shit."

"You made a promise, Inez." Rini's voice is booming all over the rec room. "I make a promise too. If Rauden tries to sell the child to anyone else, you will all go to jail." .

Now, I want to say something here. I would never tell my own child I only took her so we won't all go to jail. But I say this, to you. It's for her own sake I didn't want to take her. It's true I bonded with Ani, but she died, and after that I thought who knows how good I would of been for her, anyhow?

Janet Delize is totally opposed. If I take the child, that's asking for trouble. If the baby and I were together this increased the danger someone would find out she was, you know. Someone could Alert the Authorities.

Rini heard her. "If you do not do as I say, I will Alert them, myself."

"Rini!" I just kept trying to change her mind. "How can I keep a child alive?"

But she already changed her mind as much as she is going to.

"The way you keep yourself alive. It will work for her the same way it works for you. And I will send you credit."

Then we lost the connection.

Janet argued, "Rini's in Delhi. How will she even know what happens?"

Rauden told Janet it wouldn't work anyhow to just sell the baby and say she was not what she is, because her genes are what people will pay for.

Janet says it's better to cut a bad deal than end up in jail. If someone else took the baby, just as a regular baby, no one would know her details. No one would ever see the kid and me side by side. If I took her, they would. What if this baby grows up? She is gene for gene my living replica. If she's living as my daughter, it could show.

Rauden called Henry in Albany. Henry says what does Inez want?

I said I didn't know. It all happened so fast. All that time trying to make the viable, then all those months in the tank, changing the bags, checking the lights and thermometer and monitor, then whoosh!

Henry said, "Well, I think that used to happen even the regular way. Even when it was planned. You plan and plan, then whoosh! Right, Janet?"

Well, Janet knew what he meant but did not like to agree. She wants us to go to someone named Fergie across the Pennsylvania border. Fergie will see the kid gets a good home.

So Rauden says, well, let's just look into the situation, and we pack up blankets and bottles and powder Process and get in the truck with Janet holding the baby, but we don't even get past the gate, because some stranger is waiting there with a paper from Rini's brother's lawyer. I didn't even know Rini had a brother, let alone the brother has a lawyer, which I'm not even sure what a lawyer is. It could be a Toronto thing. Janet thinks it's a bluff.

But Rauden thought, better take a few deep breaths. So we went back inside and down to the basement. Janet fed the baby again and lay her in the little glass box. Then all three of us stood in the rec room and watched her through the window, sleeping.

"I don't even know why that poor child was born," said Janet.

She was six days old and sleeping. Wrinkled and bald. She got the veins all over the great big head. She got the skinny little body in a fuzzy yellow suit. Whoa! What is this? Her little arms and legs go shooting out. She's spazzing out! Spazz! Then it's all over. She calms down and twitches.

And she is still alive.

In the end Rauden said, "Just take her. Leave me the ones in the freezers." Janet and I said no, but he said, "Take her."

So I did.

I did what Rauden said. I did what Rini said. Look, I never claimed I got any character. I did what people said. Maybe I got it as environmental factor from Edgar Vargas in Queens. Maybe I got it from some other broker. Maybe I got it from Cissy Fardo. Someone told me what to do, and I did it. I'm even letting Rini pay credit for me to bring up my own child. How much character could this poor kid end up with, with an environmental factor like me? I sold Rini my own daughter, even if I didn't know she was my daughter.

But remember when Rauden said, well it's hard enough to be a good mother but harder if you're dead? I had some good points as a mother, and the best one was, I was still alive. My own mother—my birth mother? That was her big problem as a mother. She was dead.

So I did what Rini said. I took her child.

The last time Rini called, I only heard her voice. She was calling somewhere totally without vid. "They are doing as I said?"

I told Rini's voice, "They have to give her Supplement. Madhur has a weight problem."

"Who is Madhur?"

I waited. "I thought you want to call her Madhur."

"The child I want to call Madhur is not your child. Madhur is my child."

Sometimes I think Ani was the last unplanned child anyone heard of. Madhur was planned. Ani was a kind of accident. We all planned for Rini to have Madhur. Rini's baby was planned. Mine was not. So because she was unplanned, I had to come up with a name in a hurry. Ani was the only one I had.

We moved into Janet Delize's temporary. Stay off the Farm, because Farms are always what gets raided first—whether it's Albany Inspector or K of L or whoever. We could be in real danger, even with Ani out of the tank, looking like a regular baby. But what are we even doing with any kind of baby? Janet really wanted us out of her house yesterday. But we can't leave until I know how to keep Ani alive. I got to learn the ropes.

Because we made history here. That's what everybody said. Even Janet knew it.

And maybe something was wrong with it. Maybe it was even a crime against nature. But whatever it was, they want to be sure I don't do something stupid with it. They were pretty sure I would. I was too.

But one thing I was sure of. I wasn't going to sell her. Never even crossed my mind. And I can tell you this. I never sold a single part of Ani, ever. Teeth, soma, nothing. Not even fingernails.

So I guess that proves she wasn't me, right there.

3 THE ROPES

MY LIFE AS ANI'S MOTHER STARTS RIGHT HERE.

It's true I knew her from the tank but she was Rini's daughter then. I still sometimes thought she was. I still sometimes forgot she's not Madhur.

She was still Rauden's Project. She used to be my job. She's not my job now. I don't get paid. Well, Rini will send credit later. But I'm still going to be the mother. Henry is going to fix up both our swipe IDs to prove it.

They put us in Janet Delize's basement with cots for me and Janet too till I learn the ropes. They put a cloth on the window so no one could see. They didn't want anyone but us to know. They're really worried that if word gets out, there could be a raid from an Inspector, let alone Knights of goddamn Life. They didn't even try to find a crib for Ani, because that could call attention, if someone happened by. They just put her in a regular box on the floor.

And she was very good.

Janet Delize said so. She slept through the night. Remember when we first looked at Lucas's tank, Rauden and Henry were like, oh! Violet 4! This is like, oh! Slept through the night! They are worried to say too much on the phone, but this is such a big deal Rauden even tells Henry on the phone. Rauden made history but come on—one week old, still alive, and slept through the goddamn night!

Henry says, well if she sleeps so good, will she miss some

feedings? Then everybody worries, oh! Miss some feedings. Well, it's ok with me. I'm the one got to do the work. I got to learn the ropes. That is the big thing. Learn the ropes. Rauden made history here, and everyone is concerned, could she breathe, could she respond, but the big concern is I'm going to be her environmental factor and do something really stupid. I was concerned too.

Rauden is researching what he calls a Haven, in New Jersey, where Ani and me will be safe and have help and Support, but even so, her main environmental factor is going to be me. She is a Sylvain hardy, and as far as they could tell she's not getting Luzon, Avian, Typhus, Marburg, Ebola, Polio, TB, Hep A or B or C or D or HIV or HP51 or any of that. But drop her, it's over.

And watch out for the neck.

When I pick her up, Janet Delize is like, the neck! And watch out for those wrinkles! Clean them really good! The neck! The vagina! Clean them really good! Boil the water you mix the Process in. Boil the nipples on the bottle. Boil everything. Or she could get something. Wrap her up good. She is a Sylvain hardy but do what Janet says.

Remember in the trailer, Rauden was fussing, am I warm? Am I safe? Like, I'm so hardy, be very sure I am ok? Ani's so hardy, be very sure she stays alive. She is the history Rauden made. And guess who got to pick her up?

Look, this kid spent pretty much her whole life in a tank. She might rather stay in her box. She might even prefer the freezer in the other room in Janet's basement. She spent a lot of time on ice before she was born. If she prefers the box, or a freezer, I wouldn't take it personal.

She preferred me. I don't know what that proves.

Between me and Janet Delize, I'm pretty sure she preferred her. But Janet said, do the feedings, she will bond.

Just get it in the mouth.

You have to hit their back after, or they will get wind. I didn't even know what that meant. But I don't have to know. Just do it.

Rauden used to take notes and say she was just like any baby. I had the feeling he didn't know that much about any baby. He knew baby pigs and cows. Remember Rauden used to say he might be out of his depth? He was out of his depth. We all were.

Even Janet Delize was out of her depth. Like now that it was ok to bond, in fact I was supposed to bond, she would say how much the baby looked like me, then freeze up and said, well! Not exactly like me.

I mean, she didn't look like me at all. She is red. And wrinkled. Watch out for those wrinkles. Watch out for the neck and make sure she can breathe.

We all spent a lot of time watching her breathe. Henry watched too, now he came down from Albany. Breathe! Well, look at that little belly puffing up! Breathe! It empties out till you can see the ribs. This is regular. Sometimes she puffs in and out fast.

Whoa! Spazz Alert! It is not my fault. It's regular. Spazz is regular. Green shit is regular. Rauden calls the shit "stool" or "it." Like, "Her stool can be green, but if it has blood, call a professional."

"But just a lot of blood," Janet Delize said. She really rather nobody professional see Ani. Do not call attention. Someone might notice something. Janet calls shit "poop" or "business." I mean, she will say "stool" but cough first. Clean it off with cloth. Wash the cloth. If you don't, the kid will hit the roof. Remember the hormone used to send a message, do this or that? If a baby is dirty, she sends a message herself. The way she sends it is, hit the roof. If this kid got a problem, she will hit the roof and if you don't fix it, she could go totally ballistic.

So clean her. Feed her. Pick her up. Walk her.

Mariah left paper dydees but Janet makes me use cloths and pins so I could learn how it works. You got to wash the cloths.

By the time I was the one doing all this for even two days, Ani stops being so good. She woke up in the night. She starts to cry. Well, I can tell you this. She didn't get it from me. Maybe I cry once in a while, like from hormones, but this? She cried so hard, you feel as if your head will blow off. It was like a whole human being got inside my head and cried. I don't think it is about, you know. No one could stand it.

When Ani cried, Janet, Delize and even Rauden would get into the picture. They would try anything to stop her crying, and everybody acts like they are the only one who could. They are like, let me handle this, she will stop crying. Let me pick her up. They couldn't keep their hands off her. Even Rauden. And Henry was the worst! He walked her from his wheelchair! It worked.

Later, when I was back in Queens, I noticed that this would happen with total strangers. Total strangers would tell me what I was doing wrong, how I dressed her, or carried her, or what Zones I carried her to. Maybe they were right. What did I know?

What did any of us know? When she was Madhur and not even born, no one was thinking this far ahead. Keep her alive till she's born, then it's Rini's problem. It's our problem now. Is something wrong with her? How would we know? Bernie's in jail. All the other shady OBGYNs disappeared. Rauden could weigh Ani and do bloods, but he was just a DVM. Well, he wasn't even DVM, Janet said, he just had credits. Lucas didn't even have credits. But a regular MD could ask questions. Even a shady one might notice something. What if they examine the birth swipe Henry forged? What if they examine me? I wasn't the Host. I wasn't the birth mother. Someone might ask for proof she's mine. Is she me? Well that could be a problem later but for now the main thing is, is she mine?

Well, that and, keep her alive. That's the main thing. Feed her, clean her, walk her. When she cries, do something. Maybe it works. If it doesn't, get Janet.

I been learning the ropes about a week when Janet woke me up one night and said get dressed fast. K of L riders were on a rampage, heading right this way. They already burnt two barns—I could smell the smoke when we went out her door at dawn. She hid me and Ani in her car and took us on the front roads over the county line to a little hybro Stop where she gave me instructions while we waited for the first hybro out. Take it to the Jersey border. A Haven contact will be waiting. Don't tell them how Ani was born. Act like she's regular.

The hybro pulled up, I climbed the steps with Ani in my arms and the bag Janet fixed on my back and off we go.

ii

Am I scared? On my own with Ani—vigilantes behind us in the woods, and who knows what ahead?

I was mainly scared to be on my own with Ani, period. I was so worried I will do something stupid.

The hybro's full of smoke. The driver's coughing under his mask. A passenger is coughing, in back. I'm coughing. Ani's wrapped up so she won't cough. She does cough. I don't know what to do but hit her on the back. It worked. She stopped. She stopped so hard she didn't make a sound. So I'm like, oh man, I did do something stupid. I hit her too hard. I killed her. I pulled her cover off her face—is she still alive? She was still alive.

Whoa! A rider speeds across the road. The driver hit the brakes. Ani and me got bumped around so hard I checked again, is she still alive? She's still alive.

The whole trip I am checking, is she still alive?

By the time we made the border, I already figured out that being on my own with Ani, I wasn't alone. So that is one more way to explain she was not me.

The Haven is in Netcong. The contact never showed. All traffic got rerouted but not because of vigilantes, it is Mumbai cautions. I spend two hours in the border toilet with Ani yowling so bad some man knocked on the door and said, "Get it out of here," so I jumped on the next hybro and end up in Passaic, and, man, it's creepy. It is totally empty. Janet had gave me an old Mobile for the trip, but it didn't work. Ani went ballistic, a hybro pulled up with a sign for Hudson River jitney, and I just jumped on with Ani and the bag.

We end up at the Terminal at ten at night. One person got off too, but we're the only ones who took the jitney to the west side Manhattan Lock. I was worried someone will notice Ani on the Manhattan side, but nobody else seemed to be even out.

With the bag Janet gave me fixed on my back and Ani tied in front, I climbed up the spiral Lock ladder to the catwalk and headed to Queens the other way from when I went to New Jersey in September, stopping in the middle to check if Ani's still alive. She's still alive. It is very dark. It's like the last time I came home from the Farm. Something seemed different, but I been gone so long I couldn't tell if it was me.

When we got to the East River, it was so dark you couldn't even see the other side.

So Queens is in outage. At least nobody's going to notice us. I lugged Ani down the spiral ladder, flagged a gypsy ferry, jumped on board, it shoved off, and I just stayed on deck and held her sleeping while we go across the river and around Roosevelt Island to Queens. "I must leave you in Queensbridge," the skipper said. He was wrapped up from head to foot, except his eyes. "Be careful, Miss. They have an Exodus from the Projects." Then he shoved off.

Now, I don't know if they have Exodus where you live. An Exodus could be from some flu or Epi. It could be from anything. It could be just from panic. People will hear some rumor, then they panic and flee. It was ok with me. In Exodus, who's going to be around to notice us? It is very late. There is not even a shaw in sight. So I am not getting back to Zone North tonight.

"GET IN YOUR GODDAMN RESIDENCE!"

Oh, man, they got cruiser cops, with the loudspeaker. I do not want this guy noticing us, so I ducked into the first door of the first building that is not all burnt, and when I got inside, I will tell you, I never been anywhere as dark as this, even when Rauden turned the truck lights off.

At least it's Exodus. We got the place to ourself.

It is really hot inside. It got a smell. I felt my way up the stairs till the third floor, then down the hall to one open door to an empty unit, stood in the dark till I was sure it was really empty, went in, laid Ani down, checked she is still alive, then crashed beside her on the floor.

Now, I don't know if they got Projects where you live. It's not the way Ani was Rauden's Project. It's a bunch of buildings all the same. People say this Queensbridge Project used to be rough, with gangs. Even in Exodus, there could be wild dogs in the hall. Am I scared now?

I was mainly scared Ani would wake up.

She did wake up.

I did the feed/clean/walk thing, which is hard even if you could see the mouth or butt or vagina or anything. She finally conked out, I put her down, crashed, and she woke up.

I woke up too.

She fell asleep before she finished half her next bottle. The whole building was quiet. I was nodding off.

Then I heard some noise. Not in the hall. Up from a different floor. I don't know if it's dogs or all it means is we're not the only ones in this Project, but I got scared then. Not a lot. All I'm saying is when I got scared, Ani cried, so I don't know what that proves, I just know she woke up, I gave up, tried to mix a bottle in the dark, wrapped her good, and headed out in the night to message Rauden, we're still alive.

It took me one hour lugging Ani through the dark, empty streets of empty Queensbridge and empty Silvercup in the total dark to find out no Board was working.

I used one of those El floaters at Queens Plaza for Signal off the Dome, but Janet's Mobile still didn't work. I swiped coupons to call Rauden from the floater's Mobile, really scared he will be mad we didn't go to the Netcong Haven, but Rauden just picked up at the Farm fast and said, "Thank God! Thank God you're still alive!" The Farm was ok. The K of L burnt down Walter's shed but not the big house. Walter was ok. The Netcong Haven turned out to be some kind of shady setup and who knows? Maybe they would of stole Ani, so just as well how things turned out. Try to make ends meet until he finds some other Haven. Do my best to keep Ani alive till then.

By the time we head back to the Projects, it was light enough to see how empty the area was, even for dawn. Stores were boarded up, even right under the El. I did see one dog but no people until we turned down 30th Avenue, where one person was standing all wrapped up, and the eyes were watching Ani. I began to run. Ani began to cry. She cried till we got inside our building, but by the time I got up the stairs to the unit, she was conked out.

Until I conked out.

Then she woke up.

I woke up too.

The way it seems to work, when I walk, she sleeps. When I run, it could go either way. If I keep walking, she keeps sleeping. She wakes up if I lie down.

Remember Rini said it would work for Ani the way it worked for me? The way it works for me is, when I'm tired, lie down. The way it works for Ani is, when I lie down, cry. The way it works for me is, when she cries, get up. Pick her up, walk her, till she sleeps again. Then lay her down. Lay down too.

She woke up.

Here we go again.

I slept maybe half an hour all day. When it got dark again, I just wrapped Ani and headed off to Mobile Rauden we're still alive. I just didn't know what else to do. I kept close to the side of buildings. I don't want to call attention. Even in Zone North, you never saw a baby. In this Zone, I hardly even saw adults. On the Mound, there was usually at least somebody out, even if it's someone you rather not see. Here you could go an hour without seeing anyone. Even from Powell's Cove, you could walk to a Board, and even if some flu or even Epi came through, there is sometimes a store open on Northern Boulevard, or at least a Locker. What good does credit do if there is nothing to even buy? How do I get the credit in the first place, without a working Board?

I guess you must be thinking, why don't I head back to Zone North if things is so bad here? Even Zone North was better than this. Well I will tell you, I don't even know why. Maybe I was too tired to make a plan. Remember Rauden never slept and could still drive for hours, work all night, and even with no sleep, come up with some sort of plan? I did not have that in common with Rauden. Maybe the walk/clean/feed business got in the way. It was a full-time job.

I did have a few supplies Janet gave me, and a unit in the Project, and a working floater on the El. I used the same floater the next night. Henry had gave me a special code to tap in so strangers can't get inside the call. Rauden says he still didn't hear from Rini. He wants a report every day, is Ani still alive? She's still alive. She does the breathing, and moves, and I mean, eats? She's scarfing down bottles like there was no tomorrow.

There is, though.

The water is the problem. It is running low. Remember how, till she is born, the main thing is, will it work? And it is about, you know, hardy, Rini, raids, whatever? Now the main thing is, feed her, walk her, clean her. How do I feed her Process without water to mix it? How do I clean her cloths? We have water jugs but only one is boiled and that is running low. The tap water is brown, if it comes. You are supposed to boil even the regular bottle water but the stove is off and I don't want to call attention with a fire.

So now I got to look for water, with Ani tied to me in front under my shirt and the bag on my back. There is no store. I found a water Locker near 30th Avenue. It's empty.

I walked all the way to Socrates Park with Ani and the bag, and we looked across the river through those things they have there, to the Manhattan Dome, shining in the sun. I found a water Locker. It was empty. I didn't see any other Locker the whole time. I didn't see any people. Even for Exodus, this is very, very empty. On the News at the Farm, Mumbai kept getting closer all the time. Did it get to Queens?

I thought I should wrap Ani up really good. I don't even know why. She's a Sylvain hardy. But sometimes I got the feeling, Sylvain or not, they are not totally sure how this will work. I wrapped her so good I had to duck in doorways, unwrap, check, was she still alive? She was still alive. Seventeen days old. Rauden is keeping count. He tells me how old she is when I Mobile from the floater to let him know she's still alive.

He heard from Rini! She's still alive too!

He didn't hear Mumbai came to Queens. Even if it does, don't worry. It will work for Ani the way it works for me. I'm a Sylvain hardy, she's a Sylvain hardy. She's not going to get anything. Except hungry.

He is working on more Haven research. Rini's working on the credit.

Where am I going to load it down from, without a working Board?

I'm getting hungry too.

I'm down to one jug of regular unboiled water. I just mix the water unboiled in her unboiled bottle with the unboiled nipple and she scarfed it down. She didn't get anything. I don't know what that proves.

I didn't tell Rauden though. I think he could handle it, but what if he told Janet?

I found a hydrant leaking, came back with an empty jug and filled it, drinking from the puddle where it splashed. What am I, going to get cholera?

I used the hydrant water to soak macaroni I found in some empty unit where I went to use the toilet to keep the smell down in our own unit. Just chew the macaroni good, holding Ani. Walk her while I chew. I still have red jelly, from Janet's bag. Eat it with one hand.

What I'm saying is, ok, it's going to work for Ani the way it works for me. I don't even know how it works for me. The way it used to work for me, I used to work the Mound. If I need food, I sell something. Blood. Piss. Teeth.

Where do I put Ani while I do that?

I'm not saying I was so crazy about the Mound. But the work I did there is how I used to stay alive. If I bring Ani to the Mound, someone could steal her. They might even use her for a Subject or even Donor. Small as she is, take something from her, what's going to be left?

I'm not leaving her with someone else. I don't know someone else.

And what about deCon and Opening? By now I lost my contacts, if they are even still alive. I probably got to go through Interview again, and where do I put Ani then? Even if I sneak her through, how do I do deCon holding Ani? I am always holding Ani.

I'm not saying I ever want to go back to those V brother combos I used to work for, the Vertovs, the Vargases. You got to do what those guys say, until they die. But even so, it wasn't like, I couldn't use both hands. It wasn't like, I couldn't lie down. Sometimes I can't even stand in one place.

I thought I heard a baby once, on a walk to look for a store. I stood on a big empty street trying to figure out where I heard it. Maybe this kid had a regular mother who could pass on some details Janet did not have time to teach me, like when does the mother sleep? How does she lie down? How does she use both hands?

Then I thought, whoa. Just because they got a baby too, that doesn't mean they won't Alert the Authorities. What's someone like me doing with a kid to start? Then I see a cop in a bubble cruiser and I'm thinking—shit! They did Alert somebody! The loudspeaker belts out, "HYGIENE SPRAY ALERT!" and then, "GET IN THE GODDAMN RESIDENCE. GO IN THE GODDAMN BASEMENT." I duck inside before the spraying starts and am just going to head up to our unit for supplies, but a bubble cop is standing in the lobby with one of those stupid lights on his head, pointing to a door, and if I go the other way, it's going to call attention, so I just went down the stairs with Ani and the bag, then more stairs, then a door, then more stairs to the basement in the total dark, and when I fell down on the basement floor, you can be sure Ani hits the roof. So she is still alive. Find the bottle in the bag. Get it to her mouth in the dark. I was so busy dealing with the bottle, and the dark, and Ani, it took me a while to realize we weren't the only ones down there. I don't know who they were. All I know is, one of them lit a match. I saw eyes. Maybe ten.

Then the match went out.

So great, I'm in a room with who knows how many total strangers in the total dark with Ani.

At least I don't have to worry they will notice anything.

I just have to worry they will steal Ani.

Somebody lit a candle and like three, four people approached with the candle and stood watching Ani go to sleep on my lap. · They watched for a long time, and I'm like why do they watch her sleep? Are they waiting for the right moment to steal her or do they notice something? It took them quite a while for any of them to talk. Then one of them said, "How old is it?"

Twenty-two days old.

Still alive.

Another one said, "You put her down wrong."

She is face up on my lap. She should lie face down. Or she will get wind.

No, says another. Face down, she gets SIDS.

So that's it. They just wanted to watch what I do and tell me what is wrong with it.

I turned her face down, and everyone calls out, "Watch out for the neck!" That woke her up.

So, great, I have to pick her up and walk her. That is wrong too. Do not pick up a baby when she cries, or she is spoiled. She has to learn. Somebody else says, nobody does that any more. I mean, nobody does anything any more, but anyhow, no one could stand it when she cried, they all want to pick her up themself, and to tell the truth, I would of let them, so I could take a break, but somebody else says no, don't let them pick her up, she might get something from them. You can be sure I didn't mention why that wouldn't be a problem. Anyhow, maybe it would, I don't know.

All I know is, we stayed there, all of us, for two days. When she cried, everyone told me what to do. When she slept, even if just for ten minutes, it was like whoa, I have a head. I have space in my head. Let's party. We had water, MREs. For two days, I fed Ani by candle with everyone watching, mix the bottle, clean the vagina, lay her down, whatever I did, everyone watched everything I did and told me what was wrong with it.

When it was over, we all got water and MREs to take away with us. In fact, the next day I found extra water at our door, outside, in those mega jugs.

Ok. By now I worked out when I'm scared, put a bottle in her mouth and walk, so she won't cry.

Because I was scared now. Worse than with the K of L on our tail. Worse than from the wrapped-up man watching Ani.

If they put the water at our door, of all the doors on the floor, all the floors in the sector, they noticed where we live.

I packed up what I could, even the mega jugs, wrapped Ani really good, and headed out where it still stank of Hygiene spray to Northern Boulevard as fast as I could. If they know where we live, they could tell someone about us—cops, some kind of Authority, which I still do not know what that even is but I was pretty sure it will not turn out well.

I saw a group shaw heading east, ran after, jumped on, and took it to Jackson Heights.

iii

Remember environmental factor? How Rini said the child will not be me, because of different environmental factors? Well, I am Ani's environmental factor.

But she is mine too.

At Jackson Heights, I jumped off, hid till the shaw left, and walked to Elmhurst. Not East Elmhurst. There is two Elmhursts. This is the other one. I walked there now.

Before Ani, I was no one's environmental factor. Now I'm hers. What I'm saying is, that is an environmental factor back to me, and here is how you know. I never used to worry like this. I worried now.

Elmhurst looks better than Queensbridge. There are people. No cops, that I saw. I worry about cops.

Before Ani I wasn't exactly like, oh? Want to call a cop? Great. It was more like, try to find one. Throw me in jail? Try to find one. Now I'm like, where do I put Ani then? I'm pretty sure they did not put babies in jail. Well, I never even saw a jail. Well, I never even saw a baby. I mean, before.

I did see kids before, a few, like I told Rauden. In Francis Lewis Park just by the Mound, they would hide in the toilet with their mother when an Inspector showed up.

So even regular mothers hid regular kids. Now that I thought about it, how did I even know how regular they are?

Before Ani, I never would of gave a thought, are they regular or not.

I gave it now.

In Elmhurst, we found a unit upstairs in a house, with a balcony. There is a lot of bike wheels and metal and some nylon in big rolls.

There is power! They have a working Board! The credit came through! They even have a store. I got all the water we want. Rice too. The store has a working stove and for extra coupons the Singhs let you cook on it.

Rauden is ok about no Haven. She's four weeks old. She's still alive. I could tell her age myself, now that I got Board access. Just press UpDate button for what day it is, then count back from there to her birthday. Then you know how long she is alive. Rauden's big thing now is, get her weighed!

Well, I'm not going to do that.

The Singhs have a scale. And they were pretty nice. But come on, they never even saw her, except the bundle I carry under my shirt. I'm not saying they don't suspect what it is but they do not want trouble. Put that bundle on the scale, it's going to hit the roof, and there could be trouble. The Singhs do not want trouble. They say, "Queensbridge. Trouble, trouble, trouble. All the time Exodus, and it is just panic." There was some big vaccine drive and the Queensbridge population panicked and fled to the beach.

The Singhs do not fear shots. They take shots.

When the Singhs run to the Ridgewood clinic in such a rush they leave the store unlocked, I sneak in, put Ani on and off the scale so fast she doesn't know what hit her. Three kilos.

Still alive.

This is what I mean about is she me? If she was me, I would just say, whatever. What do I care how much I weigh? Now I'm like, three kilos. Is that regular? She is so small she fits right under my shirt.

At least under my shirt, I don't have to worry, does she show? I just have to worry, does she breathe? I keep ducking in doorways to pull her out from my shirt and check, does she breathe? She does breathe.

Then I start to worry, did someone see me pull her out to check?

In Elmhurst they have services, the streetlights work. Some of them. Someone could see her. Nobody got that close though.

Anyone sees anyone, they pretty much cross the street to the other side. They are worried they could get something. I crossed the street too.

So this is different too. I used to think, if I thought anything, oh, I'm a Powell's Cove hardy. I'm not going to get anything. Whatever!

I didn't even used to know I was a Sylvain hardy. If I knew, I would of thought, whatever.

Now I was something else. I was an environmental factor.

I worried now.

When I stopped worrying so much is she alive, or does she breathe, or show, I am so used to worrying, I worry if I don't worry. So I come up with something else to worry about. Is she regular?

Come on. How regular could she be?

But I would like to see a regular baby. I would just like to see how regular it looks.

One day I saw a pile of springs and broken plexi on Dry Harbor Road. It's almost like the parts of the tank that Ani grew in. I started to look closer but heard somebody coming, and I left.

I came back next day. The whole street is closed, caution tape's everywhere, and there was a smell I recognize, like heavy-duty Hygiene spray, antiPatho strength. So someone had got something. I don't know what. If anyone grew in that tank, I don't know if they had it.

I don't know if the Singhs had it. They didn't come back

from the clinic. I sneaked in at night and took their scale. Still three kilos. Still alive.

Still bald.

I saw a sign in a park one night, you could get work mornings as Courier. Next morning I came back to check it out. The park is caution-taped. We just went home.

There is more of that smell around.

I don't need work anyhow. The credit is coming through. I don't even need credit. With the Singhs gone, I can just go in the store and help myself. They even got dydees.

At least if I don't have a job, we don't deal with anyone. No one will notice if she's regular or not. Except me.

Like, Ani cries most of the time. She goes crosseyed. She goes ballistic.

I go to the nearest Board to ask Rauden is that regular, but the Board crashes. I walk to the next Board. It has already crashed.

I go so far to find a working Board I have to cross a Zone checkpoint, and this one has crossing guards. And I was really worried now because Ani started to fuss, and we will attract attention, and—oh, shit. A cruiser cop is cruising toward us. "Get it out of here," one guard shouts at me. "They're doing quarantine sweeps." It is a long time since I ran into quarantine sweeps. I almost don't remember how they work, let alone, with Ani. The guard doesn't even check our ID.

If you want to get through checkpoints fast, bring a kid. A baby's even better. They just want to get you out fast. They are afraid it's going to cry. No one can stand that. Even a guard can't stand it.

By the time we got through the checkpoint, Ani is going nuts. Wah, wah! Where are we? It could be Middle Village. There is a cemetery. There seem to be a lot of cruiser cops. There is a toilet in the cemetery. I just duck in, like I used to see mothers do. What is it with Ani? Yowl! Yowl! She's coughing. She's going red, spitting out the bottle, nothing is working. I'm starting to worry she's so loud, even from the toilet, a cop could hear.

Then I hear a kind of crackling noise. A stall door opens. A lot of plastic is inside, with something inside that, and it has a bundle. The bundle's moving.

I just froze where I stood. It's a mother with a kid.

I could hear the cruiser horn approach.

All I'm thinking is, so this is a regular mother.

She isn't even the only one. Another mother comes out of the other stall with a smaller bundle and a smaller kid inside.

This other regular mother has a bag. She reaches in the bag, gets out a pin, a safety pin. I am worried she is going to stick Ani, but she just takes the bottle, sticks the pin in the tip, makes the bottle squirt, and sticks it right in Ani's mouth. Ani sucks it so hard she is, like, panting. Then she conks out.

Then it is really quiet.

And it's like, in the Queensbridge basement, when she slept, it felt like a party? Like, oh! I have a head. Now it is like, it's so quiet, I can hear everything, and what I hear is a cruiser horn. Shit! It's getting louder. I'm not the only one thinking, shit. We all are. Now it's like that time when Rauden and I were in the truck in the woods, quiet, while the Knights of fucking Life rode by on horses in the dark. Even the kids are quiet. The cruiser's right outside. Then it is a little less close. Then I'm pretty sure it's further off than that. When it's totally gone, these other mothers look at each other and nod. Then they looked at me. You can be sure I looked at them.

I was waiting so long to see a regular mother. So this is a regular mother! I haven't seen a mother at all, this whole time, regular, nothing. I wanted to see a mother, any mother, just to compare. Here are two.

The first one wears one of those, you know, plastic burkis, like are supposed to keep off germs but they don't work? The second one just has a plastic raincoat, which also doesn't work.

The first one's face was sort of red, the second sort of brown, but you couldn't see much of either one except the face, and how the faces looked was, tired.

So. I had that in common with them.

Their kids seemed pretty young, young enough to bundle up and hold. Still, Ani seemed to be the only baby. The mothers seemed really interested in her. They leaned right over her. I just unwrapped her, so they could see. And I'm thinking, why did I do this? They're going to notice something. Still, they're not going to call a cop. Call a cop, they'll be in quarantine.

Anyhow, they didn't act like they noticed something. They said she was cute.

So I had that in common with them too. I thought she was cute.

They ask if Ani had her shots and I say I don't know. So they look at me funny.

The second mother finally says, "It's ok. Mine didn't either. Look." She unwraps the bundle, so you can see her kid's legs. They hang like, I don't know, worms. "That's what happen if they don't get their shots."

"Mine did," the first mother says and unwraps her bundle. The kid was totally gray. "That's what happens if they do." It was cute though. Its hair was red.

The other kid wasn't gray. He had shiny eyes, brown skin, and long curls.

He was cute too.

I really think Ani was the cutest one. I got the feeling they thought so too. She got the little tiny face, the crunch-up eyes and little tiny stickout mouth. She is a regular color now, not red. Still bald though.

The one whose son didn't have his shots was nice. She didn't worry what he would get from us. He already got polio. At least he was alive. You know how everybody tells me what I'm doing wrong? This regular mother said, "If your kid's still alive, you're doing something right."

What she had in common with everybody else is, if I did it right or wrong? She knew. They both knew what was right or wrong.

Like, one asked did Ani get the Check Up? Bring her to Pomonok Center, in South Flushing. They have free Check Ups with a regular MD.

The other mother said right, but they give you a hard time about shots. They are not allowed to force the shot but if you refuse, they could say you endanger the kid's life and are a bad mother. They could Alert the Authority and take your child away. Go to the Myrtle Avenue Center, this mother says, in Ridgewood. They do not make you take the shot and also they give free Process, the green kind, you feed it to your kid by hand.

The first one said but watch out for Hygiene. Your kid could get something from some other kid who had something. I didn't even know there was enough kids to get anything from.

Whatever I do, both mothers agree, don't let them give my kid the shot for Mumbai. It is experimental. Maybe she won't get Mumbai. But she'll get something else. They call it Stealth Virus. You end up with challenged Immune and that will cause problems as bad as Mumbai. She won't be able to have her own baby.

As far as I heard, she wouldn't be the only one. But I did not say that. I mean, I got no idea how these mothers got theirs.

One of them peeked outside. The cops was gone. The mothers left one by one, with their kids. I was the last to go.

After that, I walked all the way back to this same cemetery toilet a few times to see if these regular mothers were there. I don't even think it's to compare. I just wanted to see them. They never showed.

Two months old. Still alive.

Here is what I worry about now. Should we get the Check Up? Ani was alive and all but cried so much.

Here is what I worry about next.

What if they make her take a shot?

She's a Sylvain hardy, come on! She is not getting Stealth or any kind of virus.

It could work the other way though. Hardies don't get anything if we don't have a shot. What if we do?

I had a shot when I did vaccine trials. I wasn't a baby when I took the shot though. I was thirteen years old. That I heard.

Ani is two months, one week old and crying night and day.

When she is two months, one week, four days old, and crying so hard I almost thought one of us is going to pop, I put her in my shirt and walked to Ridgewood. You have to go on Grandview Avenue. The trip took like one hour, and you pass a lot of empty houses, most of them not even burnt, and when I finally get to Myrtle Avenue, so many mothers is lined up I could hardly even believe my eyes, though with the Hygiene thing, they are so wrapped up you could not see them or the kid. The nurse at least just wears a mask when she calls out, "Ladies! Behave!" because they are all pushing and shoving. "There is a pile of free Process, just hand in your swipe and your child's swipe for ID check," and I'm like, ID check? I'm not doing that. I just squeezed through the line, grabbed Process from the pile and ran. Another mother did too. We ran to Grandview Avenue. The other mother sat down on a curb, pulled her wrappings off and fed her kid green Process with her hand. I did too. Ani stopped crying. She slept all the way home.

She cried again when we are back in our unit. I gave her more Process, with my hand. It wasn't hard at all.

She cried again.

I gave her more.

Cry. More. Cry. More.

This time it didn't work. She wouldn't take green Process. She just cried. I mean, she really cried. It is late now, night. She didn't stop crying once. I just walked right out in the night with her crying, all the way back to the Center. It was closed. I walked around the whole building with Ani crying and thrashing till somebody comes to the door. I don't even know who she is. She says her name is Sonia and she is a nurse. I don't even know if she is. She puts her hand on Ani's head, then stomach, says, "Wind," and goes off to get something for wind. So this is wind. So Ani got wind. Sonia comes back, puts something in Ani's mouth, and Ani conks out. Sonia didn't even ask to see ID. I don't know why she didn't. I don't know how Sonia knew it's wind. I don't know if they all get wind, all babies. They had to get it sometimes, or Sonia wouldn't know.

So that is one thing Ani had in common with regular babies. She is a Sylvain hardy who got wind.

She is a Sylvain hardy sleeping all the way back to Elmhurst and when I put her down on the floor she keeps sleeping, and I am so tired from two trips to and from Ridgewood, I could hardly keep myself from crashing beside her but I'm pretty sure if I lie down, here we go again, but I must of done it anyhow because I woke up in broad daylight. We slept the whole night through. It is the first time in two months we slept the whole night through.

Everything seemed different when we woke up. Like, look at the sun! Look at the dirt!

Ani already woke up and didn't even cry! She is lying in sunshine staring at me really hard, like, look at I! Like, whoa! I never saw anything this interesting before. So that is something we had in common. I thought she was interesting too.

Her face is three, four inches from me on the floor with

sun all over, and her eyes popped really wide, so wide her lips popped open too. Pop!

She never made that noise before.

Then she gave me a look, like, oh! You think I didn't do this before? Well that is one more difference between us. Come on. I do this all the time. She gave a kind of wink.

It was very cute.

Then she did it again. Pop!

It was so cute.

She did it again. Wink!

It was so cute, I had a thought I never thought before.

If she got wind, she has that in common with regular babies or how else did Sonia know what it was? So she could pass for regular.

But just the same time I thought that, I felt a, like, squeeze? Like how I felt when Rini said she's not coming back for Madhur?

If she got wind like regular babies, what else does she get?

I threw Ani under my shirt and rushed out to message Rauden from the Roosevelt Avenue Board. It crashed. I ran all the way home and when I got there put her on the scale and weighed her. I don't even know why I did. Three point eight kilos. Still alive.

I laid her on the floor, on a cloth. She went pop.

She followed me with her eyes when I walk one way by her. When I walked the other way, she followed me with her eyes the other way. When I stopped walking and looked down to where she lay on the cloth on the floor, she went pop.

It was so cute.

What I'm saying is, she is a Sylvain hardy and it is going to work for her the way it worked for me because it's in the genes. But when did it start working for me? When I was two months, one week, five days old, was I a hardy yet?

How would I even know? I was inside Cissy Fardo's basement. Inside, what was there to get?

I was in the basement a long time, too. All the kids were. It was the Big One. People kept their kids inside until it is safe. Even post Big One, it was Luzon or some other Epi, or they are afraid someone will give their kid a shot or steal them. Cissy Fardo was so old and scared, she kept me inside more than most.

What I'm saying is, Ani's a Powell's Cove hardy, a Sylvain hardy. But she is three point eight kilo. When I was three point eight kilo, I was inside.

She is a three point eight kilo hardy on the street.

Should I keep her in?

Well that is really going to work. I have to bring her out to even ask Rauden if I should keep her in? I'm not leaving her alone.

I make a burki from some nylon and wrap us up—at least now we look like everyone else, but it is really hot and took a really long time to find a working Board and message Rauden what to do. He messaged walk around. See what happens. So I walked around. I saw what happened. What happened was, we didn't get anything. I don't know what that proves. It could prove she's a Sylvain hardy. It could prove I am a bad mother. Maybe I am.

On the street, they show posters, here is what happens if you do not give your child the Mumbai shot. It is a dead baby. It has turned blue.

Three months old. Still alive.

She had the little blue vein beside the eyebrow. I guess it is ok.

On the street, someone has crossed out "not" on all the posters, like, here is what happens if you do give your kid the shot.

Fourteen weeks old. Still alive.

She ate green Process. She sat up.

She fell over. It was so cute.

It hits me, when Cissy Fardo found me on the bus that wasn't a regular bus, I was outside then. I was outside the whole walk from Kissena, where she found me, till Corona, where she lived.

So it could be ok to take her out to forage.

When we foraged, we saw no one out at all, even though Mumbai is not confirmed. Elmhurst is looking as empty as Queensbridge. On Roosevelt Avenue, they have the caution tape. They have the posters of the baby who is blue over a whole wall.

Fifteen weeks old. Still alive.

She had the really round head, the little bug eyes. Her eyebrows went up in the middle, like—surprised! She was so cute.

She didn't look like me at all. Maybe she never would. Things happened to me that didn't happen to her. I got scars. I got hair. She got me.

What else would she get?

Rini said the child would not be me, don't worry. Like it is a bad thing, if Ani is. Well, of course I don't want her to be me. And I don't even know what it means.

But here is one thing I did think I knew. If she's me, she won't get Mumbai and die.

Her mother will die though, if she's me. That was the birth mother though. I wasn't the birth mother. I was the Original. I didn't know what that means. I didn't know what most of this means.

All I'm saying is, if I don't know if she is me or exactly like me or a Sylvain hardy or what, when it turned out Mumbai did hit Queens, and everyone started to panic so bad they just do things that made no sense? I did something that made no sense. I had that in common with everyone. I panicked too.

iv

I heard a noise out on the street one very hot night. A crowd is in the street, shoving, pushing, carrying bags. I never knew so many people lived here.

Next morning, they didn't. Nothing is on the street but what everybody dropped. There was a lot of food. MREs, Beverage, cereal, water in jugs. I tied Ani to me with a cloth and forage, forage, forage. There was clothes too. On Dongan Avenue, I found baby things in plastic bags. Sheets and little stretchy suits and dydees. I brought them home, put Ani in one little suit. It was so cute.

In the middle of the next night, I woke up, pulled everything off, and scrubbed Ani so hard she went nuts. I threw the whole bag out. I took it a block away and left it on the street. Then I came back and scrubbed her again. So that did not make sense.

I just thought, why not leave Elmhurst and move to Flushing? I don't even know why I did. I just packed our bag and took Ani out on the street, carried her all the way to Flushing and found a unit with a balcony a lot like the Elmhurst one, but no wheels, no nylon. I wished I brought the nylon with me. I almost went back for it. Then I thought, better not.

A few people were out lugging bags in Flushing too.

Now, supposedly Mumbai is related to Luzon Third, the one that killed Rini's original daughters? So some say people who didn't die from Luzon could be Immune to Mumbai. So maybe

Mumbai won't be so bad. On Board News, they say the numbers are only like twenty thousand, so far. We all seen worse, in Queens. Well, when there was more people alive, to start, more people died. Anyhow, I didn't really panic. Not yet.

I went to message Rauden what to do. The Main Street Board kept crashing and the line of people waiting in sheets or robes or plastic is so long it is the middle of the night before I reached Rauden. He was still awake. I think he had been drinking. What it came down to was, he didn't know. I didn't panic though. Even though the crowds are getting bigger and louder, and people are yelling back and forth, whatever numbers they heard. Eighty thousand!

But that is counting Brooklyn and the Bronx too. We all seen worse in Brooklyn, Queens, and the Bronx. Even when the numbers keep getting higher, and the crowds on Main Street are bigger, lugging bags and yelling and pushing, I didn't panic.

I didn't panic until they are in bags, themselves. Then I took Ani in my arms and our bag on my back and the nylon burki over everything, joined the Main Street crowd, and started walking.

There was a lot of people walking. All this time, they were inside, so you could never know how many people there are alive? Now they just fled to the street and walked.

Why do we even do this? What is the point? We're better off inside. It is the panic.

They wore sheets and burkis, parkas, hoodies, raincoats, saris, and they carried bundles. Sometimes the bundle is moving.

They had sealed the bridges and the tunnels that were not already closed. We headed east, to the Nassau County City Line.

There were bodies of people who just died walking on the street. They weren't blue when I passed them. Maybe they were blue before. Bubble suit squads came to take these bodies off in bundles and melt them. They piled them on shaws. Every size of bundle. Some were small.

Not as small as Ani.

They made us stop at a Zone. They put us in a room. They let us go. We had to stop at a Zone further out. There was a doctor here. She never saw us. They put us on a truck.

Then someone came on the truck and told us, "Get off, get off."

There were a lot of bodies now. It was hard to walk, and then you saw they had sandbags, because they made a fence, chicken-wire, with barbwire, so you couldn't get across. It was the City Line. It was vigilantes from Nassau County, who piled up all this stuff and stood on top with sticks to hit us if we try to cross. They want to stop the Exodus at the City Line.

Some people tried to flee by water.

They have cruiser policeboats off College Point and, I don't know, nets. I mean, people was jumping into Powell's Cove. What am I, going to jump in Powell's Cove? I can't even swim, let alone with Ani and the bag.

They try to flee the other way, to the Manhattan Dome, but they have vigilantes waiting at Manhattan, on the waterside, at the east side Lock, with sticks in case we try to come over in boats.

They put us in trucks to the Flushing General quarantine. Then they took us away from there.

We are in triage.

A doctor is doing intake. Name. Age. Symptoms. Then she looked hard at Ani. "Where was she born?"

I told her in the sticks.

She looked hard at me. "A rube?"

I didn't know what to say. I didn't say anything.

"Full term? Nine months?"

I said I didn't know.

"Who is the father?"

I just said something stupid. It is the panic. "There is no father," I said.

She didn't get it. "No, no. For the genetic history."

I repeated, "There is no father."

"I see," she said. But she took a quick look at Ani's face. She took a quick look at mine.

Finally I just said, "I don't even know if I'm the mother." Then she did look at both of us hard. I don't even know why I told her.

Remember they used to do that me/her thing back at the Farm? She did that now, looked at me really hard, at Ani fast. Then she looked, I don't know, inside her own mind. Then she just looked tired. She shrugged. Like, whatever. It was none of her business. Maybe she's better off if she doesn't know.

Then somebody calls her. They say should they put us on a truck but Dr. Martinez said no. No. Don't go on a truck. Wait here. Then she went somewhere. Then we just walked out of triage by ourself. I don't know why they let us.

She just left the door open and we walked out. We headed further east.

We walked way out on the Expressway, passing bodies on the road. I kept heading for the City Line, walking. I was trying to get away from the Pandy. Instead of getting away, I carried Ani right into what they called the epicenter. They swept us in quarantine. They call it Creedmoor. When they let us out, Ani's five months old. Still alive.

So, we had that in common.

I was too.

V

Let me say a little about quarantine, which maybe you heard of or even went in once. But if you don't know what it is, I can tell you how it works, or worked back then, in Queens. They seal you in like it is jail. I never been in jail but heard when you are in it, you can't go out.

The way it's not like jail, if you're outside when they seal it, you can't go in. Your kid could be in there, your Parent, whoever, you can't go in with them. They have to stay locked up in quarantine till everyone who is going to die dies. Sometimes they have a doctor in there. Sometimes the doctor dies too.

When everyone is finished dying, wait two more weeks. Then who is left could go. Now all you have to do is stay alive the regular way, and there is smoke and dust and antiPatho spray, and they put you on trucks to some kind of Center but the trucks are commandeered and you are on Union Turnpike, which is a mess. Rickshaws, bikes, more trucks, cops in bubble suits, and everywhere, crowds on foot, running and shoving. You want food? Get on a line. Want shelter? Get on a line. Watch out for vigilantes. Watch out for stampedes. They are stampeding so they don't get swept in quarantine.

Now, if you were in quarantine, you get a certificate, what they call hard Proof, you were in quarantine and are still alive. They put it on a plexi card, in case they can't read your regular ID because the Boards don't work or whatever. Maybe this certificate will keep you out of quarantine next time. If you want to stay out of quarantine, hold it high.

Well, let me tell you, the first time we went in quarantine, I was so scared. Even the second time. I was really scared what will happen to Ani in there, with everybody dying.

You are probably thinking, wait. Second time? And I got certificates to keep us out? Might do something stupid? How stupid can you get?

Well, here is something maybe you don't know about quarantine. If you have a kid, they put you in a special room. If you don't have a kid, you share a room. If you have a kid, you have your own room. They lock you in. But they leave food at the door. Maybe they leave clothes. How stupid is that? The truth is, in quarantine, it was the first time since the Queensbridge basement I had a square meal.

The next part of our life, we spent in quarantine. We moved from quarantine to quarantine. Metropolitan Avenue. Harry Van Arsdale Drive. We didn't get anything. Except food. Clothes, shelter. Proofs.

Sometimes they quarantine a building. Study what building got body bags coming out. Go in before it's sealed. Even if it's just a few units where the body bags come from, a lot of times they quarantine the whole building. You can stay there for a month, maybe six weeks. You get another Proof when they let you leave. If you want to go back in quarantine and got a Proof? Hide it good.

Watch which way the stampede's going. Then go the other way.

She spent her first Christmas in quarantine. They put a toy in a bag on the door. It is candy.

In one of these quarantine rooms, in Metropolitan Avenue, Ani started to crawl. Backward.

They let us hear the News. A quarter of a million dead in

Queens, the Bronx, and Brooklyn. So far. No message Board though. No vidPhone. It's for security.

Around the time she began to crawl forward, they let us move to a Resettlement, what they call, Resettlement, at Flushing Meadow Park, which was a little different. We still can't go in or out, but it's more like living somewhere regular, and people don't die. You sleep in pods, what they call, honeycomb pods, around a transition Zone, where you could practice, you know, being exposed to others, see what happened. They have a yard. They let us grow potatoes in the yard. Which I enjoyed. Ani enjoyed it too. The way you grow potatoes, you put what they call the eye of the potatoes in the ground, and it makes single Donor viables, which are gene for gene the living replica of the potato. And which was ethical, because it was Nature, and because they are plants.

Ani enjoyed the potato area. She even stood up in the field. Then she fell down again, in the potatoes. She got pretty dirty too.

When no one was dying any more, they put us on trucks and sent us back to Flushing.

She didn't remember Flushing at all. Well, it was hard to see what it even looked like, because of so much smoke. A lot of buildings were burnt down. Our old unit was gone too, the one with the balcony. A lot of streets are roped off.

They had a shelter on Bowne Street, in case your home was burnt or sealed. It's not a quarantine. You could come and go. You had to show your Proof, then they gave you a cot. They had meals too. They had a working Board and when I did upDate, it is one week till Ani's birthday. So she is almost one year old. Man! She was still alive.

When the shelter people saw Ani, they put us in a room all to ourself, just like in quarantine. When we went on the street though, everyone noticed us. I tried to keep quiet but we stood out. There wasn't many kids to start, and so many had died. I mean, you would see people just staring at their hands, like they were lucky to still have hands. Just staring at a tree, a plant, like they were lucky to see anything. Imagine what they think seeing a baby. Once when we went out to find a Board that worked, a little group began to stand behind us and clap.

She was very cute.

She got a thin body and a big round, round head. You can be sure someone will tell me I should put a hat on her head. I should put different shoes on her feet. She is too cold! She is too hot! Man! How do they know these things? It was interesting though.

She didn't talk at all. She just sort of peeped, like an Endangered. Well, I guess she is.

If you hold her hand, she takes a few steps. Otherwise, she falls down. She held my hand.

Her brows go up, like, not surprised but, you know, how worried looks? She looked worried. Maybe she got it from me, I worried so much. I was less worried now than before. She was still alive. She was almost one year old, and I was still alive. I was pretty sure my own mother had been dead almost one year when I was almost one, myself. My birth mother. Like Rauden said, I wasn't Ani's birth mother. If Ani's me, I'm Cissy Fardo. She gets me for nine more years, till I die in a fire, when she is ten. We could deal with that then.

I found a working Board and reached Rauden! He said thank God we're still alive! He wanted to hear all about the quarantines. He told us to come straight up to the Farm and posted tickets. With credit I still have left from Rini I bought crackers and drink for the trip. We went up on Ani's birthday! We had to go up through the Bronx and cross the Newburgh bridge. We had to wait in line to get a hybro, because so many people were on the way out. Our Proofs got us through all the Zones though. Ani enjoyed the hybro. I was very happy to see Rauden, and Janet Delize, and the others, and the Farm. Janet even had a gift for Ani. It is a Bonnet. It almost fits. I was very proud to show off Ani, who was still alive. Rauden was proud too.

I had missed the Farm. I missed Rauden. He was very excited about the Proofs. We had four each. He was on the Board right away, for clients. We got a track record now. We got Proofs.

And that is just one thing that's different this time.

vi

The first ones were from Santa Sofya. We met them at a safe house in Dwaarkill, because Rauden worried they would come back to the Farm and steal Ani and me if they know where it is. I was worried too, but what I worried was, Rauden will sell Ani to them but he said no. No. Don't worry. She's more valuable to keep around. She *is* the track record. She's the goddamn Proof!

Well, I did not know where Santa Sofya is or what they had there but everyone thought my genes and Ani's would not get it and Rauden sold them fourteen frozen viables and threw in some bottles of my blood they could use for the Compatibility, which who knows if it will work but that's their problem. Henry made them a copy of my code ID that he sent down from Albany. He was up there fixing gizmos and systems because Albany needed all the help it could get, after Mumbai. It is a mess. We don't even have to worry would any Inspector come around. They are too busy fixing up the mess. We don't even have to worry will the K of L raid us because they took a hit when Mumbai jumped species and wiped their horses out! We just have to worry, will other buyers come.

Which they didn't.

I mean you always do a lot of waiting in this business. Remember how long it took to hook up with Rini? And the outreach is always tricky because you have to watch your language in a public post, even now everybody's so busy just being alive.

Still.

It's almost June and after the Santa Sofya brokers, nobody else called.

"Junior?"

It's a sunny day. Ani, me, and Janet Delize are on the orange sofa, watching a TV program called *Fresh Start*, about life after Mumbai that people used to watch back then if their TV worked.

"Junior," Janet calls to Rauden, who is in back, "you should take a look at this."

This week *Fresh Start* featured Parents whose kid died from Mumbai but they saved the skin and want to clone him—nobody but us ever said nuclear Transfer. But it was pretty much what Rauden does, whatever you call it. These Parents are so mad with grief, they didn't care if it's a crime against nature or ethical or what. They just miss their kid.

Rauden called to Janet, "Turn that shit off."

Janet said turn it off himself.

Rauden came in and turned the TV off. Then he went back to the Box Room.

Janet went after him. "Oh too busy to look?"

Rauden said, "That is necrophiliac shit! Those Parents think they can bring their dead kid back to life. That's not how it works!" and he went down the hall.

Janet followed. "What's the difference? It's a business Opportunity."

"The difference is," Rauden said, and his voice is getting louder, "I only work with hardy product," but I have to deal with Ani for a minute. She went to the TV and is hitting it so hard I'm afraid she will break it. She really liked TV and would watch it day and night if she could, even though Janet is on my case about fresh air.

By the time I get back to the doorway where I was trying to hear what they're saying, Rauden is yelling at Janet, "Unique?

You don't know the meaning of the word! I work with hardy product! That's what buyers goddamn come to me for!"

Janet said oh she really noticed that. She really noticed so many buyers came, we're turning hundreds away. Like, buyers are just coming in droves!

Rauden came up front wheezing so hard he is almost falling and pulled the TV plug out. Ani started to cry. I just picked her up and we went outside in the sun and stood on the dirt road under those trees out there until things quiet down. I could hear them yelling even from here.

They already had one really big fight the first day we got here, about where Ani and me should stay. He said with Janet. Janet said well that is easy for him to say—it is a lot of extra work, and he was like, oh really? He didn't notice her doing so much extra work. She was like, no, he didn't notice anything—he did not ever stop to think what if he has an emergency? Say, Daisy 5's time comes and he's gone for days? Then Janet will have to deal with everything. "Why don't they go stay with you at the clinic," she said, "if they are so important to you?"

"Oh give me a goddamn break," Rauden said. "Sook is already going to throw me out because I took so much time off last year. I suppose we could put them in the trailer." Janet said you can't keep a child there. I don't know why not. I don't want to ask. She does not want us on the orange sofa, someone could walk right in on us. The rec room will not work because it got expensive equipment—what if Ani gets up in the night and broke something? She never broke anything! I keep an eye on her! And by the way, she keeps an eye on me—follows me around all day and night. I can't even get beefed up for a new Harvest without her pulling on my arm so hard Rauden could hardly get the needle in my vein.

He was hitting the bottle quite a bit.

When Henry came down from Albany to help during the Harvest, he fixed us up an empty room near the kitchen, where Ani and me could sleep, with a special gate so she won't escape in the night and break something. He also showed me how to check the generators and systems, if Rauden goes away. That kills two birds with one stone, whatever it even means. Henry was very nice to Ani. He even brought her a toy, which she enjoyed but would not let him touch her. She won't let anyone touch her but me. I have to touch her all the time and when I go off to the new shady OBGYN in Callicoon for the Harvest, she makes such a racket they are thinking of giving her a shot herself. It was a really bad Harvest, just two eggs.

Rauden got drunk.

"Bro!" Henry told him. "Don't be depressed. You already made history! Someone will call!" Then he went back to Albany. But he was right.

Someone did call the next day. From Buffalo.

So, we're off to Dwaarkill to meet this broker in the safe house in June. He looked at Ani. He looked at me. Checked our vitals, studied all the Proofs. Then he looked at Ani very hard. Thirteen months old. Still alive. He says he will call and goes off in a van.

Janet said don't hold our breath and Rauden got that look like he is going to hit something, but he just took a deep breath and got in the truck, and we all squeezed in the front with Ani sleeping on my lap and drive back to the Farm in the late afternoon and been driving maybe five minutes when Janet goes, "If he wants to go through the whole shebang, he's gonna think, why not get something special for it?"

Man! What is it with her?

"She's a Sylvain hardy!" Rauden goes. "How much more special can you get than that? Get off my goddamn case!" He smacks the steering wheel till the truck goes sideways. It is a long time since I saw him do that. At least it shuts Janet up a while.

But when we're on the regular road near the Farm, she starts again, and this time it is my case she's on. How I bring Ani up it is not good for sales. Ani watches too much TV. I do not show her who is boss. If you do not show her who is boss, this is not a favor, to either of you. I'll be sorry later. And don't forget, when she's two, Ani should do her business in a pot. I mean, great, that is really going to work.

Rauden's yelling, "She's a goddamn Sylvain hardy." By now we're at the turnoff to the Farm, and he has got out to fix the blinking light, then got back in. "No one is going to fucking care if she is toilet trained." Now we are at the Quonset. "It's not her they're buying."

We went inside and he is yelling and banging around so much, Ani wakes up from her nap and starts yelling too. She's scream-ing, Rauden goes in some room and slams the door. I bring Ani to our room to calm her down and I just hear a lot of noise through the walls, doors slamming, banging around. He is on a bender. Slam, bang. We stay in our room. We can hear him banging around all night. Something falls down. I think he falls down.

Next thing we know, he's waking us up in the night, breaking our gate. The Buffalo broker wants in! He has a client! They want the works—tank, blood, live babies. The broker under-stood our situation and will put cash down up front. He wants the work to start ASAP. So now we're all in a better mood, even Janet.

The broker wants ten viables. So this is another difference from before. There will be two tanks, the old one and a brand new model Rauden will make with Henry. Lucas will not be involved. Remember the viables Rauden made to stay sober? He will thaw some of these out.

So now we're in a rush, and with Lucas off the Project and Henry going back and forth from Albany, everyone got to pitch in. I'm going to clean the old tank, and Ani comes with me because where else could she go? I haven't been in the tank room since she was born, and right away it all came back—the tubes, the track. The nesting, the lights. The names on the sections. This time there will be no names, just a) to j) so we won't bond and it won't bother us so much when they die. But when they do nest, it's just as big a deal for all of us, even Janet. I didn't even cry when d) and h) died right off. I'm too busy working out how to deal with Ani while I'm giving product hooked up to the IV. So that's another difference from before. I must deal with Ani. After all that where do we sleep, we're both in the rec room now.

j) died in July. I cried then. A lot. It's like Berthe all over again. And what about Chi-Chi! I start to cry about Chi-Chi, even though she's dead more than a year. I cried even more than when she died. So that is another difference from before. I cried more.

I'm more tired too. It could just be because now I must deal with Ani. I used to take a nap. I don't take a nap, now. When I take a nap, guess who wakes me up? Fifteen months old. Still alive. I'm crying from the hormones but trying to hold her but my arm hurts where the IV is hooked. I'm trying to show her the viables, like, oh, look, there is a), b), c), e), f) g), eight weeks in, still alive. I don't know if she noticed when c) died. I just say, look, a), b), e).

Janet gave us a look when I said that to Ani. Then she just looked the other way. She is always giving looks. Like, do not let Ani watch the TV. Show her who is boss. Usually when she gives looks she will tell me what I'm doing wrong, or once she even told Ani, "Tell Mommy, I need fresh air." I mean, give me a break. Ani does not even talk and anyhow I will have to unhook everything to take her out. I am the only one Ani will even let take her anywhere, and I am so tired.

When the viables are ten weeks in, the Buffalo broker calls. He got clients! It's a man and woman who lost their kid from Mumbai. They want to meet me and Ani. We don't want them to see the tanks direct in case they report us but Rauden makes videos to show them. We got cleaned up, I put Ani in a little red dress we got from charity in Resettlement and some little shoes Janet found for her, which almost fit. Rauden unhooks me from the IV and we go meet the couple at the safe house so they can see how Ani looks at sixteen months old. The Buffalo couple seem really nice. It was like when I met Rini—they were crying. Another thing like Rini was, they changed their mind. The difference was, when Rini changed her mind, she had already put her money down.

What I'm saying is, they declined.

So we went back to the Farm. The rain started on the way back. Whatever. The broker pays Rauden, no matter what. It's the broker's goddamn problem.

I went straight to the rec room with Ani and hooked myself up. I checked the viables in the tanks. I gave Ani a cracker we left on a table when we left, and I took her on my lap, and I can tell you, if the Buffalo couple do not like our genes, whatever. But if they don't like Ani, that is so whatever, I want to really shove them, hard. Something is wrong with Ani? Well, what is so great about *you*? Ani is alive. Could your other kid say that?

Rain started pouring to the floor through some hole in the Quonset wall. Janet came down to help wipe it up. She checked where my IV is in place, with a bandaid and a big bruise. Ani watched very careful, what Janet did. She was interested, she touched the bruise. I thought she was worried. I thought she was too young for me to tell her what it is, even if she talked, but it was very cute.

So, a few minutes later, Ani got off my lap and is playing with the toy Henry gave her. It is a sort of box on wheels with a string. She was pulling the string, then she like puts the string on her arm and walks away. Then she looks over her shoulder. The box didn't move, the string is on the floor. She tried a lot of times. Then it hit me, she is pretending her toy is a little IV cart like is hooked up to me. She is pretending to be me. I thought that was so cute and looked at Janet Delize to see if she thought it's cute too. So, right now an environmental factor sets in, and let me tell you, it's going to be there for years. For years I wondered what would of happened if this didn't happen.

Because what happened is, Janet was already giving Ani a look. To tell the truth, she's staring. When she saw me looking at her staring, she looked away fast. I looked away too. But when I looked back at her in a minute, she was staring again, this time at the viables. Then she stared at the ground hard, frowning till she saw me look at her frowning and she just got up and pretends she's busy, like, oh! Better clean the leak on the floor again.

Now, I was used to getting stared at. Ever since I got to the Farm, someone is staring or at least looking at me hard— Rauden, Bernie, Rini. Lucas. Ani always got a lot of looks in Queens. Well, she's a baby. It is usually about how cute she is. This was not a look like that. I didn't exactly know what kind of look it was. But I was pretty sure it was not a good look. It's like Janet is thinking what's happening here, something is wrong with it.

I don't know why she would think that. I looked around the rec room. It was cozy. The rain made a nice sound. I'm giving blood to the IV. Ani is playing with the pretend IV cart. So then I look back at Janet, who is pretending to be busy cleaning up the leak, but sneaking looks at Ani, who is pretending to be me.

Then it hits me what Janet thinks could be wrong. It could be wrong if Ani is...

Me.

Man! How stupid is that?

A person could not be another person. Rauden said so.

Well, maybe it's hormones or how tired I am or how the Buffalo couple declined, but while I'm thinking how stupid Janet is for thinking Ani's me, I look over at the viables and think something stupid too.

Is she them?

Man! She's not them.

Right then Ani stopped with the toy and sat on the floor in her red dress and started to bounce—she really liked to bounce. Here is the next stupid thing I think. If they were her, how cute would that be if they all sat in a little row on the floor in a little red dress, bouncing. That is so stupid. That's not how it works.

She had a little bunch of hair right in the top of her head. When she bounced, it bounced. It was so cute. I pictured them all with a bunch of hair, bouncing. How bad would that be? If she wasn't the only one. Of her.

Then I thought, I! *That's not how it works.* Rauden said so. Ani is gene for gene my living replica. That doesn't mean she's me. Or them.

She could be *exactly like me.*

But if someone was *exactly like you* but not you, hello? Isn't that a pretty serious difference? So then they weren't even exactly like you. But wait.

If the only way for someone to be exactly like you is if they are, does that mean if they're exactly like me, they are. Me.

I was getting a little dizzy here.

Ani stopped bouncing, got up, went to the toy again, and pulled it on the string.

It's not like I never been through this before, in Elmhurst. If she's not me, she could get Mumbai and die. But if she is, that's even worse—she's me. And Janet is right, something is really wrong with that.

Now, let me say this. I done a lot of things something is wrong with. It's pretty much how I stayed alive. And maybe something is wrong with me that I did those wrong things, and maybe that is why the Buffalo couple declined. But I could handle it.

I just didn't know if Ani could.

And that is one more way to prove, you know. If she's me, why would I care?

I was getting really dizzy.

She left the toy, lay down, and kicked the rec room wall.

Rauden said and Rini too the child will not be me because of environmental factors. Well back then they thought Rini will be the environmental factor. Now it's me. Genetic factor, environmental factor. Should I give her back?

Well, that is really going to work. She goes ballistic if I even leave the room. She liked me.

I liked her too.

She stopped kicking the wall now. Her breathing got more slow. Her mouth is open. Her mouth is like, if pink is purple. She has really small teeth. If she is me, she's going to sell them on the Mound.

I just don't want her to.

She conked out, and her feet slid down the wall and left a mark. She just lay there on the floor. I got a Beverage. I stretched the loop out from the IV tube so it was long enough to reach the ground and I lay down too. I didn't kick the wall though. I don't know what that proves.

It is really rainy.

There is an outage. They get the power back in time. The backup generator pulled us through.

I got unhooked and took Ani out for fresh air. It is raining. We don't have a parka. Janet says she will catch her death of cold. Give me a break. Ani's a goddamn Sylvain hardy who is sixteen months old, been exposed to Mumbai, quarantine, who knows what else, and she is goddamn still alive—how hardy is that? And she's going to die from a cold?

It keeps raining.

There is a problem with g) and i). They are not growing right. Rauden thinks it's a lining problem—maybe the outage caused some damage. g) and i) could be at risk. He will intervene. He moves g) to an empty section in tank 1. If it works, they are going to move i) too.

It didn't work.

It also didn't work to keep i) where she was.

So.

We're down to four. How hardy is that?

What I'm saying is, they are all gene for gene, you know, but how does that really work? Gene for gene, they are a goddamn Sylvain hardy, all of them. What good did that do i)?

a) isn't looking so great. It's October. Remember when the Ani group used to swing on the cords? Some of them swing. a) just hangs there. Then she's gone.

Ani didn't notice. She hardly even looks at the viables.

So now I start to think why didn't she notice? Would I of noticed? I'm pretty sure I would. When I was her age, I was locked inside so much, I would be glad to look at anything. Like, one time Cissy Fardo forgot to lock the basement door, I headed up the steps and Cissy was after me so fast, yelling, "Man! I am going to knock you from here to kingdom come!"

Well, that is a difference right there. She's not locked inside. I do not yell at her. Still, I worried.

I worried she could be upset they died. I unhooked my arm and took her out more, so she doesn't have to see them die. We got cold. Janet is at the door calling, "Inez, she will catch her death. Take this for Ani." She gave me a coat to put on Ani and we run around on the mud road. Janet didn't bring a coat for me but whatever! It's one more thing we do not have in common.

And I could intervene about the rest. I could change her environmental factors.

Except me.

But I could goddamn change the rest. I did not pass school? She would. I worked the Mound? Keep her off the Mound. Who knows if it is even still in business, after Mumbai? We would have to have a few things in common, my best points. My best point was, I was alive. Ani was the only one I passed it on to of all the five in her set. So that was a good start right there. She had my best point.

In the new set, the Buffalo viables, only one did in the end.

Six died before October. Two went in November. When it was down to two, the broker came with a crew before Christmas and made an early birth at twenty-five weeks. Rauden gave Ani a shot and put her in our room so she won't get in the way.

It's a really different birth, the tanks don't even rock, they just cut straight through the lining, put the two survivors in a dry tank, Ani wakes up, we have to go to Janet's and stay there until e) and f) went off to Buffalo in a van. They messaged when they got there. e) was still alive.

Rauden didn't even get drunk after. He just sat and stared at the empty tanks. Then he stared at Ani, like, of all the ones who could of been the only one that works, why is it her?

For Janet it is probably more like, of all the Parents who would get the only one that works, why is it me?

Myself, I was thinking, if the main thing about me is I am still alive, none of them are me except Ani and e). If e) was still alive.

Then Janet got depressed too. I don't know what I got. Ani was ok. It rained all the time.

The winter holiday is almost here. Janet wants us out. Her relatives are coming and they will notice Ani and me. Rauden wants us to stay but settles on taking as much product from me as he could, but when I went to get scraped in Callicoon, Ani flipped out so bad I had to hold her for hours after. She wouldn't even go to sleep. She wouldn't even let me leave the room after that. I was starting to wonder how great an environmental factor the Farm was for Ani. She has a predisposition to be me. This could clinch it. Then she ends up making viables which are just like her. And so will they. And so will theirs.

And who would buy any of them? It's not like buyers are knocking down our doors.

So we went back to Queens, in rain.

They handed out masks at the City Line North, below Yonkers. I fell asleep then all through the Bronx and over the bridge. We got off at Main Street Flushing and headed for the Main Street Board. I had told Rauden I know where I am going but I honestly got no idea.

The Main Street Board was down. We slept on the floor. I didn't know where else to go. In the morning we went to a church that still is open and they give breakfast if we wear a mask. What is this with the masks? Is Mumbai coming back?

I almost wish it would. At least in quarantine, the expenses are covered. I'm trying to make a plan here but even when I find a working Board, the credit from Rini does not come up. I try a few times. Nada. I don't even know when it ran out. I was at the Farm for so long I forgot to check and before then was in quarantine. I already missed quarantines. At least they give you bed and meals.

I try to find a listing for some quarantine. They are all out of town. Like, Buffalo still has quarantines. But I don't think we should go there because of e). Akron, Ohio, has quarantines. I could figure out how to get there but to be honest, the fresh start I had in mind—I was picturing one of those Queens Domes—Maspeth, Jamaica Estates. They are not so fancy like Manhattan but it is a better crowd than Powell's Cove or even Flushing. Believe me, we're not going back to Powell's Cove.

But how could I pay Dome prices even if the credit came through? I don't know if it's ever coming through again. All I have is a few coupons Rauden gave me when we left. I already missed the Farm. I'm never going back though. Too bad for Janet and her stupid looks. She's never seeing us again.

We could squat in the old honeycomb pods in Flushing Meadows. I wrap Ani and me in plastic I found on the street and try to go there in the rain but cannot get a shaw or vehicle of any sort it's raining so hard. Nobody's even out except refugees from the City Line Zone, that had been a major Mumbai epicenter, near Creedmoor. It seems they had some new problem, maybe it is just about the toxic antiPatho spray. Whatever it is, there is a major Exodus. People are leaving in droves.

And then it hits me. Exodus? Droves? Nobody wants to stay there? Hello? It is like quarantine all over again. I know how to work this. See which way they flee from. Then head that way with Ani. I turn around and start walking east.

It is raining and raining and raining. We have to keep ducking into a church or Camp or Board shelter to get dry, and in one Camp, in Auburndale, refugees are selling keys to their old abandoned units by the City Line. One refugee, Honey Vitale, just gives me her key free, to what she calls a garden apartment, so deep in the bad area there is no services, nothing. So they have food drops. So I don't even need credit. This could work. I took a few keys from other refugees and contacted Rauden to let him know my plan before we go, in case the Boards don't work where we're heading.

Rauden wants me to come back! He thinks he got some new clients and has a new plan for how it's going to work. Just come up, get scraped, take shots, and he will draw a lot of my blood. Then he's going to set up a chip he read about that could translate my blood into hormone messages so the next lot of viables could grow totally without me. I could be in and out in less than two months. It might not work but Rauden thinks we have an

Opportunity here. Let's just see what happens. Well I will tell you what did happen. I answered back, "Decline." Then I put a jam on my ID so he can't message me again, wrapped Ani and me in plastic, and headed toward the City Line, in the rain.

Now let me explain, because I want you to understand. I would of liked to see what happens. I would of tried the translator chip. But I just thought, we have an Opportunity here, ourself. In two months it could be lost.

We crossed Bell Boulevard.

Maybe you think that is unfair to the others—the viables back at the Farm who are not even born. All I'm thinking of is Ani's different life. What about their life? Look, they might end up with a better life themself if it doesn't start off with this translator chip that between you and me sounds even more cockamamie than the goddamn tank that, for all Ani came out of it alive, nobody else did that great.

I did care about all of them. I still do.

241st Street.

It is just very hard to know what is the right thing to do. It's hard to be a good mother, but Original is no walk in the goddamn park.

I just know I declined. I kept carrying Ani toward the City Line, on Northern Boulevard, in the rain.

Man, it's like Projects sideways out here. You could really get lost. It all looked the same.

57th Avenue.

And empty? What are the chances anyone is even here to notice us? Let alone figure us out. I was having trouble figuring myself out. Is Ani me?

251st Street.

I didn't even know if I was me, these days. I used to be a Subject. I would do anything. Slept in bins, went off in boats with anyone, anywhere. Now it's all worry this, safe side that. It's just—

60th Avenue.

—I got a one year, seven month daughter at risk of being me. Well, that is not going to happen. I'm going to goddamn intervene. I will keep her off the Mound. Make her pass school. Here's a no-brainer—I'm not dying in some goddamn fire. That alone could do the trick. And if it doesn't?

61st Avenue.

Out here? Who's even going to know?

So I turned at empty 256th Place and went to Honey Vitale's empty apartment, in the empty garden, in the rain.

4 THE GARDEN APARTMENT

IT'S NOT REALLY A GARDEN. NOT A REGULAR GAR-
den, like where Rauden grew corn on the hill or Janet got flowers outside her house.

It is more like mud. The mud has grass in it. The mud and
grass is in a square, and brick goes around that square, what they
call, a Walk, with two brick buildings on each side, and they call
the whole thing Courtyard 2. Next to Courtyard 2 is Courtyard
3, then 4, then 5—you get the picture. Twenty courtyards total.
16 units in each one. 320 total units. In the whole thing, there
could be fifty people still alive. In our own courtyard, we were
the only ones.

There used to be a little pool in the garden but it was drained
and filled with dirt so it won't breed something bad. I planted
potatoes there when the rain stopped, from garbage I found by
the City Line.

And let me say this about the life we started now, in Honey
Vitale's garden apartment. I never had a life like it before.
Neither did Ani. I don't know how that works for Ani's different
life if we both get the same different life. But I can tell you this.
These next years, in the garden apartment—Ani's early years?
It's pretty much the best part of our whole life together, that we
had. Ani and me.

We got a two bedroom unit on the first floor of the second
building on the left. This unit came with furniture, which was, I
don't know, plaid. Believe me, I never even saw furniture like this,

let alone sit on it. Where I generally lived was a mess or picked clean. This place, there was even candy left, in glass dishes, with tops. Tables with glass tops. Mirrors on the walls. Nothing is even broken. They even had TV, the old kind, in a cabinet. It worked. Someone already rigged the TV to a cable from Nassau County, on the other side of the City Line wall. We used to watch TV all the time, if the power worked. If not, we just got into bed all day and hug. I found blankets in a closet.

At that time, after Mumbai, most of Queens was pretty quiet. Believe me, it was quiet out here too. But we saw people sometimes, like when we went to food drops. We never went too far. Ani is getting big to carry, and I was nervous who we will meet. It could be vigilantes. I heard they got vigilantes by the City Line wall. At least I don't have to worry about Ethics inspectors. Ethics took a bad hit when the Staten Island Dome cracked, from people trying to break in to escape Mumbai. You might see cops once in a while on the Expressway or Northern Boulevard, but generally it was just regular people, and even those are old. I don't know what oldies are doing still alive out here at the City Line, which was close to Creedmoor and had been a Mumbai epicenter. Maybe they're hardy oldies. Maybe they're lucky. Either way, I was pretty sure they were not going to steal Ani, or if they tried, they would move so slow I could catch them. But man, they stared!

Sometimes they follow us. Like, I will look behind us when we walked to a food drop and some oldie is following us. It will be the woman oldie, not the man. At first I ran away. But in a while, I got used to it and would slow down and let them look and they would say she is so cute. I thought she's cute too. She got hair now and is even cuter than before. Well, I think they would of thought she's cute no matter how she looked. As far as I could tell, she was the only kid in the garden apartments, and maybe the whole City Line Zone. Supposedly, Mumbai's over, it's safe to go out, and in our Zone, some people did. They didn't bring kids. I would of liked to see another kid. But we're the only ones

I ever came across. I would of liked to see another Parent, how they do it, so their kid gets the kind of different life Ani should have. Most kids in those days, they got no life, period.

They had a program on TV we used to watch—*Gone Too Soon*—just pictures of babies and small kids who died from Mumbai. It was really sad. Ani liked it. I worried is it wrong to show her all these kids who died, but she didn't know they're dead or even what that is. And how else are we going to see another kid? I used to look at these pictures of regular kids who died, to compare. Does Ani look like them? I looked at the little clothes they wore. Puffies, stretchies, little caps and Bonnets. One kid even wore a shirt and tie. It was so sad.

One day I heard a knock on our door. I just grabbed Ani so fast and hid with her in a closet till the knocking stopped. Then I come out, open the door very careful, and look around. Well, what is this? It is food. Process, crackers. Water in bottles, which we did not even need—there are already big pots in the courtyard to catch rain. I got all the water I need. I could use the bottles, though.

Well, I start to find little things at the door. Little clothes. Once somebody left dydees and I saw an oldie running off. I think it's Alma Cho from Courtyard 5. She is really small. Old Norma Pellicano from Courtyard 8 would sometimes leave things too. Sometimes they both did, and I would hear them talk outside our door. They mostly talk about what is wrong with what the other one brought. After a while I start to open the door and let them look at Ani. I didn't let them touch her.

Well, one day when it is a little warmer, Ani gets a big environmental factor. I hear a noise at my door, and what is this?

It's one of those bubble carriers you used to see. I think I see Alma Cho scurry away. Man! Where did she find that? I just put Ani in a little sweater and hat one of them had left, set her down in the carrier, wheel her out the Walk, down the street, and here we go. I'm so glad I don't have to lug her, I didn't worry about cops or vigilantes or even how it's raining. I just push the carrier and run and run in the rain—almost to the end of the City Line Zone, past Alley Pond Park till we come to a ramp and up we go till, whoa! The ramp just stopped. A drop went from the edge of the ramp to a big empty road below. I think it is the old Expressway. I think the ramp used to be a bridge that broke. You got a great view from here—Alley Pond, mist, sky, I even think Little Neck Bay. I am so busy with the view, at first I don't see someone standing on the other side of the Expressway, in a mask. Well, I start to wheel Ani away fast—you never know who is behind those masks. But I look back.

It is just a woman holding a bundle. She's just standing there, carrying a bundle.

So I turned around, and just stood there a while and so did she, her with the bundle, me with the carrier, each of us on the other side of the Expressway. I really want to see what's in her bundle. I got the idea she really wants to see what's in my carrier.

So I opened the carrier and picked Ani up and held her facing out. The woman really stared. Then she took her bundle and, well, she did not unwrap it, but when she held it out, I could see it move. Ani could too. She really stared. What could it be but what it looks like?

Tiny newbie. Still alive.

It started to squirm, the way Ani used to. The woman has to hold it close and bounce it. She has to walk it. It squirmed more. So she shook her head, waved, and walked off down the ramp with the bundle. We watched them go.

Well, here is what happened now. Ani reached her arm out where they had been and starts to cry. I mean she howled. She looked right at me, howling, with tears down her face, and then she did something she never did before. She said, "My." I never heard her say a word before. I don't know how she knew it in the first place.

When we got home, I put the TV on for her to watch while

I am putting out our things to dry. *Gone Too Soon* comes on. She put her arm out and said, "My." When the show was over, she said, "My." She even pointed at the TV when it's off and said, "My."

The whole next day, "My! My!" and then the next day, "Mani." That is me! Man! Where did she get that? Here is something she will say. "Dis." She will point at something and say, "Dis." I think it means, like, thing. Sometimes she will say, "Mani, dis." She wants me to give it to her, the thing. "Mani, dis." It was very cute.

Well, the weather warmed up and the rain stopped. I would push Ani in the carrier to different places. So there is an area with grass they call golf course, where old men and women used to sit on a bench in the sun. So I would sometimes wheel Ani past, and she is like eating a cracker or holding a bottle. The old men used to pretend they would steal her bottle and said, "Gimme dat!" like this was funny. The women did not say it. Ani didn't think it was so funny. It got so when she even saw some old man on the street she hid the bottle.

One day, I'm wheeling Ani down West Alley Road, and one old man is sitting on the curb. He starts to point one shaky finger at the bottle. Ani stuck the bottle right out at him, like she will hit him with it. She yelled, "My!" She was mad. I got us out of there really fast and turned the corner. She gave me a look I never saw before. She showed me the bottle, said, "My had dis," and laughed so hard she cried. I thought it was funny too. I didn't even know what it meant.

Well, one day she comes to me with her arms up and goes, "Pick you up, Mani." So I thought that is cute too, but I want her to know who is who.

So I go, "No, Ani. Pick *me* up."

Well, that does not work. She tries.

"No, Ani." I want her to say it right. I want her to get it right, who is who. I don't want her to mix us up.

"Pick you up! Pick you up!"

I hit her. I didn't know what else to do.

I will never forget how she looked—shocked, tears just rolling down her face. I picked her right up and held her. She did not even hit me back, just cried in my neck. I can tell you this. I'm never doing that again. I don't care who is who or what. I don't care if I don't show her who is boss.

I just don't know how this is supposed to work. One reason I watched TV, I thought I can find some program with kids and Parents in it, get some ideas, how it is supposed to be, the different life I'm going to give her, if I could.

It's true I also put on *Fresh Start* sometimes, because I hoped it will show that program we watched with Janet Delize that time, about those Parents who were so mad with grief they want to make a new kid the same way Ani was. I want her to have a different life, but to tell the truth, I sometimes want to see someone else with a life like us. We were the only ones I ever heard of.

The News would run stupid stories about the baby crisis and what they call Alt Repro. Someone is always sure there is a booming business in what they call clone factories or nests, which is supposedly so unethical they want to call a raid. They never show a real case. They never show a picture of a real clone. From what I could tell, nobody ever even saw one. Or if they did, they wouldn't know. Like, Ani and me? If someone saw us, what? I'm going to spill the beans? So there could be others like us, Ani and me, who did not spill the beans. To be honest, I wished there were. Maybe something is wrong with it. Maybe it is a crime against nature. But I wished we weren't the only ones.

I watched a lot of News. I don't know how new the News was or if it's even true. Norma Pellicano says it depends what boat it got transmit from. Alma Cho thought it's transmit from some Dome. She thought Memphis. Norma said that Dome cracked. A lot of Domes cracked besides Staten Island. The Cincinnati PharmaDome cracked, plus some Process Domes in New Jersey. Moscow and Johannesburg Domes cracked bad. Rio cracked long ago. Beijing Dome still worked. Manhattan too. Sometimes the News said terrorists cracked those Domes. Alma Cho says. "No. It not work." She means Domes do not work. She talked like that.

The News is mostly still about Mumbai. They would show a map with blue on it where the Pandy had hit or was hitting now. It is still spreading overseas. Some place called Grozny was hit bad. In America, besides Queens and Brooklyn and adjoining areas, St. Paul, Minnesota, still had it, plus Kansas City and San Diego. Buffalo was a mess. I wondered how e) was doing. The baby crisis is global. It was bad for years but now it's off the charts.

Sometimes I thought the whole clone panic was made up. Like, this is going to get people's minds off everybody being dead. Like, come on, even with everyone dead, no infrastructure, no kids, even no Ethics, at least in New York, we still have too much ethics to commit crimes against nature like nuclear Transfer.

The Horror show I told you about—*Them*? Where nuclear Transfer works like bingo? That is totally made up. This show was so stupid, I worried Ani might see it and it's a bad environmental factor. I only watched it if I'm sure she's asleep. I honestly don't know why I even watched it myself, it is so stupid. If you believe this show, clones are pale and do things in a group, facing forward, like an army. None of them could think for themself. Twins could though. Look at Rauden and Henry. Well, on this stupid *Them*, clones can't think for themself, because they are not real, because they're clones. They cannot even bleed.

Ani did bleed, I guarantee. I mean, when she bleeds, she hit the roof.

How do you prove a person's real? Like proving was she me?

How do you prove either of those things, either way? I really thought about this a lot. As environmental factor, that look from Janet went a long way. Well, I had a lot of time on my hands out in the garden apartment. I don't even know if it was Ani's time or mine. I don't know whose hands it's on, if you want to put it that way.

We sometimes slept at different times. But what does that prove? Maybe she is just me in a different place. We sometimes disagreed. I mean, once she learned to talk. Like, she didn't want me to go anywhere without her. I disagreed. I sometimes just want to go somewhere by myself. I mean, a different room. She did not want me in a different room.

Sometimes I carried her to the other bedroom when she's already asleep. She would wake up and sneak back. I don't know what that proves. When she stole back, she woke me up. Then I'm awake, even when she goes back to sleep, and once I'm up, I'm up for good, except when she would take a nap. But she would not take a nap. So I can't take a nap. Who's going to keep an eye on her? I'm the only one in charge.

Sometimes I worry, does she want to be with me all the time because, you know? But come on, if I'm her, why does she care? If I'm her, I'm there already.

She wants me to carry her too, I mean, all the time. She's getting so big. She's almost two years old by now! How do I carry her, if she is me? In the Horror show, clones are always all the same age and size, so it doesn't come up.

When I used to live with Cissy Fardo, before the baby crisis got really bad, they sometimes had what they call Dramas, that are not scary like Horror but are also not based on fact. In this one Drama I saw with Cissy, someone is adopted, so the only thing they care about was their real background, which meant who their Life product came from. In Dramas where they are not adopted but are regular, it did not come up. They care about their life. If they're regular, their Life just did not come up. They already knew where it came from—the Parents. At least back then it did.

For myself, it was a little different. I was not exactly what you call adopted, because there are no papers. So I guess it is not a real adoption, even though Cissy Fardo took care of me for ten years, until she died. Her real kids already grew up and I never knew if they were even still alive because they moved out long before the Big One, so as far as being different from her real kids, I didn't know how real I was because I was the only one around.

Maybe it just proves something is wrong with me, but as a kid I was not that curious about my Life or background or any of that. I was mostly curious if Cissy Fardo would stay alive, and she didn't.

If Ani is me, or exactly like me, she will not be curious about her background or Life. If she's not me, it won't even matter. She'll be regular. She can think what she wants.

Sometimes I just thought it is too stupid to even worry about. Rauden thought so.

I missed Rauden. But I was afraid to be in touch. I thought he will be angry I declined to come back. I was even afraid he will make me change my mind, and we'll end up back at the Farm. He was always trying to keep me in his sight. He was as bad as Ani.

But I missed him, and the Farm too.

On Ani's second birthday, I went to a message Board way up Little Neck Parkway, which worked good, logged into Universal Guest, so no one can reply, and sent Rauden this message: "Still alive."

ii

She even did her business in a pot.
   Sometimes.

   Here is something funny Ani did. The sofa in the living room has plaid cushions? So, one cover got loose so you can see the foam inside? She took a big bite of the foam! Here is what she did next. With the big bite in her mouth, she hopped one two three to the mirror and spits the foam out. Man! What was she thinking?

   I guarantee I never did that. Cissy Fardo, if I did something like that, she would knock me to kingdom come. So maybe I would of done it if I could.

   Here is something else. She got lost. She had trouble finding the door. It happened a lot. She will be like in a chair? Then gets up to go somewhere, then stops. Then she will look around, worried. Then she will walk around again and stop. Then again. Then she will sit down on the floor and cry. If she is outside, well, I could see the problem. Everything looked the same in Courtyard 2. How could you know what is our door? But inside?

   I was concerned. I would like her to find the door, of course. Still, that is one more difference between us. I did not get lost. I could find the door.

   Maybe I couldn't when I was her age. Maybe I would of had a problem with a door if we had more than one room. We just had one room in that basement, and Cissy Fardo never let me out. Nobody let their kids out. Maybe I would of got lost too, if Cissy Fardo let me out.

I thought about her a lot, now I was bringing Ani up. I wondered how she even stood it, locked up in the basement with me all that time? Ani and me, we could go anywhere—courtyard, foraging. It still sometimes got on my nerves.

Here is something else I wondered—the time she left the basement door unlocked? And I was heading to the street, in Corona? She got up those stairs so fast. Before, if I thought about that time—I mean, once I knew I was a hardy—I would think, all that for nothing. She could of let me out. I'm a goddamn hardy, I could drink water from a puddle in the street and not get cholera. I could kiss someone with Luzon on the mouth and still not get it. Now I thought a different way about it.

How did she get up the stairs so fast? She was old.

And with those legs. Her legs were so big and swollen they spilled over her slipper. It is like you see in a picture in a book of elephants. They were so big, in the end she couldn't climb the steps at all. She had to let me out to forage for food. She couldn't walk at all, even from a fire.

I thought about her legs.

I guess I thought two ways about them. One is, keep an eye on how my legs are doing or I could die in a fire. And there goes Ani's different life. The other is just Cissy Fardo's legs, period. It is a really long time since I thought about Cissy Fardo's legs. I thought about her hands too. How they are white and swollen. How they fixed things. Food. Buttons. How she fixed my hair in the little bunch. I thought about her smell.

It is a really long time since I thought about Cissy Fardo's smell.

I thought how she took care of me. I thought how I felt when she died and I was just a kid and was like, where is Cissy? Who will take care of me now? And then, what happened next? Well, I'm not even going to tell you about that. It's bad enough

Rauden figured it out. I just don't want it to happen to Ani. I want her to have a different life, and not even so she won't be a crime against nature and we're all in jail. I just don't want her to feel that way I felt.

She did seem to have a different life. So far.

Two and a half years old. Still alive.

She's in the courtyard, playing with leaves that fell from one tree that nobody cut down for wood. She is scooping leaves up and pouring them on her head. She is rolling in them. I guarantee I never did that.

Sometimes I got really sick of thinking about it all the time. Sometimes it didn't even mean that much to me one way or the other is she me or like me or e) or even the Santa Sofya ones, if they were born. They could all be her if they want.

Just let her be the one of her I get to keep.

She got a little jacket Alma left for her. Little tiny jeans and, oh man. Tiny overalls. I wish Rauden could see her in them. She was so cute.

Three years old. Still alive.

Ani is playing with some wood with nails in it I hauled back from the City Line.

"Do not touch! It tetanus." Alma Cho. Where did she come from? You would look up and there is Alma Cho in the corner of the courtyard. She is really small and bent and wears a blue hat and, like, apron.

I yell back, "Do not butt in. She does not get anything." Oh, shit. She doesn't know we are a Sylvain hardy. She will think I'm a bad mother. So I said, "Ani, no. Do not touch." Then I check back if Alma Cho heard. I think she did.

So maybe it worked. Maybe she thinks I'm not a bad mother.

I don't even know why I cared. Alma Cho is not going to Alert anybody. She is probably worried someone will Alert somebody about her.

Still, I thought be on the safe side. Once, I had brought some forage back from Douglaston Estates and Ani is playing with some antiPatho spray she found in a box. I looked down the courtyard entrance and here is Alma Cho again, watching. Now, I don't get sick from the antiPatho spray and Ani neither probably, but Alma Cho does not know that. I'm pretty sure she never heard of Sylvain hardy. So I do the thing again, like, "Be careful, Ani." I say it loud, so Alma could hear.

A few days later, Alma Cho is right at the door. She got tapes and pamphlet. Do chores for her. She will give us tapes and pamphlet. What do I need that for? What even is a pamphlet? She says, "Ok. Coupon." She talked that way. Which I enjoyed. She means she will give me coupons if I do chores for her. Go in some units where people died. Get forage. Spray with anti-Patho. Ok, she figured us out, at least the hardy part. She isn't going to Alert anyone. She just wants us to do her chores. So I got some dishes and chairs for her in Courtyard 4. I did pretend to look out for Ani, be careful, do not touch. I can't make Ani stay away though. She followed me even in the units.

One day I have to lug out a generator cycle from a unit in Courtyard 6 and inside is two bodies, or what used to be two bodies. They still smelled. I lugged the cycle to Alma Cho's unit where Bernie Cho is sitting in the dark. Ani is more scared of him than those dead bodies. What really scares her is if I'm not there. Like when I went into those units for Alma, and I will tell you, they really smelled, she followed me in. She doesn't even want to watch from the door.

Once when Alma Cho had me climb the City Line wall and rehook our cable to the generator on the other side, Ani flipped out. I could look down from the wall and see her jumping up and down and howling while Alma and Norma Pellicano and some other oldies tried to shut her up. From the top of the wall, I looked down and saw Nassau County. I never saw Nassau County before. It's all personal Domes.

What is the point of that? Every time you need something that is not in your personal Dome, you will have to go outside to get it. How Hygienic is that? The regular Domes, they have one big Dome with services, hydroponics, Process factories, whatever. Some Domes even got chute tunnels that pipe in from other Domes, like the ones that make Process or meds. You don't need to leave for anything. The personal Dome—well, remember Ani is an unplanned baby? The personal Dome is like that. They did not think that far ahead. They built them personal because they did not want to share. Then they saw that didn't work. Too late now.

A lot of Queens is like that—too late now. Somebody should of built a big Dome for us when they could, but too late now. We're dead.

I mean, not Ani and me. We're still alive.

The tapes from Alma Cho worked. They are cartoons. I remember these from when I was a kid. The cartoons was to teach kids Education, like, a, b, c, d, e, in case school is closed from some new Epi. Which it generally was.

I never saw the pamphlets before. They are like Education for the Parent. I looked at the one called *My Healthy Child*. I think this was old, because the kids in the pictures are in a group. Your healthy child needs stimulation. I could use some stimulation, myself. I am so sick of walking to the City Line but where else could we go? Bodies still wash up in Little Neck Bay. I didn't think Ani should see that. I really thought it could be stimulating for her to play with some regular kids, if I saw one. And for sure it would be stimulating for me to talk to their Parent. I never saw a kid though. I did see living people out, even besides oldies, like at the food drops. No kids though.

The drops come about once a week, and you really have to get to the drop fast, because the food disappears. So this one windy day, I'm hurrying to a drop that fell near Queens Village barricade. They put up the barricades to protect the safer Zones from Zones like us—City Line was a very bad epicenter. Man! It's over. They still thought they could get something from us. Well, I will tell you this. They didn't mind getting food from our drops.

This one day? I saw two masked people scramble over the barricade, steal Process Paks, and scramble back. I was mad! This is a City Line drop! Get your own drop! I scrambled to the barricade after them. A big sign said, DO NOT CROSS. Well, you crossed to my goddamn Zone. I could cross to yours.

So now I scrambled across the barricade carrying Ani in the bubble carrier but this took so long by the time I made it across, the masked people got away. Well here I am in Queens Village Zone. And nobody's even here to stop me. Let's check it out. It looked a lot like City Line, except you are supposed to wear a mask. You could read that on another sign. WEAR A MASK. I closed the bubble trap on Ani and pulled my coat over my face and pushed the carrier down Springfield Boulevard. So this is Queens Village! It is a windy day just before spring. The Boulevard is totally empty.

Some vehicle is parked in the middle, like Ani's bubble carrier but bigger, with two sails on top like one of those sailtrams you would sometimes see? But smaller. Let's check this out! Well, I got more stimulation than I bargained for. I carried Ani into this vehicle, pulled the bubble top shut and whoosh! The wind came up and off we go down Springfield Boulevard. Whoa! How do you stop this thing? Ani cried but pretty soon fell asleep. When the thing finally stopped I got us out as fast as I could. Dizzy! Where are we? 115 Road. I saw some kind of Dome not too far off. Cambria Heights Dome. I heard of that. How are we getting home from here? Ok, just push the carrier back the way we came, up Springfield Boulevard, but the wind came up against us so strong I could hardly push so I get off to a side street, but old torn caution tape is up, so I try a different side street that is a mess, like they had a Hygiene fire here. There was such a big pile of burnt stuff you could hardly push a carrier through. I turn around and tried to get back. The carrier kept getting stuck in burnt stuff, in heaps. Behind one heap was a, like, wall with no building and these words painted on in white. "WHY WAS I BORN?" I turn us around. A different wall has these words painted in black. "WHY AM I STILL ALIVE?" I turned around again and kept pushing through the mess. Way off in the distance I saw some big thing that I think was once a famous quarantine, called Belmont Stadium, at the City Line. If I keep it on my right, I think we will head home, but the carrier wheels keep getting stuck. I pick the carrier up and plow through the mess till I come to a whole side of a building with these words, "because it is God's Will." Then we are getting hit with something. It is bricks. Ani is screaming so hard I have to pick her up and drag the carrier till I finally saw a clear street and got us on it and ran almost the whole way home.

When I told Norma and Alma about it, they said we're lucky to be alive. It was Fundy vigilantes. Well, I heard we had something like that in Queens but never thought I'd see them so close. Norma said these guys run around in robes and burn down anything they think is not God's Will. A lot of times, what they mean by that is how you were born, or your kid was born. They was very big on being born the regular way. Well, what those vigilantes got a problem with, Ani is it for sure. Not that they could tell just by looking. And by the way, these nuts don't seem so regular, themself. Ani and me are more regular than them. Even how Ani was born, she came out more regular than them.

Even regular kids are not as regular as they were when I was born. A lot of kids are not born the regular way. Vaccine Syndrome you heard about and there are problems from the spray. Now it is Stealth Virus which those regular mothers in the Middle Village toilet talked about that could challenge your auto

Immune so you could not have your own kid though you could have someone else's kid, but even that was hard to bring off. If those Fundy nuts are going to burn down every kid that did not come the regular way, they will be pretty busy. I really kept an eye on the News.

I still never heard of anyone like us. You mainly heard about Donor intervention. You could see about it on TV. I saw one program where the mother bought Donor everything. She bought a Donor viable, then paid some girl to Host it. This Parent was great. She did not even use a virgin Host. She was not afraid to go public. She said she's going to tell the whole world the truth how her kid is born, including the kid, once it could talk. It's the kid's Heritage! The kid should not be ashamed.

I never thought of that.

I don't want Ani to be ashamed.

But how could I tell the world? We could end up in trouble with the Authority. Or worse, with these Fundy nuts so close. And that's just about nuclear Transfer. What about the tank?

I thought about the kids I had seen in Ani's life. I thought about those Middle Village toilet kids with their regular mothers. I thought about the plexi and springs out on Dry Harbor Road. Was that part of a tank a kid was born from? Why was that kid born? Why were any of them? Those Fundy vigilantes really got in my head. They're as bad as Janet Delize's stupid looks.

Why was Ani born? That is a nobrainer. She was born so Rini Jaffur would have one child to stay alive. And that is one more difference between me and Ani. I don't know why I was born. And I don't know if it's God's Will I'm still alive. But I can tell you this.

I am.

Ani too.

It's already spring. Ani's in the courtyard, playing with dirt. She likes to build a pile of dirt, then jump in it. I really wish I knew of any kid who did that. I wish I knew of any kid period. I wish I could take Ani to Middle Village. Maybe Myrtle Avenue Center. But it is such a long trip. Norma Pellicano said they are going to make a podtram all the way to Hunter's Point. One day we could take that trip. Maybe we could get out at Elmhurst.

Norma says a lot of infrastructure got improved at last. The sailtram will start working again any day, on the old tracks Ani and I sometimes walk on, for the view. You just go up a ramp at Northern Boulevard. I decide to take her for a walk up there on her birthday. The view from there, who knows? Maybe we could see a kid.

I got us up early on the birthday. Alma Cho is already waiting outside with a toy for Ani. Ani just threw it away. She prefers the dirt. I put Ani in the bubble carrier, wheel her to Little Neck Board, and send Rauden his birthday message.

Still alive.

Then we walked to the sailtram ramp. I had packed us food and water. We go right up the ramp. There was a bench up there. I sat down on it and gave Ani a drink and just look around. It was a great view. Golf course. Creedmoor. Even some Nassau County personal Domes, way off. The tracks start shaking. The sailtram's working! Here it comes. WHOOSH! We just sat watching the sailtram pass, with its sails shaking in the wind. It was great.

A little ways down the tracks was a sign. INSERT COUPON, PULL FLAG FOR COLLEGE POINT. Well that is right next door to Powell's Cove. I'm not going there again in a million years. We cross to the other side. OZONE PARK BY WAY OF SPRINGFIELD GARDENS. I heard of Ozone Park. Let's see what happens! I always got some coupons in my pocket, from

Alma Cho or my own forage activities. I insert one, pull the flag, and we just wait and wait. So, whatever. The view is still great. It is still a great day.

Then the sailtram came! It stopped! I had been on one of these a long time ago. You just walk on. So I just walk on, carrying the carrier. I didn't see anyone else but us. Well, once this thing got started, it's so fast it makes that Queens Village bubble vehicle seem as slow as Ani's carrier. I can't even read the signs we pass. Whee! It was great. It's like we will fly right off the tracks. We don't even stop for Zone crossings or anything till the tram overheats. Then that's it. Where are we? I took Ani off the sailtram and we are in a great big empty space with great big burnt things. Then I saw—I think it is a plane. We ended up in JFK! What else is it going to be? Everyone heard of JFK. The Big One started here, on a plane, the same year I was born. And I am here with Ani on her fourth birthday. And she is still alive.

You could smell water. You could even see water shining behind the burnt buildings.

I pushed Ani in the carrier till we came to a bunch of army tanks that must be here to guard the place, though no one's in them. We went right up to the tanks. I told Ani, "Tanks." She mouths it back. *Tanks.* At least now she heard the word.

We come to a ramp, I push Ani up the ramp to a regular street and right away a big group shaw goes past with two pumpers in front, and you cannot believe how many riders. Nobody wears a mask. What is this? A stadium? And—I could hardly believe my eyes. It is a horse. I was a little nervous. But it seemed to be the only one, and nobody's riding it. The horse pulls a tiny shaw. So out here by JFK they got a horse that got no vigilante on it and is still alive. Ani really stared. The horse and shaw head toward the water. I pushed Ani after, till the tiny shaw went somewhere else.

Well, here are two old men. I think they are fishing! We go right up and look. One man says, "Do she want to touch the fish?" Ani is scared. She won't even get out of the carrier. I try to put her on the ground, which is sand and grass. She just hangs on to me so her foot can't go on the sand. She was scared of the sand! I let her ride my back and kept heading out on the X Bay Boulevard, dragging the carrier. The Boulevard is a narrow strip between water on both sides, and you can smell the water really strong. Way out on the water was a boat. Way ahead on the land I could see tents. I feel like I am in a dream.

I could see people jumping up and down. I heard music. I start to think about the Exodus that moved to the beach from Queensbridge. Was this them? I really want to check this out. Some of the people jumping up and down are so small, what are the chances they're not kids? Some of them jump right in the water. I felt this is a place I always wanted to be, but Ani hangs on to me so tight I could hardly breathe. A copboat cruiser comes right up through the water with a speaker and everyone runs away. We ran too, but the other way. Where are we? Is this Ozone Park? Well, look at that. It is a sailbus! We got right on! Even Ani liked that.

A sailbus, you have to not care where you end up. The tram, they don't have a driver and it's full of surprises, as you saw. But it stays on tracks. The sailbus, you could end up anywhere. This one ends up at a Dome I'm pretty sure is called Jamaica Estates. There are three residence Domes in Queens—this one, then Maspeth, and Cambria Heights. They are all smaller than Manhattan Dome.

We just stood outside this Jamaica Estates Dome, trying to look in. It's starting to get dark. You could see lights come on, inside. You could see people on a bench. You could even see trees. I wait a long time, hoping to see kids, till a Dome cop comes up from nowhere. Where is the mask? Where is the swipe ID? The cop looks at Ani hard, then me, then back at our swipe IDs. What are you, she says, from the City Line? What Zone, Northeast?

I was too tired to lie. Maybe I should of lied. Maybe nobody ever will notice us if I lied that time. I just told the cop where we are from. She punched it in her Reader gizmo then said go home. She didn't have to say it twice. I was really tired. I just kept pushing Ani home. By the time we got home in the dark, I could hardly drag Ani up our steps. We both slept the whole next day, but when I finally got up and thought about what happened? I think I never had a better day, my whole life. I just want to do it again.

And that is one more difference between Ani and me. I could hardly get Ani to leave the courtyard after that.

"Ani. Want to forage?"

She wants to stay in the courtyard and play with dirt.

"Want to go to the food drop, Ani?" She will not even go to the food drop. I have to pick her up to even get her in the bubble carrier, and she is squirming, and when I try to open the bubble trap, she kicks it shut. "Ani!" I say. "We got to go to the food drop."

She looks up at me and says, "Ani! We got to go to the food drop."

So what is this?

"Ani, for real."

"Ani, for real." So this is the new thing.

Like, when I turn the cartoon tapes on and go, "Don't you want to learn ABCDE?"

She goes, "Don't you want to learn ABCDE?"

It made me nervous. Why is she talking like me? Maybe she got too stimulated. Maybe it is a Phase. In one of those pamphlets from Alma Cho, I read about the Phase.

The dirt Phase is still on.

Here is something Ani does with dirt. Digs, builds a heap, then hops one two three to the heap, points one finger at it, and says, "Do she want to touch a fish?"

Man!

Then she hops three two one away. Then she mouths, so you can hardly hear it, "Tank!" What is she thinking?

Still alive. That's the main thing.

And I will tell you this. She's not the only one. The time when we could walk a half an hour and be the only ones we saw was starting to end. Even by the City Line you saw people on the street sometimes besides oldies, and I'm pretty sure once I saw a kid by a house behind caution tape, off Douglaston. Someone was pulling the kid back inside a door. I definitely saw a kid once when Ani let me go over the Flushing barricade. Nobody stopped us. The kid wore a mask.

Norma Pellicano said lots of new infrastructure finally came back to Queens. Central Dome has been promising it since Mumbai ended. Some schools in other Zones already are working, plus Norma said they are going to open a school out here that been closed since Luzon Second. They got working transportation in some parts. Podtrams, sailtrams, sailbuses, and I think some new kind of regular hybro, with different fuel, that even had a driver. Trikes with bubbles! Trikes without. Skates! Boardies! They had a bubble boardie too.

Well, look at that. It is one of those pigeon fleets, for messages! I guess some pigeons are still alive, even without Larraine's intervention. They seem to be a little challenged. They just drop message Capsules wherever they are.

Man! She's already five.

Alma and Norma brought a Princess dress and fixed her hair. Norma even brought a crown but Ani refuses to wear it. To tell the truth, I have to get her out of the courtyard very fast before she pulls the Princess dress right off. I stuff her in the carrier and went up the hill to send Rauden the birthday message. Still alive. I sometimes think I should pull the jam off my ID so he could get back to me, tell me how he's doing. I'm just afraid he's still mad, I declined to do the work. Maybe another time. I just left the message and off we go.

I'm going to treat her to a podtram ride. A podtram is a tram with pods, so you are not getting TB or SARS from some other traveler. I really wanted to go to the beach by JFK again, but Ani still hardly got over last time, and I thought she would like this. I just stick a coupon in the podtram Reader, climb in one pod, shut the gate.

A pigeon fleet was dumping message Capsules in Alley Pond behind us when the pod took off. Not that bright. Still alive.

The tram is heading toward Manhattan Dome. I want to show her places on the way where she has been, or I have. I really thought about what that mother with the Donor everything said, about the Heritage.

Here is Kissena Boulevard, where the bus stopped but it wasn't a regular Stop or bus, and Cissy Fardo climbed on, took me off, and carried me to Corona. I never told Rauden that. I didn't tell Ani that. I just told her the word as we passed by. *Kissena.*

Here is Flushing Meadows, where we had Resettlement.

Here is Elmhurst, where we stayed in the unit with the nylon. I didn't make a big deal. I just said the word. *Elmhurst.* We passed three big cemeteries, then Sunnyside, where neither of us ever been. We got off at Hunter's Point and looked across the river at the sun shining on the Manhattan Dome. I didn't see it so close since Ani was a baby, at Queensbridge. Now she is five years old, and I was so proud. She talks. She walks. She does her business in a goddamn pot. What I'm saying is, ok, Rauden made history with Ani.

You tell me this. Who kept her alive?

By now I was so used to my life with Ani, I didn't worry all the time. Maybe I should of worried now. Like, why is that pigeon fleet dropping a Capsule in our courtyard when we got back, tired, from our long day? Maybe I should of thought, better hide that Capsule before Ani saw it. But maybe when you see what's coming it's just as well I waited to worry. I will have lots of Opportunity to worry, after today.

Ani scrambled from her carrier, grabbed the Capsule, and opened it up. In the Capsule is two little papers. She hands one to me.

REPORT TO DESIGNATED CENTER FOR ID CHECK AND HEALTH PROFILE.

I turned it over.

CHECK LOCAL BOARD FOR DETAILS.

Ok, it is some kind of stupid scam. I bunched it up and put it in my pocket. "It's a scam, Ani."

I should of done the same thing with the second paper. I should of bunched it up and hid it. I wish I did. I wish I threw it in a heap of worms. I wish I burnt it. I wish I did anything but read it.

But I did.

On one side it said, CITY LINE BOARD OF ED.

And on the other, PARENT SCHOOL AGE CHILD.

Too late now.

What it is, it's the end of the time it's just us two.

iii

Look, I try to be a good mother. I want an Education for my daughter. But, come on. ID check?

In the night, I made a pile of what we will need. Clothes, pots and dishes, blankets, food and water. I think I could fit it all in two really big bags. I still got the bag Janet sent us off with. I will forage for another up past the Little Neck Board. They got some really good forage left in the big houses up the hill.

I wheeled Ani up Little Neck Parkway the next day, after lunch. There is one big house up the hill that got very good forage plus this thing in back called a patio where Ani sometimes liked to play but this big house does not have a big bag and the house beside it just got small ones. Ok, I will have to make do with one big, two small. I will just stuff as much as I could in those. Then move to the beach. "Time to go, Ani," and she climbed in the carrier and I wheeled her out the door. I was pretty sure they will not have school at the beach.

Ok, I know. I know. This sounds bad.

Here she has an Opportunity I never had in my whole life to get an Education. She could learn something. She could be somebody. And I am moving to the beach?

I wheeled Ani to the sidewalk.

Well you are right of course, but try to see my point of view. What are the chances no one will notice something? We could really get in trouble. Alert the Authority? These guys *are* the

Authority. She is a crime against nature. I helped commit it. I just thought it's better to move to the beach. And that is really going to work.

I sat down on the curb and put my head in my hands. What was I thinking?

Ani did not even like the beach. She hates the beach.

I was just so mixed up.

Ani fell asleep in the sun.

I sat on the curb a long time. Then I got up and pushed the carrier back down to the Board to check out these so-called details. She really outgrew the carrier but for trips this long I just stuff her in and her legs stick out.

HELLO! WELCOME TO CITY LINE BOARD OF ED. Chancellor Hugo Murcia is delighted to inform Parents that the City Line Disaster Fund finally came through after just four years! And guess what?

EVERY CITY LINE CHILD OF SCHOOL AGE MUST REPORT TO PS 263, 261st AVENUE, 8:15 SEPTEMBER 5.

And not only that.

IT IS MANDATORY THAT PRIOR TO THAT DATE YOUR CHILD REPORT TO DESIGNATED HEALTH CENTER AT PARSONS BOULEVARD WITH ID FOR COMPLETE HEALTH PROFILE.

Complete Health Profile. Oh, that is really going to work. I just bumped the whole thing off and wheeled Ani around empty houses down the hill and big flat burnt-out lots all the way to the grass and sand at the edge of Little Neck Bay, where I parked the carrier on the grass with Ani conked out. Then I lay down beside her on the grass, just Ani and me.

That's what it has been all these years—Ani and me. Foraging, exploring Zones, planting potatoes, watching TV. The whole time, just two oldies even knew who we are. No one knew what we are. What if somebody finds out?

She is on her side, flopped in her carrier, breathing. I just watched her breathe, like when she was a newbie.

I was just so worried what will happen. I'm worried they will take her away. I'm just so worried they will give her to someone else.

Then I fell asleep too.

When I woke up, everything looked different. The water looked different. It has lines in it. I got up and walked over to see it up close. No bodies. A barge was paddling past. I haven't looked at the water this close since the old days on the Mound, when I had a different life.

I looked back at Ani, who is starting to wake up too. She was rubbing her eyes and stretching. She was so cute.

And then I start to think, wait. What about *her* different life? All she does is spend her time with me. She even watches the same cartoons I watched when I was as young as her. It's true I went to school myself a little when it was open between Epis till it shut down for good, but it was Catholic School. I never went to regular school. She could learn a skill. She could meet another kid. She could have another goddamn environmental factor besides me!

And come on. It's not like we never took a risk. Fundy vigilantes, quarantines, not to mention it was pretty goddamn risky for her to even be born. I took deep breaths like Rauden said to do. That calmed me down enough to come back to Ani, who is still yawning. Ok, give it a shot. "You want to go to school?"

She blinks. "You want to go to school?"

"Ani, don't start."

She goes, "Ani, don't start."

Man! I could hardly wait for this Phase to be over. I walked off and took deep breaths till I am calm enough to think of a plan. Then I come back and say, "I'm going to school too."

She fell for it. "I'm going to school too."

Me, "We're going to school," her, "We're going to school," so that's it, it worked. We're going to school.

Wait. Do we want to go to school?

Too late now.

It took a month till I got my nerve up and brought Ani for the complete Health Profile all the way at the Parson's Boulevard Center, and I can tell you, I was so scared I have to breathe deep the whole way. But the scanner didn't work. So nothing came up. We even came back another time. It still didn't work. The person gave me a card and a map to find PS 263 and said, "These scanners never work. Just bring your daughter to school as indicated. They will have a scanner there. It probably won't work, either."

I start to think we could bring this off.

I start to get excited. Really excited. I start to run around jumping up and down. I'm not the only one excited. Word of the new school spread all over the garden apartments. I think it spread all over the Zone. Alma Cho starts bringing school forage. Backpack. Crayons. Norma Pellicano left a ruler. Lunchbox. Little plaid skirt. Well, look at this. It is Jellies.

Alma Cho brought a regular clock. She shows me how to wind the button so it works. Now Ani won't be late to school.

Not much chance of that. I lie awake that whole night before September 5 with the clock beside me. When it says seven, I woke Ani up, cleaned her good, put her in the plaid skirt and Jellies, stuffed her in the bubble carrier, put the clock in my pocket, took the card and map and headed out. Alma Cho is standing on the corner, waving. She is smiling but I got the feeling if she didn't see us on our way to school, she'd turn us in. We waved back.

At 74th Avenue, I saw two people at a window, waving. We waved back. I had been in this part of City Line northeast before. I never saw so many people out. One oldie is in front of a house that is covered in plastic. She is covered in plastic too. She waved and we waved back.

By the time we got to Union Turnpike, I started to hear a sound. At 259th Street, Ani heard it too. The closer we get, the bigger it is. It's only when we turn the last corner we find out what it is. Kids crying. A big bunch of kids and Parents are standing near an old brick building, under a flag. The Parents are crying too. And watching the whole thing is more people than I saw at once since the Mumbai panics. Some of them are crying too. They just want to look at kids. Some of the Parents hid the children's faces. Some wore masks. We should of worn a mask too. Then if something showed, no one would guess. No one looked at us funny though. We walked through the door.

The swipe Reader didn't work! Everyone got through. The scanner for Health Profile didn't work. Everyone's crying so much they just want to get us in fast. We got through!

They put us all in one regular room, with pictures on the walls, and books, and toys, and a teacher, and a smell. I mean, it was all interesting. But the most interesting thing was, kids. I didn't see so many kids since the Myrtle Avenue Center that gave green Process so long ago. I guess there was fifteen Parent/kid combos. The kids are in like blankets and shower curtains for Hygiene but after a while the kids got hot and cranky so the Parent took the wrappings off, and inside was, you know, kids—different color kids, brown, pink, tan, gray. Some of them are totally white, like they never even saw daylight. Some of them had a big head. One had a sort of pipe to help her breathe. One wore a helmet. I don't know why she wore a helmet. All I know is, compared to those kids, we seemed regular. Ani began to cry.

She flung a hand out at the others. I thought she would say, "My," the way she did with that newbie on the bridge. She just cried. The others cried too. Most had never seen a real child except themself. They were the only ones they knew. The Parents cried too. They wouldn't even leave the classroom. They wanted to hold their kids. Finally the teacher let us stay in the room, holding our kids. We stayed all day. The next week, we had to wait out in the hall, if the kid would let go of us. We sat on the floor in the hall. You could hear the kids cry through the door. They could hear us cry too.

The teacher found two rooms with a door between and put the kids in one and us in the one beside, so our kid and us could check each other. The rooms are not so big and as far as I could tell Ani did not get lost.

So the next part of our life, this is it. We all come in every morning, pry the kid out of the carrier or off our back, or, you know, peel them off our leg, or sometimes you peel the Parent off the kid, anyhow, once we are pried apart, the Parents go into our room and, you know, wave at the door. It was great. To be on the safe side, two of us took turns watching the other door of the classroom where our kids were, so no one would steal them. Sometimes the kids stopped waving long enough for, I don't know, meetings. The Parents had a meeting too. So one mother is like, where is the arm guard? She was the only one who cared, the rest are like, everyone knows what is wrong with that. Everyone except me. Everyone knew more than me.

A lot of these Parents are, like, Grandparents, the Parent already died, so they are from another generation and were old enough to remember the old schools, before the Big One. They really knew a lot about school. I'm not saying they had the same opinion. They disagreed. Like, a good school is a Stretch, but others knew what is wrong with that, it could be a Strain.

Remember all the things I had to learn to be a Parent, the wrinkles, the neck, wind? Now I had to learn this, what was wrong with everything. It was interesting.

Like, indoor/outdoor? In that time, there was a new idea, it is more healthy to do things outdoors. You will not get the germs. It wasn't just about school. They are starting to think Domes are not that great, period. Like, ok, inside the Dome, you're not going to get something. But leave the Dome? You're going to get everything. It is an Immune thing.

So then some other Parent explains what's wrong with Outdoor Schools. Like, what about rain? Maybe they won't get TB or SV. They could still catch their death of cold.

Another Parent said, how they went to school indoors, it was good enough for them. If it was good enough for them, it was good enough for the kids today, but another one said, they want their kid to have a better life. So when they said that, I learned I wasn't the only one.

Here is something else I learned. Remember how I worried, what will happen if Ani goes to school? How I was always worried someone will find out what's wrong with us? I wasn't the only Parent who worried. I'm just saying this because maybe in your life something could happen that makes you think something is wrong with you and you're the only one in the whole world that it is. Well I will tell you, what was wrong with us, Ani and me, it's not the only thing that could be wrong. What was wrong with these other kids is they are not a hardy, they really could get something bad. Whatever is wrong with us, it isn't that. These Parents took their kid's life in their hand, just to go to school.

We went to this City Line school for about five months, then one morning, it was blocked. Caution tape, signs. One teacher had got sick. They didn't say what it was, but a kid got sick too. They are required to shut down.

So I got what I thought we wanted. It is just us two again. I didn't like it now.

This was a gray and windy day, and when Ani and me got back to our courtyard, I started to dig a little in the froze-up ground where the potatoes have been, and Ani is hopping in the cold. Then she just stops. I just stopped too. And I don't know what this proves, but Ani looked at me and said, "Ani? Let's go to school."

I put her in the carrier, took her back to 261st Street, and ducked under the caution tape on the steps to the school door, which is covered in boards. We weren't the only ones there. About eight Parent/kid combos gathered at the front, even though it was a windy day. Remember those Parents who worried would their kids get something from being out of the home? I'll tell you what these Parents got. They got mad. Think about how nervous we were in the first place, to even bring our kids out of our homes. Now this.

Somebody said, if this one school closed, we were entitled to a list of schools our kids could go to instead, even in other Zones. Man! How did they know that?

Someone else said, everyone else thinks something is wrong with us, by being City Line. The City Line kids have rights too.

So someone shouts, "City Line kids! City Line kids!" So we all shout, "City Line kids! City Line kids!"

We marched up Little Neck Parkway toward the Bay and are going to get on a boat and sail to Nassau County and force them to put our kids in school there, but a cop stops us for our own, you know, sake because the vigilantes in Nassau County are going to shoot us. They got someone to put us all on a group shaw and some hybro pulled it all the way to the Temporary Center, in Sunnyside, a really long ride. A few people came out to stare.

There was masks for all of us when we got out. The Grandmother named Doris Goodman went in with one other Parent, the rest of us waited outside and met three other mothers who told us what was wrong with most of the schools in Queens. In one hour Doris Goodman came out with a list of Out Of Zone schools that are Legally Obligated to accept our kid, if the kid doesn't have something, so the other mothers look at the list and between them they knew what is wrong with every school on the list! So everyone cheered. The Catholic School is a Strain, the Utopia school is not even a Stretch. There is also the Jamaica Estates Dome school, which is the only really good school in Queens but they give you such a hard time why not go to this one Manhattan school that is Legally Obligated to take everyone, even us. There was a Zone crossing Pass for every Parent and a copy of the list. We even got travel coupons! Then we all got pulled back to the Alley Pond barricade where we all climb off and make a plan to meet here in the morning, eight Parent/kid combos.

Well guess what? Besides Ani and me? Nobody showed but Betty Feeny and her daughter Carmel. At least we got each other for Support. So off we go. We're going to start off with the Catholic School. It is the closest. We walk there with our Pass.

It was a little hard to find but seemed ok and different from what I remembered from Catholic School in Corona. Besides that there is just eight kids in the whole school, the teachers make you change your clothes and leave them in a bag. The Parent too—they give you a kind of uniform and mask. It didn't work, not even for fifteen minutes. Ani would not wear the uniform, she would not wear the mask, she would not sit in chairs, she could not even tie her shoes, she is expelled. Carmel is ok but scared to be the only one she knows so Betty pulls Carmel out and next day we meet again and try the school that the Sunnyside mothers said is not a Stretch. It's on Utopia Parkway and even harder to find than Catholic School, but we see somebody climbing a fire escape so we just hide our carriers and follow them up to the roof where a young guy is in charge of five kids or so, all older than Ani. Man, I am getting used to kids! The young guy said hello and explained his plan. He did not intervene. He didn't know how these kids had stayed alive. He did not want to rock the boat. Whatever that means, they did not have chairs in this school. So Ani did not have to sit in them. I think they had chalk.

We been here like half an hour when a girl who seemed regular in other ways starts walking backward. She did it for a long time too. So Betty goes up to the teacher and says, hello, she's walking backward. So the teacher did not think he should intervene. He said she is just being herself.

So Betty asked the teacher, "Is she the only one?"

"Walking backward? In this group," he looked around, "she could be the only one. But there are others. We think it serves some sort of purpose. We don't know why they do it. We don't want to absolutely forbid it. We don't want to damage the cerebral flow."

Well, Betty and I don't know what that is and are not sure the teacher does, so Betty agrees with the Sunnyside mothers about the Stretch and wants me to come with her to Jamaica Estates. I don't even know why I didn't go. Later I really wished I left right then. Although the guy said the girl was the only one, in that group, I noticed others who walked backward, and pretty soon Ani began to do it too. They would put one hand against the chickenwire while they did it. They did it fast too. Ani practiced it at home, inside and out.

Look, I know the teacher wants them to be themself. But I don't know if this is Ani's self or the others'. She never walked backward before. At least she's not myself. Still, if she is going to be like others, maybe it should be others *who walked forward*. Maybe others *who could tie their own shoes*.

And then, if she walks backward, someone might think something is wrong with her. With others, it was just, ok, they are themself. But if Ani is herself, who knows where that will lead?

So now I don't know what to do. She already has trouble finding her way. How could this help?

I walked us all the way to the Jamaica Estates Dome, but we could not get through their Lock, we have to pass a health test first. There is some other Parent trying to get her kid in, saying, we already passed a health test! That was the Hollis health test. This is the Jamaica Dome health test. Go to Jamaica Health Center. So we went with this other Parent, Ismirna, and her son Winston to the JHC which was really close. We pass the health test and go back to the Jamaica Estate Dome, get in the first Zone, what they call transition Zone, which is a new idea, for immunity, it has Vitamin D. Two other kids are playing there. Right away, Ani starts walking backward and it's like, call the marines. Two mothers come up and hello, your child's walking backward, and I'm like, "She's not the only one! There are others!"

So one of these mothers says, "Well, maybe she should play with them."

The Secretary comes out and says, "Your child is City Line, yours is Hollis, they are Special Needs kids." I don't even know what that is but Ismirna is like no way Jose, she is yelling, "My son's Special Need is for a regular school!" I just take the Pass the Secretary gives me to the Special Needs school on Sutphin Boulevard and on the way I told Ani, as far as walking backward, there was nothing wrong with it. *She should just never do it around other kids.* Never. She could do it in the courtyard if it was so important.

I guess that shows how a little environmental factor can go a long way. The roof school was a factor, by which she walked backward. My saying she shouldn't walk backward was a factor, by which she felt something was wrong with her.

The truth is, I was starting to wonder if there was. I was starting to wish we never went to school in the first place. If we never left the garden apartment, none of this would of happened. If something was wrong with her, I would not even know.

The Sutphin school for Special Needs is a rink with kids hitting themself on the head. Ani starts to shriek, I mean really loud. She is climbing right up me, she is so scared, so I decide, let's try the Manhattan Dome school where the Sunnyside mothers said they have to take everyone.

Maybe I should of gave up right then. Maybe I should just bring Ani to hang out on the boarded-up school steps and hope some other City Line kid would show up and at least they could play. I guess I just thought the Manhattan Dome Opportunity might not be there forever. Better grab it now.

We go back to the Temporary Center. They give us a Pass to get into Manhattan so Ani can take a test.

I thought it had to take everyone.

Everyone who takes a test.

Before she even takes that test, she has to take the Dome health test. She already took the Dome health test! That was the Queens Dome health test. This is the Manhattan Dome health test. Go back to the Sunnyside Center, get a Pass to take the health test for the Manhattan Dome, at South Brother Island.

So this next part we spent taking tests just to be able to take a test. I mean it practically took up the school year. This test you take to go to the Manhattan Dome, you take it at nine a.m. in South Brother Island Dome. It took three hours to get there, with ferries. We had to leave at six, to get there at nine.

We had to wait on line for two more hours once we got there. Then Ani was hungry. We already ate everything we brought. We couldn't leave the line. We would lose our place. I'm squeezing her hand so hard to keep her from walking backward she was crying by the end.

She cried from the test too, even though it was just blood and urine—nothing invasive. A little spit. But she got so wild they want to make her take a pill. I just hide it in my pocket and give her a look till she calmed down till the test was done and they said here is your Pass for the Dome. By the time we get home, she never wants to leave again. The Pass only works two weeks, we cannot wait very long.

By the time I get her on the podtram to the Hunter's Point

ferry to the east side Lock next day, she is a total mess. We can't even bring the carrier, it is not allowed in the Dome. To get inside Manhattan Dome, they hose you three times! By the time we get through with our Pass, Ani is already upset. So this is the Manhattan Dome! Is this Opportunity or what? It is really dark and full of tunnels and everyone wears a kind of mask even in the Dome so what is the point. The Center is like a Dome inside the Dome. As soon as we get inside for the test, she walks backward. So they say, she needs a different test, go back to the other Center. It is not the health test. She is so tired I have to carry her back to Sunnyside Center, and it is closed. We're so tired we just sleep in the yard. Then when the Center opens in the morning they say, oh! We were supposed to go to the other *Manhattan* Center.

She does not walk backward in the other Manhattan Center's waiting room but so what, they don't even run a test, they just call our name and give us a Pass. Go to Mill Rock Island. I mean I have to practically hold Ani down to keep her from bouncing off the walls. If I take her home now I'll never get her out again. How about crossing the catwalk by foot, we are so far into the Dome we're almost by the west side Lock, so that works except I have to lug her on my back and she is strangling me, but we make it over the catwalk to the east side, grab a ferry to Mill Rock Island where a big flag says EVERY CHILD IS SPECIAL, and I'm like, shit! What is that going to be but Needs? Sutphin all over again. *No way Jose.* I just jump back on the ferry, we are going back to Queens, let her walk backward, let her play with dirt, whatever, but the ferry ends up at Roosevelt Island, it is stopping there. So we're at Roosevelt Island and have to swipe the Reader to get the ferry back to Queens, but it is some kind of really SOTA setup because when I swipe Ani's ID, up pops one of those name/age/condition things, and it goes Special Needs. So I don't want that on her ID. I swipe my own ID in fast to wipe hers off like Henry said sometimes could work.

Instead now Special Needs pops up on my own swipe ID. I try manual override like I used to use to wipe my own ID with but it is so long since I tried that, I crash the screen, and when I try to call it back, the whole Board crashes. The ferry cannot leave till it's back up. Nobody's getting to Queens. A paddle barge is by the dock. Sometimes they take a passenger if you will help paddle but the skipper says, sorry, we are heading upstate. When he turns his back I just jump in with Ani and hide under a tarp. I mean, what is he, going to throw us overboard? When Ani starts to shriek he's so mad I start to think maybe he will, but he says he will take us to Newburgh but she really has to shut up, and she is not walking backward but is making so much noise I just give her the pill from my pocket and she is out cold. Out cold. And I'm like what did I do? What did I do?

All the ride up river I am checking is she still alive and when we climb off at the Newburgh pier in the early morning she's still out cold. I have to carry her to the local hybro. I even carry her down the big road where a farmer gives us a lift on his cart, and up the county road where she is just starting to wake up. On the dirt road she is awake enough to lift her head and see the trees over our head.

I go up to the door and press the buzzer. No one replies. Two trucks are parked in front. I try again. I'm worried they are not going to let us in. Like, oh, want to come in? Too bad. I declined to do the work when Ani was so small. We'll be sleeping in the trailer. If I could even find the trailer.

The vidCom finally comes on, the static goes up, and then a voice.

"Well!" I can tell right off it's Henry's voice. "Bro! Come quick. You really want to come and see who's here."

iv

It's a long, long time since we have been here at the Farm.

While I am waiting for the door to open, I count off from Ani's age how long. Four and a half years. It looked the same. Some old pails were lying in a heap around the Quonset side, like they used to.

"Chee!"

It's a long time since I heard that sound. I looked up overhead. An Endangered is crossing the morning sky.

"Chee! Chee!"

A breeze blew. Some branches moved in the breeze.

Then the front door opened. And there was Rauden, in a bathrobe. He looked different. He had new glasses. Henry wheeled up behind in a minute. He looked the same.

I don't know how I looked.

I just stood outside the door, holding Ani half asleep, and they were on the inside, and we all just looked at each other, in the morning, while the Endangered went, "Chee!" further off. And I could hear those things and smell those things you heard and smelled at the Farm.

The orange sofa where I used to sit or sleep was still where it used to be, though more beat up. The chairs are there, and the paneling. Janet Delize showed up in her vehicle soon after, with buns. I guess Henry called her. We all went in the Box Room and ate buns. The Box Room looked the same.

Janet looked the same.

The Box Room even smelled the same.

Ani hid in my neck.

We all just sat there chewing buns. It was so quiet you could hear us chew.

After a while, Henry wheeled his chair beside Ani and me, leaned over where she's hiding in my neck. He grabbed her hat.

She looked up fast, he put the hat back on her. He wheeled away, and she hid again. Then she peeked up again. He wheeled up again, she hid again. I could hear her, like, giggle. Then he wheeled away, grabbed a bun, put it on a dish and set it on the floor. She peeked up, climbed off me, grabbed the bun, and scooted behind my box. She ate the bun there, on the floor.

When she was scooting, everyone stared so hard, they forgot to even speak. She's going on six years old and still alive. When they saw her last, she wasn't even two. Of all of us, she looked most different of all.

Remember she liked to bounce? She didn't bounce now, she bobbed. She would stand behind me, then bob out. Then she would bob back.

When she bobbed out, everyone stared at her till she bobbed back again.

After an hour or so, she would take a few steps away from me, then come back fast and hide. If she lost sight of me, she got lost.

Her eyes still went pop, like they used to, and they were puffy underneath and red around the rim. But it was cute. The eyebrows still went up, like worried. She didn't look worried though. They just went up.

The other kind of Puffy, that you wear? She wore one, plaid, and the hat she wore matched the Puffy and had flaps. Alma Cho had left this at our door.

Her hair stuck out on the side of the hat. She was thin and narrow. Five years, ten months old.

Rauden said he was mostly doing DVM work. He would of liked to do more human Projects. He was consulting on some tank Projects. For livestock though.

Larraine died of natural causes. Lucas was in jail. Walter was still alive.

Nobody mentioned Bernie, so I didn't ask.

Henry had made a livestock Chimera called Dookie but it disappeared.

I told them about the garden apartments, and the City Line school that closed, and the other mothers, and the Manhattan Dome.

When we were finished saying all that, no one said anything much. We had more buns.

I really noticed how quiet it was. When I wasn't here, I thought of the Farm as a place where a lot was happening. Now that I looked at it when no Project was in place, I mean, for most of the time, nothing was happening. If you came here because you wanted to see what would happen, it would be a long wait.

I could hear that wind you hear. I think I heard a cowbell.

Finally Rauden said, "How's Ani doing?"

I said I didn't know.

No one said anything.

Henry asked Ani, "Want to ride my chair?" I don't know why she got on. They rode off down the corridor.

When she was gone, I began to cry. "Something is wrong with her," I said. Remember the hormones used to make me cry? Since then, I almost never cried. Ani cried. I didn't cry. Even the worst of Mumbai, I didn't cry. I'm crying now. Maybe there was still hormones in the air at the Farm. Maybe it's just how everybody cries up here. I cried five minutes. It could of been ten before I told him, "She has Needs."

He wasn't even mad. He just went out of the room and came

back. I could smell it on his breath where he had went. "What Needs?"

I said I didn't know.

This time he went out longer. When he came back I told him it could be Special.

"Ah!" he said. "A Board of Ed thing."

I agreed.

This time he brought the whole bottle back. "The B of E," he said. "B of fucking E." It was great to see Rauden again. I had forgot what he was like. His beard. His booze. But mainly how he just kept talking.

Like, after I told him about the transition Zones, the test on South Brother Island, the Sunnyside Center, the Manhattan Center, the other Manhattan Center, he said, "The B of E. The goddamn B of fucking E," and even banged his fist on his desk, like he used to. "I mean! The city's a goddamn wasteland. Even with whatever so-called infrastructure improvements they're bringing to poor goddamn Queens, it was a total mess even before Mumbai—population wipeout, neighborhoods burned to the ground. And with all that, the goddamn B of E is going to drag you through so much red tape you're going to wish they goddamn burned down too! I mean, talk about fucking hardy! Dewey Sylvain was barking up the wrong goddamn tree. For hardy fucking bullshit, the B of f E's red fucking tape makes a Sylvain hardy look like a goddamn wuss." Then he went out again and when he came back his hair and beard was soaking wet, the way it was when he put his head under the tap the first day I was ever here, so long ago.

We were all pretty quiet for the rest of the day, even Rauden. We ate beans and watched TV. I noticed Rauden gave Ani a lot of looks though. Everyone did. Janet, Henry, Rauden. Rauden watched me too sometimes. Everyone else just watched her.

They wanted to be sure she's still alive. She's still alive. She did get lost twice, in the Box Room. Everyone noticed that.

Rauden said we should stay for a while, now we made the trip. They would put us in our old room, with the gate. Rauden was sleeping on a cot in one of the old lab rooms. I don't know if Sook threw him out, or what. I didn't ask. Our old room was a mess. There are plastic tubs, 10-gallon tins, a lot of plastic garbage bags. They put a TV in, for Ani. They brought some new covers for the cots and had a picture on the wall of a cow. They put a lot of things in. We were going to have to stick around for a while to figure out what to do about the B of E.

Henry said he could hack the Special Needs out of her file, but stick the swipe in any B of E scanner, it's going to pop back in again.

It was interesting, how it worked for Ani. Like, Henry gained her trust. Even Janet Delize gained her trust. She took her out to see a cage of Endangereds. And Janet was nice to Ani. She was not nice to me. And that is one more proof, you know.

I even think Ani enjoyed the Farm. She enjoyed the toilet, and the faucet taps. She enjoyed the big TV. She said, "Hey Krazy Durg," and watched for three hours. Hey Krazy Durg was a TV Character she enjoyed. Henry liked it too. He had a gizmo, it could run a Program backward. She thought it was really funny. So one day after he run Hey Krazy Durg backward, she showed him how she walked backward. Then she walked forward. Then she walked backward. She did it really fast. She did it down the hall too, all the way to the green light, then all the way to Lab 3 and back to the sofa in front. When she saw me watching her, she stopped. Rauden saw it first, though.

I told him, "She's not the only one. There are others. She picked it up from them."

It's funny, when I saw her do it back home, I took it really hard. When Rauden thought something was wrong with it, I had excuses. "She's not the only one who gets lost! She's not the only one who cannot tie her shoes or sit in chairs!"

It did seem to bother Rauden though. He said we ought to get her tested. She could have some anomaly.

I said no. I didn't want her to be tested any more. She already had all the tests she will need for her whole life. I wanted her to be different from me. I was tested all the time. That was what Subjects did. I don't want her to be a Subject. I want her to be like anyone.

Oh, man. I'm crying again.

Rauden just waited till I'm done. Then he said anyone could take a test.

I shook my head. If she tests wrong, they might take her away.

I could see Rauden thinking about that, like, maybe they would. He went to his screen for a long time punching keys and when he came back out, he said he had a tester in mind who won't take her away. This guy won't even tell anyone, no matter what he finds.

The tester's name was Suresh, and it took a week to get him down from Ithaca. He was very nice. He was like a nurse, except he looked, I don't know, soft. He had wet eyes. He asked Ani, "Do you have a special way of walking?"

So Ani nodded hard and got up. But she just walked the regular way.

So Suresh waited awhile, then said, "Very good." Then he said, "Do you have a regular way of walking?"

So Ani nodded hard. But she just walked the regular way again.

Suresh said, "Very good."

Everything she did, he said, "Very good." Which Ani enjoyed. She began to think she was very good. Every time Suresh came down from Ithaca, she walked the regular way and said, see my special way of walking. Forward, backward—she didn't know the difference. She didn't walk backward again the whole time we were there.

If Rauden hadn't seen it, maybe we could of gotten away with it.

Anyhow, I guess Suresh found other, you know, anomalies, because he determined, she might have Special Needs. He wasn't sure exactly what it meant in her case. It could mean what they call LD. It could even just mean City Line kid.

The good part was, this is some sort of hard Proof, she was not me. I didn't have Special Needs. That I heard.

The bad part was, if Rauden plans to market any other viables, this is not exactly going to help sales. It's true she survived Mumbai but she cannot tie her shoes or sit in chairs or find her way out of a room. So that could be a problem. What kind of price could he get for a child with Needs like that, hardy or not? Between you and me, I thought why not find a country where they go barefoot and sit on the ground and maybe don't even have rooms for her to find her way out of, but I suppose they also would not pay the best rates, so I kept this to myself.

And I mean, nobody said this to me but I got the idea Ani's Special Needs are not all that great even for her.

Henry thought maybe he could invent a special block to keep the thing out of Ani's ID, but Suresh thought, do not be hasty. If things still worked the way he heard they used to, she can use this to her advantage. It can give her access to Special Resources she might not be able to access another way. That is, if things still worked that way. None of them really knew how any of this stuff worked now or if it even did. Rauden wasn't even sure where the whole B of E came from now. He thought it could be some anomaly in the system that kept turning out Resource, funds, rules, whatever, even if no one was at the other end.

But Suresh said, well whatever was true now, it is always

true that you have to what they call work the system, to get the Resource. Well to get anything in the B of E. Needs was as good a way as any to do that.

And everyone agreed but me. I said no. No. "I want her to be a regular kid. I want her to go to school with regular kids."

Suresh went back to Ithaca. Rauden drove him to the Terminal.

When he came back, Ani was asleep in our room. Rauden sat down with me on the orange sofa and said, "I, a lot of things can go wrong with a child. Even regular kids sometimes have problems. This Mill Rock thing might work for her. It might help her."

I just hung tough. No, no, no. I did not want to call attention. They might find out what is really wrong with her.

Rauden didn't say anything more about it. He just went and did some Box Room work. So I'm heading for bed later but saw him standing by the freezers where the viables are stored. He had his hand up on one freezer door. I don't know who they were, and if they were ever born.

But whoever they were, or were going to be, Rauden had his hand over their freezers and really looked sad. I got the idea he is thinking, what is the goddamn point? We always thought these will be very special kids but not this way. If they are just going to walk backward or get lost or cannot tie their shoes or sit in goddamn chairs, hardy or not, why should they even be born?

Well, I want to say something about those viables, or some of them. They are the reasons they were born.

Because, look, if something is wrong with Ani, Rauden's not going to kill her. It's ok Ani was born, because she is. But they're not. If it's not ok for them to be born, they won't.

But if it's not ok for them to be born, and they're so similar to Ani—this is what I'm saying. Then it's not really ok for *her*. Even if she is. Born.

I really wanted it to be ok for her to be born. What else did she have?

And then I thought, well, no one will goddamn take that from her. I'm going to intervene. Work the system? I will do that. Take another test? Whatever. I'm going back to Queens and make it my Project to get Ani fixed. And when she is fixed, it's going to be ok for the whole goddamn lot to be born.

So I told Rauden, and he told Suresh. I am ready to do this. Suresh checked Mill Rock out and said it is ok. So that's what's going to happen. We're going to do what we must to make this work.

Henry cleans up our swipes. He updates our codes. And remember, he says, if there is ever a problem, like a pure code Reader could read her as me? Punch some keys he shows me. It will crash the system. Someone could bring it up again, but this will buy time.

Before we left, Rauden brought me down in the basement to look at some new tank he was tinkering with, while Janet Delize took Ani off somewhere to look at rabbits.

The new tank could convert to a mini strap-on unit, which was a great idea because these days most hardy sales are overseas and Transport is an issue. You still couldn't bring live children across borders without papers, so it had to be viables, like the Santa Sofya ones, and you had to smuggle them, so this mini unit will get strapped to the Courier's belly, like she is a Host. Make the unit from soft plexi so it won't set off alarms, and come on, who's going to be poking around there? If Ani's anomalies get fixed, and they work out some details, there could be some serious Transport here. If they got any calls. Which so far, they didn't.

It's funny, remember how when I declined to come back I was afraid to even talk to Rauden, because I worried he would make me come back to the Farm and do the work? I wanted to do it now. I didn't want to leave.

It wasn't only that I wanted to do the work again and try the new tank. The truth is, when Henry took Ani on the wheelchair for a ride? It was the first time in more than four years she had been out of my sight, even at the City Line school. I felt like I been holding my breath for five years. With Henry and Janet to pitch in, I could sometimes take a break. And then, they all understood our real situation, even Janet. They were the only ones in the world who did. Besides me.

But we have to get Ani fixed, and anyhow, she wanted to go home. She liked Henry, and she got used to everybody else. I really would of liked to stay, forever. But Ani hung tough. And maybe it would of been better if we stayed, and maybe not, but either way, we left.

Henry said don't be strangers, and when we're getting on the hybro home, Rauden said if it turned out there was any work in the future, maybe I could come back from time to time for that.

And I will tell you, when he said I could come back to do the work? It wasn't about the money at all. It just made me happy. I'm just saying, how things turned out—well, I'm getting ahead of myself, but when you find out, maybe you will think it was only about the money, but it wasn't. I just want to say this now, so you could think about it when you see how things turned out. It just made me happy.

v

To get to Mill Rock Special school you got to take a bus. The bus is one of those alt fuel things, they call it cuchifrito. You smell it first. It has dark windows so no one can see in. You got to wait at a Stop on the old Expressway, near some kind of broken wall, at 7 a.m.

The driver is Kurvinder. The bus goes a short way on the old Expressway, then overland to Astoria. You cross maybe three Zones. Door to door, including ferries at the end, it's about two hours each way. Ani gets the whole trip free. It makes no sense but Suresh said those B of E things never did.

By the time she finished all the tests she got to take to start at Mill Rock, it's January. They let me come in with her on the bus for two weeks. Then someone named Melanie, who seems to be in charge, says Ani must start coming in alone, like a big girl. Ani just stands there, stiff like wood while Melanie is saying this. And I am stiff too. Because I can tell you, that is not going to happen. She's never coming here again.

But, remember when I knew what Rauden's thinking? Melanie knows what I am thinking. She grabs my hand and gives me a long look. "Ani is a very Special kid," she goes. "But she's not the only one. These Special kids need to own their lives."

I don't even know what it means. But I don't have to know. Melanie is like Rini Jaffur. She is so nice. Then you end up doing what she says.

Monday morning the cuchifrito bus goes off with Ani alone on it, and I'm just standing by the broken wall, in a freezing wind. And it's like when I gave her that pill. What did I do? What did I do?

I look to Alley Pond. I look to Little Neck Bay and then the other way, the way she's going. Flushing, Jackson Heights, Queensbridge, Manhattan Dome.

WHAT DID I DO?

Remember when Ani went to sleep as a newbie and I was like, oh! I have a head. What do I do with my head? Now I'm like, here is an idea. Bang it on the wall till it breaks. I want to break my head. Why would I do that?

Then I won't feel this way.

Hello?

If I break my head on the wall, who will be waiting when she comes home on the bus?

I went back to the garden apartment and all day I'm like, lie down on Ani's empty bed. Go out the door and wait on our empty front steps in the cold. Lie down. Go out.

I get to the Stop an hour early and wait in the wind by the wall. The bus is one hour late. I am stiff like ice and it's already night when I smell the cuchifrito. The lights approach. The bus stops. The doors open. No one gets off.

What did I do?

I tried to give her a different life. Now look. They took her away and lost her. I'm never seeing her again. No one is even on the steps.

Except Ani Fardo.

On the steps.

Six years, eight months old.

And even today, if I close my eyes, I can see her like that. In her little Puffy. On the steps.

She got new mittens! She holds one up to show. Climbs down the steps, shaking. Reaches ground.

We just stood there a minute, in the dark. Then I took her little mitten hand and swing it. We go off in the night, swinging hands until her legs give out. Then I just carry her home in the dark. All the way, I feel her little body through the Puffy, shaking. Still alive.

I was too.

5 THE EDUCATION

SHE WAS USUALLY ONE HOUR LATE COMING BACK. I was usually half an hour early, waiting. Sometimes I was one hour early. Sometimes she was two hours late.

Maybe one day you will hear the stupid things people say about what we are, Ani and me. Is it ethical? Are we real? Is she me? Like that is all our whole life will ever be about.

Well, at this point, our life is pretty much wake up, get Ani dressed, put food in her, drag her to the cuchifrito bus. Sometimes she's crying all the way to the bus.

Wave goodbye.

Sometimes I am crying all the way home.

Mill Rock is an Outdoor School, and I mean really outdoor. Most of the rooms do not even have a wall. It's windy. When you get off the ferry at the dock, that banner, "EVERY CHILD IS SPECIAL!" is flapping so hard it makes a noise.

Well, she has hardly been at the school two months when she climbs off the bus in Queens, still alive, and says, "You do not know what I am."

So I'm like, oh shit, oh shit. They already figured us out. They will turn us in.

She is just trying to skip away. "You do not know!"

"Stop skipping. Stop skipping." I'm a Sylvain hardy, I don't get anything. But I'm getting a heart attack here.

She, like, tries to twirl. It doesn't work. She just runs back to me, and, remember how she mouthed "tank" when we saw tanks at JFK? She mouths, "I am Special." And she hands me a Note. Then she tries to skip off. That also doesn't work, she has to hop. At least she does it forward.

I read the Note. Well, it is just a lot of words about how our kid is Special because every kid is. Whatever it means, it's like Melanie said. She's not the only one.

Special is a big deal. They really cannot shut up about it.

All I really wanted for Ani, besides be alive, and not me, was be regular. It turns out every child is a Special child.

But at the Conference that every Parent must attend two times a goddamn year, Melanie does that squeeze my hand thing, like Rini. Then she looks so deep in my eyes I get dizzy. Then she says, "That doesn't mean Ani isn't Special too."

Whoa!

They're all supposed to think they are Special, whatever they have.

Maybe she is more Special than the others. How would I know?

At April, she is getting off the bus, still alive, and says that, "I am Special" thing. But she waits till we are past the golf course till she pulls me close and tells me why. "I could tie the shoe. Migan cannot." Then she puts her mouth right to my ear and whispers, "So ha ha ha." Then she just turns around and tries to skip away. She has a problem skipping, and these new purple boots she took from the Mill Rock Sharing room do not really help. She wears them pretty much day and night.

Well, I have a problem skipping, myself, but I was almost skipping too. They're going to fix her! She will be ok. She could tie her shoes, Migan cannot, she's going to have regular Needs, how Special is that?

You could say, well I could tie my own shoes and did not have to ride four hours on a goddamn bus to do it. And that is totally true.

But you could also say, come on. Is this a different life or what?

What's Special about most of these kids is, they have a wiring problem.

Some have a scam. This one kid, Don Park, he is supposed to be Asperger, what they call, Asperger. It turns out he just tested wrong, he's Gifted. His Parents said, oh, he already made friends. Let him stay. Melanie is so nice she says Gifted is a Special Need too, but to tell the truth I think it is the Parents' scam. They come from out of state, this school will not ask questions, he will mainstream out and some really good school in the Dome will let him grandfather in. Maybe the whole family could get a Pass to even live in the Dome. This kid gets brought to school in a skiff. I think they camped out on some other island. They aren't the only ones. A few families did that on the weekdays so they don't have to travel so far.

Besides Don Park, there is a real Asperger kid too, who likes to say, "Is this the rehearsal?" So you are supposed to say, "Very good."

Don't let them think something is wrong with them. The good part is, the teachers all know something is wrong with them, so when the kids do not do what they say, they are not expelled. Most of the time, the teacher does not even make them do anything.

When I ask Ani, do you do what Melanie says, she doesn't even know what that means. Melanie usually says, oh! Want to play Nature today? Magnet Alley? Where Is The President? But nobody has to do what Melanie says. I guess that is good because Ani does not do what anyone says anyhow. A lot of these kids don't. So the teachers do Strategies. This one kid, Tensin, is Oppositional, what they call, Oppositional? To take off her coat you have to say, put on the coat. So then she takes off the coat.

Ani, it doesn't work either way, but she is not expelled. They know something's wrong with her. They think they know what it is. Give me a break. What's wrong with Ani didn't even cross their mind.

These kids all get lost, so Ani's not the only one. I really don't think anyone but her is Special from nuclear Transfer. They just have wiring problems. So the teachers let them play with magnets. The kids put on a Special belt with metal on it, then the teacher has the magnet and the kid does not get lost, he sticks to the magnet. These kids do not know where they belong. Some of them, I think it is a kind of vaccine Syndrome, but also Mumbai messed up whatever infrastructure was even left, and then with the reproductive crisis, Hosts, gene splicing, Donor everything, they could end up with a Boundary problem. This one kid, Itzhak, has so much trouble with Boundaries, he could hear a conversation in Yonkers. He just couldn't hear what the teacher says. So they are devising a Strategy for Itzhak. Should they have walls?

That's the big question, walls. This Boundary thing, is the wall going to help or get in the way? It also is a problem because it is an Outdoor School. It is about the Funding. Like they must be an Outdoor School or the Funding goes. As Outdoor School they could have walls if they do not have a roof or the other way around but not both. One mother thinks she could hack Funding and maybe change the Funding rules and we could have both walls and roofs, but so far it didn't work.

So Melanie finds out they could get away with an awning for rain, but these kids need something to bounce off or they're going to land in the East River. So they put up a few walls with insulation against injury but some have to wear a helmet anyhow. For Ani this is not the problem. Maybe that is why they think she is so Special. I don't even know if they really do.

Ani does, though. She thinks she is more Special than me.

Remember Rini Jaffur said, if you are gene for gene her living replica, how is she more special than you?

Well, it could be the self-esteem she is learning in school. When I went to school, we didn't learn that. So it is a difference. Another difference is, she is passing in school. They don't call it that because of the self-esteem. But she is not expelled. How Special is that?

She already made it to her second year at Mill Rock. She is seven years, five months old and still wearing the purple boots, even though it is warm. She loves those boots. She climbs off the bus, hands me a Note, and says, "You do not know what is a Project."

I go, "Oh! What is a Project?" Believe me, I know what is a Project. Give me a break here, *she* was a Project. But I go, "Oh! I do not know!" for the self-esteem, and open the Note.

She's like, "Oh, Ma, you are silly. You don't know anything! You don't even know where is the President."

I go, "Nobody does."

"Oh, Ma, you are silly. Wichita Dome!"

So that is news to me.

"Ma! A Project is How Was I Born?"

Well, I go, "Very good!" because you have to. But I am having another heart attack here, because I'm reading the Note, slow, while Ani is trying to climb the broken wall, and I will tell you, I don't know how to work this. Ok, the Project is about Heritage. Whatever it is, they have to own it. They have to have Pride.

"Ma!"

Like you could have Donor product, gene splicing, ok. I notice they did not mention nuclear Transfer. They do not even call it clone.

"Was I born the same way Migan's born?"

What are the chances?

I guess I could of said anything. Maybe I could even tell the truth. It's just, I had to think fast. "How was Migan born?"

"The regular way. From a dish."

So I said so was she. It is not a complete lie. They both started from a dish.

Well, it seems to work. "Migan and I was born the same way! We are Special!" She's so pleased she almost skips while we head up the ramp, and I'm like, great, it is going to be ok, now let's think about something else, but before the week is over, she climbs off the cuchifrito bus asking, "Were you the Host?"

Here we go again. What do I tell her? Ok. I told her no. I'm pretty sure we weren't the only ones where the Parent is not the Host.

But she goes, "What was her name?"

Shit! I really boxed myself in here. What do I say? We're not the only ones who had a different Host but this tank thing could be a problem if it got around.

I think about it now, sometimes I wonder, and maybe you wonder too, come on, the people at this school, they are so out to lunch, what difference would it make? Like if I said, "She is nuclear Transfer. You could call it SCNT." Half the people won't even know what it is. Maybe none of them will.

I wish I did tell her the whole truth right then.

If I even knew one situation like ours, maybe I would of. But we were still the only ones I ever heard of, except rumors.

I told her Rini Jaffur was the Host.

Well guess what? The very next day, she gets off the bus and says, "Itzhak was grown in a tank." So then I'm like, I could of told the truth. She wouldn't be the only one.

Maybe you are thinking, why not tell the truth now? Maybe I should of. At least part of the truth. Nuclear Transfer was too big a risk but I could tell her about the tank.

Then how do I explain who Rini Jaffur was?

The day before the winter break, Ani gets off the bus saying, "Migan is Chosen. Am I Chosen?"

Migan's Parents made her from Donor product in a dish, then gestated her in a Host, then they died and Lore and Dana Chose her and are her Parents now, so Ani says, "Am I Chosen like Migan?"

The truth is, originally, Ani was. What Rini Jaffur did was pretty much Choose Ani, when Ani was a viable. Then she changed her mind and said I had to take her or we're all going to jail. So I thought better just say I do not know. I think it's better for the self-esteem.

Well, that is bad enough, but in March, she climbs off the bus, hands me Art and said, "You do not know what is a clone." Then she goes, "Ma?"

Because I'm so surprised, I forgot to say I didn't know.

"*Ma?*"

I'm not saying anything, I mean, all the way home, nada, while Ani's going, "Ma?" and staring at me funny till we get inside.

Then I just went ballistic. "A clone is like anyone else. *Anyone else.*"

She goes, "Ma." She looks scared. "It is not real."

I just don't know what to do here. I don't want her to feel ashamed. "ANYONE ELSE!" I know what is a clone.

"Ma! It is current Event. It is not real."

"*ANYONE ELSE!*"

Now she starts to cry.

I feel terrible I made her cry. It's just this Heritage thing, I don't know what to do. I don't want her to feel ashamed. I just don't know what is safe. And like she said it is just current Event. It was in the News, I heard it too. Some Parents in Florida claimed they did nuclear Transfer. You can be sure they called it *clone*. The minute the story got out, the Florida Authority took their baby because they are bad Parents, they endangered their child by it being born.

Well when the kid gets tested, guess what? It is not a clone. Then the Parents could get their baby back.

Why does someone say it is when it isn't? Were Ani and me the only ones who said it isn't, when it is? There had to be others. I wish I knew what they told their kids. I didn't want Ani to feel ashamed, but this Florida thing, the Parents was in custody for two weeks. The child too. I didn't know what would happen to Ani in custody. She is so attached, she still was learning how to get through the day without me. Two weeks, I don't know what she'd do. I was attached too, but I was adult so, whatever. And suppose some Fundy found out. Those God's Will nuts, or the K of L, if they ever find horses again. I just thought, better keep her Heritage to myself.

She seems to be ok without it. At the Conference, they said she is doing really good and will do even better soon. She ties her shoes and, well, she is a little Oppositional but they all are. It's going to be ok.

I decide to buy a really special gift for her eighth birthday. I still felt bad I made her cry. She cannot own her Heritage but she could own a gift. I looked for extra coupons in empty units but it is not enough, and Rini's credit stopped so long ago it's like it never happened. I find a notice on the Little Neck Board, they need cleaners in public areas. One day I earned some coupons doing deCon by the City Line. I could of done some at Flushing Cemetery but it is all-day work and ran so late I would miss her bus.

Still, I have enough coupons from the City Line for a toy. I bought it from Norma Pellicano's friend Darleen. It is a Treasure box and it is pink and has a dancer. Ani never had a toy like this. Well, neither did I. She is so pleased she wants to bring it to school to show it off. She comes home from school, it is gone. Where is the Treasure box?

She left it in Sharing. So I did all that work for something she is just going to share?

Ani says to share something, you have to own it. It has to be yours. You can't share something that belongs to someone else.

I never heard of that.

"Oh Ma, you are silly. You do not know anything."

Well maybe that is true. But I will tell you what I did know. I broke my butt for that toy.

She just goes hopping down the ramp and we went home.

How to sit in chairs. I knew that. How to find my own way home.

Melanie said a magnet belt could help. It's fall Conference, Ani's third year at Mill Rock. By now the dock guard lets me through without checking my swipe. It's not worth the trouble—Ani and me crash the system all the time. Ok, I will find some way to buy a magnet belt. I had heard of a hole in the City Line fence you could squeeze through and do hardy work on the other side. The rates are good. Wait on a line, they will hire you for a day. With the personal Dome setup there, they like a hardy to get on a pulley to deCon the outside. They don't even ask for Proof you're hardy, they're just like, if you die, that's your problem.

So now I had regular cleaning work in Nassau County, over the City Line. The deCon work dried up. Still this is pretty good. I just have to run all the way to the bus Stop when my work is done, in case this is the one time she got there first.

I also spent a lot of time keeping the Health Profile up-to-date. Sometimes I had to go all the way to South Brother Island. They really want Ani there to be sure she's who I say she is, but I can talk my way out of it. Sometimes I spend most of a day getting this done and must rush to get back to the Stop in time. Catch my breath. Remember to say very good and all that.

I found a bubble trike I could use to get back and forth in

Queens. I never got two-wheelers to work. I cannot bring the trike through the hole to Nassau County but it definitely saved time. I hide it in garbage at the City Line wall and hope it is still there when I'm done with my work.

One day I blew a tire and have to leave the trike and run to the Stop by foot in case she gets there first. I look back and see someone stealing the trike. I start running back to the trike. Then I smell the bus and run back to the bus. It is not the bus. I run back to the trike. The trike is gone. It starts to rain. The bus is one hour late. She is never coming home! She's lost! The bus is lost! When it chugs up, she climbs off in the rain, hands me a book—a, you know, regular book, but the Special kind they give kids who read backward, with words that go both ways. She is proud she could read it and wants me to say how Special she is, like that is something I could never do.

I just opened the book and read, "MOM POP WOW. Very good." I don't even know why I did. I guess it's just what a hard day I had, and I was very sorry.

Because she got very mad. "You do not know how to read!" She says I got one word wrong. "You said COW."

I told her and I'm telling you, I did not say COW.

We just go home in the rain. But when we are inside and got dried off she will not read. She lost the self-esteem. She will not read at all until I say, oh, I do not know how to read. Then she goes, I will show you how. MOM POP WOW. Well how Special is that. She can read three words. I can read three words. But I am adult. I do not need the self-esteem. So, whatever.

And I will tell you this. It works.

It is her fourth year at Mill Rock school. She is reading forward! She is walking forward, at least that I saw. They tell me if she catches a break, she could do anything. She could be anything.

My dream is she would be a Tech but it's ok if she is anything. Except me.

How's she going to feel if she finds out she is?

All the kids are doing great. Don Park got in to a private Dome school, as Diversity, whatever that even is. Others could mainstream soon. Ani could too. She will pass. She will have regular Needs, the whole shebang.

She rides a bus four hours a day. She sits in a chair. She ties her shoe. She reads forward. I mean she is so proud.

Nine years, ten months old. Still alive. So was I.

Sometimes I was a little nervous though.

In two months, Ani will be ten years old. I'm pretty sure she has a different life than I did when Cissy Fardo died in the fire, when I was ten. We been through this before, right? Ani's not me. Nobody's Cissy Fardo.

Still, even Rauden was never totally sure how this is going to work.

ii

Ten candles. One extra for luck. Janet Delize made the cake.

The party is in her kitchen, with those green covers over everything. It's one month after Ani's real birthday so she could finish the school year, and it's a very big deal. There are marshmallows and hats and as a special treat here comes Mariah Delize who put on a lot of weight. She gave Ani a Purse. Henry couldn't come. He sent regular money. Man! Where did he find that?

Ok. We're all around the table. Everyone sings Happy Birthday. Then Ani makes a wish and blows the candles out. I don't know what she wished. But I know what I wished.

She will stay alive, be regular, and graduate. And one more thing.

I don't die in a fire.

Everybody cheers.

"Well!" Janet says. "Our little girl is growing up."

You can see how I was thinking on her tenth birthday. Will I die in a fire like Cissy Fardo? I was so busy thinking about that, it took a while for me to notice everyone else seems to be thinking something too. Janet Delize is giving Ani a look. That is never good.

It's totally quiet. You could hear the generator hum. The windows are open—you could hear an Endangered somewhere in the sky.

Now Mariah Delize is doing it. She and Janet look at me, then Ani, then me. Then everyone's doing it.

Except us. Except Ani and me. Sitting at Janet's table side by side.

Ani is looking at me like, what is this? I shake my head like, whatever. It doesn't mean anything!

But personally, I was pretty sure it does.

It's like the looks they used to give when Ani and the others were viables in the tank. Ani/me. Ani/me. In the same room, side by side. And then it hits me what they're thinking.

Ani is growing up. She's ten years old. I'm thirty. She's going to change a lot. Me not so much.

I think they could be thinking, how long could we pass?

After a while, Janet says, "Well! Who's ready for cake?" Everyone says they are. Pretty soon everyone's talking again.

Except me. Ani and me.

We generally don't say much anyhow at the Farm. Ani even less than me. She just jiggles her feet. I mean the whole table jiggles.

Janet goes, "You may be excused, Ani." Ani is looking at me like, for what? I'm just moving my eyes, go to the TV.

Ani leaves the kitchen and turns on the TV in the Den. The rest of us clean up.

I still can't leave Ani alone so much at the Farm, Mill Rock is pretty much the only place she doesn't get nervous if I am out of sight, so while we are cleaning up in Janet's kitchen, I have to check is Ani ok watching TV in the Den. She is ok but got frosting on her birthday dress so I took her to the toilet to clean the dress and while we're in there I check how we look in the mirror, could we still pass? We definitely could. She is much smaller and smoother. Even the hair is different.

So, I'm like it's going to be ok, but this birthday, man! Things just keep happening. A little later I am on the way down Janet's hall to check again is Ani still ok with the TV when Mariah Delize comes behind me in the hall and whispers, when did I start to ministrate.

So I'm like, oh, I don't know. Could you excuse me a minute? I want to see is Ani still ok. She is.

But on my way back down the hall, Mariah Delize stops me and whispers, the age you start to ministrate, Ani could start to ministrate.

I'm like, well, ok, but she's just ten years old. Could you excuse me? I just want to get out of there. But Mariah Delize blocks my way, in the hall. You really cannot get around Mariah Delize in a hall.

Ani has to know what is going to happen, so she is not afraid. It could happen any time, she goes. Ten, eleven, twelve. She has to know it's part of nature. It's part of nature girls must ministrate, or no one will be born.

Well, between you and me, how Ani was born? If that is part of nature, I don't know what part. But I just say, oh I will be sure to tell her what you said.

Here is what happens now. I am facing Mariah, in the hall? Janet Delize comes up beside Mariah and says, "Well we don't actually know if she's going to ministrate at all."

So Mariah turns to look at Janet. Then she turns to look at Ani, who is looking at TV. Janet does too. We're all squeezed in the hall. They are both looking at Ani. Then they are looking at each other. They don't look at me. Instead of Ani/me, Ani/me, it's Ani/them, Ani/them, till Mariah finally goes, "Well, either way, she should not have unprotected sex."

Janet goes, "She shouldn't be having sex at all."

I wake up on the floor.

Rauden is kneeling beside me in the hall. Am I sick? I only fell down. I am a goddamn Sylvain hardy. I don't know why they make me lie down. They even put me in one of Janet's regular beds, in a room I never saw before. There is a puff on the bed. There is curtains on the window, with big designs of flowers. Janet shuts them tight. She tells everyone, leave Inez in peace. Even Ani must stay out. I hear the door shut.

But in a while, I hear it open. And who comes running to the bed across the room? Ani Fardo, in her birthday dress. She puts her head on my breast. She nestles right up to it. She stays there a long time. She even pats my hair, till we hear footsteps in the hall outside. Then off she runs.

It's Rauden, to check up. He takes my temperature and my, you know, the pulse on the wrist. He even does intake. Did I have Episodes like this before? Any symptoms? Give me a break. I'm supposed to sleep some more and stay in bed. I'm not even going in Janet's basement until tomorrow. They do let Ani spend the night with me but make her sleep on the floor. She holds my hand, from the floor.

In the morning, Rauden comes in to do temperature and pulse, then stays sitting on the bed beside me and clears his throat. Am I still regular?

I'm pretty sure I never was but he means something else. "You do still have your," he coughs, "menses?"

Oh, man. He wants to talk about the periods too. Mine. Where is this leading?

He just coughs a lot and goes, "It might be prudent to pull a few more ova. Since we don't really know how long it's going to be available at all."

Ok. I get it now. He thinks I'm going to die. He wants a Harvest first. "Do you have a client?"

He said, "Well! No! But! You never know what will happen. I can always freeze it."

I guess I was pleased. If he thinks we could be marketable, he thinks Ani is ok. She isn't mainstream yet, but at school they say that is just a matter of time.

He says let's be on the safe side. Pull a few more ova out. God forbid something should happen to me but, even if it didn't, I'm not going to have eggs forever. After how much they stimulated the system, who knows what could happen?

So I said fine. The school year's over. I got two weeks off from my cleaning jobs. We could stick around a while. Rauden always gives me some Compensation for Harvest. I'm just glad to get out of bed.

They start beefing me up the next day.

What happens now—ok, I have done this many times, though not for a few years. Ok, they gave me all my shots and now I'm in the new OBGYN's garage, in Basher Kill, a pretty long drive away. Ani has stayed with Janet. They have everything set up, the table, the scalpel, the plastic and everything. Before they knock me out, I just grabbed Rauden's hand and said, "Promise, if something happens to me, you and Henry will take her."

He was really surprised. "I, you've done this a dozen times. Nothing is going to happen."

"Promise."

He shrugs.

"Don't give her to Janet Delize."

"Nothing is going to happen."

"Promise you'll take her."

"I, you know I can't keep a child. I can hardly keep myself."

"And don't sell her."

"I'm not going to sell her, I. But nothing is going to happen."

He was right that nothing happened. It was not a great Harvest, just four eggs, but I was still alive. I know, I know. I already did Harvest dozens of times and nothing happened. Well, it was not the Harvest I worried about. I was worried if I die in a fire. I know, I know. What are the chances? I'm just saying.

We stayed a few more days. Then we went home.

But from now on, as far as things that could happen, they pretty much did.

The same week we got back from the Farm, I woke up early one day to a lot of noise. Alma Cho is in the courtyard running around, yelling, "Build a fire! For the body. Build a fire!"

So I come down in my pjs and am like, calm down.

"Bernie Cho died. Build a fire!"

So I'm like, "Alma, calm down. I'm sorry for the, you know, loss. But I'm not building a fire."

She is like, "For the Hygiene. Build a fire!"

Calm down. I will dig a hole. So I get dressed, go to Alma's courtyard where she keeps a shovel and some other things, and I dig. Ani came too and watched. It is a pretty hot day.

Alma goes, "She should help."

So I go, "Ani, want to help?"

She does not want to help. She thinks I should just build the fire. I'm not doing that.

So Ani and Alma Cho just sit and they both watch me dig. Then I drag Bernie over in the bag Alma made and put him in the hole and we all cry.

When the whole thing's over, and we are in our own unit, and I am tired, Ani comes right up close to me and whispers in my ear, "You could of built a fire."

I don't say anything.

She goes, "Ma."

"It's hot," I say.

Well, you have guessed by now, it's not about the weather. If I would of built a fire, how much hotter could I be? I'm dripping sweat here. No, it's about if I die in a goddamn fire, and I'm not saying that's going to happen. I'm saying I worried. I worried so much I had a hard time thinking straight. And the way this year starts to turn out, it would be better if I could.

When school starts, Alma Cho tells me be careful, there is some new pathogens around. It could be local flu. Well, thanks, Alma, but who cares? We're not getting anything.

But Kurvinder did. The new driver said so. She wore a mask. I never learned her name.

And Melanie got something too. She didn't die but is too sick to work. A substitute, Anton, is in charge and was not that great. I always liked Melanie, and she was very nice to Ani, but until now I never saw it really clear what she did. A school like Mill Rock, with all those Special kids and magnets and who knows what, there is a lot of things to deal with. It turns out Melanie was the only one who could.

Like, at the fall Festival? This is a regular thing they invite Parents to every year to show the skills. Like, remember that kid who hears the conversation in Yonkers? He really improved, he just hears it from the FDR Drive. So we all clap. The Asperger's kid walks on the stage and says, "Is this the rehearsal?" So we all clap. This is regular stuff. They do it every year. The lower functioning ones demonstrate they could tie their shoes. They are really cute.

Well, Migan's shoes have Special magnets so she won't get lost, but she finally learned to untie them, so now she ran around barefoot and what happens is, she starts to float away. Ok, what it is, it's about the magnets. This year the infrastructure had improved so much it has some new Energy Saving Device, with magnets too, for transportation, called MagLev. It is two magnets with a train between, which floats on tracks, how special is that, and now they even have it for boats, they call the boat AquaMag, but with all the magnets at the school, the East River AquaMag could go off course so they set up these anti-gravitational devices on Mill Rock Island, which sort of work, except when they forget to cap them and it makes a, like, current. There was already one injury, a minor one.

So, someone forgot to cap the anti-grav and this time Migan, who is very small and light, starts to float away. She only went up like five or six feet and is caught in some trees and rescued, but Lore and Dana went ballistic. It is because she's Chosen. They're always afraid she's going to float away. Come on. What are the chances it's going to happen again? But Lore and Dana pull her out of school and are going to homeschool her. Ani is really upset. Melanie would of dealt with it. Anton is just afraid he's going to lose his job.

It starts to look like he could.

The Parents generally have an outside meeting after the regular Conference. So it turns out Anton is telling most of us our kid is ready to mainstream. Well Tensin's mother, whose name is also Tensin, thinks he is just saying that because the school could get closed down. It is about the Migan incident, but also with Melanie so sick there could be a Hygiene issue. Well it's true Anton did say Ani could mainstream and is grandfathered to a school they call Ward Island and could take the Tour even today. It is one of those island schools they like for outerborough kids so we will not give any other kids what we have. If we do.

I had looked over the water to where he said Ward Island school is. Some smoke came up from it. That could just be somebody burning leaves like they do this time of year, but I had said I rather take the Tour another day. Be on the safe side. Anton said she is also Zoned for IS 243 at Corona, a good local school.

Corona! She's not going to Corona. I got a little too much history from Corona. That is where the fire thing began, when Cissy Fardo died in it. I just said thanks, Anton, I will get back to you on that.

Well it turns out Anton told all the Parents their kid could go to Ward Island. Well, except the really low functioning ones. I don't know what he thinks those kids should do.

Remember how the Parents used to talk out at PS 263 in

Queens about what is wrong with everything? These Parents do that now. It really brings back old times. It is even windy like that time the Parents got mad outside PS 263 when it was boarded up for Hygiene. These Mill Rock Parents are glad to share what is wrong with Ward Island. It is a tough school. They make the kids do what they tell them to do. What are the chances a Mill Rock kid could bring it off?

So Tensin's mother asks me, "Inez, what did Anton tell you?"

I don't even realize at first she's talking to me because generally the other Parents don't. To tell the truth my mind had wandered and where it had went was whose name did I put down for emergency contact? Alma Cho. Does that mean Alma gets Ani if I die in a fire?

I look up. I say Ward Island. Or IS 243 in Corona.

So some Parent heard that is a good school, but Itzhtak's mother says well here is what's wrong with local schools. They are tough too. The way local schools are tough, kids punch each other in the halls. At Mill Rock they never let the kids punch each other. They also do not have halls.

So now they get their teeth into the main thing, what is wrong with Mill Rock. The kids never learned to punch each other. Their Education will suffer. I never thought anything is wrong with it but these Parents seem to know.

By the time I take Ani home, I am pretty depressed. This is the first time it really sank in, she would ever leave Mill Rock. Now I have to work the system all over again and it is hard enough trying not to die in a fire.

Ani heard from her friends about how all the kids might have to change school. I guess they are talking about it too. She got really excited. "Ma! I could homeschool with Migan." She missed Migan.

"Come on, Ani. They live in the Dome."

We're waiting at Queens Plaza for the podtram. We have to take the podtram home because the Conference ran so long we missed the cuchifrito pickup and have to take public Transport home, which takes forever, but I'm glad they have public Transport at all in this part of Queens. I remember when they didn't.

"Ma!" The podtram finally comes, we get seats. She is jiggling like crazy. "Ma, we could move to the Dome!" She doesn't get how it works and I don't want her to feel ashamed, but, give me a break here. When you live outside the Dome it is hard enough to get a day Pass, let alone move in.

I just say, "Ani! Enough with the jiggling."

She is like, what? She is upset I said that.

She gets over it, though. When we get back to the garden apartments she is running up to our unit. Then she is yelling down at me, "Ma! The plumbing works!" There are some infrastructure improvements at the City Line. The plumbing sometimes works. "Build a fire and boil water for the clothes."

Here we go again. I say it is too late for a fire.

"Ma! I smell!"

"It is too hot!"

"Ma! It's not hot. It's cold!"

Ok. I will do it. I built a fire in the courtyard and boil the clothes, and spread them to dry. When the water cools down I let Ani jump in the pot. Then I pour the water on the coals when she is out and dry.

Then I wake up in the middle of the night and run out to check the ashes. I can't get this fire stuff off my mind.

Like I'll be on a pulley scrubbing a Nassau County personal Dome and will notice I didn't do anything for like ten minutes because I was thinking, could I put Rauden's name down for emergency contact in case I die in a fire? Well that will never work. He's living at the Farm and Janet would never let me use the Farm info. She doesn't even like it when I try to reach his Mobile phone.

I did get my cleaning work done. I'm just saying it was pretty hard to concentrate, and the way things are turning out, I need all the help I could get.

Because what happens now is, Melanie died.

Well, when they had a ceremony for her on Mill Rock, everyone went ballistic—kids crying, Parents complaining, and Anton saying do not worry but everyone does. At least they are not building a fire to burn Melanie's body, but when we get home after the ceremony, I think I smell smoke and make Ani stay inside while I go sniffing around the area, but she keeps coming to the door and calling, "Ma! I'm cold!"

I am busy.

"Ma! Where is the fire in a can?"

I just lose my patience. "Much as you are jiggling, what are the chances you will not knock over the can and start a fire."

"Ma!" She is almost going to cry. "I did not jiggle."

So then I felt bad. I came inside and put the fire in the can. I guess it is ok. When we wake up in the morning, we are still alive.

She keeps jiggling though.

At Christmas, look who shows up? Lore, Dana, and Migan. They are giving a party for all Migan's old friends. They come back with a boat and bring everyone around the island in the freezing cold. Man, they are rich. They have a hydroponics franchise.

It turns out Migan is not in homeschool any more, she is in another Special school called Free School, where they also let them get away with everything, just like Mill Rock, though in the Dome. You have to pay for it. And you can be sure Ani is like, "Ma! Could I go to Free School with Migan?" She really misses Migan.

Well Lore and Dana say, oh! It is a really good school. And I'm like, thanks, but I don't think it is going to work, because what a Free School like that charges, hello? I can't pay that in a million years! The Dome is like a different world.

Lore and Dana say, oh! She could get Aid. Which I never heard of. Oh well, these schools have Aid to admit Diversity so their regular kids will know what it is. Don Park got it, as Asperger. Maybe Ani could too, as City Line kid. They will check it out as a favor, but it turns out Free School has all the Diversity it needs, we could maybe get a Partial but how could I even pay that? Diversity, Partial—like I have any idea what any of this means?

Still, I'm disappointed when Free School doesn't give us Aid because I was already thinking if I die in a fire while Ani is at Free School, what are the chances Lore and Dana would not take her? Then I'm like, hello? By the time she starts school she will be eleven years, four months old, and then I'm like shut up, I. Shut up.

Ani is so disappointed she bursts out crying. "Ma! I wanted to go to Free School with Migan!"

And I say, "Oh! Ward Island is a good school." I'm just trying to cheer her up.

It doesn't work. She just keeps sobbing, "I want to go to a Dome school with Migan! Ma! I do not want to go to Ward Island," until it gets on my nerves so bad I just go, "Much as you are jiggling, who else is even going to take you?"

So then none of us says anything. I could see she is really upset. I don't even know why I said that.

It's just, I could hardly stand the suspense if I'm going to die in a fire. I am doing the deep breathing and trying to think straight.

"I did not jiggle!"

It is like you do not know how to read all over again. You just have to agree. So in the end I just go, "No. You did not jiggle."

She did though.

Sometimes, when I think of everything that happened in the next few months, I think, who started what when? Was it me, about the jiggling or even about the fire? Was it her? What changed what?

What happened now, Ani and me get invited to the Diversity Fair on Roosevelt Island, in case some Dome schools need more Diversity than they had, so we're all set to go, but there is a rumor of some lesser flu from Bushwick, so the Fair is postponed. At this point she is ten years, nine months old.

And maybe you are thinking, come on, just three more months till she's eleven, it's going to be all right. Well, the closer she got, the worse I worried if I die in a fire in the last stretch that is almost the worst of all.

When they finally let us on Roosevelt Island for the Fair, it's just two months till she turns eleven and I'm in such a state about the goddamn fire I don't even care if Ani jiggles or anything. Right away they hose us down. Ani is really upset and I'm like, ha, ha! They used to do it all the time! When our name is called, I'm just going, oh, hi! Ha, ha. We didn't really need the hosing! Because we're Creedmoor hardies, here are our Proofs. I'm sure they're going to go, oh wow, a Creedmoor hardy! It's going to be like the Mound all over again, next thing you know they'll want to sell Ani's teeth and hair, but it turns out the school with one place open already has a Creedmoor hardy. By the way, I forgot to worry about anybody noticing anything, because I was too busy worrying if they admit her to the school, then I die in a fire, who will put her on the bus?

But they didn't.

Ten years, eleven months.

She is Waitlisted for one Diversity spot.

Like I even know what that means. What was I thinking? A Dome school is even letting Ani in? We already tried.

Ten years, eleven months, twenty-nine days. I am staring at one of the clocks Alma Cho had gave me. Ani's already in bed but I am staring at the clock.

Ok! She's eleven years, zero minutes old! I'm still alive. I start to run and jump until Ani calls out from her bed, "Ma! I know it is my birthday but calm down."

So then I just lie in the bed and look at the ceiling, in the dark. So ha ha ha. Is this a different life or what?

So, it's a beautiful summer night. She is eleven years, one month old. She graduated. They all did, because the B of E shut the school down, so all the kids get a flower and diploma and the Parents cry because the only thing the B of E ever thought was special about our kids was, Needs. I'm putting the diploma on the wall while Ani is getting ready for bed. She graduated. I did not die in a fire. Am I happy now or what? Well, maybe I would of been but it is always something.

"Ani? Are the yellow pjs on?" I go in her room, where she is standing in the beautiful summer night with the yellow pj bottoms in her hand, wearing the yellow pj top, and looking down.

What happens now is, she got hairs.

iii

I know, I know.

I KNOW!

It's nature.

What did I know about nature?

I went and did the head under the tap thing that Rauden does. The plumbing worked. I came out, breathed deep, and told her it is part of nature.

She is like, ok. She just looked down at the hairs.

I went back in the bathroom, did the tap again, came out dripping wet, breathed deep, and said, "The bleeding is part of nature. It is how they used to get kids. Do not have unprotected sex."

She stares up at my big wet head. Then down, at her little hairs, between her legs that are not as little as they used to be.

Then she goes, "*Ma! I know!*" She pulls her yellow pj bottoms on and starts to hop. She hops down the stairs to the courtyard. I go to the kitchen window and watch her hop. She hops all around the courtyard in the dark. It is a long time since she hopped. I don't know why she's hopping now.

At least I got this over with. It's true I was stiff like wood, I said bleed, not ministrate. At least I did not say, the Curse. At least I didn't try to pull the hairs out.

I wanted to though. I cannot get it off my mind.

Man! What is it with me? My little girl is growing up. I didn't die in a fire. She graduated, it's the most beautiful summer I ever saw. And I am like, ok, the fire thing is off the table. Here come the hairs. It's nature! I want to pull them out. Why would I even do that? What do I, want her running virgin Cures?

I had an Episode.

"Ma!"

I got up off the floor. "*What?*"

She stared at me. Then she hopped away. I went in the kitchen to start dinner. What is this with the hopping? She's hopping all the time. I just don't think she should. I don't even know why.

I don't even want to see her with her pants off.

Well, it is June. I'm trying to message Rauden from Little Neck and set up our regular summer visit, but I stop to read something from the B of E, one of those PARENT SCHOOL AGE CHILD things the pigeons used to drop. HELLO! YOUR SCHOOL AGE CHILD IS ENROLLED IN IS 243, CORONA MIDDLE SCHOOL.

What happened to Ward Island?

"Ani! Stop hopping!" She is hopping all around the Board. "Ani!" She does not stop.

I bump the message off and try again. The Board crashes. This one always does. We just walk home. But I can tell you this. She's not going to Corona.

Next day the Board works and I message Rauden we are coming up. No time to lose.

Corona! That's where the fire was. That's where the foster care was Edgar Vargas bought me from, after Cissy Fardo died. I could of been Ani's age by then. I could of had the hairs. She's not going to Corona. I am going to make goddamn sure of that. Henry will hack the B of E and put her in Ward Island where she is supposed to be.

Well, here is what happens now.

"Ani! Time to leave." I'm just shutting our door.

She is hopping on the Walk, in some little shorts.

"Come on, Ani." I am coming down the garden apartment steps. "We're going to miss the MagLev."

"I hate the MagLev." She just keeps hopping.

"Ani! Come on!" I'm checking everything, clothes, swipe IDs, Process Snacks for the trip. Ok. "You know we never even took the MagLev."

"I hate the Farm." She is just hopping and hopping around the Walk.

"Ani! Stop hopping!"

So this is when it starts—and I don't even know what it is. She does stop hopping. Then she turns to face me and screams, "I hate the MagLev!"

Whoa.

"I HATE THE FARM!"

So, what is this? "Ani. You like the Farm. They give you gifts."

But she just totally lets it rip. "I! HATE! THEIR! GIFTS!"

Ok, ok. Take a few deep breaths. Could she of got something? That flu that took Melanie is not totally over yet. Could this be something she gets? I go to feel her head. It seems ok. I try again. "Look. We could take the podtram on the way back." I'm talking really soft. I don't even know why. "Want to take the podtram on the way back? You love the podtram." I pat her shoulder with my hand.

She pushes it away! "You think I love the podtram! You do not even know!" Now she started to cry! "I HATE THE PODTRAM!"

Whoa.

So in a while I say, and I don't know why I even said it, "Want to hop to the Expressway?" And I don't know why it works. But it does. She stops yelling right away and hops to the Expressway.

We grab a shaw to the Bronx. By the time we're out of Queens, she is regular again and enjoys the MagLev or seems to. I did too. So what was that? I have seen Ani Oppositional but not this way. I guess it was a new anomaly. I'm just relieved she stopped at all because if Rauden sees her like this, well he is still trying to market whatever viable he made last year, after my big Episode, and what does this do for the track record? But she is ok.

What happened at the Farm, well, even Henry could not hack the B of E till September 1, but while Ani was busy baking Bars with Janet and I'm in Lab 3 getting soma scraped, Henry hacked some Diversity site. It turns out this one Dome school, East Side Girls, its Diversity died and by charter they must fill the slot with some Diversity. We just got to show up at their Meet and Greet for this to work.

He also hacked us free Passes for the MagLev so we could come upstate any time.

East Side Girls! This is better than Ward Island. It's better than my wildest dream! It is a totally different life. It's in the Dome! The rest of the summer, I'm a nervous wreck. I am fussing all the time, like, "Ani! When we get there, do not hop! Do not jiggle!"

She just looks at me, like, what?

"Ani! Ani!" It's already September. Time for Meet and Greet. "Ani!" Everything is going wrong. "Put on shoes. Where is the swipe ID? Ani! We must leave!"

And I am just running around, hairbrush, ID, shoes, when Ani says, "Oh! I'm not going."

"Don't start."

"I will not go."

So I breathe very deep and say, "Ani, it is a long trip and we must leave right away. It is a long walk even to podtram to even get the ferry to the Lock, and you can be sure there will be some kind of tie-up at the Lock with our stupid temporary Dome Passes."

She just goes into her room and slams the door.

This is a great time for another anomaly.

I open the door and try that backward thing you do with the Oppositional kid. Like, you do not have to go.

She just says, "Very good."

"Ani!" I'm not saying it was ever easy to get her to do what I say but till now, worst case, I could pick her up and make her. She is getting a little big for that. "This is not a joke."

Now she starts to cry, like she did about the MagLev.

"Ani! No! What happened?" I run and take her in my arms. "What is wrong?"

Finally she gets it out. "You are wearing the wrong thing."

Well! At least it is another difference between her and me. I'm like, Meet and Greet, hairs, different life. She's like, you are wearing the wrong thing.

"*Ani! It is not me they Interview.*" I am trying not to lose it here.

So that's another difference. She totally lost it. "Ma! Ma!" Sobbing, sobbing. "They will stare."

I just do my best to breathe deep till I think of what to say. "Oh! Want to go to Ward Island and get expelled? Want to go to IS 243 and get punched in the hall?"

It gets her out the door.

And I will tell you this. Maybe I did wear the wrong thing. Maybe I said the wrong thing. What did I know?

"Nobody else wore a mask!"

They used to.

It doesn't matter either way. Once they finished spraying us for Hygiene at the door to East Side Girls, which is a small white building inside a kind of miniDome inside the regular Dome, they don't even look me in the face. They hardly even look Ani in the face. They just accept her, with Aid, because she is the only Diversity that showed up, because none of the other Diversity who could of showed up knew how to hack their files. So ha ha ha.

Well, we just got to scramble to get everything we need. School starts in a week, and we must take a new bunch of South Brother health tests for the Manhattan Dome. The whole trip, she is going, "I hate that school."

"Ani!" We are on the ferry back to Queens. "Do you know what I would of done to get in a school like this?" Then I go, "What did you say?" because I think she said something I could hardly believe she even said.

"I SAID GO YOURSELF!"

I grabbed her so hard she started to cry. Then I let go.

But she kept crying. "I hate that school! No one is like me there. Ma! I don't want to go to that school!" Crying and crying.

I just say, really quiet, "Well, you are." And I will tell you this. She does.

The first day of school, they let me go in with her through the Lock and to the door of East Side Girls, where the guard sprayed us with antiPatho and checked her South Brother tests all over again before they let us in. This guard has a gun. So this is an arm guard! It is a really indoor school, I mean dark, and very near the Lock so you don't see much of the rest of the Dome. The guard brought us to the office, where Ms. Regina Chaffee is the Principal. Remember stiff like wood? Ani was stiff like wood. But I was proud. She doesn't have Special Needs any more! She has regular Needs! So ha ha ha. You have to take her now.

Once she's settled, they make me go out and kill time till three. I don't get to wait in a room, like at Mill Rock. I don't even get to wait inside the miniDome. I have to wait on the street. At three some other Parents are at the door with me when the girls all come out in Hygienic uniforms, navy blue, with a little tie around the neck that could double as a mask. How cute is that? And look who comes out in the uniform too, with a yellow tie because she is a First Year girl. Ani Fardo.

Still alive.

We walked to the Lock, took the ferry, rode the podtram, walked home, and when we got to the garden apartment she just lay down on the floor, in her little uniform, with the little yellow tie. So I have to undress her myself and carry her to bed. And when I lay her down and start to pull her cover up, she stretched her little arms to pull me close so she could whisper in my ear, "Ma?" And here is what she whispered. "I hate that school."

It is the first thing she says when I meet the little van she comes home on. Sometimes she even cries. She does not cry on the way to the bus the way she used to, that first Mill Rock year.

She waits till we are home.

Sometimes she just falls in a heap in the courtyard, on our steps, sobbing so hard she can't even say why, and I'm on the steps with her, holding her. "What happened?"

We just stay like that, me holding her, her sobbing, in her little uniform, with the little yellow tie, till she could get it out.

No one will sit with her.

So I just sit with her on the steps while some leaves fall on our head. I don't know what to say here. I don't want her to cry but this is a really different life she's starting and I got no idea how it works. I got her in a good school but the sitting part is over my head. When I was her age, no one sat with me. They still don't. Except Ani. All I could think of to say is, "Why not?"

"They, they—Ma!" Her shoulders is shaking under the uniform. "They act like something is," sobbing and sobbing, "like something is wrong with me!"

Well when she said that I went stiff like wood. Did they figure us out? "What do they say?" I honestly don't think anyone at that school is bright enough to figure us out. Still.

"Ma! They don't say anything." Sobbing and sobbing. "They give me looks."

Looks. Well I know what that is like, but it is probably ok. "They are Dome girls," I go. "They never met someone like you. They think you are unique." Like I got any idea what that is, but I thought it will cheer her up.

It didn't. She pushed me off, ran inside, and now will not sit with *me*.

It turns out in her new school, nobody is unique. They will not sit with anyone who is.

Expecially if they got the Aid.

So when a few weeks passed and no one sat with her yet, I ask Ani could she sit with others who are Aid.

"Ma! You don't know anything." She is eating Process in the kitchen. She is so hungry when she comes home, she scarfs down one, two Process Paks. And then a whole regular meal. And I got to find some way to pay for all this. "Ma, if they sit with me everyone will know they are Aid too." The other Aid girls want to pass as regular. In this school, everyone wants to. Even the regular girls. The difference is, the regular girls do pass. "Ma! What's for dinner?"

Potatoes.

She hates potatoes.

So that is news to me. I mean, she's lucky to even have that. The food drops these days is few and far between, and I am generally in Nassau County when they come. We got new expenses too. At East Side Girls she does not get the cuchifrito bus and driver because in Manhattan Dome that's not how it works. She does get a discount coupon for minivan Transport to and from the ferry. Ani still can't bring this off herself, but the school gives me Partial for an Aide to walk her through the transfers. I just have to work a few more hours to pay the other part.

I also pay the other part of Ani's Transport fare.

Also shoes.

My regular client, Mrs. Postow, sets me up cleaning for the Tomko family. So between them, Mrs. Postow, and Lorena Hutz who I already clean for sometimes, by October, I'm working so long I must bust my ass to reach the Stop in time to see her climb off the minivan, hand me her schoolbooks, and say, "I hate that school." She wore a yellow Cardigan they gave her, to go with the uniform. You can be sure she hates that Cardigan.

"Oh!" I put her books in my bag. I'm catching my breath, I ran so hard. "They will not sit with you still?"

"Ma!" We are crossing Douglaston Parkway. "The other girls are stuck up. They think they are so special."

Well this at least I know from Mill Rock how it works. I go, "Ani, you are special too!"

Well now she stops right where we are, in her Cardigan, and she goes, "Oh! You are really the world expert, how special I am!"

I will tell you, for a minute there I'm like, well I'm going to knock you from here to kingdom come. I have to take a lot of deep breaths to calm down. But I do. This is a different life. I'm not knocking her anywhere. I just held her books, took deep breaths, and we walked home.

It turns out world expert is the new thing.

In November, another kid starts using the same Northern Boulevard Stop, Agosto. He goes to school in Rego Park. Me and his mother, Yselma, wait together at the Stop. So one day Yselma says, well how does your daughter like her school. I say, well she hates it. Yselma says, oh everyone hates middle school.

I told that to Ani while we were buying Process from some oldie on Northern Boulevard. I thought this will cheer her up, she is regular.

She goes, "Oh. You are really the world expert, what Everyone does."

And I will tell you, if Cissy Fardo would knock me to king-dom come? Well, if I talked like that to Edgar Vargas, he would make me regret the day I was born. Which I did.

But that is not going to happen here. That was my life. She got a different life. I just pay the oldie, put the Process in my bag, and we walk home, and when we get inside, here we go again. She hates that school, and this is why, it is about the Flip! The other girls all have a Flip. They will not sit with her because she does not have a Flip. They go to a special Dome salon to get the Flip. Oh, Ani, I'm having trouble enough paying extra for the Aide, plus the Transport balance, plus what about Christmas gifts? I will cut the Flip myself. No, Ma, no. I will get Alma Cho. So Alma Cho comes by with scissors and cuts the Flip. When it's finished, Ani looks into the mirror wall and starts to wail. "I hate this Flip!" Goes in her room and slams the door. "Ma!" Sobbing through the door. "Nobody's Flip looks like this."

Alma Cho says wet it down. Wet it down.

I say, through Ani's door, "So it is a little different, but the Hygienic uniform is the same."

But Ani's coat is not the same. She only has an old coat Mrs. Postow gave her. She hates that coat.

For Christmas I bought her a fancy one from Norma Pellicano's friend Darleen.

She hates that too.

Yselma said it is the age. What did I know? When I was Ani's age, I didn't know anyone my age. I was the only virgin Edgar Vargas ran. I don't even remember who pulled out the hairs. At least I do not have to see how many hairs Ani has now because she hides them. If I come in while she's getting dressed, she covers them up.

Almost spring. She is getting tall. The new thing is, do I know you? She is so busy not knowing me when she gets off the minivan that she trips and falls in the street and when I go to help she does not know me all the way home till we get in our living room with the plaid furniture and the glass tabletop and mirrors. Then here we go again. She hates that school! And this is why, besides that she is Aid and the Flip did not work plus she hates her coat, well it is about a special backpack the other girls have, that is shiny and has an airbag so it could sort of float, and, I mean, ok, that is practical, because you do not have to lug the backpack but what that kind of backpack sells for, this is out of the question. She goes in her room and slams the door.

I hear her crying from her room, in the night.

I'm already cleaning extra hours just to pay her school expenses! And what about the magnet belt!

But she's crying so hard. I just don't want her to cry like that.

Now maybe what I'm going to say right here could hurt somebody's feelings. I'm just trying to be honest. Remember how Janet Delize said about Ani, when she was six days old, "I don't even know why that poor child was born." Well, that stupid backpack Ani wants so bad? There is probably a kid somewhere, that's why they're born.

iv

Whoa! Out of practice.

I woke up very dizzy in an RV outside Newburgh. Some new shady OBGYN is washing his hands. Rauden is holding up eight fingers. Eight solos. Good but not great. I'm paid by the egg.

I just got dressed fast and head for home. I don't want to be late for Ani at her Stop. The way this Harvest worked, I beefed myself up at home to save time. It was not hard. I bought my own cryoKit at Iron Triangle. If everything works, viables should be on the market by the end of the week. I will get a cut of any sale. Rauden also gave me a few coupons today on spec.

I ran across the bridge and made it to the MagLev in time but from here on, everything went wrong. The MagLev got delayed. I missed my hybro to the Bronx. Why did I take the sailbus? The wind changed. I ended up in Yonkers, in some really shady neighborhood where people in masks come right up to the sailbus whispering, "Blood? Life?" One guy even gives me a card when I climb off. "Good rates on the Change," he whispers. By the time I got back to the Bronx I was so late there goes all the spec money on a shaw to Queens, and when I made it to the Stop, Ani was crying in the street. The minvan came early for once.

I say I will never be late again. I'm going to get you something really special for your birthday, you will see.

But when I message Rauden in a week, no sale. Two weeks. No sale.

It's Yselma who explains the Change but first she says I must swear to never do it or let Ani do it. I'm like, ok, whatever.

So she says, "You know if a girl with Stealth Virus tries to Host a child from her own genes, her Immune is so challenged it could bump the kid off and herself too?" I sort of knew. Well, she could get around the problem a few ways, like rent a Host or do Host swap. But maybe she's afraid the Host will run off with the child. Then she could buy what they call the Change.

When Yselma said the word, she spat, right on Northern Boulevard, where we are waiting for our kids to come home.

The way it works, Yselma says, they tweak the mother's DNA so it is not what it was. So she is not gene for gene her original self. She freezes a bunch of her original eggs first so they stay their original self. Then she does IVF with those original eggs, but she is not *her* original self, so her challenged Immune does not need to be so confused, who is who. It is a little hard to follow. The main thing is, nobody dies. Well, if it works. It doesn't always work. Girls sometimes even die from the operation because the sleazy guys who do the work aren't MDs or even Techs. Yselma thought the whole thing is dangerous and stupid. I thought it's stupid too. It's true Ani is not going to have this problem because she will not get SV but Yselma and her friend Xochitl have it. They both have Stealth Virus and did Host swap with each other's kids and all of them are all still alive. They even plan to do it again. She asked me where I heard of the Change and I say Yonkers and she says oh she heard of that. They deal hardy product, if you need that sort of thing.

Well, then the van showed up at last, our kids got off, still alive, and we all went home.

But what Yselma told me was an environmental factor. In more ways than one. But we are way, way ahead of ourself.

One week before Ani's birthday, I went back to Yonkers to sell blood while Ani is at school—I don't know what else to do. I been messaging Rauden but the Newburgh product did not move. I brought my old quarantine Proofs to Yonkers, for quality assurance. I thought it's going to be a simple in-out operation. It didn't work. The first dealer said, oh did I mention you must give a hand job? I walked out. The next only dealt blood in combo with organ sales. They say nobody does blood solos any more. They offer top dollar for certain organs but sleazy as these guys are, something bad could happen to me and if I die, there goes Ani's different life, fire or no fire. I walked up and down the strip till it got really late, but all the rates is so bad I'm almost going to do the hand job but froze at that dealer's booth. So I'm a bad mother. Instead, I sold to a different dealer at a rate so low I couldn't buy anything good at all, at least up here.

I end up buying a used backpack from Norma Pellicano's friend Darleen. It hardly floats at all and was not new. Maybe a good mother would of done the hand job and maybe not but either way, it didn't work.

On the morning of her birthday Ani climbed on the mini with the birthday backpack. In the afternoon she kicked it all the way home. No one will sit with her.

"Well," I say. "It's still a nice backpack."

She doesn't say a word to me. She doesn't have to. I could think it myself. Like I am the world expert, what a nice backpack is.

Twelve years old. Still alive.

Well, I can tell you, when Ani's bleeding starts at Mrs. Postow's personal Dome where I bring her in summer to watch TV or play Games while I clean, compared to Year One, it's a walk in the goddamn park. She just comes out to me where I'm scrubbing the Dome roof and tells me what happened. I don't have an Episode. I don't even talk about nature. I just tell her how it works and show her what to do. I give her some cloths for the blood and say, "Don't tell Rauden," and she gives me a look like, why would I?

But when we made our summer visit to the Farm, it came again while we are there, and what happens is, she got so Oppositional, Janet figures out what is going on, tells Rauden, and while Ani is calming down with a Game in the Box Room, Rauden brings me to Lab 3, shuts the door, and starts to ask the details—this is medical history, she achieved menarche, what is the timing? Well, I don't know what happened here, but next thing I know, I start to talk a way I never talked to Rauden before. It's like Janet Delize talks to him. "Oh," I go. "She's going to be the Subject now?"

Rauden is so surprised how mean I sound, his mouth drops open. "It's just for the records, I."

Well, I was surprised too but just kept going. "Put this on the goddamn records, R." I'm like, who is saying this? Me? I never talked like this to him before. But I keep going. "You want ova?" And I hit my ovary, the one. "Here it is! You want soma?" I hit my breast. "Come and goddamn get your soma!" Rauden is holding his hands up like, don't shoot, but I am off the charts. "Who's going to get beefed, get poked, get scraped, R, who is the Subject here?" And I stick my face right next to his. "I'M GOING TO BE THE ONLY ONE!"

By the end, I'm shouting so loud Ani comes to the lab room door. She looks scared now. So Rauden and I shut up. I'm scared too. I never was like this before. I forget to even ask about the viable sales from the Newburgh Harvest.

And I really need the money.

So, on the MagLev home, I'm just going over it all in my mind, what happened, why did I act like that? I almost don't notice Ani going, "*Ma.*"

"What?"

"Is Rauden my Dad?"

"Rauden?" Where does this come from? "Who told you that? No. Rauden's not your Dad. Did young Phil tell you that?" This is Janet's grandson. He was visiting. "Young Phil doesn't know anything. Rauden's not your Dad."

But when we are almost home, getting off a shaw at Marathon in the dark, she goes, "Is Henry?"

"Is Henry what?" Then I get it. "No. Henry's not your Dad. Rauden's not your Dad. Neither of them are."

I'm not saying I didn't sometimes wish they were.

The rest of the summer was so nice I wished it never ended. But it did.

So. It's the first day of Ani's second year at East Side Girls. This one day, I'm allowed to come with her. We will take the podtram in together. We're waiting for it. She is wearing the Hygienic uniform, with a new red tie because it is her Second Year. She looks so cute.

I got her new white shoes, they call them Crewes. Her feet grew so much in the summer, I had to shell out for another pair from Darleen. Ani really grew a lot. But not in the breast. Maybe she never will. I never did. Anyhow, the Hygienic uniform fits. At the end of First Year they give them a new one for Second Year. But not shoes.

We took the pod to Hunter's Point, and now we are waiting for the ferry to the Lock. I was like, so! This year it's going to work. The other girls are going to sit with you, like that.

Well, it didn't work. From now on I don't think anything did.

v

The Dome Lock was closed. Some bug is going around. We have to get tested again at South Brother Island to get in the Dome. So this is the first day of her Second Year at East Side Girls.

When we get the South Brother tests sorted out, it turns out over summer East Side Girls changed its scanner to read pure code. We have to go up to the Farm again so Henry could fix up our ID swipes to make our pure code readings track separate, which he does but says even so, watch out because if we both scan in the same system the same day, the first person's files could get wiped out by the second one's. Just punch in a special reverse code he gave me. That will crash the system. It will buy time.

When Ani finally gets back to school, no one will sit with her. They say she has Cooties. When Ani tells me how prejudice they are I say I'm going to complain at the fall Conference but Ani says if I say anything she's never going to school again. Well anyhow at the fall Conference it does not even come up, because Ms. Chaffee says Ani is failing Humanity. She does not do the work. So that is news to me. I must stay on Ani's case and help her do the work, though a tutor would be better. Could I manage that?

Totally, I say.

Whatever it even is.

"Ani!" I say when we're home. "Do your work," because what else could I do but stay on her case, but after I did it a few times, she burst into tears.

"I can't do it, Ma. I don't get it."

So I will help.

"No, Ma. No. It's English."

How hard could that be?

"Ma! It's Diagram. You have to know what is the Subject."

Hello? I *am* the expert here. So I helped her do the work.

Two days later, she gets off the minivan and hates her school because she failed Diagram. And she is so mad at me. "Ma! The Subject is who does it."

That used to be the Tech.

It happens to the Object.

That used to be the Subject.

"You do not know anything!" She ran into her room crying and locked the door. "Neither do I! I got it from you. I'm stupid!"

So that's it. It's my fault. She doesn't know anything because I don't know anything. It's in the genes. I should of gave her to someone else. Next thing you know, I'm going to cry too.

But that is not going to happen. Not going to happen. I pull myself together. "Ani!" I call through the door. "It will be all right. I will buy a tutor."

"You don't even know what it is."

But I don't have to know. I just have to pay for it.

I message Rauden the next day about the sales. No sales. Man! What is going on? My new client for cleaning says she will ask around for other clients but it could take a while. Wait—I could ask Alma and Norma to hook me up with other oldies who need help with chores. That should bring in a few extra coupons. Ok! This will work.

So now this is the life. Year Two, month four. Wake up, do

breakfast Process. Race to get to the minivan on time. Race to Nassau County, scrub Domes. Race back to get Ani at the Stop, go home, get supper, and the minute that is over, race off to do chores for oldies. Lug boxes on and off shelves they cannot reach. Move the furniture around. Don't forget to race back home and stay on Ani's case. Did she do her work?

Yselma's friend Xochitl who was Agosto's swap Host says I could not pay the going rates for tutor in a million years but did I notice the East Side Girls had gizmos to help them with the work? Now that I think of it, besides the magnet belt, some had sort of a mirror on their head so they won't read backward. Xochitl says go to Iron Triangle Bazaar, where I did the Interview for Opening and deCon, so long ago. I could get every kind of gizmo Ani needs. Discounts on everything—that is where she and Yselma bought the male factor for their kids. So after Christmas, I brought every coupon I had saved to Iron Triangle, which was great. The tutor gizmo is a tiny chip you put on your regular swipe ID, so when you swipe into Readers at school or anywhere, it tells you the answers, but you must also buy a cheap Reader to do the work at home, so it cost quite a lot in the end. Xochitl helped me bargain and put the gizmo on the swipe.

Well, guess what? Before the week is over, Ani lost her swipe! The school office sent a Note. She cannot come to school without the swipe.

I could hardly believe this. And I just put the gizmo on it. *And* got a new cleaning job. Now I must go up to the Farm so Henry could rig up a new one. "Ani, you can't be losing your swipe. It is important."

She just said, "I hate my swipe."

How could you hate your swipe?

Henry makes a new one, but I lost two days of work not to mention the gizmo software that was on the old one, so I will have to pay all over again, and even from Iron Triangle, it's going to clean my coupons out. I am already having trouble paying Partial on the travel Aide. I got to find out what is going on with the sales. I tell Ani to go help Henry fix your swipe ID, then I follow Rauden to the kitchen where he is cooking up some Beverage.

"What is the problem, R? There is so many Epis overseas, the Newburgh viables should sell like hot cakes. Come on. I really need the money, R."

He just says, "Well there is a complication. Let's give it a little time."

"For what?" I said.

Well, I don't know how Henry rigged Ani's new swipe so fast but next thing I know, he has wheeled to the kitchen doorway. "Bro," Henry says. "You have to tell her."

"*Tell me what?*"

"Tell her what?" It's Ani in the doorway, behind Henry. So that's it for the talk about the sales.

On the MagLev down, Ani asks me, "What did he look like?"

"Who?" I'm just trying to grab a nap here in my seat.

"My Dad."

Oh, here we go again. "Why?"

The other girls are telling her she does not know who is her Dad.

Well, I am going to tell her she should tell these girls she's not the only one who doesn't know her goddamn Dad. But who's going to sit with her if she says that? So I just say, "He looked like me." For all I know, it's true.

I mean—if her Dad is my Dad. If that's how it works.

Then we didn't say anything the whole way down. She just looked at the window, where you could see her face, in the glass. I closed my eyes. When I opened them, she's looking at my own face. Then her face in the glass. Her/me.

More and more I thought maybe it's better if she never knows. She already didn't fit in with the other girls. At least there are other City Line kids in the world. But what she is—she could be the only one she ever heard of. How's she going to feel about that?

In fact not long after we got back there is a story in the News, a baby born in Idaho who seems to really be cloned. I think the mother Hosted it herself. The kid died in four days because clones die young, and the Parents died two days after that because Idaho vigilantes set their house on fire. The TV showed pictures of both Parents, then the baby clone. Then they have an Interview with some Idaho Neighbor who tells the News, "This poor kid should never of been born."

So Ani and I are watching this and I say to the Neighbor's face, "Well, you are the world expert on who should be born."

But then the TV person looks out hard and goes, "Sadly, we must agree."

What happens now, I don't know if I'm getting an anomaly myself or what, but I went ballistic. "This goddamn cretin! He doesn't know anything. *Anything*. ANYTHING!"

Ani is so surprised she starts to cry. She's crying like she did when she was eight years old and I kept yelling, "A clone is like anyone." And I feel terrible, like I did back then. Why did I make her cry?

But she is not eight now. She's almost thirteen. When I was thirteen, I did not cry at all. So great. It's one more way to prove, you know.

Still, I start to wonder if something *is* wrong with her. She is really crying all the time.

She cries when I get another gizmo and she can't make it work. "I hate this gizmo!" she sobs.

She's crying on her thirteenth birthday, because she hates her knees. How could you hate your knees? It's true they are a little big but maybe they look big because the legs are narrow. She is narrow all over. Except the face. I mean, the face is narrow but not so narrow like mine.

"Ani, nothing is wrong with your knees." I have to say this through her door because she locked it.

"Oh!" she sobs, through the door. "And you know this because?"

So this is the new thing.

Like the last day of school, when her stupid report card comes with a Note she did pass but just barely, even with the gizmo, and if she does not do better will not get into Upper School—which I never even heard of—and I go, "So. Next year, you will do the work."

She goes, "Oh. And you know this because?"

So that's the end of Year Two.

We usually go up to the Farm in June, July, or August, and I want to get on Rauden's case about viable sales, maybe run another Harvest because I really need the bucks. But I don't want Rauden to know how bad she's doing. I'm worried it could affect the sales. I message Rauden I got no time off and will try another time.

Right away I wish I went. This summer is a nightmare almost from the start. I don't have to rush to meet Ani after work but I still got six jobs, then when I'm through I have to do chores at night for oldies. I always need more coupons. And then I have to deal with her.

On vacation she used to be glad to follow me to my jobs and enjoy the Nassau County Domes but this year she's like, "Ma. I am too old for Games. Let me stay home alone." Well, that is not going to happen. I don't like to worry Ani but between you and me, this Idaho vigilante stuff with the baby clone and the fire has me nervous. You did sometimes see those Fundy nuts in robes around. I just don't think she should be alone. So I have to drag her all the way to Nassau County with me. And we are always late.

8:12 a.m. We're just leaving. "Come on, Ani. Come on." She is so slow.

"Ma, I don't want to go. It's boring."

"So bring some summer schoolwork with you." We're hurrying up 255th Street. "That could really help Year Three."

"And you know that because?"

"Because Ms. Chaffee said so."

"I hate Ms. Chaffee."

"I am not crazy about her myself, but if you don't do what she says you could lose the Aid."

"I hate the Aid." Then she just sat right down on the street.

"ANI! Get up, Ani." Oh, man. We are going to be late to Lorena Hutz. "WHAT IS WRONG WITH YOU?"

So now she is crying! Right on the street.

"You think something is wrong with me! Everyone does! Everyone thinks something is wrong with me."

"Ani, get up. Nothing is wrong with you!" We will be so late.

"Oh!" She is sobbing. "And you know this because?"

"Ani! I'm just saying!" Man! Better not say anything. I just go, "Hey! Ani! It's so hot—on the weekend, want to take the sailtram to the beach?"

She hates the beach.

"Want to do something else?" I'm just trying to get her up off the road.

"I want to go to Migan's school!"

Where is this coming from? She didn't see Migan for years. But now that it came up, this does not seem like such a bad idea. She hates East Side Girls. I was not crazy about it myself. Maybe they used up their Diversity at Migan's school and could use some more. I could try and track down Lore and Dana, but what if I need to come up with Partial? Let's see what's going on with sales from the Farm. It's more than a year since the Newburgh Harvest. We should of got some call by now.

When we finally get to Lorena Hutz's personal Dome, late, I sneak off while Ani watches TV and message Rauden from her personal Board. WHAT ABOUT THE SALES?

While she is playing a Game at the Tomkos' personal patio Dome, I sneak back to Lorena Hutz's personal Board for Rauden's reply. WE NEED TO TALK.

While Ani is home in bed, I sneak off to Oakland Gardens, where they still had floaters like the kind I used in the old Queensbridge days, and I finally got through to Rauden who is like we cannot talk. I go, I thought we have to talk. Not This Way. It is not safe to talk This Way. Come up to the Farm. So here we go again! I do miss the Farm and Rauden but am nervous what will happen if he finds out how Ani is doing.

I tell Rauden I will get back to him. Then I start to walk home. Then I think I see someone in robes! I backtrack, go zigzag, then take the long way home around the golf course. By the time I get to bed it's so late I wake up almost too tired to do anything. But I must get up, get dressed, mix breakfast Process, and here we go again.

"Ani! Time to leave."

"Ma! I'm hot."

Sometimes I started to think Janet Delize was right. I should of showed her who was boss when I had the chance. Too late now.

Thirteen years, three months old.

"Ani! Want to help me with my chores?"

She does not want to help.

Cissy Fardo showed me who was boss. Edgar Vargas showed me who was boss. That did not work out so great—I ended up with *my* life. Do I have to let Ani show *me* who's boss so *she* will have a different life? I just don't know how this works. In the morning before she wakes up, I study Alma Cho's old pamphlets on the steps. It turns out the Parent is supposed to be a role model, what they call, role model.

But what if I don't want her to be me?

I don't know who to go to for advice. I'm not going to ask Janet Delize or she's going to say I should of shown Ani who was boss. I'm not going to ask Rauden or he's going to say, oh! Oppositional? That's it for the track record.

Thirteen years, four goddamn months old.

Still alive.

I goddamn was too.

We are on Northern Boulevard waiting for the Transport for the first day of Year goddamn Three at East Side goddamn Girls, with Ani in the Third Year Hygienic uniform, with the Royal Blue new goddamn tie. I don't even know how I got to September. It's still goddamn hot, one of the hottest. We're the only ones at the Stop this year. I don't know what happened to Yselma and Agosto.

Ani is just standing away from me, squinting at the ground. This is the new thing. Squinting. She squints all the time. She just takes a few steps to the road to check is the Transport coming, in this year's new Crewes I bought her at Iron Triangle for school. She got lipstick. Man! Where did she find that? I think she got taller. We still could pass. She really has a whole different shape from me, in the uniform, and the tie, and the lipstick.

She looked so cute.

I go, "Very good. So this year it could work. It is a Challenge but an Opportunity."

"Ma, you don't even know what that means."

The Transport finally rolls up, she just gets on alone and off she goes.

Then I am bouncing off the walls at Mrs. Postow's and Lorena Hutz's and all my jobs until it's time to race across Queens to the Stop, the minivan pulls up, the doors open, and who's that coming down the steps? Ani Fardo, still alive.

vi

Well, maybe you are thinking, come on. How bad could things be now? It's Year Three at East Side stupid Girls, just one more year to go. It's going to be ok.

Well, I thought so too. But it's not even October when I get a message through Lorena Hutz. Get to Ms. Chaffee's office right away. I made it in record time, running to the pod, the ferry, the Lock, then up the school stairs. Ani stole a girl's swipe. Make an appointment with Ms. Chaffee's assistant, Don, for a special Conference. Ms. Chaffee is concerned Ani could be a Bad Influence on the other girls. That's it. So I ran across Queens for this? I'm still catching my breath when Ani and I go down the hall to Don's office in the next room over, behind a little plexi fence, and he is really busy but will schedule a Conference once he calls up my daughter's files. He punches Ani's name in. Then all at once, he freezes at the screen.

Oh! Shit! It is always something!

Remember the problem of who swipes in last with pure code? I was in such a rush when I swiped in at the school scanner, I forgot to crash the system. So her name called my files. He punched in Ani's name and it came up me.

I think fast and pretend to feel sick. He hurried off supposedly to get me water but I guarantee he will come back in a Hygienic mask. I run around the plexi fence to his system, crash it fast, and when he returns—wearing a Hygienic mask!—I'm already back on my side of the fence and say, oh thanks for the water, I feel better already.

Ani is just staring at me.

Don too. "That's funny," he goes. Because now the screen's black. He gives me a look, over the mask.

Then he gives Ani a look. But I guess the problem is fixed because when his system reboots, he peers at the screen and says, "Hmm. Ok."

Then all at once the eyes look back at my face, hard, over his mask. Then Ani's face. Then me. Then Ani.

I turn my face away, like, oh, what is that on the wall?

In the end, he just shrugs. He gets over it. Still, that's the first time since Ani started kindergarten I took it serious, someone could notice something.

I really need this complication. Ok, I will start to wear a scarf. If somebody looks at us funny, I will hide my face.

On the ferry back, I say, "Ani? Why would you steal a swipe?"

She didn't say anything, just squinted until we got to the pod-tram, which is delayed from some new lesser flu caution and we just wait and wait and I try again. "You have your own swipe, Ani."

Then she said, "So? That stupid girl got three goddamn swipes at home," and after that not one word the whole way home.

So from now on, Conference this, Conference that. And I just got a new Nassau County client to pay the new balance I must spend this year on Ani's transfer Aide! The new client pays me in vegetables she grew, and I must sell or barter them at Iron Triangle Bazaar which takes another two hours out of my week. I already got all the vegetables I need from the chores I do for Norma Pellicano's friend Mort. I tell Don I am having a problem scheduling the next Conference and he is like, and I should care because?

At the next Conference I saw a sign posted, all Year Three girls and their Parent should fill in forms for where they want to go to Upper School. Ms. Chaffee says, oh no need for Ani to be concerned BECAUSE WITH HER GRADES SHE'S NEVER GETTING IN!

Thirteen and a half years old.

It is already cold. She grew so much she will need a new coat, and where is the money coming from?

Still alive.

Ms. Chaffee says Ani might do better to transfer somewhere else, even at this late date.

She is almost graduating!

Well, we will see about that. Would I consider Armory Prep?

I never heard of that.

Ani rolls her eyes like, Ma, you never heard of anything.

Well, it seems there is a lot of complaint, the Diversity that gets into these fancy Dome schools, what good does it do? They don't learn useful skills for their own life. Why not start a really special Diversity school just for Diversity? They put it inside an Armory in the Bronx with very high walls so nobody runs away. They sleep there on cots. The fees are token and they learn useful skills. They could even go on to a career in Enforcement.

Well, that is really going to work. Ani is a crime against nature. What is she, going to bust herself?

I just say, well Ani is not ready for sleepaway school.

Ms. Chaffee says there could be some other school where she could learn skills more useful in her Zone.

Hmm, useful skills. She already could forage, a little. She could grow potatoes. She could stay alive. In our Zone, that is pretty much the useful skills. She already got them.

I say, "I was hoping she could be a Tech."

Ani squints so hard her eyes shut.

Ms. Chaffee says, "Yes, well I can see in your Zone there might be a need for Techs but that work takes character."

Well, I don't know if it is in the genes, but I did not punch Ms. Chaffee's lights out.

Is that character or what?

"Ani!" I'm in the kitchen, opening Process Paks. Outside, the wind is blowing so hard the windows shook. "Do your work!"

She is on the sofa watching TV. "Why? I'm not getting into Upper School anyway." Then we both say, "Shit," at the same time. The power went off.

"Get the wick, Ani."

She gets the wick, and I light it with an Iron Triangle gizmo I traded vegetables for.

"You know what Melanie used to say. You could do anything." I bring food to the table with the glass top. "Maybe you could find some other way to be a Tech."

"Ma! What is it with the Tech? You don't even know how dangerous it is." She is scarfing Process down. "A Tech gets exposed. A Tech could get something bad!"

Sometimes I almost want to tell her why she won't. But how do I explain without spilling the beans? Without the gene for gene part of the story, Sylvain hardy does not make sense even if she knows I am a Sylvain hardy unless I make up some lie about a hardy Dad but I'm not going there. She could figure something out. Sometimes I think she already did.

Sometimes I see her look at me hard like Don looked at me hard. Like if we are both near the mirror, side by side, she looks at us both. Her/me. Her/me. I can tell you this. I'm not wearing some goddamn scarf at home.

Christmas will be here soon.

Xochitl is missing too. I look for her when I'm coat shopping at Iron Triangle. Maybe she knows what happened to Yselma and Agosto, but somebody said Xochitl got something. They didn't know if Yselma got something. Someone else said, no, a Fundy torched them because they were trying to do another Host swap. I don't know which it is.

I heard from Alma Cho some new flu was around. Well, it's true there are more fires, and the caution tape is getting so bad, I got to work my way around it on my way to the next stupid Conference, just before winter break. Ani is failing three courses and must do them over. She will not get Aid for the do-over.

"Please! Could she even get Partial Aid? I would pay the balance."

Ms. Chaffee is like, that is really going to happen. But ok. I must bring the first downpayment when we come back from winter break.

Ferry to Hunter's Point.

"Ani! You must do your work!"

"Whatever."

Podtram home. I am really tired.

But I must do chores for oldies. Fix dinner. Stay on Ani's case, will she do her goddamn work. "I'm busting my tail to keep you in this school. And do not say it, Ani."

So she doesn't. She doesn't say she hates that school.

Thirteen years, seven months old.

Alma Cho says old Norma Pellicano died. She didn't get any-thing, she was just old.

And I would like to go to the ceremony, but I am too busy picking frozen potatoes in the dark for Mort's friend Pandit, then cut them up, then rush home to make dinner and breathe down Ani's neck, did she do the work.

When the next message comes from Ms. Chaffee, after winter break, at February, I think it is because I was a little short on the Partial balance I must pay. I get a coupon advance from Mrs. Postow and Loretta Hutz and head off in a rush. You cannot get on the Bell Boulevard podtram Stop. The pod is taped all the way back to Flushing Meadows! I grabbed a shaw to make our way around the tape. Northern Boulevard is totally blocked. We took smoky side streets till we saw body bags on Cherry Avenue. Body bags! It's been a while since I saw that. The driver just dumped me out and went the other way. I just run the rest of the way to Flushing Cemetery, where the pod still worked. By the time I got to East Side Girls, I'm two hours late, but it's ok! I do not need the coupons! It is not the problem because guess what?

Ani punched a girl.

I'm standing in the office panting and soaked in Hygiene spray they sprayed at the door, and I'm like well it will not happen again, and Ms. Chaffee is like you are really right. Ani is expelled.

Ani is just squinting at the floor.

I am just in shock. I am just breathing deep. "Please," I go. "*Please*." I even went on my knees. "Please give her one more chance."

Ms. Chaffee waits like maybe she would, but she is just breathing deep herself. Then she lets it out. I GAVE HER EVERY CHANCE I COULD! She got the Aid, the Aide, the Partial, the uniform. That is the problem with Diversity kids, they think they are the only ones in the entire world. They think they are the only ones who count. I have done what I could for your daughter but she is a Bad Influence on the other girls. I am responsible to them too. "I will tell you this—as Oppositional as Ani is," Ms. Chaffee goes, "no wonder they won't sit with her."

Well, Ani looks up now. And I am hoping she will say, please. Please give me a chance. Guess what? She looks Ms. Chaffee in the eye and goes, "Well that's their goddamn problem. I hate this school."

Ok, there goes the different life.

Don took the Passes off our swipes so we cannot get in again or even through the Dome Lock.

They will let her keep the uniform. That's it.

"Ma!" Ani is at my bedroom door. "I could plant potatoes."

I'm just lying in the dark. I didn't fix dinner, nothing.

"I could sell them at Iron Triangle. Ma."

What do I tell Rauden? What do I tell Janet?

At least I don't have to tell Rini Jaffur.

I got up at last. I went into the kitchen. She is already in her pjs. She tore her uniform and threw it away. So I could not even barter it. She hated that school.

"Ma," she goes. "I could do Projects at the Farm."

I turned on the tap. The plumbing worked. I put my head under then shook it like Rauden used to. Then I come right up to her so close I don't even have to raise my voice. "Well, I can guarantee you, that is not going to happen."

Next morning, while she is sleeping late, I go through the City Line hole to my jobs and reschedule everything.

I'm going to show my daughter who is boss.

vii

"Get up, Ani! Get up, get up." She is trying to hide under the covers but I just pull them off. "We're going to Ward Island. Get up, get up, get up!"

She is tugging the covers back. "Ma. No! Oh, Ma. I don't want to go."

"And I should care because?" I drag her to the table. "Eat your Process!"

"Ma! Look!" She is pointing out the window.

It's always something! It's snowing. First time in years it snowed out here. To get to Ward Island is a hard trip even on a good day, with a lot of waiting for the hybro in bad places. This is not a good day.

But it's the only one I could get off from work.

By the time we get to Northern Boulevard, the snow turned to rain, we're soaked, let alone, with the caution tape, there is no public Transport unless we take the cuchifrito that runs almost to Powell's Cove and we are goddamn not doing that. We did not come this far to end up there. So we have to go another way, wait for a hybro in the rain, and Ani is whining and whining.

"Ma, I don't want to go to Ward Island. It is a tough school."

"Like you are the world expert," I go, "what is tough."

When we finally get to the stupid bridge to Ward Island it's snowing again and no one is even around to tell us how to find the school, which is totally boarded-up when we do find it, closed for more than a year, and Ani is so mad because I didn't know. We're standing by the boarded-up school in the snow and I'm like, if you did the work I wouldn't need to know. If you didn't punch a girl I wouldn't need to know.

"She called me Shitty Line Ani," and I will tell you, I would like to punch that girl myself. I would like to punch Ms. Chaffee when I had the chance. "Ma! Why do I even have to go to school?"

We're heading for the bridge back to Queens, across empty Ward Island, in slush. "For Education."

"You don't even know what that means."

Well I just stopped and leaned on some sort of wall by some stupid shut-up stadium near some pile of mud and slush. "Well I will tell you what I do know. The Opportunity you have just threw away, I'm pretty sure you will not get again. The Education you could get even now, not everyone does. Ani! I never even finished third grade!"

That was the total wrong thing to say because right away she goes, "Oh! You never finished third grade. And I should listen to you tell me what to do because?"

"BECAUSE I WILL KNOCK YOU FROM HERE TO KINGDOM COME!"

It shuts her up.

The snow has stopped.

The bridge is shut. There are no Boards. It's going to take an hour for us to get off Ward Island. I flag a gypsy ferry to take us through the Riker's Channel even though it's going to clean my coupons out but what else could we do? Guess what, the Alert spread to the old airport, the boats has to all turn around, and I am so sick of how long everything took, I say drop us at the Power Plant in Astoria, and the skipper is like, it is unsafe, they have fleas and pathogens, you will get something bad, I'm like, LEAVE US OFF.

"Ma! It's dangerous."

"We're not getting anything." I make the skipper let us off

and pull her through the Plant, which is, you know, burnt, like those big things that stick up are black, and there is funny powder around and a green mud in snow, and I guess there is fleas, and one bit her on the hand, and Ani is so scared she slips in the green mud and falls and gets green mud all over her, and she is crying she is going to get something. "You're not getting anything!" I really had it by now. I even say, "Because I'm not getting anything!" I almost spilled the beans right then and there. But then I shut up.

She stops crying and looks at me. Then she looks at her hand with the bite on it.

All the way home she is doing it. Hand/me. Hand/me.

I'm going to find her a school.

I can't reach Lore and Dana.

You can forget about Ani helping me scrub Domes. She just stays home and watches TV if the power works. She says she is too old to come with me and play Games. I'm panicked all day long with her home alone because I kept hearing stories of vigilante activity, though it is mainly in the sticks. Still if these local Fundy nuts went after Yselma for Host swap, what would they do to Ani if they find out what she is? I tell her, lock the door and let no one in! Especially in robes!

Almost fourteen. Still alive.

One day I open the door and she's turning the TV off fast and I say what was that and she said she doesn't know. But if I had to guess?

I'd say it was a rerun of that old stupid Horror show. *Them.* The one about us. Clones.

I found a local school in Bayside. At least in school she will be safe. Bayside is a walk but we could make it without going through the new road blocks and podtram shutdowns which are worse every day. They have an outdoor summer program.

I message Rauden we cannot make our regular summer trip this year either. So that's it for sales. The good part is, Rauden and Janet will not learn she got expelled.

Rauden says ok.

The bad part is we will not see him for another year. It's two years since we came up in the summer. He doesn't say anything. He does not even care. I try to message him from Little Neck. I can't get through. I miss Rauden. I miss Yselma too.

At fall Ani's in the regular Bayside indoor program. It is a big school, built so long ago it could hold two thousand kids, if you can believe it. Ninety-three are in here now.

And guess what, none of them will sit with Ani. On the other side of the river no one will sit with her because she is from our side of the river. On this side they will not sit with her because she been in school on the other side of the river. I really want to get her out and am trying to reach Lore and Dana from Nassau County Board using a search technique Henry showed me but so far it didn't work.

I spent some coupons on a trike so we don't have to walk so far but guess what, nobody else gets triked to school. So I have to leave her off a block away. I just hold my breath she will make it to the door. After school, I have to wait a block away and hold my breath till she shows up. Still alive. Then I just trike her home.

I still can't track down Lore and Dana. I even had trouble reaching Rauden. He did message me once. WE NEED TO TALK. CAN YOU MAKE A TRIP?

I could not reach him back. His ID line is jammed.

Fourteen and a half years old. Still alive.

She seemed to get Adjusted to Bayside school. She does not do the work but nobody else does, either. She even found a friend to sit with, Narj Oonnoony. The pair of them are caught playing hooky near the old Flushing airport. Do you know how near that is to Powell's Cove? I really lit into her, what danger she could be in. She does not get how dangerous Queens is, she been in the Dome so long. I say Narj Oonnoony is a Bad Influence, and she is like, Ma, you don't even know what that means.

I must find her a school that does not let them run away. I'm sneaking away from my Nassau County jobs all day to do search this, search that, but the Board problems all over the Northeast are so bad I heard it is sabotage. Terrorists sabotaged the Boards. Mrs. Postow says it is not terrorists at all, it's vigilantes.

Then I saw on the News about some vigilante trouble somewhere in the sticks, and it is Four Corners! That is where Lucas lived, in that Quonset we saw that time. That is really not very far from the Farm! That's why I can't reach Rauden, vigilantes torched the Farm!

Then the News shows a map. It is not that Four Corners. It is some other Four Corners in some other state. So it is not an issue, did Rauden get torched. So he is probably still alive. I'm still alive. Ani is still alive. It's three months till her fifteenth birthday.

I finally sneaked out at night while Ani's sleeping, triked to the Oakland Gardens floaters, and got through to the Farm. Rauden says don't come. Wait till things calm down out here, it is not safe.

It's already getting warm when Ani comes home with a Note, show up for special Conference in the office Friday. Well when I make it to the office Friday, I'm not the only Parent there. It turns out eight kids, including Ani and Narj Oonnoony, also Walker Lopes, Dennis Oh, Sophi something, Joe something, and Jaraine and Murry Khan escaped from the school and went all the way to Francis Lewis Park, where they were going to take a boat ride with Narj Oonnoony's uncle in Powell's Cove!

I must of had an Episode, because I woke on the floor. Somebody gives me water. Everyone else is talking about what is wrong with Bayside school. Some Parents are going to pull their kids out. Others are considering Armory Prep. In Armory Prep, the kids are not running away. They really make those kids do what they say. One mother thinks they are even locked up. Another says, I would never send my daughter to Armory, it is practically a reform school, but the first one says, well at least they are not having unprotected sex. Then I'm on the floor again but no one even cares so I just get my own water but am still shaky for the Conference, with the kids all squinting, and the Parents furious and dragging their kids away, because they got Probation, and when I find out what that is, I drag Ani down the stairs too and throw her in the trike. She's going, "Ma! Everyone saw!" And I should care because!?

I just trike us home as fast as I could, drag her through the courtyard, and the minute we are in the door I yank her jeans down and tear the panties off.

"Ma!" She is standing in the door with her jeans at her feet.

I sniff the panties hard.

"*Ma.*" She's pulling up her jeans and crying.

I'm pretty sure it is not unprotected sex.

She just sits down in the door. "I don't want to go to school!"

"YOU HAVE TO GO TO SCHOOL!" I am so mad! I'm going to make her regret the day she was born.

Which I'm pretty sure she already does.

What happens now is, she says something she never said before. "Or what?" Then she stands up.

She is almost as big as me.

I'm going to knock her to kingdom come. I pull myself taller. I have the extra inch.

"Or what?"

Maybe a half.

And she leans up really close. "*Or what?*" Like, make me.

I don't even know if I could.
I broke the tabletop.
Now we're both crying. We liked the tabletop.
I put her in Armory Prep.

viii

Now, maybe some of you are thinking, why did I do this cruel thing? Why did I make her leave that school where at least some-one will sit with her? When I remember what I did, I wish I could take it back. I almost wished it even then. I just want my daughter to be safe. It's really hard to be a good mother. Maybe you will get that. Maybe your own mother will get that. Maybe it is not my fault that I cannot work the system—it is the system's fault. The system does not work.

Well, believe me, I'm not saying that it does. I'm pretty sure it doesn't. I don't know if it ever did. I'm just saying, if it worked, there is some kids who would never of been born.

Maybe even you.

But I'm getting ahead of myself.

The bad part of Armory is, it is so far away—practically Yonkers, inside what used to be some Armory, whatever that even is, way up in the Bronx. I miss her so much I could hardly stand it. I really, really miss her.

But I work really, really hard. I don't have travel Aide to pay for, let alone those top dollar ESG Partials, but there are still fees, even if the fees is token, like Ms. Chaffee said, and there are new expenses. With Ani so far off I need money for a Reader or Mobile. Lorena Hutz lets me use her personal Board for emer-gency contact, but not all my clients have one. And you can be sure there is no Board or even Signal at the garden apartments.

With the sleepaway thing, I am generally not even at home. I'm mainly working all the time.

That is the good part about sleepaway, I could work all the time. I sometimes work nights. I paid off what I owe and am starting to save. Maybe I could go up to the Farm. It's a long time since I even heard a message back from Rauden.

On Monday morning, a cuchivan picks the Armory girls up near their Zone. It brings them back Friday night.

When she climbs off this cuchi by Alley Park, I'm waiting with the trike, very good, how was school, but to tell the truth I could see by how she looks it's not going to work. She doesn't say anything. She just goes in her room. She doesn't walk any direction at all. Fifteen years and change.

Still alive.

But not so you would know.

At Armory, we don't have to worry who sits with her. They sit where they are told, and if they don't, they make them stand up all the time, and if they don't, they are expelled.

She hates that school.

They all hate that school, all the girls. They get scared. One girl is so scared, she bit everybody. They all have to have tests, did they get something from her. This latest Wave of lesser flus has everyone Alert.

I tell Ani, "Don't worry, you won't get anything." But I never like to go too far with that, or who knows where it will end up?

"Hello? I got bit!" Then she holds up her hand, bit. It even has the pink mark on it. It is the same hand where the flea thing happened. So Ani goes, "*Again!*" Then she goes in her room and pretty much stays there until I bring her to Alley Park Monday morning and say, "I'm going to do extra work. I'm going to bring in enough to pay Partial and put you in a better school— better than Migan's school."

She just gives me a look, like that is really going to happen. Then she gets on the Armory van and off she goes.

I still can't get through to Rauden. I am really suspicious he put a jam up on his system.

Summer is over. She came home with a Note saying she must be more careful with her swipe. She was caught trying to destroy it with some scissors in Art.

Here we go again. What is it with the swipe?

At first she wouldn't say but finally it comes out. After the biting thing, the tests came back and when they checked hers against spit code it came up she was twelve years old and lives in Bucharest.

I just tell her it is an anomaly.

But as soon as she went off on the Monday van, I rushed to the City Line hole early for my job and sneak into the public Board they have there that reads pure code. I run my own pure code to see what happens. It says I'm twelve years old and live in Bucharest.

I wipe the reading out with my regular swipe ID, take a walk, and try again.

It says I'm twelve years old and live in Grozny.

I wipe that out with my regular swipe, take a walk, and try again. This time it doesn't say anything. It's just access denied.

The cheap Reader I already got from working overtime? I try to reach Rauden on it, while I am up scrubbing Mrs. Arular's Dome. That doesn't work. To kill time I am fiddling with Search and put in Bucharest.

I just fix it with Mrs. Arular to get the rest of the day off so I could go to the Farm right away.

I head for the Bronx, get lucky with a sailbus, MagLev/bridge/local hybro/farmer vehicle all the way to the Farm. I'm not even giving Rauden the heads up. I'm suspicious if I let him know I'm coming, he is going to slip away—and that's if I even managed to get through.

"I!" Rauden says, when I finally get up the dirt road where leaves is falling from the trees and he finally opens the door. He looks a little different but it's so long since I saw him, I honestly don't know what was different, Rauden or me. His hair is totally gray. His face is white, white, white. "This *is* a surprise."

I just ignore how he looks and go, "As far as I could tell, to reach you these days, R? Surprise is the only way I even had. Come on." I just headed back to the Box Room without even saying hi. "How's your pure code software working these days?"

He is slow on the uptake but shows me where the slides are for the scanner, and it didn't work at first but after an hour or so I got Bucharest. "Want to see a map?" I said.

So he's just sitting there. Man! He is tired.

"R, wake up. It worked."

Then he's putting his head in his hands like he used to.

"R! It's the Santa Sofya lot, has to be." I pull up my Reader beside him and show him the map on the screen. "Look how close it is. Maybe they have tanks there too or better virgins or Compatibility, all I know is, we got a track record. R! I know we could be in trouble but we could make a killing here. It goddamn worked!"

He is just looking around while I am pitching. Look how many new Waves of Epi there is overseas. There are serious Epis in some of those overseas Stans and even in other places, Uruguay, Uganda, whatever, and, man, with the Santa Sofya lot track record, we could really move viables!

Finally he gets himself together. "Let's talk, I."

Come on! What is there to discuss?

"Sit down, I." And he brings me to the kitchen, where there are some chairs near the window.

I'm going, "R, please. Let's move some viables."

Maybe it's because he is right at the window, with light right on him, I notice he really is looking different. Like, his gray hair is so thin. His skin is thin too. You could almost see through it when he finally sits on a chair and faces me.

I go, "What?"

He just holds his hands up. They are swollen.

"*What?*"

They are shaking bad. His neck shakes too. His whole self is shaking. I never saw him shake like this before. Finally he says, "I can't do it any more." He just keeps his hands in the air, shaking. "I just can't do the work."

I'm staring at the hands, and then it hits me. Boom.

So that's what Henry meant Rauden should tell me.

He just starts to cry.

"Since when?"

He's just crying. Oh, come on, R.

"*Since when, R?*"

What is this? He's like he's thirteen years old. Everyone I know is crying.

"The birthday was the last time that it worked."

I'm just sitting there.

"I can hardly even take a tissue sample, let alone somatic fucking nuclear Transfer."

"The tenth birthday? R! That's more than five years!"

"I'm sorry, I."

So then I'm like, "I can't believe you never told me. You let me make my plans around the sales."

"I'm so sorry, I."

So. I'm like, I'm almost going to have another Episode, breathe deep. Whoa. "So what about Henry? Henry could do it."

He shook his head. "Henry doesn't have the hands for it. He never did. You saw how Dookie turned out."

"So Lucas could."

He shook his head.

"Mariah Delize." I don't even know why I said it.

Neither did he. "I'm really sorry, I. It's over."

So we're both just sitting there in the kitchen, on chairs.

"I can't believe you never told me."

So what is going to happen with Armory Prep? She hates it. She is going to be expelled again. She's going to end up selling hardy product on the Mound—teeth, nails, piss. The next thing I knew, I hit the roof.

"You fucking show me how to do it."

He puts his head in his hands.

"She hates her school! She needs the Education! Maybe I could find her a school where she is safe but happy too—a really good school—but I need more bucks! We have a track record! We could do this! You fucking show me now!"

After a while he looks up and says, "I suppose it could work."

"It goddamn will work!"

He seemed to get a little energy here, goes off to the sink and turns the taps on, always a good sign. He comes back dripping wet and says, "You have to do what I say, though. Exactly what I say."

I don't even know what he means. "What else would I do?"

"Like I even know," he says, and laughs. It is a long time since I saw him laugh like that. Pretty soon I'm laughing too.

The room where Rauden used to do nuclear Transfer is where it used to be, down those three steps, but it is a real mess. He hasn't even done SCNT for livestock all this time, he is in such bad shape. I get out mops and water and, hello? I am the expert here.

We take a break, and I walk around outside, where leaves are falling from some trees on those old green steps we sat on that first time, so long ago. When I came back in, he already went hunting in the freezers and got four cryoPaks. We go to the room. We suit up.

This time I will be in the room and he will talk me through it by mic from the viewing closet after he sets things up first. The ova is already out of the Paks, in dishes. He quik-thawed them and put one in the machine with a viewing scope and a gizmo to work the, you know, stick. You don't need steady hands just to thaw and set things up. So that part he could do. Then he goes out and I go in and he shuts the door. I'm in the room alone, in the semi-dark, on the chair with wheels he used to sit on to do this, himself.

He's already in the little viewing closet, on the stool, gets the mic to work, which takes a little doing. He tells me where everything is. Then I hear him say, "Sit tight."

So I sit tight. I guess he sits tight too. We are face to face through the glass, and his eyes are closed.

"When I give the word," he goes, "gently poke the egg with the stick. NOW!"

I poked the egg.

It didn't work.

"Harder! But gently. Poke it harder!"

I poked it harder. But gently.

"Harder!"

This time I poked it really hard. But gentle too. It worked! The stick poked through the outside circle to the inside circle. After that, it's easy to make the stuff inside skoosh up the stick, then do it with the, you know, somatic nucleus thing, and finally skoosh that back in.

It worked!

I almost forgot about the shock. But Rauden forgot nothing and told me what to do. It was easy.

We didn't have Sonny Rollins later, nothing. We just do the work. We don't sit on the steps and have a cigarette. When it's over, we don't sit around at all, we have to race to get me to my ride to the last MagLev so I could get to my cleaning job early the next morning. He's going to let me know if it works, and if it works, I'm coming up next week to do it again. I make it to the Mag just in time. But there is the usual Bronx problem and by then it is the middle of the night and by the time I make it through the City Line hole it's morning and I'm late to the early job, I'm fired. I needed the work. Why did I do this. I'm never doing this again.

But when I head home from the afternoon job I didn't lose, when I get back to the empty garden apartments, when I walk in our empty unit and start missing Ani really bad, I start to think something else.

Did it work?

It's all I can think. Did it work?

It did work.

It worked. It worked.

For three of them. One didn't make it.

It's like how I felt when Rini Jaffur let me know it worked, the very first time, so long ago. It's like I'm floating.

And maybe you're thinking, hello? I just committed a crime against nature with my own hands so my daughter could go to a really good school. Doesn't it bother me at all?

I'm not saying that it didn't. I'm not saying that it did.

I'm just saying I wanted to do it again. It was all I could think about. Suit up, go in the room, sit, get the stick ready to poke, NOW! Skoosh! I just wanted to do it again. And again.

And again.

6 THE HERITAGE

THE WAY I DO THE WORK—WELL, FIRST OF ALL, I got to fix my schedule of Nassau County jobs. It's better if I could work at the Farm say three days straight on a weekday while Ani is at school and time that around a Harvest—then I don't need two separate trips, but it is a problem because you time Harvest from your period, and mine is not that regular these days, and neither are the roads—with the latest flu Alerts, some road is always caution-taped off. You never know how long a trip is going to take. Some say this latest one will be as bad as Luzon Second.

Meanwhile, Rauden is working on sales. You do not need a steady hand for that. He lost his old contacts so he got to advertise. We check out other hardy or Life product sites. People was not afraid to go public now—you could even offer viables as such if you watch your language. They sometimes will post the Donor's picture, and I notice some Donors that bill themself hardy are missing teeth. So I'm not the only hardy who had sold teeth. I think I am the only one pitching hardy viables this pure, because what are the chances anyone but us cloned the Original? Even so, we aren't going to risk going public with that. A quiet One on One with a client or broker, we could go into more detail.

Some of them post a picture of a kid the Donor had, supposedly—an Example, how the kid could turn out.

I am really not putting Ani up there.

Henry puts up a picture of me. The main thing is to make the contact with the client, then feel out the situation. There could be a problem with a picture of Ani anyhow, because she is starting to look so much like me, that could raise questions we rather avoid until we are sure who we are dealing with. Unlicensed Life sales are not such an issue these days because everyone's doing it, ethical or not, especially overseas. But clones are always going to bother someone. I mean Ani doesn't look exactly like me. She is narrow like me but not as narrow so, ok, the eyes? Because the face is not so narrow as mine it stretches the eyes so they are not so close and beady like mine, also she is smooth generally. I am not smooth. The hands are, you know, familiar but smooth. The hair, I don't know how my own hair looked when I was fifteen years old. Hers sticks out. Mine is more flat, even when I fluff it. And the knees? I know she is skinnier than me, but where does she get those knees? And, come on, the teeth. That is a difference right there.

I'm not posting her up there though.

Even with the new lesser flus locally, the big sales in hardy product go on at auctions overseas, like Berlin or Istanbul, and that is out of the question because of the fare, but there are some new alternatives. Like they are working out a shipping route to Reykjavik and setting up an auction there. It turns out that auction is serviced by floating markets, they call them Lifeboats. It is like a convention of brokers on boats. It would not be hard for me to go on one of these Lifeboats with our product. To tell the truth, I am the only one of us who could, because Rauden is shaky, Janet Delize is, you know, she's Janet Delize so that is not going to work, and, what are we, going to hire our own broker?

To prepare me for the floating market, they have to fix me up with lipstick and an outfit like when I first met Rini Jaffur, but don't worry about the teeth, that is practically a Proof, itself. I was a little nervous getting to the Lifeboat, because it doesn't dock in Queens. I have to get all the way to Red Hook with the cryoPaks in a carrier, then ride some little paddleboat out to sea—by now it's November, man, the wind is off the charts—and then the way the crew is looking at the Paks, I have to look right back at them like, you try to take this Life away, I will goddamn take yours with it. Once I'm on the Lifeboat though, it all went great. It was full of brokers. I show my old Proofs and Ani's Proofs from the Mumbai years. The Proofs have details about Ani's age when she was in quarantine, and that makes it all seem more bona fide. Some brokers carry the portaLens, that could check the viables, be sure they are alive. They are alive. Some are asking for a picture of how the kid could look, but no way, Jose. One of these guys, I think I could tell him the truth. I mean, they are all shady but you never know if one of them is going to turn you in. But this guy seems like, I don't know, like he has something in common with Rini Jaffur? You know, the open mind.

I throw in the cryoPak carrier as a Bonus and cut a deal with this guy. They drop me off near some beach but I got no time to look around. I just make my way around a bunch of burnt-out blocks till I find a shaw and take it to the nearest pod connection—I'm not messing around with any sailbus, especially what a mess it is out here. It took a while before I got Signal to tell Rauden I am still alive. And you can be sure Rauden is like, thank God, thank God. This guy! He worries all the time.

But this was a great trip, and this broker is going to give us more business. Next time I could just meet him at the pier at Boston where the Lifeboat docks before it heads to Reykjavik, and if this lot gets a good price in Reykjavik, there will be a Bonus. So I am going to Boston next! See what's left of Boston!

We have to put the first payment back into Project expenses but the next time we will clear a profit. Next time, I will also bring fresh-scraped endometrial product to sweeten the deal. For now I still need some other paying work to cover my regular expenses. Then I have new expenses because I have to keep upgrading the new Reader so Armory could reach me in more locations in case of emergency—these days who knows where I'm going to be. So I have to take extra cleaning to cover that. That cuts into my worktime upstate. I also do the oldies' chores plus a little local deCon and I will tell you by the time Ani gets off the Armory van Fridays, I was pretty tired. I still tried to be upbeat.

"Ani, my new income is almost coming through. Just wait a little more. I promise we will get you out of Armory. I will put you in a really good school—better than East Side Girls."

She said, "If you put me in one more really good school, I promise I will hate it too." She just went into her room and stayed there pretty much till Monday morning, when I took her by shaw to the van, put her on it, and waited till I saw it go off to the bridge to the Bronx. Then I went over the same bridge, made my way to the Yonkers MagLev, crossed by bridge at Beacon, and if Rauden can't pick me up in Newburgh, I must wait for the hybro, though I could sometimes get a lift part of the way to the Farm. I hardly even say hi when I get there. I just suit up and go straight to work.

I think about the difference between this time and the times before, when Rauden did the work. I'm not saying it wasn't exciting too, when Rauden did it. I always wanted to see what happened. But this time, I was, I don't know. Not proud, exactly. It's like, satisfied.

The first time, with the Madhur group, when I didn't know anything, it was interesting because I didn't know anything. But this time around, it was more interesting, because I did.

Like I am sitting in the room waiting for Rauden to say NOW from the closet. And I start to think I forgot everything, this will not work. It's like I never did it before. Then he says NOW. And I remember—right! It's always like I never did it before. To tell the truth, I didn't. Not exactly. It's different every time.

Sometimes when Rauden talks me through it from the closet, that thing he does, when he gets so still, before he goes NOW! I sometimes got still too. Totally still. I even shut my eyes. Then boom! I am poking the stick *exactly* when he says NOW! I don't know how I knew.

Once he had to go answer the Alert just when we are about to start? I did it all myself. I didn't even need him coaching me. I got good numbers too. I liked it more when he's there, though. It was more interesting.

I never told Ani that. That I found it interesting. Well, I hardly really told her anything. It's true I needed the income and even true I liked doing a good deed for the Parents who were going to get children who would stay alive—well, it was good for the kids too, because they will *be* alive. I liked that it was a Project. I liked that with Ani too. I never told her that. I tell you that.

What I'm saying is, I loved Ani. That doesn't mean I don't enjoy the work. I loved Ani, I enjoyed the work. Sometimes I think I even loved the work. Rauden did too.

At Armory, they do some serious follow up on those blood checks. They send the labwork way out to a Westchester County lab that is so SOTA, they figure out she is a Creedmoor hardy.

She is fifteen years, seven months old! She doesn't want to be a Creedmoor hardy. None of the other girls are Creedmoor hardies.

"Ani! You should be proud!" We're walking home from the Friday dropoff. "Do you know what people pay for product as hardy as that? You're even hardier than a Creedmoor hardy. You are a Sylvain hardy. Ani, with all this hardy in your file, what are the chances you could not be a Tech?"

Well that didn't work. She didn't say anything all the way home. But when we got inside, she just says, "Who was my Dad?"

I said I didn't know.

"You just bought his product without even meeting him?"

I said I would tell her another time. Go to bed.

And when she did, I just locked the front door to keep her safe, then triked up to the Little Neck Board to check in on the latest viables, see what happened to the ones that worked. They're still alive. Then I triked home, tiptoed to her room, and checked if she is still alive.

She's still alive.

And by the way, at Armory Prep? She does not do her work.

All in all, I got 100 viables. That's including multiples Rauden showed me how to make with the sound-wave process, so you get four from one. Believe me, I didn't have 100 eggs, even with the solos on ice. In fact the Harvest is way low. Maybe they stimulated me too much all those years. I have to get on Rauden's case, up the goddamn dose, R. But he's afraid this ovary is going to break like the other one did.

We don't know much about what's going to happen after the sale. I think sometimes the brokers have a contact for a Host. Maybe the Parent sets it up. Rauden says somebody has to of figured out how to make better tanks, or maybe they got Compatibility under control and human Hosts could work. Something did work in Santa Sofya and Grozny. Anyhow, I didn't have to worry, would they change their mind like Rini Jaffur, and give the kid back to me. It just was a whole different marketing structure. The broker brings the viables to the Life auction in cryoPaks, then they go somewhere else to gestate. It could be pretty far away. Wherever it is, I'm two or even three or more steps from the Parents. If the Parents change their mind, that's their problem.

Don't take this the wrong way. At this point in my life, I'm just not in any position to bring up another child. It was just a different time.

When Ani comes home for her weekend, I am in a good mood but she is so quiet I am like, oh, look, I found a new tabletop, hey, they put a food cart on the golf course, whatever. She doesn't say anything. Something seems different about her. Like, she does not even eat. She does not watch the TV if it works. In the mornings, I could hardly even get her out of bed. Now I really start to worry. This is not going to work. I have to find a new school ASAP. Lorena Hutz says there is a really good regular school nearby in Nassau County, we could use her address. It is not even that far. Like, Nassau County, City Line northeast, two different worlds but we could walk there. Even if their system is a little SOTA, I could probably work my way around it. But I am worried if we could sneak in so easy, how safe could it be?

I finally got Lore! She was still alive. They all are. Migan already transferred to another school, Country Day, in Connecticut. They all moved up there so Migan does not have to do sleepaway. Lore tells me who to contact and I find out this new school is a unique educational Opportunity. They do not even have walls because the school is so far in the middle of nowhere you don't have to worry is your kid safe—in fact Lore says Ani's safer there than my own neighborhood, from vigilantes anyhow. Ani would have to do sleepaway even on weekends but think of all the extra work I could get done at the Farm.

The person at Country Day sets me up for Interview for next month and says send them a link to Ani's files. I'm not going to tell Ani yet. I'm going to keep it a surprise. If I make some sales in the next weeks plus my regular cleaning, by the time she would start school, I could have enough saved for some kind of downpayment. With the extra hours of work from her being gone, my income could practically triple—the school investment will practically pay for itself. I finally persuade Rauden to megadose, because I really got no time to spare.

If I double up on my cleaning to clear my schedule for five days of hard work at the Farm, I will go to the Boston Life dropoff with a really big load of cryoPaks and do the sales there. I timed this very close. I give myself the extra shot early Monday before Ani wakes up, and by the time she gets up I am so puffed and ready to burst. I could hardly wait to see her on the van at seven Monday morning and get on my way. It's not that I don't miss her. I'm just ready to burst.

As soon as I wake up on the Newburgh OBGYN's RV table, I know something went wrong.

The OBGYN is looking at me, and Rauden is looking at me too.

I ask, how many eggs?

"For God's sake, I," he says.

Oh, man. Bandages and blood. I try to sit up.

"Will you fucking stay down. We could of lost the whole shebang."

That means they didn't. So I could still have eggs.

Rauden is shaking his head. "I can't believe I let you talk me into the megadose, with your history."

Shit! I've been off Signal for hours. Mrs. Ridenhour is buzzing me. I never told her I couldn't scrub her Dome. Shit! Rauden wants me to rest but I need to take this job. Country Day is buzzing me. I get dressed fast and say you are right, R. I'm going home to rest, I will come back later in the week to start the viables at the Farm. He really doesn't want me to take the long trip back to Queens, but how could he stop me?

I nap on the hybro from the bridge. I am a little dizzy so I stop in Yonkers at a Beverage Locker near one of those shady operations that does the Change. Then I buzz Country Day. They are really nice. They say they wouldn't bother me but they are having a problem with my daughter's files. I go, let me look into this but I'm so groggy, I forget. I just take a shaw back to

Queens, head through the hole to Nassau County and though Mrs. Ridenhour went ballistic, she accepts my story that Ani had an emergency. So I scrub her Dome in the dark and drag myself home and man, I conked out. Next morning early I'm heading back upstate by the Bronx. Oh shit. I forgot to follow up with Country Day. I reach them from Yonkers. So I say, oh, sorry, and they say not a problem, our system is so SOTA we got her files only now it is saying she is twelve years old. Shit! They got Grozny. I do some hanky pank with manual override and blow the system out, message back and say, I do not understand what happened, they go, not a problem, our system is so SOTA we called her files up again only now it is saying she is thirty-five years old. I go, oh, must be some sort of anomaly. They go, no, we don't think so. It looks more like it read her as you. So I go, oh, I accidentally put my own swipe in. Then I just blow the system out again.

Shit! Someone is buzzing me. I'm too busy to see who it is. I have to get back to Country Day. Oh, sorry, I tell Country Day. The systems are such a mess here.

They say, not a problem only it looks like you are sisters. This is intriguing, what do you know about your own origins? Can you find a pure code Reader and we will try to sort this out? Can you find a spit code Reader?

To tell the truth, I am not that far from Wappingers Falls, which is spit code central as well as they run every kind of sleazy operation but Country Day does not know where I am so I play for time and say, yes, I will try to find a spit code scanner but, you know, and I will tell you I was pulling the answers out of the air, in Diversity neighborhoods like ours, the scanners is few and far between, so it could be tomorrow before I bring it off.

They go, we really understand, and by the way, we are ready to offer better than Partial for the right Diversity.

So I'm like, great.

So I'm going up to Wappingers Falls and use their spit code Readers. Maybe I can put a jam on my ID.

Country Day says, oh, and do not worry about anomalies. Our system is so SOTA, we will be sure to check for anomalies, even in the telomeres. That should clear things up.

Ok. Like, oh! Great! Clear things up. How special is that!

They say, ok! We will look forward to reviewing your codes! We just want to make sure you're who you think you are. For your own sake.

I'm sitting there, still dizzy, in the Board shelter of Wappingers Falls, and then it hits me, this isn't going to work. Any jam I put on, they are so SOTA, they can knock it off. If they was just coming up with Grozny or Bucharest, I guess I could say well I bought her product from some broker who also made over-seas sales, from multiples. But if my own ID is involved, they're going to get suspicious. And this telomere business, how can that be good?

So that's it for Country Day. They welcome unique kids but are they honestly giving Aid to a crime against nature? What will the other Parents think? With fees high as these Parents must pay, they are probably going to expect Ethics too.

I'm just sitting there in Wappingers Falls drinking my Beverage, looking at all the sleazy operations, wondering what I am going to do goddamn now, and then it hits me. I will get the Change.

I'm almost out of eggs anyhow, so as far as losing hardy egg sales, not an issue. Rauden has a lot of my soma on ice, enough to mix with the eggs still in storage.

While I'm at it, I could even wipe my files out, the ones that come up from my own swipe ID. So my own history will be gone.

Now that I think of it, if I am changing my genes, should Rauden scrape some extra soma? It is a long time since I left soma. Maybe I better scoot across the river and leave extra at the Farm. There is still time to get it done today. Then come back and do the Change in Wappingers Falls. Sleep in the Terminal and go back to the Farm Wednesday morning to finish doing the SCNT with whatever's on ice.

I don't even know why I never thought of this before. One of us has to be someone else. I always thought that should be her. It could be me. The Grozny business we could talk our way out of, though it is always going to be an issue. But between Ani and me? As far as who is going to be gene for gene the original me? Let her be the only one.

ii

When I let myself in at the Farm, Rauden is lying on the sofa in front, in a bathrobe. It is a gray day and the light is funny. He just sat up fast. "What happened, I?" Man, he is looking white.

I said, "Nothing, it is all good. I just had a little time between Interviews and thought I'd come back and leave some soma."

He just blinked. Remember he never slept? Now he sleeps too much, and when he woke up could hardly do anything.

"What Interview?" he says.

"I have an appointment. I only have time to scrape the breast."

So he has stood up. "What Interview?"

I said, "You can't have too much soma."

He's looking at me funny. He heads to the kitchen to boil a Beverage, and I go with him.

"I do not have time to scrape for endometrial product, but for soma, the breast tissue would work."

"I, we have plenty of soma. What's going on here?"

I didn't say anything. I just sit down on a chair because I am still a little tired from the Harvest and running around.

"Where is this Interview?"

I said I didn't know.

Then all at once he got very quiet. "*Where is this Interview?*"

I said I didn't know.

There was two chairs in the kitchen, and he just sat down on the other one, hard. "Oh, my God. You're doing the Change."

Whatever.

"Jesus, I. What's wrong with you?"

I said, "Oh, R, what is the big deal? The ovary is used up anyhow. I mean, take extra soma just in case, but once I stop giving eggs, it's over."

"I." He is rubbing his eyes, to think. "*I!* Listen, I." He is rubbing his whole head. Then he looks up. "What are they paying? I'll match it. Whatever it is. I'll pull something together. It will take a few days, but—"

"I'm not getting anything."

So he's blinking.

"It is for Country Day."

"For?"

"It is the Heritage check for the new school. Otherwise, when they do the Heritage check, they're going to notice something fishy. The really good school has SOTA systems. They are going to figure us out."

So he is still confused.

"They are so goddamn SOTA, R. I can't crash their system. They're going to figure out we are gene for gene the same, but a different age. R! They are doing telomere checks."

He really looked confused now. His eyes are going back and forth. Then he got it. "You amaze me, I," he goes and laughs. "Look, can't you find a different school?"

"We ran out of really good schools, R. Anyhow, the systems in the really good schools is all getting SOTA. I mean, I guess the really experimental school could be open minded and accept her as some new kind of Diversity, but then Ani has to know."

So he is thinking hard. He almost speaks, then doesn't. Then he does speak. "Well tell her, then, if that's all it's about. She's old enough."

I shook my head. "I don't want her to know."

He stops and is going to speak. Then he looks at me. "I," he goes. "Listen to me." Then he goes really soft, like that would help me hear, "*Listen to me.* These guys who do the Change are a whole other can of beans than me."

I'm running out of time here. I just want him to start with the soma.

"Listen to me, I." He grabs my wrist. "These guys don't know what they are dealing with."

Whatever.

"I, you have no idea what might happen."

"R! If it doesn't work, I will try to get it done somewhere else."

"I! For God's sake, I. I'm worried that it *will* work."

I finally sit down. I'm not having an Episode or anything. I'm just tired. "R. Come on. We did enough. It's not like we want to take over the world."

He just sat there blinking. Then he looks up at me. "Dear God, I. What are you thinking? You think it's about sales? I, this is not about sales."

What I'm thinking, I will never get back to Wappingers Falls in time.

He is just going on and on and on. "I, this is risky. You have no idea. We know you are a hardy, I. But nobody ever figured out how it worked. If these bozos tweak you the wrong way, you won't be a hardy any more. You could die."

Like I am really going to die.

"I! For God's sake!" He's pulling his own hair. "This is dangerous!"

Like I never did anything dangerous before.

"*Will you fucking listen to me!* We don't even know how it's going to affect the healing process. You're still bleeding from the last Harvest. You want to get scraped for soma now then hop across the river and get Changed? You could have open wounds for the rest of your life."

"So don't scrape," I said. I was too tired to keep arguing. "Use the old soma."

"You're not getting this, I." He is almost going to cry.

"Ok, R. If you really want endometrial, go ahead. But you will have to do it yourself. Just do it fast. I would throw it in for free."

So now he does cry. Here we go again. "You think this is all about the money! Obviously there were always ethical issues—the Life Industry is full of ethical issues, even without our contributions to the messy ethics of the goddamn thing.

"But, I. What we're talking about now, it's your *life*. I'm not talking about genes, or viables, or telomeres—which actually are a bit of a problem—or even the goddamn tanks we grew them in. I mean, I!" He is like, splish splash, down his face, through his beard. "How does someone get to be like you? I'm not talking about Mumbai or whatever goddamn pathogen had the misfortune to penetrate your goddamn body. I don't mean Sealed Room goddamn tests. I mean, I! I'm talking *personally* here. The things that you survived—dear God, you were just a child! And OF COURSE I KNOW ABOUT THE CURES." He's crying so hard he starts to wheeze. "Do you think I'm stupid?"

I didn't say that.

"You're not stupid, yourself. How else did you manage to stay alive with what you've been through? Some New Life idiot hacks your reproductive system to shreds, and what were you, sixteen?"

Fifteen.

"And then, after all that—dear God!" He's mopping his cheeks with his bathrobe collar. "You still like to see what happens.

"What I'm saying is, if there are others remotely like you," he's wringing the collar with his hands, "bring 'em on! But—well, I'm hardly a world traveler," he's wiping his hands on the robe, "but," he has to stop and wheeze before he finished, "you're certainly the only one like you *I*'ve seen. You're the most amazing person I've ever met!"

Then he goes out of the room and I'm just like, what is this?

When he comes back he's wearing regular clothes and looks pretty clean. I guess he wiped himself off. He looks me in the eye and says, "I might be a little out of my depth here, and ethically, I have my limits. But, I—if you end up dying just so Ani gets into the right school, that would seem a bit unethical, even for me."

So, maybe more of Rini rubbed off on me than I knew, as environmental factor. When Rauden put it that way, I changed my mind.

Maybe I *am* a bad mother. I mean, nobody's that good a mother if they're dead. But even if they are, as far as who had a life, Ani wasn't the only one. I had a life too.

All I'm saying is, I changed my mind, and ok, if I had character, maybe I would not change my mind. Or maybe I would. I'm not exactly the world expert, what is character. All I'm saying is, if I did the Change and lost the hardy genes, when the next Epi came, who knows? I could of got sick and died. The viables that are in the freezers would still be born, because they are already made, but let's just say I ever wanted to find those viables and tell them what happened. Who I am or who they are. If I did the Change and died, I never would.

Maybe they don't care. Or maybe they rather not know. All I'm saying is, I have a life too. I have a Heritage too. I want someone to know what it is.

I really felt different after Rauden said what he said. I felt so different I just wanted to take a walk outside. I don't know why! But it's cold and he's already shivering, so I just took a walk inside. I walked to the back of the Quonset. Rauden walked with me, wheezing, till I said, "R? Remember when you first did the work with my product, you used to run conventional IVF with my eggs and sperm from Sylvain's hardy, just to see what happened? Did you ever do it with, you know, yours?"

He didn't say anything. He just looked down at his socks.

"You never did it, right?"

He just looks at his socks, in the sandals.

"R. Come on. What? I could handle this."

He just says, "It didn't work."

So when I heard that—because it meant he wanted it to work—I don't know how to explain this. It's like, inside my head is the sound the MagLev track makes? Hum!

All this time, we are both walking. It is a little stupid. But we are just walking the Quonset, back and forth. By now we reached the green light hoo-ha and turned to walk up front.

"When?" I said.

"A few times."

"More than once?" Come on, I. Hello? That is what a few times means. Hum! "When was the first?"

"After the Buffalo series, when you went to Queens and declined to come back and do the work." He is hanging his head.

That far back! Hum! "You mixed my egg and your sperm, in a dish?"

He is whispering, "It didn't work."

We're at the front and are turning around to walk to the back again. "And were there other times? Other times you tried?"

So he is stopping to check a doorknob. Like that is so important. "I also did it after you had the Episode. From the Harvest after the birthday party."

"The tenth birthday? But, R. There was only four eggs," I said. "You used up one of four?"

"Two." Oh, boy, he's smiling now.

"*You used up half the Harvest?*"

"It didn't work." So he is almost giggling now.

I am like, oh! Didn't work! Tell me something I *don't* know. I was like, you used up half the Harvest? You knew it isn't going to work!

Then I guess I was laughing too. I thought it was pretty funny too.

I said, "And were there others you tried with? I mean other eggs from other Subjects, that you mixed with your sperm in a dish?"

He shook his head and smiled. "No, you're the only one."

"I guess no one had product as hardy as me."

So then he says, "It wasn't a hardy thing at all. I just liked doing it." Then he smiles again. "I missed you."

So when he said that, it is not even a MagLev track thing, it is like one of those antigravitational devices, next thing you know, it's going to push me to a tree, like Migan.

"I did use other male solos with other eggs of yours, from Sylvain's collection," he said, "but that never worked. I didn't use Henry's though. You probably wish I used Henry's. It might have worked with his."

I said, "You are the only one I would of wanted it to work with."

And to tell the truth, until I said it, I didn't even know that it was true.

"Show me how to do it, R. Come on. How much harder could it be than nuclear Transfer? I could do it right now, if you want to teach me," I said. "If you have any more sperm on ice."

He looks like he is near some antigravitational device, himself. "I might. Or I might be able to," he coughed, "produce some."

Remember airborne pathogen? We are like that. Remember hit the roof? At least the roof is there to stop us, if we are airborne now. We're like the goddamn MagLev, we do not touch ground.

So he is checking out the freezers when I notice for the first time that a message came to my Reader. Who knows when it came? I didn't check in all this time at the Farm.

It is some kind of hospital in the Bronx, and it sounds like they have Ani. Then they are breaking up.

Rauden is saying, what, and I tell him. So we're just standing there.

He says, what hospital.

I don't even know. I can't get through.

So we're just standing there. He says there could be Signal up the hill, where the corn grows in summer. We both are running up the hill, near the frozen corn fields, and try again. It doesn't work.

It is so cold up here, Rauden has a hard time breathing. "They did say she is still alive?"

I forgot to ask.

So we went further uphill to the top, where there is some kind of backup generator gizmo, and I get Signal. "Ask them." He is wheezing.

I ask them, "Is she still alive?"

It's hard to hear but sounds like she's still alive. I tell Rauden, "She's still alive."

So that's it for the IVF with Rauden's sperm.

We're already running back down for the truck. We just race all the way to the bridge. I don't even remember to tell him I'll be back to do the IVF. I don't even think about it till Yonkers.

I thought about it then. To tell the truth, I think about it now.

Then I forgot while I was running around the Bronx City Line, chasing down a shaw.

Then I'm in the hospital, trying to prove I'm Ani's Guardian. They won't even tell me if she's still alive before I prove it. They got some fancy ID filter I never saw before, and the Guardian part on my ID is not coming through. They won't even inform me, before the Guardian thing clears, she tried to jump off a bridge. I can't even follow this. On Monday morning, the Armory van broke down right on the bridge. She climbed out a window and tried to jump over the side.

By the way, she is expelled from Armory Prep. She is a danger to herself or others. I can't even see her till morning. They let me sleep on a chair out in the public room.

When I finally get into her room, she is out cold. They gave her a shot. They won't even tell me what it was. They are going to keep her one more day for Observation. So I go outside to call Rauden. But I can't get through.

When I'm back in the hospital, the Supervisor who cleared my Guardian thing went off shift. The new one has to start from scratch. Am I the Guardian? Am I myself? Am I qualified to make sure Ani is not a danger to herself?

When they finally let me take her, I'm so glad to see her awake, I'm almost jumping, but, I don't know if it's the drug or what, she just looks away. She will not talk the whole way home. And it is a long, long way. It is the usual problem of transportation in the Bronx, and some kind of ash is blowing in some kind of wind. The whole trip I am like, is she going to be a danger to herself? Is she going to jump off something? And all this time she doesn't say word one. I am almost falling asleep on my feet but I keep myself awake. I don't even let go of her hand. I try to keep myself awake by blabbing this, that. What kind of Process does she want for dinner? She doesn't say anything.

By the time we finally got to Queens, I was so worried I can't stop blabbing. What does she want for dinner? If the power works, what TV does she want to watch? She doesn't say anything. By now we're almost at Courtyard 2, and I'm like, please, let her say something, I will never leave her side again. I won't do IVF with Rauden's product. I won't do SCNT. I will even give up my cleaning jobs. Well I will tell you this. When she did say something I almost changed my mind. She said, "You're not my mother."

Whoa.

"You're my sister."

So what is this?

"The ID filter said you're my sister. The first Supervisor said so."

"Ani, you know I am your mother. I brought you up."

"Did I ask you to?"

We just have to get through the Courtyard 2 entrance and cross the courtyard in the dark and we will be home. There is still some wind and ash. "Ani. It is about the ID filter. It's not about us."

"My mother would not let them lock me up."

We just have a little more ways to go. "Ani, they never even reached me all day. They never let me through when I was even there because the code Reader would not let me through."

"My mother would not send me to this school to start."

"I will find you a better school. Country Day is not going to work—well, you don't know about that, but I will find you something else."

"Did I ask you to?" So we are in the middle of our courtyard, and it is dark and cold with some ash still falling. "You don't even know what is a good school. You don't even know the driver hurt me."

So this is news to me. "When?"

"He grabbed me really hard!" And she shows the bruise on her wrist, which I can't see in the dark.

At least she is talking at all. "When?"

"When I am trying to jump off the bridge."

So I am like Rauden was when I tried to explain the Country Day thing, I'm just trying to follow this. "I think he saved your life."

"DID I ASK HIM TO?" We're almost at our door, but she is stopping where she is. "I hate my life! I HATE MY LIFE!" Then she goes, "I hate you."

I just sat down on the steps in the dark. I didn't know what else to do, I'm just so tired and she is just going, "I hate you! I hate you! You send me to schools where no one will sit with me. I'm glad it isn't going to work with stupid Country Day!"

So it is just as well I didn't do the Change.

"I'm glad I am expelled from Armory stupid Prep! Why do you even find these stupid schools for me?"

I am so tired. "I just want you to have a better life."

"You don't know anything about my life."

"Ani, let us go inside."

She just keeps going on. "Whatever school you put me in, no one will sit with me. No one will sit with me anywhere. You don't know anything about anything! You don't even know who is my Dad!"

I really want to get inside. But she keeps standing in the courtyard in the dark, going on.

"No wonder I can't do anything! I got it from you! You can't do anything! You can't even pick me up on time! So don't tell me what to do. You don't know what to do, yourself. You don't know anything!"

I was just so tired.

"Anything!"

So tired. I been running for days. To the hospital, the Nassau County job, the Yonkers Board, the Farm. I been running for years. To the Transport Stops, all the trips to all the goddamn islands where you get the goddamn Passes, the MagLevs, the cuchis, the hybros, the goddamn Lifeboat. And these last four days? Let alone this one day, the hospital, the Country Day stuff, the Change stuff. Maybe that wasn't even why I said what I said now. Maybe it was all the things Rauden said, and the whole airborne thing, the hum, I don't know. I just know I told Ani, "You do not have a Dad."

Then she got really quiet.

"And I know why."

I don't know if I thought it was good for her or I was mad at her because she thinks I don't know anything. I don't know who I thought it was good for. I don't know if it is just, you know, from all the things that Rauden said, I finally got some self-esteem and do not want to lose it. I just know that I told her.

I don't even know why I told her. Maybe I was just too tired to make things up any more.

It is dark in the yard. It's getting darker. The ash had stopped. But we just stay there, on the steps, in the courtyard where she spent so much of her life. Now look. She hates that life. It's not so dark I can't see how her face looks. I wish it was that dark. I wish I didn't see it. I wish I didn't see how her face looks when she said, "So I *am* a clone."

"There's a lot of things you can call it," I told her. "You can call it what you want. I prefer human being."

iii

Now maybe you think this night here, and the next day that follows now, it is the worst time of my life. Well, I will tell you this. I wish it was.

She pretty much cried the rest of the night. She is shut up in her room.

I don't know if she even slept. At least we are home.

I just stayed in the living room the whole time, on the plaid sofa she bit, so long ago. I'm not going to go to any of my jobs. I'm afraid what she will do if she's alone.

She cried so long I go to her door and call her name. "Ani?"

She just cries.

I come back in a while, and try again.

She will not say anything. She just cries.

"Ani," I tell her. "When all is said and done, it's just another way to be born. It could happen to anyone."

I don't hear anything for a while. But then I hear her right up against the door. "Then why am I the only one I ever heard of, that it did?"

"You know what?" I'm saying this through the door. "I never figured that out. I'm sure there are others. They just didn't tell. Until they do, no one will know."

She is talking so soft I can't hear.

I have to say, "What?"

She yells, "WHY DIDN'T *YOU*?"

So I am, you know, rubbing my ears where she shouted that. "We could of been in so much trouble. People think terrible things about people who do what Rauden and I did."

"You could of told *me*," she said.

"You were a child, Ani. It was a really dangerous secret."

I just hear noises. Then I don't hear anything. Maybe she is going to sleep.

So I go back to the sofa and maybe twenty minutes later her door opens, she is in the hall and says, "Like it wasn't dangerous to go through the Astoria power plant and slip in the mud!"

"Ani." She still doesn't get it. "For us, it's not. We're Sylvain hardies, Ani. We don't get anything."

She just stops where she is, in the hall. She lifts her hand up where fleas bit her that time at the power plant. She looks at her hand a long time. Then she looks at my face. Then my hand. Then her hand. Then my face. Then she went back in her room and shut the door. She got it now.

Then I fell asleep and when I woke up, she is standing in the kitchenette in the dark, eating Process straight from the kit.

I go, "There is a spoon."

She goes, "Talking to yourself?" Then she went back in her room and shut the door.

At least she wasn't crying. At least not then.

So now I'm awake. "Ani, you know how twins work? Like Rauden and Henry? It's really like that." This is also through the door.

"So you are not my mother."

"Well! Ok. Not exactly like twins. It is my egg."

After a long time she says, "With nothing in it."

"Well! Mitochondria!"

It's even longer till she comes up with what she says next, which I'm pretty sure is, "So what?"

I guess I went to sleep again because next thing I know I'm on the sofa and she is standing there. "Why was I born?"

Whoa.

"Who was Rini Jaffur?"

Oh, shit.

"Why did you say she was the Host?"

So she remembered. "She was not the Host."

"You said she was."

"She wasn't."

"Why did you say she was?"

I said I didn't know. I was starting to think I should not of told her anything. Nothing at all.

Then I was thinking, or I should of told her sooner.

Then I was thinking, or later.

Then she goes back in her room and locks the door.

I go, "You know, you're not the only one you know who had the artificial Host. Itzhak also had the artificial Host."

She didn't remember Itzhtak. "Who was Rini Jaffur?"

"You don't know her."

"Why did you tell me she was the Host?"

I said, "She would of liked to be the Host. I would of too. It just didn't work. The tank was all that worked."

I don't know how many hours this took.

All I know, she is spending so much time in my face going, "WHO WAS RINI JAFFUR?" I finally just went, "She was the client."

That really stopped her. She sat down. "You weren't even the client?"

"Ani. The prices people charge for work like Rauden did— how could I ever pay?"

"So. Rini Jaffur bought me?"

"Well! No. I mean—she was the client."

She is going to cry again. "You didn't even buy me, yourself?"

"I was the Donor! It didn't work that way."

"How did it work?"

"I was selling solo eggs. Well, soma too. Anyhow, they paid *me*."

So she is crying again. I never heard anybody cry this much. "Why would anybody pay to make a baby like *you*?" She is sobbing and sobbing.

"It is the Sylvain hardy thing. People pay for that." Well, how it turned out later, I wished I didn't put that in her mind. But I didn't know that then. "It was a terrible time, Ani. Well, it still is. Rini Jaffur lost four daughters in one month. She was mad with grief. She just wanted one child who would stay alive."

Ani is sobbing, "So that is the reason I was born? So Rini Jaffur would have one child who would stay alive?"

It sounded bad. "Well not the only reason."

"What was the other reason? You needed work?"

"It was more than that."

"Oh. Rauden needed work too?"

"Ani, the money was just part of it. It doesn't prove anything. Come on, everyone needs to stay alive."

"Oh. I was born so everyone could stay alive?"

I'm running out of answers here.

"So I guess she was pretty disappointed, to get a child so much like," and she just points at me with her hand.

"Ani! She was not disappointed. She just changed her mind."

But she is looking at her hand.

Then she is looking at my hand.

She's doing that her/me/space thing everybody does. Then she makes a sound. She goes to the mirror and stares in. Then she puts that hand on her cheek. Then she scratches straight down like Rini Jaffur used to do, until the blood drips.

"Ani! No!"

Now she is running to her room and locking it again. She is hitting things and making noise. "I should never of been born!"

She calls out, "I don't even know if what I was even counts as being born."

I call out, "Well, a lot of people didn't even get that."

"I wish I was them! I wish I was anyone! Anyone but me!" And then she is really quiet. "Except the one in Grozny!"

So she figured it out.

But maybe Grozny is the only one she knows about. Maybe she doesn't know about the others. I'm pretty sure she doesn't know about them. I just didn't think I could tell her. I'm sorry if you wish I did. I just didn't think she could handle it. At least not then.

Because even now she made a sound so terrible I'm ready to break the door down, but she opens it herself, wearing a coat, and blood is dripping down both cheeks to the coat, and, I'm like, "Ani! Let me fix that."

"Don't you touch it! The blood is on my face so people could recognize the difference between us," she said. "Until I get the Change." And she is heading for the front door.

And I will tell you, I intervened then. "Ani!" I'm trying to grab her. "It is dangerous."

She is trying to pull away. "Let's just see what happens. Like you did with me!"

I have her by the arms. "Let me do the Change myself. I'll end up with the different code. It will work either way."

She goes, "Oh, talking to yourself?"

"Ani, stop."

She goes, "Ani, stop."

Now it's me making a noise.

She goes, "Ani, stop."

So we're just standing there, me making a noise and trying to hold her.

She pushes her face right close to me and goes, "Why did you tell me Rini Jaffur was the Host?" Then she pushed me so hard I fell back on the wall and while I'm trying to stand up she ran out the front door. By the time I get down to the courtyard she's already gone.

This time right now, it's worse than the time right before. I couldn't even do a thing. I couldn't leave the unit. I go to the courtyard to look. Then I go inside and wait.

Then I go out to the courtyard.

Then inside to wait.

I can't go to my cleaning jobs in case she comes back. I can't go find a Board in case she comes back.

One day Alma Cho comes running to tell me of a new lesser flu. It is larger than the last lesser flu. A lot of these new lesser flus are. And there is new caution tape around, and smoke. So now I'm really worried. How is Ani going to get anywhere? She already has a problem getting anywhere.

There is even talk of one quarantine at St. Albans.

What is she going to do in quarantine if they sweep her in? How will I find her?

I did hear noises from the direction of the old Expressway, like a lesser Exodus is going by but I can't leave to check in case Ani comes back. Alma says lock the door, lock the door, a stranger could come! I'm not going to do that. I have to keep it open in case Ani comes back. I just sleep near the door to guard it.

It's the middle of the night. Alma Cho is banging on the door. She saw a stranger in my courtyard!

I come outside and we look all around in the dark. Is a Fundy in my yard? I send Alma home, go back in, and hear a noise, like someone is opening a drawer that has a knife. Who is in my kitchen?

Ani Fardo. Still alive.

She is eating Process standing up. "I had unprotected sex," she said.

I did have an Episode, because she is kneeling by me on the floor.

When she saw me wake up, she stood up. "It was just a hand job, Ma."

So then I stood up.

She says, "Technically, three hand jobs. I had to, for the Change."

Now I am almost going to have another Episode but she goes, "It didn't work. I went to a shady operation at Richmond Hill. I had to get around the blockades, that's what took so long. They put the genes in on a virus, that's how they do it, so the genes could mix with my regular DNA. The virus died." She is really scarfing the Process down. "It was embarrassing."

So she goes on the sofa and just sits down and turns on the TV. She just sits there and watches. So I just sit beside her and we both watch News of the lesser flu until the power goes. Then we just sit in the dark. We're just sitting there in the dark until she says, really quiet, "Why did you tell me Rini Jaffur was the Host?"

"I didn't want you to be ashamed."

"It didn't work," she said. Then she went into her room.

She left the door open this time, though.

So I went to her doorway and stood there, in the dark.

So I thought she's asleep, but she called out to me, from her bed, "What *did* happen?"

"When?"

"You know. When I was born." She goes, "How did it work?"

So I leaned against her doorway. I could almost see her, in the dark. I think I could hear her breathe. "Well, at first it didn't work. The first thing that happened was, it didn't work.

"I mean, they tried. They spent months trying to even get one viable embryo, with soma from my ovary and breast and Rini Jaffur's empty egg. It didn't work. They tried with my egg and my soma and it did work. They got viables." I sat down in the doorway, on the floor. "They spent two more months trying to make the viables stick in a Host. It didn't work. They tried a virgin Host. It didn't work. They tried Rini Jaffur. They tried me. It didn't work. They tried the artificial Host, the tank. It did work. They started with five viables. Every one died but you. You were the only one who stayed alive."

She doesn't say anything for so long I thought she fell asleep, but in a while I hear her go, "What were their names?"

"There was Lily and Berthe. Chi-Chi." Now I am crying, myself. I really liked Chi-Chi. I mean, not more than Ani. I loved Ani more. I did like Chi-Chi though. A lot. I never told Ani that. I tell you that. "And Ani and Madhur."

"I was Ani?"

"Well, not at first. Originally you were Madhur. Well, not the *original* Original, who had died of Luzon Third, but, you know, in this lot. Then when Rini changed her mind and gave you to me, you became Ani. The original Ani died. There were other Madhurs too, in India. Rini adopted them. They are her daughters now. I mean, if they are still alive.

"In that lot, you were the only one who stayed alive." I thought a minute. "In the next lot, there was e), who went to Buffalo, but to tell the truth, I've never been sure how great she turned out. I think it could of been a bad lot. Even if she worked, it is just one of ten. Your lot, one in five. The Santa Sofya lot, the Bucharest and Grozny thing? I think that is a really good lot. I think their numbers were really good."

So this time, I was pretty sure she did go to sleep, but she calls out, "What happened to her though?"

"e)?"

"Rini Jaffur. Why did she change her mind? Did she think something was wrong with me?"

"Ani, she never even saw you born."

Now she gets out of her bed and comes right to the doorway. *"Ma! Did you steal me?"*

"No, Ani, no. You were a gift."

So she just slides down to the floor beside me. "What was she like?" And she leans against me, like she did when she was small.

"Rini Jaffur? I never met anyone like her. She was very original. She cared how you feel. She was always asking, How do you feel? She was brave too. She didn't believe in Fate. She thought Fate was what happened. After something happened, you say, that was Fate. If you change what happens, you change your Fate. But I think it was just too much for her. I don't think it was you she changed her mind about. She changed her mind about Fate. She gave me her Fate. I don't know whose Fate she got in the end.

"You have to understand. None of us knew what we were doing. But, Ani—I don't honestly know if anyone ever does. Even when they used to do it the regular way. Rauden had a plan. Most people don't even have a plan. Even if they do, it doesn't mean it works.

"She gave you to me, Ani. It was my luck she did. My life really began then. If she didn't give you to me, Ani, what are we talking about here? I didn't know I wanted you. I couldn't pay that kind of rate."

She was already asleep. She slept for a really long time.

I got myself settled in the doorway and lay there so if she runs off again at least I'm going to know. She has just nestled on my breast, like she used to do. Then she slid down, lying sideways, with her body in her bedroom and her head on me. I just lay there and try not to move so she will stay. I don't even want to go to sleep. But I do.

And when I woke up later she is in her own bed.

In the morning, we're out of Process and she says, Ma, get it. I'm not going anywhere.

When I come back, she says, "I don't want anyone to know. Nobody."

I said ok. "It's going to be tricky though. And by the way, if you go public about it, we could maybe use it to get Aid to one of these experimental schools for unique kids, like, we are unique in not being unique."

"No one would sit with me anyhow."

"Well, it is experimental. The experimental school, sometimes they don't have chairs."

She just shook her head. "I want to find Rini Jaffur," she goes.

So I just go, ok. We are eating Process. "She is in India though."

"I will do the nuclear Transfer and sell viables to pay my fare."

"Ok. I'm not sure Rauden will let you do that though until you are of age."

"So I will find someone less ethical than him. I will use your ID with manual override and say I am thirty-five and live in Queens."

I mean till now I'm handling it ok but this is just too much. "I wanted you to have a different life."

She said, "It's my life now."

"You could do so much with it, Ani. You could be anything."

"Ma. Be a Tech yourself if it's so important. This is my life, not yours. It's not up to you."

I guess she was right. It's her life, not mine. If she wants to be me, I couldn't stop her.

7 ANI FARDO

SO. THE PART ABOUT ANI'S LIFE WITH ME IS ABOUT done.

I mean, not at first.

At first, I'm getting her to stay till it is not so cold. Then we're just trying to get to the Farm. There was a big deal getting out of Queens with the Alerts and checkpoints and blockades even though supposedly it is such a lesser flu. And there is some problem getting through to Rauden. We took the inland route by New Jersey because of bridge blockades upstate and we have to keep changing hybros and get dumped just over the New York border, at Sparrowbush. There is still snow on the ground. I figure out some back road way to walk toward the Farm. There is no public Board, plus no Signal for my Reader, and then I smelled smoke. I thought, let's come back later and turned around, but I heard hoofbeats, or thought it is hoofbeats, oh man. I even saw the horse. Where did these nuts find a horse? I saw the rider in his cape! We hid in a bush. We went back to a dirt road, and there is horse droppings. There is a fire on a hill. She says, Ma, let me go alone. And I'm like, no, no, it is so dangerous.

She goes, Ma, if these nuts find us together and figure us out, it is more dangerous than that.

I just don't want to leave her. But I see what she means. If they find us separate we could be regular. She could be regular,

I could be regular. Together, who knows? We could be what we are.

So I say, let's go off separate for now but meet up somewhere else and Ani said, no, she must do this on her own.

I go, Ani! Just at first.

She goes, "Ma. No. It's time. Ma, if you try to stop me, I will turn myself in. I will say I am a crime against nature. We will both end up in jail."

Man! Where did she learn to hang so tough!

So. That's it.

She did let me walk her to the county road.

She also let me walk her to the regular road.

Then she just said that's it.

Now maybe you are wondering, this India plan—how is she even getting there, with her problem getting anywhere? Maybe you already wondered, hello? How did she even get to Richmond Hill to try to do the Change?

Well I will tell you what she told me, right before she went off on her own. She said, "I walked backward. Ma! It's not an SCNT thing, it's an LD thing. The Special kids, the ones like me? We don't know if we're coming or going. So we walk backward. I'm not sure how it even works. To tell the truth, it could just be a placebo. But it seems to do the trick."

So the last time I saw her, leaving, on a regular road a few miles over the border from Jersey, it was her face I saw. And right, maybe she stumbled a little, putting one hand on bushes or fence posts to guide her as she walked away, and ok, she looked scared. But so proud!

Not the last time I saw her face, period. I saw her face when she made the vidCall, seven months later, from Massachusetts.

Also the Northeast Kingdom, a year later, when she could find a Board.

And from Canada, I saw her head to foot!

But not at first. At first I didn't even get to hear her voice. I didn't even get a message, though I checked every Board I saw. She jammed her own ID so I can't message her and that even jammed my own ID until I rigged up a different entry. But she sends no messages to that.

I'm sneaking off three, four times a day from my Nassau County jobs to check the big Board there—that's if I'm not in a personal Dome with a personal Board. I'm trying for Signal on my Reader from a personal Dome roof. Nothing. From Queens, I keep running up to check at the Little Neck. Nada.

I'm up on Mrs. Postow's personal Dome roof when I got the first message, and it is just two words, STILL ALIVE. I almost slid right off the roof. I just am jumping around all day. No picture. No voice. No reply. But still alive.

It's like when you are thirsty, you are so glad to have anything, you just gulp it down. It was like that. I just gulped her down.

Still alive! Still alive! All night I'm running all over the garden apartment.

Then nothing. Nothing so long I start to wonder if it was just some old message of mine that I had sent to Rauden long ago, bouncing back.

Nothing even on her sixteenth birthday. I spent the whole day out at the Little Neck Board. It was a Saturday, I had the day off. I had brought food and water. I even slept there on the ground. Nothing.

But the next morning, a message is blinking for me. Still alive. It is even the kind where you can reply!

I reply, "WHERE ARE YOU?"

Then I have to keep checking for *her* reply, which doesn't come for two more hours.

"MA I DON'T EVEN KNOW."

Then the Board crashes.

I pretty much camp out at the Little Neck Board till the system starts up again. There is no message even then. Then there is nothing but News Flash because they say lesser flu pathogens was IDed in the President's Dome, then also in whatever Dome they transfer him to, and I'm like, I should care because! But the News went so ballistic, it's already Monday morning before you could get any regular messages, but nothing from her. I try a few reverse codes Henry taught me that could hack recent message history, in case I missed something. The Board crashes.

When it finally comes back, this message is waiting. "I WANT TO GO HOME."

Then it crashes again.

I hate this Board! I hate this Board!

I'm rushing back to Nassau County so I can try my clients' personal Boards! Nothing. I never can get Signal from the garden apartment or even nearby. If I could move full time to the Farm, I could use Rauden's system and keep trying night and day. But I can't do that.

I went to Oakland Gardens but the area is closed off. In the end I found one right in Alley Park, set up an open line with a regular time she could phone me, if she could find a phone, and keep trying at the regular time. It worked! I mean, this is weeks later.

"Ma!" I hear her voice! It sounds different.

I'm like, "Ani! Ani! Thank God you are alive!"

She goes, "Ma. Come on. I am a Subject now. Don't intervene."

"Ani! I will come and get you!"

She goes, "If you try to intervene I will not ever message you again!"

So first I'm like, ok. Then I'm like, very good?

"Ma, you will be so proud! I did a Seal Room test. What Subjects call, Seal Room test."

But she is just a minor! But with the new lesser flu interfering so much with who is available for Subject, I guess the guys who run those tests do not have a problem bending the rules. Well, they never did.

And I don't know what happened but, well I'm not saying she knows where she is but she says it's ok. "New York! Vermont!" she goes. "What does it matter?"

She does not want to go home. She is going to find a vidPhone!

Then the City Line hole is blockaded from the new lesser flu panic. I cannot even get to work, let alone the Nassau County Board with vid capacity. I end up at the Main Street library Board, but the screen is out. Still, the sound worked.

You probably want to know how the Seal Room test went to find out if it is in the genes, and, yes, she passed the Seal Room test. It was nothing bad, just some flus, like HP51, H1N1v, HP53, H274y. She didn't get anything.

A lot of this stuff it is mixed up in my mind, what happened when. I guess at that time, it is July, August, and she is sixteen years, two or three months old and I am always wondering, is she still alive?

Then it's fall. She's in Massachusetts, doing another Seal Room test. So I'm like, oh, very good. I'm really trying not to intervene. I go, what pathogens?

She goes, they call it filovirus series.

Well, I will tell you this. You know how I used to do the Seal Room test, and I was like, what, I'm going to die? Well when she messages from Massachusetts she is doing the filovirus series, Ebola, Marburg, slatewipers, I could hardly move. I said, "Ani. Do you have to do this?"

"Ma. *We're Sylvain hardies*. I'm not getting anything."

"Please do not do this test." So that is one more difference between her and me. If it was me, I would not bat an eye.

So what? Either way, she did the filo series. And she's so mad at me for intervening, she doesn't contact me for a really long time. The City Line blockade did loosen up and I could take a message at the vidBoard there again but nothing comes. I have no way to message her. I'm like, that's it. It's over—she did the filo series and got something, the Sylvain hardy thing is not in the genes. I could hardly even move, I could hardly even walk till I finally got the message blink at the library Board and made the vidContact, she's still alive. And I could see her face! The screen worked!

She goes, "Ma!" Her hair has grown. "Come on, Ma. I passed with flying colors!"

So this time I'm like, very good, how special is that but would she be a little careful what she gets into?

She's like, "Ma! We're Sylvain hardies. What! I'm going to die?" So that is one thing we do have in common. I was just like that when I was her age. Sixteen and a half years old!

Still alive.

She's back in Vermont.

Still alive.

It sounds like she's looking for a Host farm. Is this a different life or what? Maybe you are wondering, what happened to selling viables? Why does she need to be a Host? Weren't the Seal Room tests to verify the, you know, track record so her viables would sell?

Well, it's hard to believe, but it starts to look like Rauden and I are the only ones in the whole Northeast who could bring nuclear Transfer off and for now she is looking for whatever work she could get.

So I'm on the Nassau County vidPhone, on my break, trying to show, you know, Support. To tell the truth, I'm worried she won't keep in touch if I give her a hard time but I can't help it. I know when I was her age I been on the Mound for years. I already lost half my reproductive system and was like, whatever. Now I'm so panicked she is going to try for Host, I could hardly even talk. But I manage to say, oh! Very good—but is Hosting a little dangerous?

She's like, "Ma, we're hardies and should get really good rates for Donor work. But no one I meet knows how to make viables from me. The solo egg is a really hard sell, even of hardy product. What I get paid for Hosting, Ma! I'm halfway to India. I could even be a virgin Host!"

Now maybe you are thinking, man, with all the time I put into school this, school that, do the work, very good—and she is going to be a virgin Host? To tell the truth, well, right, I would of rather she was a Tech. But what happened now, I will tell you, Ani made history.

Not at first. At first she didn't even make a sale. She was all up and down the sticks for months trying to pitch product, let alone find clients who want her for Host. At least she finally found one Board that sent good vid. She really looks different! Her hair got really long and she has a, I don't know, scarf. Not like the scarf I wore so Dan won't notice anything when she went to East Side Girls, but to keep warm. She says she chose the scarf because it's plaid, like the furniture in the garden apartment. She needs a warm scarf because she is at some goddamn Host farm in the middle of nowhere, what they call, Northeast Kingdom. She has the hardy Proofs from the Seal Room tests and I guess the clients she finally hooked up with was open minded because they like a hardy Host for the viable they carried in a cryoPak they already bought from someone else, and they sign a contract and make a promise and Ani does too.

And they don't know how lucky they are how it turned out. First they ran more tests, then they have two shady OBGYNs who blew a viable to Ani's uterus and ok it didn't stick at first but they tried again and then they try again and just before her seventeenth birthday they found out it worked! Seventeen years old! She was a Sylvain hardy who could Host a child! She was the only one I ever heard of who could. And these guys—clients, brokers, OBGYNs—they don't even know how unusual that is. They don't even know she made medical history. They don't know what a Sylvain hardy even is or how lucky they are she is one.

Because it turns out one of these new lesser flus is not as lesser as they say, in fact some people say it is such a slatewiper, it's going to be another Big One. Well it is not as bad as that. It was bad though. When it came down from Canada, the deaths are quadruple digit, which in that part of Vermont there was not a whole lot more than that to start, but when it's over Ani's still alive. The kid inside her too.

The Parents, no.

So the Host farm director, who is also still alive, is shady like most of them, and is going to sell the child to other Parents from some other state but Ani says, hello? I made a promise here. I do not Host this child for just anyone. So she ran off with the child!

This next part she is in Canada. She got through the border checkpoints and is in some kind of goddamn Haven that is promoted by the goddamn K of L, Canadian chapter. K of C L. Man! I guess Canadian vigilantes are doing better than ours because they have their own goddamn Haven. Still! What was she thinking? Who do the K of C L even need a Haven from? What are they, going to raid themself?

At least they have a good Board because I could finally see how she looks with the, you know, baby inside. Her eyes is like, I don't know, milk. Her skin is like milk too, but puffy. She still has the scarf. It's Canada. It's already November. It's cold. And there is a boy behind her I could see in the vid too, Ferron, some kind of, I don't know, he looks like some kind of mutant but she is so proud. He is going to be the father! I don't even know what she meant!

But she looked so proud!

They are not doing intervention, medical assistance, nothing, because it is a K of C L Haven, that is how the K of C L do things. Come on, the K of any L are out of their goddamn minds. She wants me to come for the birth, even though I don't know anything about how that works, the regular birth. She says don't tell them we are, you know. Just say I stole her. The K of C L steal babies all the time. This guy Ferron, who is going to be the father? The K of L had stole him, to start.

So I am figuring out how to get to Canada with my old hacked Pass that Henry fixed for me so long ago, but when I hear from her again she will get back to me, they have some problem with the Haven and she and Ferron have to flee.

So I am worried the K of C L are going to chase her on horses, if they could find a horse, and I am checking every day for messages, three times a day, and there is another problem at the City Line—they sealed the hole again! I am trying to scramble over the wall! I'm roaming all over for a better Board but I have to use Little Neck. It crashes all the time and even on a good day there is no vid there. By the time I reach her, she's back in New York State. She is in some other Haven.

They call it Canastota.

Her plans for India are delayed. But when the kid is old enough to travel, she and Ferron will take it to India, show it to Rini Jaffur, if Rini's still alive.

They have a really good Board at the Canastota Haven, and she says, Ma, try to get a good screen so you could see how big I look. She was so proud. She is still not doing intervention, even though this Haven would permit.

I go, Ani, it is so dangerous.

She goes, "Ma! It's always dangerous. Come on. How I was

born it was intervene this, intervene that. I just want to see what happens if we don't. I just want to try the regular way for once."

And she was right. It always is dangerous.

"Ma, are you angry?"

Now, I want to tell you here, they are going to say, the way it turned out, these poor nuclear Transfer kids, what they call clones, should never of been born because they will just die young. Well I will tell you this. I don't think so. I don't think that's what it proves. It just proves the regular way isn't safe either. It never was.

That doesn't mean no one should do it the regular way, just because it is not totally safe.

Sometimes you really have to take a chance.

And sometimes it doesn't work. That doesn't mean you shouldn't try.

If you think you should be totally safe, no one would be born at all.

So I go, "No! No! I'm proud." I mean, to tell the truth, I would prefer she do intervention. Maybe I should of told her, do intervention. Maybe she would of listened. But who knows? She probably would not of done what I said. And that is one more difference between us, I did what I was told. It was how I stayed alive. She did not have that in common with me. I just go, "I'm proud of you, Ani!"

And the way things turned out, I was really glad, of all the things in my mind, that was the only one I said.

So I headed to Albany on the MagLev with a load of things for the kid and by the time I got there it's already snowing so hard I got lost and missed the windtram. By the time the next one left, the snow was so bad we got stuck in Herkimer for two days till the track is cleared. Then the wind went the wrong way.

Then it went the right way. Then it stopped dead, and I have to walk a day to get to Canastota in the snow, then find the Haven in the snow, which I don't even know what a Haven looks like till I saw the smoke, and I don't even know why there's smoke or where the smoke is from and by the time they told me, it was too late. It's over. That's it.

She was seventeen years, eight months old.

ii

Why am I at the Farm?

I'm not at the Farm.

This is mixed up in my mind. The Farm came later. Ferron is there with a bag.

I think I'm running around in ashes in snow, going, "Where is Ani?" So this is still Canastota.

I think Ferron is in a message on a screen on a Board.

And I am in the snow.

"We could not do anything." That's the Haven person, in the snow too. "We could not force intervention."

"She was the only one I ever loved!" That's Ferron in the screen. He did not say she bled out.

The Haven person said she bled out. "We could not do anything. She bled out from the birth."

"She is a Sylvain hardy." This is me. "He did not need to burn her body for the Hygiene."

"You'll never make another Ani!" That is Ferron. That is why he burnt the body. He thinks I would try. I would never do that. I would not let anyone do that, even Rauden. They did not need to burn the body so I won't.

They did not need to have the ceremony without me in the snow even though she died because they did not force intervention even though they could of tried. They really could of tried. They did not need to burn her at all because she was not sick, she died from the birth. I mean they could burn her for the ceremony if they think it is so important, even though they did not need to, but they could, if it is so important to burn her for the ceremony in the snow.

They could of waited till I saw her first.

They really could of let me see her once before they did.

I just would of liked to see her, even if it's only once.

WHERE IS THE KID?
What was in that bag?

I'm really at the Farm this time.

Janet Delize is there, in ashes and snow. I told her Ani bled out from the birth. She took me home and was so nice I even wondered if she thought I'm someone else. I wish I was. I wish Ani was. I wish Ani was me. Then she'd still be alive.

I wish I was Ani. Then I'd be dead.

I don't know how I even got back home. Alma Cho found me in the yard. I wish Ani was her. I wish she was anyone.

All those years, clean her, walk her, feed her. Keep her alive.

Seventeen years. Eight months. Four days.

That's it.

I just would of liked to see her one more time.

iii

I stayed inside so long, when I open the door, it's warm. That's how long I been inside.

It is spring.

Grass is growing in the courtyard.

I walked across the grass. I went out to the street. 256th Place.

I did not remember caution tape was up.

I did not remember a Hygiene fire, but trees are burnt. I forgot if I smelled smoke. Alma Cho must of told me what it was about when she brought me the food I ate. But I forgot.

I turned on 61st Avenue.

Setauket. That's it. Setauket. A slatewiper that crossed to Queens from Suffolk County and did terrible things in between. It's going to end up a Pandy. One of the worst.

I walked to Little Neck Parkway. I walked up the hill. Burnt here too but some leaves on some trees. It's a really long time since I been up this hill.

That good house with the patio was burnt. The patio is all that's left.

The Board worked. I went in the shelter and ran UpDate.

April 8, 2079.

Then I walked back home. The last date I remembered from before was January 2, 2078. That was on my way to Canastota.

More than a year went by since then. It's one year, three months since Ani died there, in the birth.

I checked the date regular after that. I don't even know why I did. I just know that is how I know it's four years, four months after Ani died, and she's still dead, and I'm still alive, and still at the garden apartment, looking out my window, when who's that coming up across the courtyard? Someone who does not look familiar.

And who is that behind him?

Someone who does.

8 THE ONLY ONES

I DON'T KNOW YOUR NAME OR ADDRESS. I DON'T know your age or who your Parent is.

I don't even know if I should send this. You could have a better life if I don't.

Maybe you will be ashamed or scared. Maybe you will just be like, whatever, who cares?

I just think it's going to come out one way or another. Something could show up in our codes. Maybe even yours. Maybe you already wondered. People got such stupid ideas about what we are. I just think you should hear it from me.

So now you did.

Remember Ani said, if it's just another way to be born, why am I the only one I heard of? Now you heard. You're not the only one. Neither was she.

Let me just say a few more things that you should know.

The hardy thing is real. Avian, Luzon, all of them plus so many other things I been exposed to that I did not name but on the whole it is like Rauden said. If they penetrate my system it is their misfortune. And it did look like that would be true for Ani. And probably you too. I just want you to know in case you are in a situation where it could help, and not just when an Epi comes through, but if you are in a bad place like I heard some viables end up? Work Camp, sex slave? Run into epicenters. Climb over bodies. Hide in quarantines. Who's going to chase you there?

I'm so sorry if that's where you ended up, but let me say this too. That did not happen because of what you are. It could happen to anyone. Being regular is no guarantee how things will work. There are always unknowns in the Life Industry. Even the old regular way, when people got their kid from male/female unprotected sex? I don't honestly think anyone ever totally knew what's going to happen. There were always many factors, even luck.

I also want to say, in my own life many bad things was done to me, and that is how I know that when it happens sometimes you think something is wrong with you. Whoever did those things to you? It's them it's wrong with. It's not your fault.

Even if you are in a good situation, you might think something's wrong with you. Maybe someone will tell you something is wrong with you, because of what you are. That is so ignorant. Nothing is wrong with you. If someone says that to you, just say right back well I am still alive. How wrong is that?

I also want to say if you are mad, it is ok.

I know it is not up to me, if it's ok or not. I'm just saying how I feel so you will know. I don't even know if you care how I feel. I'm just saying, in case you do. How I feel is, how you feel about any of this is ok. It is up to you.

The one who looked familiar is Lucie Benedikt, who came all the way from Berlin. Nineteen years old. Still alive.

The one who did not look familiar is Ferron. I didn't recognize him with the beard. I never totally trusted Ferron but you got to understand. How he grew up, with vigilante cretins, there was a lot of prejudice about people like Ani and me. He really did love Ani, though. I'm the one he had the problem with. But I think he got over it.

When Ferron found Lucie Benedikt he was looking for me with a pure code search he was running with Ani's code that he had saved from her blood when she died. But this kind of search is very hard to control. He ended up in Lucie Benedikt's code instead. They made contact. He told her what he knew about Ani and me, and, well, she had this in common with Ani—she just told her mother however they say it in their language, Ma, it's my life not yours. And off she went to find me. She made her way to America by different boats, a very hard trip, maybe harder than Ani's, but Lucie Benedikt hung very tough. Ferron met her at Boston Harbor and from things Ani had said when she was still alive, they figured out how to find me.

She is on my case to send this out. She says I could do it with a pure code post which she will help me run.

She also wants me to put in a Comment Box so you could post in. It will be safe. We won't know who you are. You could post a Comment or question you might have. And I will try to answer though it was not easy for me to say what I already said. The Canastota part I could hardly bear to say at all.

Here is something you will want to know. Lucie has been in touch with her mother, Hille Benedikt, who was very glad to hear she's still alive. It turns out Hille Benedikt is very smart with research and looked into what was happening out by JFK in Queens when the Big One started. It is on the record that a bus escaped from a quarantine with babies on it whose Parents died. Now how the Big One used to hit people, you would just die very sudden and that is what the driver did, just keeled over and the bus crashed. The bodies were found later. The driver, seven kids, and one empty basket. The bus crashed on Kissena Boulevard.

Well, Hille poked around what files she could and there is some GI who died during childbirth in the VA hospital in St. Albans, near JFK. Nya Santiago was her name. I'm not saying that's my birth mother. I'm just saying the timing works. She was all shot up with untested vaccines and for all we know, that's what killed her. Maybe she was already dead when her kid was born by C-section. They don't know where this mother had been posted or who the father was or anything else.

So this could be my birth mother, and maybe, technically, yours. I never have been sure how that all works. I'm very sorry that she died. But I am sure of one thing. If Cissy Fardo didn't take me off the bus on Kissena Boulevard, none of us would be alive.

I got some more things to say about other people you heard about. Henry is still alive. Janet Delize is still alive.

Rini Jaffur died of natural causes. All the Nassau County group died, except Lorena Hutz. Lorena Hutz is still alive.

Alma Cho is still alive.

Rauden—

I want to think if there is anything I forgot to say about what we do and do not get. Oh! Worms. I don't know if they even have them where you are—but hook, pin, whatever, plus salmonella, hemophilus, shigella. Not a problem. I would watch out for snakes though. I personally never saw one and I think what they give you is really bad neurotoxins which as you know Ani and I were ok with, but if you see a snake, I would keep my distance. Be on the safe side.

People who are not hardy themself might not understand how this works and maybe you don't either yet, but let me make one thing very clear. Remember I used to go off in boats with just anyone? That was not a hardy thing. That was foolhardy. Sometimes you got to be on the safe side, hardy or not.

But the see what happens thing is a little different. Sometimes it is hard to tell the difference between foolhardy and that. And the problem is, the see what happens thing, if I didn't have it? You wouldn't be born. I don't even know if it comes from the genes. Ani had it in the end. I don't know if you will. Lucie

Benedikt has it, though she is different from Ani in so many ways.

I just know—well, this is about Ferron, because it turns out why he came looking for me in the first place, he wants me to find someone to clone the baby, who died with Ani, in the birth. He had saved the baby's soma—that was what was in his bag, at Canastota! He saved the baby's soma and Ani's blood and took them away in the bag, and found cryoPaks somewhere. He has the baby's soma, in storage, in cryoPaks, with Ani's blood, and wants to find someone to do nuclear Transfer from it.

The baby's name was Jack.

And this is what I'm saying about the see what happens thing. It turns out I still had it. I'm going to do it. I'm going to do the work.

Well maybe you think, here we go again. This dude wants to take advantage of me. Everyone does. Ferron is going to exploit me like everyone does. That's what they always say. They never say it's interesting. I'm going to do it.

It's not even because I think this new kid will be my grand-child because he would of been Ani's child if they lived. I hope Ferron will bring him for a visit, though.

But either way, I'm going up to the Farm and see if I can make it happen.

Sometimes you hear people talk about how great it used to be, how they made viables from unprotected male/female sex and how much they enjoyed it. Well let me tell you, what I had of unprotected sex I never enjoyed it as much as nuclear Transfer. What Rauden and I did, I enjoyed that so much. I loved it. Rauden did too. I'm not saying you would love it too, though I expect you would be good at it and might be in a situation where it was the only thing that worked. I'm just saying, I want you to know.

I don't know whose eggs we will use. Some of mine could still be left on the property, after all these years. Or Lucie Benedikt could be Donor, if that is what she wants. I never wanted Ani to be a Donor or a Subject or any of that, but it was her life, not mine. And it is Lucie's too.

Yours too.

So let me say a few last things. I'm not your mother. I'm not your birth mother. That's not how it works. You have that in common with Ani. I wasn't Ani's birth mother. I was her mother, though.

How I felt about Ani, and she is the only one I felt that way about—I really don't think it's unique, how I felt about her.

The whole unique thing—remember Rauden said what makes the baby grow is like words, that tell it what to be? Well, words can mean two things or more, like the Free School was not free, and Life is not life, but also bear the child or bear the pain or bear the animal or, you know, bear with me. Even mean can mean two things or more.

So genes could mean two things or more.

And not just Ani's and Lucie Benedikt's, and yours, but even Rauden and Henry, who had the same genes by being twins. It isn't just that one is in the wheelchair and the other was Rauden. It's more about, what Rauden said to me the last time I saw him, how he felt? Henry never felt that, and Henry even cared for me, but Rauden was the only one who cared for me that way. And what I'm saying is, the way I cared for Ani, look, I don't want to say the wrong thing here, and I do care about you and am proud, but the way I cared about Ani, she is the only one.

She even still is.

To tell the truth, I'm pretty sure it is not unique, to feel that way. I hope it's not unique.

I think I could bear to tell you about Rauden now. This was right around the time Ani and me were in Sparrowbush, just before she went off on her own. The K of L went on a raid and this time torched the Farm, and though most of the Quonset did not burn, they chased Rauden through the woods and, well, you know what he's like. He had a respiratory Episode and that's it. Janet showed me where he's buried. I knew all this a long time but could not bear to say it.

Well, something else happened in that raid that you should know. I only heard this after Ani died in the birth and Janet Delize was so nice. I heard this from her grandson, young Phil. While they were chasing Rauden, Janet went back in the Quonset really quiet before they torched it. And maybe you remember how mean she could be, the looks she gave? Sometimes I think she was just jealous because Rauden cared for me the way I didn't even know he did. But sometimes I think she really believed what we did was a crime against nature. Well, maybe she is a criminal herself. Or maybe she just saw a business Opportunity. It could even of been a plan Rauden made, that he will run distraction in the woods while she grabbed what he told her from the freezers and went off with it. Or she could of changed her mind like Rini Jaffur.

All I'm saying is, what does it matter? If you ask yourself, why was I born? It could be because it is somebody's business Opportunity or it could be they changed their mind or had unprotected sex, who even knows? It could just be about luck.

Sometimes I would like to see a scientific study, with Controls, what is luck? How does it work? When the bus crashed at Kissena and everyone died but me, that was not a hardy thing at all. It was just luck somebody put my basket in a safe place. It was luck Cissy Fardo was a passerby. And I don't know if luck is in the genes, but you have it too.

Why did the others die on the bus and I was still alive? Why did Lily and the others die but Ani was alive? Why did e) stay alive? If she did. All I'm saying is, why were *you* born? Because Rauden needed the work? So Ani could get the special back-pack or out of Armory? You were born the reason anyone was. Because you're lucky. You're lucky to be alive.

And those ones Janet grabbed that day at the Farm? She took them in cryoPaks, sneaked away through the woods, made it to the nearest MagLev, rode to Boston, and sold it at the harbor. The last anyone knew, it's heading for Reykjavik, the Life auction. The hundred viables I made, plus whatever Rauden had left on ice from what he made—I'm thinking two or three dozen—plus a handful of solo eggs along with a bunch of soma, which no one but Rauden and me ever knew how to use, so far, heading for Reykjavik. They could of gone anywhere from there.

So. Ok. About the Comment post? I will keep checking, did you post or not post. Feel free to take forever to post back, because I will keep checking, forever. And I'm not saying I'm not worried, are you mad at me, or is your Parent mad, or could I bear the pain. I'm not even saying I'm sure you will even get this message—if the pure code will work or if you even got the scanners to read where you live. I'm just saying I will keep checking back, see what happens, forever.

Ok, so I'm heading upstate with Lucie Benedikt, Ferron, and Jack's soma, see what happens. I will post the results. Here we go. I love you, Ani.

ACKNOWLEDGMENTS

This novel was a long time coming and had help all the way.

Julie Barer dragged it, kicking and screaming, to become a better book. I thank her for her persistence and loyalty, and William Boggess and the whole team for their support and advice.

It was my great luck that *The Only Ones* found its way to Two Dollar Radio, which Eric Obenauf and Eliza Wood run with such simplicity and vision. They have been a complete treat to work with, and that first little edit Eric threw my way was a game changer.

I was lucky too, that the kindness of Steve Erickson, Jonathan Lethem, and Lynne Tillman, forces of good in the writers' world, extended to me.

Many were the brains I picked and shoulders I cried on. Just to name a few—the Christgau-Levi family, who followed every twist and turn of my progress whether they wanted to or not; early readers especially Louise Levi, Julian Dibbell, Laura Tillem, Dominique Dibbell, and Laura Dolan; plus Sarah Lazin, who became my trusted advisor throughout. And then there were Janet Mendelsohn and Marc Levitt, Dominique Avery, Greil and Jenny Marcus, Tom Smucker, Laura Kogel, Linda Mevorach, John Rockwell, Ann Powers, Eric Weisbard, Tom Hull, Tom Carson, Kit Rachlis, Jon Dolan, Shellie Sclan, Joe Levy, Irene Javors, Ann Waters, Michael Zilkha, my sisters Joy Harvey and Sandy Dibbell-Hope, Lynn Phillips, Beverly Winikoff, the fabulous Bay 41 women's group, and the (virtual) Witnesses.

Special thanks to Claire Moed, who gave me a room to write in. Very special thanks to Roger Trilling, who was a guardian angel from the first. And to Nina Christgau, my daughter, who always understood what the story was about, and why I wrote it.

Finally, my husband, Robert Christgau, is a great critic and editor but even greater partner in life. The woman he knows I am is the one who wrote this book.

Also published by *Two Dollar Radio*

BINARY STAR
A NOVEL BY SARAH GERARD

"Rhythmic, hallucinatory, yet vivid as crystal. Gerard has channeled her trials and tribulations into a work of heightened reality, one that sings to the lonely gravity of the human body." —NPR

THE ABSOLUTION OF ROBERTO ACESTES LAING
A NOVEL BY NICHOLAS ROMBES

✳ One of the Best Books of 2014 — *Flavorwire*

"Kafka directed by David Lynch doesn't even come close. It is the most hauntingly original book I've read in a very long time. [This book] is a strong contender for novel of the year." —*3:AM Magazine*

MADE TO BREAK
A NOVEL BY D. FOY

"With influences that range from Jack Kerouac to Tom Waits and a prose that possesses a fast, strange, perennially changing rhythm that's somewhat akin to some of John Coltrane's wildest compositions." —*HTML Giant*

MIRA CORPORA
A NOVEL BY JEFF JACKSON

✳ *Los Angeles Times* Book Prize Finalist
✳ One of the Best Books of 2013 —*Slate; Salon; Flavorwire; Largehearted Boy; Vol. 1 Brooklyn; LitReactor*

"Style is pre-eminent in Jeff Jackson's eerie and enigmatic debut. The prose works like the expressionless masks worn by killers in horror films." —*Wall Street Journal*

THE ORANGE EATS CREEPS
A NOVEL BY GRACE KRILANOVICH

✳ National Book Foundation 2010 '5 Under 35' Selection.
✳ *NPR* Best Books of 2010.
✳ *The Believer* Book Award Finalist.

"Krilanovich's work will make you believe that new ways of storytelling are still emerging from the margins." —*NPR*

ANCIENT OCEANS OF CENTRAL KENTUCKY
A NOVEL BY DAVID CONNERLEY NAHM

"Wonderful… Remarkable… it's impossible to stop reading until you've gone through each beautiful line, a beauty that infuses the whole novel, even in its darkest moments."
—NPR

HOW TO GET INTO THE TWIN PALMS
A NOVEL BY KAROLINA WACLAWIAK

"One of my favorite books this year." —*The Rumpus*

"Waclawiak's novel reinvents the immigration story."
—*New York Times Book Review*, Editors' Choice

I SMILE BACK
A NOVEL BY AMY KOPPELMAN

✱ Now a major film starring Sarah Silverman and Josh Charles!

"Powerful. Koppelman's instincts help her navigate these choppy waters with inventiveness and integrity." —*Los Angeles Times*

RADIO IRIS
A NOVEL BY ANNE-MARIE KINNEY

"Kinney is a Southern California Camus." —*Los Angeles Magazine*

"[*Radio Iris*] has a dramatic otherworldly payoff that is unexpected and triumphant." —*New York Times Book Review*, Editors' Choice

THE PEOPLE WHO WATCHED HER PASS BY
A NOVEL BY SCOTT BRADFIELD

"Challenging [and] original… A billowy adventure of a book. In a book that supplies few answers, Bradfield's lavish eloquence is the presiding constant." —*New York Times Book Review*

"Brave and unforgettable. Scott Bradfield creates a country for the reader to wander through, holding Sal's hand, assuming goodness."
—*Los Angeles Times*

Also published by *Two Dollar Radio*

CRYSTAL EATERS
A NOVEL BY SHANE JONES

"A powerful narrative that touches on the value of every human life, with a lyrical voice and layers of imagery and epiphany." —*BuzzFeed*

"[Jones is] something of a millennial Richard Brautigan." —*Nylon*

A QUESTIONABLE SHAPE
A NOVEL BY BENNETT SIMS

"[*A Questionable Shape*] is more than just a novel. It is literature. It is life." —*The Millions*

"Presents the yang to the yin of Whitehead's *Zone One*, with chess games, a dinner invitation, and even a romantic excursion."
—*The Daily Beast*

SOME THINGS THAT MEANT THE WORLD TO ME
A NOVEL BY JOSHUA MOHR

* One of the Best Books of 2009 —*Oprah Magazine*;
  The Nervous Breakdown
* *San Francisco Chronicle* Bestseller

"Mohr's prose roams with chimerical liquidity." —B*oston's Weekly Dig*

1940
A NOVEL BY JAY NEUGEBOREN

"Jay Neugeboren traverses the Hitlerian tightrope with all the skill and formal daring that have made him one of our most honored writers of literary fiction and masterful nonfiction. [*1940*] is, at once, a beautifully realized work of imagined history, a rich and varied character study and a subtly layered novel of ideas, all wrapped in a propulsively readable story."
—*Los Angeles Times*

THE CAVE MAN
A NOVEL BY XIAODA XIAO

* *WOSU* (NPR member station) Favorite Book of 2009.

"As a parable of modern China, [*The Cave Man*] is chilling." —*Boston Globe*

CRAPALACHIA
A NOVEL BY SCOTT McCLANAHAN

* One of the Best Books of 2013 —*The Millions*; *Flavorwire*;
Dazed & Confused; *The L Magazine*; *Time Out Chicago*

"McClanahan's prose is miasmic, dizzying, repetitive. A rushing river of words that reflects the chaos and humanity of the place from which he hails. [McClanahan] is not a writer of half-measures... This is his symphony, every note designed to resonate, to linger." —*New York Times Book Review*

Novels by **RUDOLPH WURLITZER**

THE DROP EDGE OF YONDER
* *Time Out New York*'s Best Book of 2008.

"A picaresque American *Book of the Dead*... in the tradition of Thomas Pynchon, Joseph Heller, Kurt Vonnegut, and Terry Southern."
—*Los Angeles Times*

"There's a bawdy, lunatic thrill to the tale that seems somehow radical. It's the kind of book someone will stick in a back pocket before heading out on the trail into the unknown." —*LA Weekly*

NOG
"A strange, singular book... somewhere between Psychedelic Superman and Samuel Beckett." —*Newsweek*

"The Novel of Bullshit is dead." —Thomas Pynchon

"Nog is to literature what Dylan is to lyrics."
—Jack Newfield, *Village Voice*

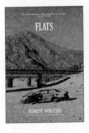

FLATS / QUAKE
* **Two countercultural classics from Rudolph Wurlitzer now available in one "69ed" edition.**

"One of the most unique and fascinating American writers." —Dennis Cooper

"Wurlitzer might be the closest thing we have to an actual cult author, a highly talented fiction writer."
—Barnes & Noble Review

On an overcast Wednesday afternoon, Patrick N. Allen took his own life. He is survived by his father, Patrick, Sr.; his step-mother, Patricia; his step-sister, Patty; and his twin brother, Seth.

Coming 2015

Written & Directed by Eric Obenauf

Part-thriller, part-nightmarish examination of the widening gap between originality and technology, told with remarkable precision. Haunting and engaging, *The Removals* imagines where we go from here.

Coming 2016

Written by Nicholas Rombes

Directed by Grace Krilanovich